THE LONG QUICHE GOODBYE

THE LONG QUIET GOODBYE

THE LONG QUICHE GOODBYE

AVERY AAMES

WHEELER
CHIVERS

This Large Print Edition is published by Wheeler Publishing, Waterville, Maine, USA an dby AudioGO Ltd, Bath, England.

Wheeler Publishing, a part of Gale, Cengage Learning.

Wheeler Publishing Large Print Cozy Mystery.

The text of this Large Print edition is unabridged.

Other aspects of the book may vary from the original edition.

Set in 16 pt. Plantin.

LIBRARY OF CONGRESS CATALOGING-IN-PUBLICATION DATA

Aames, Avery.
   The long quiche goodbye / by Avery Aames.
     p. cm. — (Wheeler Publishing large print cozy mystery)
   "A Cheese Shop Mystery"—T.p. verso.
   ISBN-13: 978-1-4104-3565-1 (softcover)
   ISBN-10: 1-4104-3565-2 (softcover)
   1. Businesswomen—Fiction. 2. Cheese shops—Fiction. 3. Providence (Ohio : Township)—Fiction. 4. Large type books. I. Title.
   PS3601.A215L66 2011
   813'.6—dc22   2010051313

BRITISH LIBRARY CATALOGUING-IN-PUBLICATION DATA AVAILABLE
Published in 2011 in the U.S. by arrangement with The Berkley Publishing Group, a member of Penguin Group (USA) Inc.
Published in 2011 in the U.K. by arrangement with The Penguin Group (USA) Inc.

U.K. Hardcover: 978 1 445 83710 9 (Chivers Large Print)
U.K. Softcover: 978 1 445 83711 6 (Camden Large Print)

LP

Printed in the United States of America
1 2 3 4 5 6 7 15 14 13 12 11

To my mother and father,
for teaching me to dream.
To my husband,
for helping me follow that dream.

ACKNOWLEDGMENTS

First and foremost, I want to thank my husband, Chuck, my first reader and my staunch supporter. I love you. Without you, I never could have achieved my dream. Thank you to my son, Jackson, who makes me realize I can't produce anything better than you. I'm so lucky. Thank you to my sister, Kimberley. Not only have you taught me to be patient when dealing with a computer or the Internet — it's a wonder these things work at all — but you have been my dearest friend since the day you were born. Thanks to Kevin, Jill, Craig, Nancy, Kristy, and all of my extended family and friends who accept that I'm different and sort of kooky. Your love spurs me on.

Thanks to Krista Davis and Janet Bolin, my fabulous critique partners, without whom I would have given up writing long, long ago. Thanks to Lorraine Bartlett, Elizabeth Zelvin, Sandra Parshall, Sheila Connolly, Hank Phillippi Ryan, and all the other Sisters in Crime Guppies. With your support, I have stayed true to my path. Thanks to my writing friends in Sisters in Crime, Mystery Writers of America, and International Thriller Writers. Your journeys continue to make mine easier. And a special thanks to my blog pals at Mystery Lovers Kitchen. Ours is a great recipe for friendship.

Thank you to my agents at BookEnds, LLC, for your guidance and persistence. To my fabulous publisher, Berkley Prime Crime, for believing Charlotte Bessette is a character worth knowing. To my editor, Kate Seaver, for your attention not only to the big picture but to the nitpicky details. To our hardworking Berkley publicist, Megan Swartz, for her inspired ideas. To my talented artist, Teresa Fasolino, for her brilliant cover artwork. To Breakthrough Promotions for putting together a campaign that I could handle and enjoy.

Thank you to all of the wonderful cheese and wine shops I've visited over the past year for the tastings and insider information about cheese. Thank you to Amish Tours of Ohio for introducing me to the Amish culture, and to the innkeepers at the White

Oak Inn for making my bed-and-breakfast stay in Ohio memorable.

Thank you to all the librarians and booksellers who ignite people's passion to read. Thanks to animal rescue groups like Pets in Need.

Last, but certainly not least, thank you to my mother and father, who smile down on me from heaven. You always encouraged me to pursue my creativity. I am blessed.

CHAPTER 1

"I'm not dead, Charlotte," Grandpère Etienne said.

"But you are retired, Pépère." I tweaked his rosy cheek and skirted around him to throw a drop cloth over the rustic wooden table that usually held wheels of cheese, like Abbaye de Belloc, Manchego, and Humboldt Fog, the latter cheese a great pairing with chardonnay. Dust billowed up as the edges of the drop cloth hit the shop floor.

"A retired person may have an opinion."

"Yes, he can." I smiled. "But you put me in charge."

"You and Matthew."

My adorable cousin. If I had a brother, he would be just like Matthew. Bright, funny, and invaluable as an ally against my grandfather when he was being stubborn.

"What does Matthew say about all this?" Pépère folded his arms around his bulging girth. The buttons on his blue-striped shirt

11

looked ready to pop. The doctor said Pépère needed to watch his weight and cholesterol, and I had been trying to get him to eat more of the hard cheeses that contained a lower fat content than the creamy cheeses he loved so much, but he had perfected the art of sneaking little bites. What was I to do?

I gave my grandfather's shoulder a gentle squeeze. "Pépère, I love this place. So does Matthew. We only want the best for it. Trust us. That's why you made us partners."

"Bah! So many changes. Why fix something that isn't broken? The shop made a good profit last year."

"Because life is all about change. Man does not live by cheese alone," I joked.

Pépère didn't smile.

Fromagerie Bessette, or as the locals in the little town of Providence, Ohio, liked to call it, The Cheese Shop, needed to expand and get with the times. Our proximity to Amish country was driving more and more tourism in our direction. The town was exploding with bed-and-breakfasts, art galleries, candle and quilt shops, and fine restaurants. To take advantage of the boom, Matthew and I decided the shop needed a facelift. We had stowed all the cheeses in the walk-in refrigerator until the renovation was complete. The sign on the door of the shop read *Closed.*

"Pépère, why don't you take a walk in the vegetable garden?" The town had a co-op vegetable garden and hothouse in the alley behind the shops on Hope Street. "Pluck me some basil. Maybe some heirloom tomatoes." I intended to sell homemade basil pesto in jars. For a simple treat, basil pesto ladled over a scoop of locally made chévre and served with flatbread and a slice of a juicy heirloom tomato is an economical gourmet delight.

Pépère muttered something in French. I understood. "Give the horse the reins and the rider is quickly thrown off."

For a little more than thirty years, I had heard Pépère's witticisms and grown in the tutelage of his wisdom about all things cheese. Today, I turned a deaf ear. I needed to concentrate. Everything for the reopening of the shop was going smoothly. So far. But if we were to finish by next week, we had to maintain a strict schedule. The decorator was due any minute with the updated kitchen fixtures and lighting fixtures, none of which had been switched out since 1957. Antiques were to be prized in a home, but not in a thriving business concern. The painter was scheduled to arrive at noon to paint the walls and refinish the

13

twelve-foot wood counter at the rear of the store, hence the need to stow the cheese and cover the display tables with drop cloths. The painter would stain the wood a warm honey brown to match the ladder-back stools by the Madura gold granite tasting counter, and then paint the walls Tuscany gold. Yesterday we had installed extra shelving that would soon be loaded with new additions like patés, chutneys, homemade jams made without pectin or preservatives, gourmet olives, crackers, and artisanal breads. I would cluster cheese baskets, gifts, and accessories on the five oak barrels stationed around the shop. My favorite gifts — the olive-wood-handled knives from France, the copper fondue pots from Italy, and the crystal cheese trays from Ireland — would sit on the largest barrel prominently stationed in the middle of the room. Over the last year, thanks to the Internet, I had "visited" many wonderful places and found one-of-a-kind items.

"Where is Matthew?" Pépère said, ending my moment of patting myself on the back for a job well done.

"Seeing to the wine annex."

Matthew used to be a sommelier in one of Cleveland's finest restaurants, but a month ago, life struck him a hard blow, and suddenly living in a big city didn't appeal to him. His wife ditched him and his twin daughters and went back to dear old Mumsie and dear old Dad to live in their thatch-roofed vicarage in dear old England. My grandparents, who never liked the woman in the first place, had urged me to take in Matthew and the girls. How could I say no? When Pépère offered us the partnership in The Cheese Shop, Matthew jumped at the chance. He arrived bursting with new ideas. A must-see place like Fromagerie Bessette should also sell wine, he argued, and Providence didn't have a wine shop yet. I had agreed wholeheartedly, and we set to work.

For the annex, we leased the empty space next to The Cheese Shop. We cut an archway between, laid travertine tiles on the floor, paneled the wine annex with dark mahogany, installed a bar and stools, and added rows and rows of wine bottle nooks. *Voilà.* In a short time, we had created an authentic-looking winery tasting room. When word got out, local vintners had clamored to provide samples.

"Progress, bah." My sweet old grandfather uttered another grumble of disapproval and fled through the rear door of the shop.

I smiled. I had prepared myself for his resistance. After World War II, he and

15

Grandmère had migrated from France and given their life's blood to The Cheese Shop. Pépère did not like me bucking tradition, but I had such dreams: cheese and wine tastings, a mail-order business come the fall, cooking classes. I even planned to write a cheese cookbook. It would be so popular that the Barefoot Contessa would beg to write the foreword.

One thing at a time, I reminded myself and chuckled. Like cheese, if I set too many slices of life on a plate, the flavors would be indistinct.

The grape-leaf-shaped chimes hanging over the front door tinkled.

"Charlotte, take a look at these beauties." Matthew bounded across the natural pine floor like a long-limbed Great Dane. He carried two mosaic bistro tables with S-scrolled legs that I had ordered from Europa Antiques and Collectibles, a quaint shop located in the building next to ours. "*Très* hip," he said. "You did good."

The antique shop's proprietor, Vivian Williams, glided in behind Matthew, carrying a pair of matching mosaic chairs in black matte finish. She reminded me of a clipper ship, aloof and elegant, sails unfurled, her chin-length hair in a flip, the flaps of her Ann Taylor suit jacket flying wide. She said,

"Take these. I'll go get to the other set of chairs."

I slipped the stools from her grasp, admiring for a second time the way the round mosaic seats matched the table. Definite conversation pieces. I traipsed after Matthew into the annex.

Vivian returned in seconds with two more chairs. "By the by, I saw the girls on their way to school. They're so adorable."

Matthew's eight-year-old twins.

"Did they make their beds?" I asked Matthew.

His mouth quirked on the right side. "They pulled up the covers."

I sighed. It was a start.

"The littlest one, Amy, is a handful." Vivian fussed with the chairs, arranging them with an eye for balance. "They're not identical, are they? Amy's like her mother, I assume?"

"Nothing like her." Thank God. We didn't speak her name in Matthew's presence.

"My great-granddaughter is just like me." Grandmère Bernadette trundled into the annex like a locomotive with no off switch, arms pumping, chest huffing, patchwork skirt swirling around her calves. She was always in a hurry and filled with boundless energy. I only hoped I could have that much energy at seventy-two. *I think I can. I think I can.* She finger-combed her short gray hair and tossed her red macramé purse on the drop-cloth-covered bar.

"What are you doing here?" I asked. "I thought you had rehearsal." I strode to her and bent slightly to give her a hug. She was shrinking but would never admit it. She took pains to stand erect. Once a dancer, always a dancer, she told me.

"Later, *chérie*. Later." She smacked her gnarled hands together. "Now, what can I do?"

I ushered her into The Cheese Shop. "The window displays."

"*Moi?*" She tilted her head in that coquettish way she had.

"Yes, *toi*," I teased.

"Oh, but I couldn't."

"Don't be modest. You know you love it." Not only was Grandmère the mayor of our little village, but she managed the Providence Playhouse, a local theater that had won dozens of regional theater awards. She had an eye for staging that was beyond compare. Sure, she could wax dramatic and she often dressed like a gypsy, but it was her ability to see the big picture in regard to set design, costumes, and crowd appeal that made her famous throughout the region.

"I'd help you, Bernadette," Vivian said, "but I've got to run. Another appointment. Oh, that reminds me, Charlotte. The decorator is on her way. She called me to say she was sorry she was late. I guess she lost your cell phone number. Ta!" She sailed out of the shop as if launched on the crest of a wave.

As she exited, she dodged my clerk, Rebecca, who hurried in, gangly arms and legs jutting from her frilly blouse and capri pants. Luckily it was a cool day in May, so the air conditioning didn't have to work overtime with all the comings and goings.

"She's here!" Rebecca waved her hands like a singer at a Baptist revival, which was unusual since she was Amish and prone to quiet displays of excitement. Like the Fromagerie, Rebecca was a work in progress. Last year, at the age of twenty-one, she chose to leave the church and step into the modern world. She hadn't lost her faith, just her desire to be cloistered. At twenty-two, her latest discoveries were the Internet and the wonders of Facebook and Victoria's Secret.

"Who's here?" I said.

"Her!" She pointed toward the front of the shop.

I noticed she was wearing red nail polish.

19

I suppressed a smile.

"Her. Zoe, Zelda, Zebra. You know, that lady with the Z name."

"The reporter from *Délicieux*?"

Perspiration broke out under my arms. The *Gourmet*-style magazine with an ever-expanding readership offered to do a feature on our family — how my grandparents, Matthew, and I were keeping the old French tradition alive, with modest changes like adding the annex and offering cheese and wine tastings. Pépère was against the idea of speaking to a reporter. He said for fifty years word-of-mouth had been good enough for his sturdy business. But with all the dreams that Matthew and I had for the future of the shop, we craved a little media coverage.

I tugged the hem of my linen shirt over the waistband of my Not-Your-Daughter's jeans. Casual chic, in my humble opinion, was always best. "Do I look okay?" I whispered.

Grandmère toyed with the feathered-cut tresses around my face, then cupped my chin. "You look radiant, as always. Just be your delicious self." She winked. "Get it? Delicious, *Délicieux*? I made a joke, no?"

I chuckled.

"She's not actually *here* here," Rebecca

said, amending her story as she gathered her long blonde hair into a clip. "She's in the Country Kitchen having coffee. But she'll be here when she's done. Some of the local farmers are there, too. Don't you have a meeting with them at ten?"

"They rescheduled. It's now set for tomorrow at eight." I glanced at my watch out of habit while ticking off impending appointments and feeling my blood pressure soar. Why did good things often happen all at once? For that matter, why did bad things happen in threes? I looked forward to the end of the day when I would curl up in my Queen Anne chair with a glass of wine and a good Agatha Christie mystery.

"That *racaille* . . ." Pépère stomped into the shop through the rear entrance, his arms filled with tomatoes and basil, and kicked the door shut.

I hurried to him. "What's wrong? Who's a rascal?"

"Ed Woodhouse." The town's biggest real estate holder. Powerful beyond measure. Ruled by his snappish wife who wanted to oust my grandmother from her position as mayor so she could take over herself. Elections were next week, set in early June because our town founder, Ed's great-great-grandfather, had wanted it to coincide with the birth of his son. Ironically, the son chose that very same date, sixteen years later, to dump a cartload of cow manure in the Village Green to protest his father's stance on a youth curfew.

"What's he done now?" I said.

"He's selling the building."

My heart leapt at the news. Pépère had been trying to buy our building for years, but Ed was never willing to sell. "That's wonderful," I said. "We'll purchase it and be rid of him for good." The man was not a nice landlord. He indiscriminately raised rents. We had to beg him to allow us to make the archway to the annex. Once, he said he wanted to put my grandparents out of business simply because they were French.

"He refuses to entertain an offer from us," Pépère said.

"What?" I nearly screeched. "Can he do that?"

"*Je ne sais pas,*" he said, then mumbled a few choice snippets in French that would make a longshoreman blush.

Grandmère grasped him by the elbow and drew him into the kitchen by the walk-in refrigerator. I couldn't hear what she was saying to him, but she had a way of calming him down with nothing more than a tender kiss. Their love was magical, like something out of storybooks, love I longed for but didn't think I could ever hope to find. A moment later, they broke apart and Grandmère rejoined us.

"I must be gone," she announced. "The theater awaits."

"What are you putting on this summer, Mrs. Bessette?" Rebecca asked as she laid out more drop cloths. Before moving to Providence, she had never seen a play.

"A ballet of *Hairspray.*"

Grandmère's events were quite unique and not to everyone's liking. Last year, she had staged *Jesus Christ Superstar* as a ballet.

Rebecca gasped. "Can you do that?"

"Dear girl, I can do anything I please as long as the town votes yes."

"I mean, isn't that rock and roll?"

"If Billy Joel can do it, so can I. *Adieu.*" Grandmère did a curtsey, then *jetéd* toward the shop entrance, arms spread wide. She ran headlong into my best friend, Meredith Vance, who was entering. In a flash, Grandmère recovered. "So sorry, *chérie.*"

"My fault." Meredith, voted Providence Elementary's most adored teacher, was lovely in a freckle-faced, natural way. Sun didn't burn her; it kissed her. Sun didn't bake her tawny hair; it glossed it with a shimmering sheen. She also smiled more than anybody I knew. But she wasn't smiling now, and she was visiting during school hours. She stood half in, half out of the doorway, her lips a hard knot.

A peppery taste of anxiety flooded my mouth. "Is something wrong?" I asked.

Meredith yanked her arm. In trotted my niece, Amy, her cocoa bean eyes wide, her pixie face lowered. What had the little imp done this time?

I hurried to them with Matthew and Pépère at my heels. I steered Meredith and Amy away from the front door, to the empty area by the display window. We huddled around the duo as if circling the wagons.

"Tell them," Meredith ordered.

Amy's chin quavered. "I . . . I . . ." Gumdrop-sized tears fell from her eyes. "I . . ."

"Ah, heck," Meredith cut in. "She hit the Woodhouses' daughter in the nose."

A light sparked. I spun to my right. A boxy woman in a T-shirt with a huge zinnia on it stood just inside the front door. She held up her camera and took another picture.

I cringed. Z for Zinnia. The *Délicieux* reporter. She was getting an eyeful.

CHAPTER 2

At seven A.M. the next morning, after packing the twins' lunches, I sat on the wrap-around porch of my two-story Victorian home, a cup of cinnamon-laced coffee in my hands, and I debated the punishment I had meted out to Amy. Matthew, afraid to discipline the girls since their mother ran off, had ceded the decision to me. Had I been too lenient? Too harsh? How could I be sure?

I set my deliberations aside and instead focused on the initial interview with the reporter from *Délicieux.* In that regard, I was quite pleased with myself. At first, Zinnia had been resistant to release the rights to the photo with the angry family huddling around tearful Amy. I had signed a model's release, she reminded me. I begged and pleaded, but she didn't yield. I asked about her career, her family, how she got her name — a hippie mother dedicated to flower power, she confided. I even offered to let her take multiple pictures of the family at the opening night party, but she remained bullheaded. However, when I treated her to a taste of Tuscan Tartuffo, the ultimate in Italian cheeses, made with raw milk Pecorino and black and white truffles, fabulous alone or drizzled with a nutty honey, she caved. That was putting it mildly. In truth, she had nearly swooned. Everybody does. Success, Pépère often told me, is a result of being persistent. And clever.

At half past seven, dressed and showered for a busy day, I scooped up my rescue cat Rags — a fluffy Ragdoll with the easiest demeanor in the world, his silver, rabbitlike fur marred by one brown spot near the tail — and I headed off to The Cheese Shop. I let Matthew deal with the girls and their breakfast.

Late May is my favorite time in Providence, when dogwoods, azaleas, and daylilies are in bloom. With a bounce in my step, I strolled down the lane of colorful vintage houses like mine and turned right. Sunlight glinted on the face of the clock tower that stood in the middle of the Village Green. The scent of lilacs growing against the Green's white picket fence was intoxicating. At Hope Street, I made a right and sauntered past the brick buildings with green awnings that housed Mystic Moon Candle Boutique, Europa Antiques and Collectibles, and Sew Inspired Quilt Shoppe. At each, I took a moment to admire the display windows and make mental notes of what I could tweak in my own.

Minutes later, I ambled into The Cheese Shop, certain that the day was going to be a snap compared to yesterday's mishmash. Was I ever wrong.

Soon after my arrival, Grandmère pushed through the front door and ground to a halt. Prior to her retirement, she often came in early, gave me a hug, then headed for the office to balance the books and pay bills. She didn't look ready to do any of the above. She tapped her tiny foot like a riveter. Rebecca slipped in behind her, mouth grim, arms at her side. Hand the girl a musket, and she could have been a soldier ready for battle.

"Good morning," I said cheerfully, my heart doing a not-so-cheerful jitterbug.

Grandmère approached with unbridled fury in her coconut shell brown eyes. "I won't have it, Charlotte."

"Me, either," Rebecca said.

"Have what?" I asked, knowing full-well what they meant. They were upset about the deal I had cut with Meredith in regard to Amy. Guess I was too lenient.

"Allowing the girl to work in Fromagerie Bessette during the days she is expelled from school is no punishment at all, and you know it," Grandmère said.

"She loves The Cheese Shop as much as you do," Rebecca added.

True. Ever since she had arrived on my doorstep, Amy had made a habit of showing up at the shop after school. She lingered over the wheels of cheese and quickly proved she could distinguish a cheese simply by its aroma. A good nose was a gift. I had it. So did Pépère. Was it wrong to let Amy spend extra hours in an environment that she loved, learning about something that could one day be her future?

Reluctant to have a confrontation where locals could spot us, I steered Grandmère and Rebecca to the little office beside the kitchen. It was bigger than a bread box but certainly not big enough for me, Grandmère, Rebecca, Rags, and the sixteen-year-old techie I had hired to create our new website.

"Bozz?" I said. "I know you just got started, but I need you to step out for a moment."

The boy sat hunched in the oak desk chair

with Rags draped over his shoulders like a stole. A set of iPod buds were stuck in his ears. His fingers tapped fervently on his cell phone, texting Lord-knew-who.

"Yoo-hoo, Bozz?"

Considering the boy's slow rate of productivity, I wasn't sure if he would finish the website in time for the grand opening of the shop, but he was the only web designer in town. I had planned to take a community college course to learn how to create a website, but never got around to it. Matthew, a renaissance type of guy, was computer illiterate.

One thing at a time was fast becoming my new mantra.

I plucked an iPod bud from the kid's ear. "Bozz, step out a moment, will you? It's tight quarters in here."

"Sure, Miss B." He offered a toothy grin, then removed Rags from his shoulders, plopped the cat onto the chair cushion, and shambled out of the room.

I glanced at the partially completed website on the computer screen and liked what I saw. Bozz had chosen a calligraphy font and set it on a golden background. Images with groupings of cheese, bottles of wine, and people enjoying a cheese and wine tasting — all captured by a professional photog-

29

rapher from Cleveland who had charged me a minor fortune — lined the left side of the screen. So far so good, I thought, eager to get the site up and running. I envisioned having to hire a second clerk just to manage the online orders. A gal could dream.

I closed the door and Grandmère lit into me. "Too much freedom leads a child down the path to destruction."

"She's right," Rebecca said. "I heard that on *Law & Order*."

I sniffed. "Oh, please, it's not like I'm giving Amy a gold medal for cleaning the little Woodhouse's clock. Anyway, the girl deserved what she got. She and her friends were making fun of you and razzing Amy because her mother walked out." I jabbed a finger at my grandmother.

She stiffened. "I didn't hear —"

"Amy whispered it to me before Matthew hustled her home. Look, Grandmère, I know Kristine Woodhouse is hungry to replace you as mayor, and now she has her child spreading rumors. Someone has got to put a foot down. Might as well be me."

Grandmère harrumphed. Rebecca folded her arms over her petite chest.

"C'mon. Let's cut Amy a little slack," I said. "She's only been here a short time. She's trying to fit in. Wanting to defend

30

family is a commendable trait."

"Not with one's fists, *chérie*."

"Okay, fine, I'll talk to her about using her words." How many times had my grandparents reminded me that words were our sharpest weapons? "She is under my roof, so I'm in charge." I didn't have a clue how to raise a child or set ground rules, but I was a fast learner. At least I hoped so. "In the meantime, I've got a meeting with the local farmers. Now, can we disband?"

"*Oui*," Grandmère said.

"*Oui*," Rebecca echoed. She knew about three words of French but was catching on quickly and was a little too curious about Pépère's more colorful phrases.

I snagged three Hershey's Kisses from a stash in the lowest desk drawer and handed one to each of them and kept one for myself. Kisses were my passion. After cheese and wine, chocolate could cure a whole lot of ailments. We ate in silence, sealing our agreement with a *kiss,* then I swung open the door, told Rags to stay, and marched into the shop. I found Pépère muttering yet another string of French longshoreman curses and shook my head. So far, retirement wasn't doing either of my grandparents any good. Perhaps Matthew and I could entice them to go on a vacation to the Caribbean. An extended vacation.

"What happened, Etienne?" Grandmère rushed to Pépère. She grabbed his hands.

I knew better than to intrude, but I kept an ear open as Rebecca and I removed drop cloths from the tables and barrels. The smell of paint and antique stain hung in the air, but with the doors and windows opened, the place would quickly air out. One thing Ohio offers is plenty of clean, crisp air.

"You won't believe what I heard at Country Kitchen." Every morning, Pépère visited the fifties-style diner across the street for an espresso. Alone. His private time, he said. In truth, as good a cook as my grandmother was, she couldn't brew a decent pot of coffee for the life of her. "Kristine Woodhouse told that . . . that . . . reporter . . ." Pépère's cheeks and neck flushed red.

"The reporter from *Délicieux*?" Grandmère said.

He nodded. "She told her that you were unfit to be mayor. She said you were past your prime, and she said . . . she said . . ." His jaw ticked with anger.

"*Mon ami,* breathe. I can handle whatever lies Kristine Woodhouse makes up. Go on."

"She said the shop is a disgrace, that we are making a mockery of Providence with our . . . our pretension."

32

"Pretension?" I shrieked. How dare she!

"She said she should have been the one to open the wine store, not us, and she said—"

"Relax." Grandmère stroked my grandfather's hair and kissed him on the forehead. "It means nothing. Do not rise to the bait."

The grape-leaf-shaped chimes tinkled and the front door opened. I turned and realized my eight A.M. appointment, a group of local farmers, had arrived. I wasn't nearly ready. *Merde.*

The crowd split and I caught sight of Jordan Pace, a rugged man with the untamed energy of a silver screen cowboy. Call me crazy, but whenever I saw him, my knees went weak and I thought I could hear movie music swell and spurs jingle. He always wore blue jeans and work shirts rolled up at the sleeves, which showed off his powerful tan arms. If he slipped an arm around my waist and kissed me hard on the lips, I wouldn't object. But that wouldn't happen. We were only friends. He supplied the majority of the shop's artisanal cheeses, all made by hand with the freshest products available. *Buy local* is another of my mantras.

Jordan left the crowd and strolled toward me with an easy, catlike grace.

I finger-combed my hair and smoothed

the front of my short-sleeved turquoise sweater, wishing I had carried a tube of gloss in my trousers' pocket so I could smear a coat on my parched lips.

"Morning, Charlotte."

I smiled, thankful that I had checked my teeth in the mirror before leaving the house to make sure no blueberries were lodged there. "Jordan."

"Place is coming around."

"Sure is."

"I like the color of the walls."

"Thanks." Could I sound more inept?

"So . . ." He hooked his thumbs through the loops of his jeans and hitched his chin.

Something inside me fluttered.

"What's with the protesters in front?" he said.

I glanced out the display window and my mouth dropped open. He hadn't hitched his chin to flirt with me. Women in dresses and sunhats were marching on the sidewalk with signs in their hands that read *Vote for Kristine!*

Kristine Woodhouse, a lean brunette with a beak of a face, led the pack, her floral dress flouncing around her stick-thin legs.

"Mon Dieu!" With the fury of a train heading downhill, Grandmère stormed outside.

I galloped after her. Of the family, she had

34

the sharpest set of tools in her vocabulary chest.

"Kristine Woodhouse, get off my property," Grandmère ordered.

Three women broke from the crowd, Kristine's coterie of snobs, all clad in summer hats and chiffon dresses no doubt purchased at Kristine's boutique. They clustered around Kristine, hands on hips, heads bobbing, mouths chattering, reminding me of a gaggle of hens.

Kristine raised a hand over her head to silence them. "Girls, thank you for your support."

Girls? She had to be kidding. Kristine's pals had to be in their fifties. She, herself, was on the wrong side of forty. The birth of her daughter had surprised everybody.

"This sidewalk is public property, Bernadette Bessette. I may walk it freely." Kristine drew near to my grandmother and looked down her nose at her. "You, as mayor, should know that, but obviously you have grown dim in recent days." She eyed her pals. They clucked with delight.

Grandmère whispered something in French that even Pépère wouldn't say.

"Speaking of which," Kristine continued, "we need someone with a clear head and an eye to the future to run this town. You and your ridiculous theater events are a distraction."

"They are works of art!" Grandmère shouted.

"They are works of a lunatic. People laugh behind your back. They want classic ballets."

"You mean *you* want them. You lobby for them."

Grandmère was right. The people of Providence had a vote in what productions were done each season, and many, other than Kristine, enjoyed the celebrity and praise that the avant garde shows engendered.

"And that great-granddaughter of yours," Kristine went on, undeterred.

Grandmère's hands drew into fists. No one insulted her family. She breathed in shallow spurts, doing her best to maintain her composure.

"She is a wild child," Kristine continued, unfettered. "She belongs —"

"Don't say it!" Grandmère raised her hands, fingernails primed.

"Go ahead. Hit me. I would expect nothing less from the likes of you heathens."

"Heathens? Why, you —" Grandmère lunged.

Pépère burst out the front door. He

grabbed her in the nick of time.

"I rest my case." Kristine lifted her pointed chin, her lips twitching with smug satisfaction. "As for you, Charlotte." She whirled on me and stabbed her finger at my face. "My husband will never sell this building to you and that cousin of yours. I'll see to it! Do you hear me? If I have my way, Ed will evict you when the lease is up next year. Evict you!" With that, she turned on her high heels and strutted away, her friends chanting in her wake, rally signs raised.

Grandmère spun around and gazed at Pépère, tears swelling in her eyes. "Oh, *mon ami,* it is finished. Kristine and her rich friends will pressure people. She will destroy everything our family has cultivated in this town."

Pépère drew her into his arms. "Nonsense. The shop makes lots of money. Ed is not going to kick out tenants who pay on time."

I wasn't so sure about that.

Pépère ushered Grandmère into the shop, and I eyed the crowd that had gathered, which included a busload of tourists on a wine tour from Cleveland. "Show's over, folks. All over."

As they disbanded, I caught sight of Ed Woodhouse standing on the sidewalk by the Country Kitchen. The man never failed to send a shiver down my spine. He always wore a black suit. The skin on his face clung to his bones. Some people said he was a womanizer, but I couldn't see it. The Grim Reaper held more appeal.

With adrenaline pumping so hard through my veins that I could hear it in my ears, I reentered the shop, wondering how I could salvage my grandmother's reputation and the future of Fromagerie Bessette. I was relieved to see that the local farmers, including Jordan Pace, had slipped away during the commotion. I wasn't in the mood to discuss artisanal cheeses, and I certainly wasn't in the mood to flirt. I would reschedule the appointment for Monday, that is, if they weren't all convinced that Fromagerie Bessette was going to be out of business within the month.

"Psssst, Miss B?" Bozz stood by the display window, his narrow shoulders hunched, fingers surprisingly not tapping the buttons on his cell phone. He swept a thatch of blond hair out of his eyes. "Got a sec?" He beckoned me with a crooked finger.

Oh, great, I thought. He's going to quit.

"Sure," I said with a forced smile and drew near.

"I know a way you can buy this building," he whispered.

CHAPTER 3

The next day, using a website, Bozz set me up as a corporation which he called Q. Lorraine, Inc., the Q for Quiche, which I thought was pretty darned clever. Via the anonymity of the corporation, which he said his uncle Luigi did all the time, I put a bid on the building, anonymous as long as Ed Woodhouse didn't look up the principals in the company. I crossed my fingers, but I didn't dwell on the outcome of the offer because I had more pressing problems — picketers who, thanks to their loyalty to the lovely Kristine, were marching in front of Fromagerie Bessette, either boycotting the reopening or demanding that my grandmother step down as mayor. If I couldn't stop the revolt, we might lose so much business that it wouldn't matter if we owned the building or not.

"What are you going to do?" Matthew asked me as I angrily swept the floor.

I set my broom aside and gripped him by the shoulders. "*We* are going to go door to door and convince people to side with us."

"We?"

"You and me. Who better to plead our cause as well as Grandmère's?"

Matthew removed his chocolate brown chef's apron, slung it on a hook by the rear door, and clapped his hands once. "Let's go."

I grinned. Matthew might vacillate as a father, but he was decisive when it came to business.

Before beginning our quest, we visited the wishing well near the center of town, as we had the day we took over the shop. Matthew tossed in the first nickel.

"Make a wish," I said.

"I hope Amy will come around."

I squeezed his forearm. "Don't worry. She will."

"Your turn."

I tossed in my coin. "I pray I won't pull an 'Amy' and punch Kristine Woodhouse in the nose."

Matthew chuckled.

In less than three hours, we convinced the owners at Sew Inspired, Mystic Moon, and dozens of other shops to join forces with us and support Grandmère for mayor.

■ ■ ■ ■

On the morning of the reopening, revitalized with enthusiasm, I threw open the shop windows to let in fresh, crisp air, and I hummed while I refaced and rewrapped the cut wedges of cheese. Pépère always says that buying cheese is a visual experience. We eat with our eyes first. My good mood fizzled, however, when Grandmère shambled into The Cheese Shop draped in a gray dress the size of a tent. Where had she found the hideous thing? She looked like an engine that had run out of steam. Pépère gave me a wink as he closed the door. He was on the case.

I hugged my grandmother and urged her to eat something. She refused. I didn't chastise her when I saw her slip Pépère a morsel of Délice de Rougemont, a succulent buttery cheese from Switzerland. How could I? She was tending to the one she loved. At times like these, I wished my mother was still alive. Grandmère often told me how my mother's singing made her forget everything that was bad in the world. I recalled a lullaby she used to sing to me.

Around noon, after arranging the platters of cheese and adorning them with the beautifully printed title cards Bozz had designed, I poured a hot cup of vanilla latte and led Grandmère into the wine annex. I eased her into a chair, set the cup on the mosaic table, and as my pièce de résistance, I sang a verse of the lullaby. Grandmère sipped the latte and attempted a smile, but I could tell she wanted none of it. I didn't have a bad voice; she just wasn't interested in drink or song. I fetched Pépère and told him to let Grandmère stay home if she couldn't handle the evening. He nodded, mouth quavering, sweet blue eyes unable to hide that her pain was breaking his heart.

For the better part of the early afternoon, Rebecca, Matthew, and I lined up wine-glasses, opened bottles of wine, and tweaked the display windows. My other niece, Clair, dropped by after school to help Amy polish cheese spreaders. Two hours before the event, Matthew, Amy, Clair, and I raced home.

In the privacy of my master suite, I fluffed up my hair, applied fresh rouge and lipstick, and changed out of my sweater and trousers into a gold silk blouse, a pair of tapered black silk pants, and beaded flats. I checked myself in the antique oval mirror and liked what I saw. Confidence. I hurried down the mahogany staircase and met up with Matthew and the girls in the foyer. He had dressed the twins in matching white frocks and white ballet slippers, although they looked like complete opposites. Clair was light to Amy's dark, and taller by a head. The light from the grape motif chandelier I had purchased at an estate sale in Pennsylvania cast a warm glow on their smiling faces.

"You look beautiful," I said.

The girls curtsied then giggled.

I gave a tweak to Matthew's tie. "And you are the best business partner I could ever imagine."

"You're not so bad yourself." He cuffed me lightly on the chin.

I made sure Rags had plenty of water, and then the four of us set off for the shop.

About a half hour before the event was to begin, Jordan Pace showed up, uncharacteristically dressed in a white button-down shirt open at the neck, and tan slacks and loafers. Handsome as all get-out. He carried a honey-colored basket full of brilliant gold sunflowers and velvet red roses fitted with fern fronds and baby's breath.

"Evening, Charlotte," he said. "The place looks great, except, hmmm . . ." He rubbed his chin. "It seems to be missing one thing." His mouth turned up in a lopsided grin as he offered the basket to me. The smile reached his eyes and his gaze hit me like Cupid's arrow. "They're from my green-house. I'd hoped to bring them over earlier. Time got away from me. There are two wrist corsages tucked in there for your nieces."

"Thank you." Heat rushed up my neck. I willed it away but failed. A gorgeous man had brought me . . . us . . . flowers!

"You look very . . ." He paused.

I tried to ESP him a word to fill in the blank. Nice, pretty, downright sexy.

"I like your hair like that," he said.

Good enough.

"Listen," he went on. "I thought if you had a moment, we could talk —"

"Charlotte." Rebecca gripped my elbow.

"What?" I said, turning red-faced in-stantly, horrified that I had snapped at her, and in front of Jordan no less, but I was certain that she had just interrupted Jordan asking me out. On the other hand, he could have merely wanted to discuss payment ar-rangements.

"Your grandmother's here."

"Oh, of course, thank you." I licked my lips and smiled. "Rebecca, would you please put these flowers in a vase and give the girls their corsages? And Jordan, why don't you try a bite of that cheese over there?" I pointed to the Cabot Clothbound Cheddar, a delicacy from Vermont with just a hint of crystallization. Jordan was the kind of guy who would like a bold cheese. I would stake my reputation on it.

"We'll talk later?" He shot a finger at me. Bull's-eye.

"You bet." I zeroed in on Grandmère and Pépère as they neared the center display of crystal cheese platters, copper fondue pots, and other accessories, and my jitterbugging heartbeat returned to normal. Grandmère looked reenergized. Her eyes were bright, her cheeks rosy. I felt confident she would have a tart comeback to anything Kristine Woodhouse might say.

"Love the outfit," I said.

Grandmère twirled. Her layered black skirt fluted up around her aging dancer's legs. She wore a lacy white peasant blouse over the skirt, stylishly cinched with a tooled silver belt. "Made the blouse myself," she said. What couldn't she do? She clutched my elbow and drew me near. "I heard you have been tilting at windmills on my behalf. *Merci.*"

"Do not give up yet, Grandmère. People will vote for you."

"Ah, but we do not know what people do behind closed doors, do we?"

I kissed her cheek then hitched a thumb at the wine annex. "Matthew and the girls are in there." Before she could voice a concern, I added, "Don't worry. I made fresh-squeezed lemonade for them, and the sitter is coming to get them in one hour."

Grandmère pinched my cheek. "You will be a fabulous mother one day."

One day. The clock was ticking.

The grape-leaf-shaped chimes jingled.

"Showtime," Grandmère said.

My stomach tightened as she hurried to the door and wedged it open with a stopper.

The first to arrive were a handful of locals, all dressed in their finest.

Vivian Williams sailed in behind them, looking as windblown as she had the other day. She wore a sea blue, long-sleeved silk dress that matched her eyes. "Lovely, simply lovely," she said as she passed by me.

I glowed. A compliment from her was a real treat.

Close on her heels came Ed Woodhouse, alone. He trundled to the rear of the shop.

Next to arrive was a group of elementary schoolteachers, Meredith among them. She looked radiant in a yellow sundress, her tawny hair brushed off her face, a pair of diamond studs in her ears. She scanned the room. When her gaze met mine, I waved. She raced to me, clutched my elbow, and tugged me to the corner of the room.

"You'll never guess," she said, breathless and starry-eyed.

"What?"

"I'm seeing someone."

"Who?"

"I'll tell you soon, when I figure it out."

"What's to figure out?"

"Timing. But he's dreamy. He reads me poetry and he spoils me."

"Sounds perfect. C'mon, who? A teacher?"

"No."

"The guy who owns the sport shop? The artist? The cabinet maker?" I knew every boy Meredith had ever had a crush on.

She locked her lips and tossed away an imaginary key, just like we did when we had big secrets in fourth grade.

"Okay, I won't pry . . . for now."

She giggled. "How're things with you-know-who?"

I sighed. "He almost asked me out."

"Almost is only good in horseshoes, Charlotte. Get cracking! And good luck tonight."

She kissed my cheek and hurried to rejoin the other teachers. As they entered the wine room, a cluster of wine tour folks from Cleveland, all of whom were dressed in

48

matching brown T-shirts, walked into the shop. The voluptuous tour guide, a bleached blonde whose name I couldn't recall, wore strands of silver necklaces that she continuously twisted around her fingers. As the throng meandered toward the wine annex, uttering oohs and aahs about the vast selection of cheeses and accompaniments, the butterflies in my stomach subsided.

Rebecca left her post behind the counter and scooted to my side, her face pinched with displeasure. "*Hmph.* That Mr. Woodhouse smells of whiskey. His palate will be ruined."

I grinned. Rebecca, the budding cheesemonger and wine expert.

She swept her hair over her shoulders. "I put the flowers on the counter. Aren't they pretty?"

They looked beautiful, a perfect finishing touch. Perhaps tomorrow I would send Jordan a thank-you note on our personal stationery and hint — just hint — at a date.

"Oh, I've got customers." Rebecca hurried back to the wood counter and presented slices of Manchego one-year cheese to a few of the bus tour people. They murmured their appreciation.

I looked around for Jordan but didn't see him. What I did see made my pulse race.

Grandmère had cornered Ed Woodhouse, or maybe vice versa, by the shelves holding honey and jam. They were arguing. In the center of the room, Pépère chatted with some of the townsfolk, ignorant of the quarrel.

Grandmère poked her finger into Ed's chest and said loudly, "You will not evict us, you old goat. Not if you want your secrets kept secret."

Ed pushed her away and marched into the wine annex without an apology.

I ran to Grandmère, who recovered her balance on her own. I said, "What's going on?"

"Bah! Ed Woodhouse." She gave an angry tug to her blouse and her belt. "He . . . he makes my blood boil."

Through the arch of the annex, I spied Ed cozying up to Meredith, who was chatting with friends at the wine bar. Ed slid an arm around her waist. She quickly stepped away. He sniggered, then moved on to the tour guide in the brown T-shirt and silver necklaces, and patted her ample rump. I ground my teeth together. Did the man have no shame?

"We pay the rent," Grandmère went on. "We have never missed a payment. He and Kristine . . . they are . . ." She flipped her hand in the air. *". . . impossible!"* She hurried around the wood counter and disappeared into the office.

I signaled Pépère, who shuffled after her as another dozen townsfolk wandered into the shop, among them people whom I had solicited for votes. As I thanked them for coming, Meredith sauntered to my side and winked.

"Looks like you've got a hit on your hands, girlfriend." She sidled over to the tasting platter, which held one of my special tortes, made of layers of Stilton and mascarpone cheese, decorated with pecans and cranberries. "Amy's due back at school tomorrow. Is she up to it?"

"She'll be there."

Using a silver-handled cheese spreader, Meredith slathered the creamy torte onto a buttery cracker and popped it into her mouth. "Oh, my. Yum. What wine goes with this?"

"A sauvignon blanc." Matthew had educated me on our choices for the evening. He was brilliant at pairing wine with food. "We have one from the Bozzuto Winery." Bozz's family had been vintners for two generations. "It's crisp with undertones of pineapple and melon."

"Sounds tasty. I'll have to get some."

"C'mon, tell me, who you're dating," I said, still dying to know.

"Say, isn't that the reporter from *Délicieux*?" Meredith said, side-stepping the question. She gave me a thumbs-up. "Have fun."

She returned to the wine annex as Zinnia made a beeline for me, her floral T-shirt replaced with a severe suit that did nothing for her boxy shape, but far be it from me to tell her that. I wanted her to write a flattering article about the shop. She held a camera in one hand, a notepad with pen in the other. Before I could object, she snapped a picture. I winced. I do not usually look good in candid photos, but at least this wouldn't be a picture of our family in turmoil.

Zinnia leaned in close. "Guess what I heard at the diner?" Her voice sounded hoarse, as if she had been talking nonstop for hours. "Ed Woodhouse sold the building east of yours to a developer. I also heard that Lois's Lavender and Lace, the B&B where I'm staying, is asking the town's permission to turn her garage into a commercial space. What a charming house, by the way, with those lovely dormer windows and the white lattice fence."

My Victorian had similar features. I had

chosen an eleven-paint scheme for the exterior in keeping with the original owner's design. The tiles surrounding the dormer windows reminded me of a roll of Necco wafers.

"And did you hear — ?"

"Well, well, well," Kristine Woodhouse said, her shrill voice carrying over the crowd and cutting Zinnia's gossip short. She strutted into Fromagerie Bessette with her clique of wealthy friends trailing behind, dressed like they were attending Easter Sunday at church, white gloves in hand. Did Kristine intend to bring gloves back into fashion?

Like a precision drill team, the women stopped near the center display table, donned their gloves, left then right, and with a nod from Kristine, they paraded deeper into the shop, fingering everything as if they were checking for dust.

I excused myself from Zinnia and approached Kristine, who had stopped at the table filled with artisanal cheeses. She removed her gloves and helped herself to an hors d'oeuvres that was one of my favorites: lavender goat cheese nested on dates, compliments of Two Plug Nickels Farm. I promised myself one before the night was through, if any were left over.

"Kristine, welcome," I said. "So glad you

could make it."

"Charlotte, dear." Kristine waved a flippant hand. "Isn't this soirée a little over the top? I mean, really, the shop is so . . . crammed. Didn't you ever hear less is more?"

I flinched. Not from her ridicule, but from the sour stench coming off her. She had spritzed on extra perfume, but she couldn't mask the fact that she, like her husband, had been drinking. I doubted she would be able to discern the difference between one of our exquisite cheeses and Velveeta. I bit back a snarky comment and turned to her friends. "Felicia, Prudence, Tyanne, nice to see you."

Felicia, the one with wild red ringlets who reminded me of an aging Scarlett O'Hara, scrunched up her mouth. Prudence, the skinniest, whispered something to Felicia, who in turn sniggered, then whispered something to Tyanne, a transplant from New Orleans after Hurricane Katrina, who was ten years younger and the stoutest of the three. She repeated the wisecrack to Kristine. All the women cackled hysterically, leaving me to wonder whether they had spent the afternoon playing Bunko and kicking back shots of hard liquor.

"Isn't that Ed, Kristine?" Felicia wiggled

her fingers.

All heads turned.

Ed Woodhouse stood at the tasting counter with the blonde tour guide from the Cleveland wine group. As if they were the only two people at the event, he dipped bread into a granite bowl filled with olive oil and fed it to the woman. She licked his fingertips then chortled.

Kristine said, "Swine."

Prudence elbowed Felicia knowingly.

Kristine cleared her throat, threw back her bony shoulders, and beckoned her companions to follow her. She paused at the table with twenty-five-pound wheels of Gruyère, looking like she was debating whether to grab a wheel and slam her husband in the head with it.

Please don't make a scene, I prayed.

After a tension-filled moment, Kristine and her friends headed into the wine annex, probably to make fun of the rest of our decorating choices. To settle my roiling stomach, I snagged a cube of Swiss Emmental, then continued to make the rounds.

An hour passed without consequence. The teenage sitter I had hired gathered the twins and left for home. The crowd thinned, most of the guests vowing to return often. As I tidied displays, I spotted Grandmère and

Pépère sitting on the ladder-back stools by the tasting counter. His hand rested on hers, and I smiled, glad to see my grandmother had calmed down. Beyond them, near the rear entrance, Ed Woodhouse was making eyes at curly-haired Felicia. Kristine would not be pleased. Through the arch, I saw Jordan in the wine annex looking incredibly hunky. A local vintner was pointing out the red wine legs in Jordan's glass.

I fluffed my hair and geared myself for a little flirting, but before I could get so far as the arch, someone grabbed my shoulder and whipped me around.

"You!" Kristine teetered on her high heels and glowered at me with blatant disdain. "You . . . I'm so tired of you and your family and your —"

"Hey, Kristine, let it go." Felicia gripped Kristine by the elbow. She had abandoned Ed for her friend. Wise choice. "C'mon."

Kristine's other pals hustled to Felicia's side and voiced support.

Kristine wrenched away. "Not yet. I have some unfinished business to discuss with this . . . this . . ."

I stiffened. My hands balled into fists until Grandmère's warning to Pépère flitted through my mind: *Do not rise to the bait.* I drew in a deep calming breath and said,

"Why don't we discuss whatever it is tomorrow?"

"No! Now. I didn't speak my piece earlier." Kristine's words slurred together. "Your niece, or whatever you want to call her, is a brute."

"A what?" I sputtered. My composure vanished in a nanosecond, which didn't please me, but what could I do? "Take it back!"

"It's your fault. You let her run around unsupervised. Your grandmother did the same with you. All of you are vulgar little —"

"Stop it, Mrs. Woodhouse." Rebecca squeezed in beside me and raised an accusative finger. "You have no right to talk to Charlotte like that."

"Stay out of this, missy." Kristine batted away Rebecca's finger then refocused, with what little focus she could muster, on me. "That rugrat you are harboring hit my beautiful baby."

"She was saying bad things about my grandmother," I snapped.

"Sometimes the truth isn't pretty."

"That's enough!" Grandmère broke into the group and gripped Kristine by the wrist. With strength bred from years of backstage theater work, she yanked Kristine toward

57

the front of the store. "I've had enough of you, Kristine Woodhouse. You are no longer welcome. Go home." She marched Kristine out to the sidewalk. Kristine's three friends scurried after them.

"Ed!" Vivian set her wineglass on a display table and stomped toward Ed, who had taken up with a woman I didn't recognize by the center display table. "Why don't you take care of your wife instead of cavorting with every other female in the place?"

His eyes shot daggers at her. "Mind your own —"

"I mind mine. You should mind yours."

He grumbled something indecipherable, whispered something to his companion, and then stormed out of the shop behind my grandmother and Kristine and her cronies, none of whom had returned. Perhaps Grandmère had taken a walk around the block to cool down. She liked to do that. Pépère had disappeared, too. He had probably gone after her.

Vivian shook her head, her cheeks streaked red with embarrassment.

I joined her. "Are you okay?"

"Ed never should have married her," she said. "Just because they both came from money . . ." She paused. "They're nothing alike. He used to be so . . . so —"

"Charlotte." Jordan appeared. "That reporter is asking for you."

Vivian squeezed my hand. "I think I'll get another bite of that lovely ham and pineapple quiche. What's your secret?"

"White pepper in the crust."

"It's absolutely scrumptious." She strode toward the tasting counter.

Jordan said, "I heard you promised the reporter an interview." He grinned, his eyes sparkling with humor. "Want to promise me one?"

Did I ever. I put the fracas with Kristine aside and said, "Sure, let's —"

"Miss Bessette." Zinnia pressed between me and Jordan. "People are raving about this place, me included."

My momentary chemistry with Jordan fizzled like flat soda pop. He bid a quick goodbye and drifted away.

"So, let's hear the dirt." Zinnia tucked her camera into a pocket and flipped open her notepad, pen at the ready. "How did you get started?"

I'd rehearsed answers for days. "When I was young, my parents died in a car crash, and I came to live with my grandparents."

"I'm so sorry."

"It was a long time ago," I said, though the memory felt bitterly fresh. "As a young

59

girl, I found solace in The Cheese Shop and became eager to learn all I could."

"By the flavors I've tasted tonight, I can tell you're a good cook."

"I take cooking classes and attend lectures." Grandpère said a cheesemonger should be expert at all things cheese.

"You've written articles for a few food magazines and websites, too. Will you pursue more of that?"

"Oh, my, I have so many plans." I chuckled as my mantra, *one thing at a time,* chimed in my mind. "I guess I —"

A shriek cut the air. From the sidewalk.

Without excusing myself, I sprinted through the crowd and burst out the entrance. On the sidewalk, just to the right of the front door, Meredith was kneeling beside Ed Woodhouse's fallen body, her hands clutched as if in prayer, her mouth hanging open. One of my prized olive-wood-handled knives jutted from Ed's chest. Blood speckled Meredith's pretty yellow sundress.

I crouched beside her and slid my arm around her shoulders. "Did you — ?"

She stared at me, her gaze haunted, then past me. At someone huddling in the shadows by The Cheese Shop wall.

Grandmère Bernadette. She looked dazed and her hands were drenched with blood.

CHAPTER 4

Grandmère huddled by The Cheese Shop front door, clinging to Pépère. I'd only secured sixty brief blathering seconds of her protesting her innocence in French before a siren blared and Chief of Police Umberto Urso, a linebacker-sized teddy bear of a man, lumbered from his car.

Fifteen minutes later, as a fine mist fell from the sky, Urso was still surveying the scene. I stood by The Cheese Shop door like a lummox, damp and unable to help the woman who meant everything to me. Why wasn't Urso saying anything? He could be so obstinate.

I finally found the gumption to approach him, instantly regretting how close I got to his massive form, because I had to tilt my head back to look up into his hardened face — not the strongest position of attack. "C'mon, U-ey . . ." I sputtered. None of us had dared to call Urso by his nickname in public since grade school. He deserved our respect. Providence had a very low crime rate thanks to him. "Chief Urso, please, you can't possibly believe my grandmother could have killed —"

"Charlotte, I don't know what to believe." Urso was the kind of guy I would want on my team for kickball or flag football. Strong, forthright, ever alert. He could probably break me in half with his sizeable hands. "Let's move back people." He flailed his arms. "Off the sidewalk. Back."

I always thought Urso would go into the family business. His tidbit of a mother, no bigger than a preteen, owned Two Plug Nickels Farm. She and her husband had emigrated from Sicily. They made the best ricotta salata I had ever tasted, and their goat cheese was incredibly smooth. She claimed playing opera over a set of loud-speakers while the cheese was processing made the difference. Their son, Urso, had taken a different path. He dedicated himself to service. He became an Eagle Scout. He served as our high school class president. At one point, when he headed up the town council, I thought he might leave Providence and go into national politics. I could see him as president, albeit the largest president America would ever know. At the very least, with his resonant voice, I thought he would have considered becoming a preacher.

The emergency medical team moved the body to an ambulance while Urso's deputy set up a perimeter with yellow crime tape.

I drummed up more courage and pursued Urso again. "Chief, please, may I take my grandmother inside?"

"Sorry, no. We're going on the assumption that the murder weapon came from your shop. If that's the case, the shop is included in the crime scene."

"Then can't you question her tomorrow? It's damp. She'll get sick."

"I'd like to get all the accounts now while they're fresh. We're under the awning."

"But —"

"Let's start with you."

Worry shivered down my arms and into my fingertips. I had not expected to be grilled on the sidewalk. What would I say? I hadn't seen a thing. I couldn't exonerate or condemn Grandmère.

All business, Urso tipped back his hat, then pulled a paper and pen from the breast pocket of his brown uniform. "Where were you at the time of the crime?"

I shored up my shoulders, and working hard to keep my voice calm, I explained that I was inside the shop being interviewed by the *Délicieux* reporter. As I said the words, I wondered where Zinnia had gone. Jordan was standing off to one side, his mouth pressed to a cell phone. I hoped he wasn't calling the *Providence Post* and giving them the scoop. So far the crowd had remained thin. Matthew had appeared and handed Meredith a glass of wine. She looked as shaken as Grandmère, worrying the diamond stud on her ear with a vengeance. Vivian, her raincoat pulled tight, looked frozen in time. Kristine and her three cronies were nowhere in sight.

"See anything suspicious?" Urso asked.

"Ed was hitting on women. Did you know he's a womanizer?" I didn't like that gossip rolled easily off my tongue, but I was too upset to be ashamed. I kept my grandmother's argument with Ed a secret. It wasn't important. At least I hoped it wasn't.

"I'd heard."

"Any one of those women could have had enough of his . . . unwanted affections." I hitched my thumb toward the diner. "Heck, Kristine could have killed him. She didn't take kindly to being embarrassed in public, and with her run for mayor, she was bound to find his wanderings embarrassing, don't you think? Aren't you wondering where she is?"

Urso jotted my musings on his notepad. "Yeah, okay, I got the picture. What else? When was the last time you saw your grandmother?"

My mouth went dry. I had hoped he wouldn't ask. I ran my tongue around my teeth to loosen my lips. "Around a quarter to nine, she went outside with Kristine. They were . . . having words." He was bound to find out. "But it was because Kristine was saying bad things about my niece," I rushed to explain.

"Anybody see Bernadette after that?" Urso scanned the crowd hovering around us. "Anyone?"

No one said a peep.

"She was upset," I went on. "She probably took a walk. She does that."

"Anybody see her take a walk?" Urso turned in a circle, arms spread wide.

Again, no one came to Grandmère's defense.

"I'll take that as a no," Urso said.

I felt like kicking him in the shins for trapping me. I couldn't offer an alibi to help Grandmère, but surely someone else saw her. Someone. Anyone! "My grandfather wasn't in the shop. I think he went walking with her."

"I asked him already," Urso said. "He

wasn't. And he wasn't here when you heard the scream and came out of the shop either, was he?"

I chewed on my lip. Where had Pépère gone to at the time of the murder? For that matter, where had anybody gone? Kristine, her friends, the tour group people? There had been so many at the gala opening. Any one of them could have lain in wait for Ed to leave the store. Any one of them could have pilfered one of my prized olive-wood-handled knives and used it as a weapon. Sharp, serrated, one quick thrust.

Stop it, Charlotte. Do not get gruesome. I sighed. Death is gruesome.

I refocused on the crime. Who'd had access to the knife? So many guests had circulated around that centrally placed display table. Were all the knives still there when I had tidied up an hour into the event? I had an eye for detail. I could remember the names of hundreds of cheeses, their countries of origin, and whether they were made in the morning or the evening. I could recall the crests of every farm I had ever visited. Why couldn't I remember something as simple as the arrangement on a display table an hour before?

A thought occurred to me. "Would the plastic box that the knives were stored in hold fingerprints?"

"Might. Might not," Urso said. "We've logged it into evidence. Could take months to get the results. We're not as fast as those guys on *CSI*. Nobody is."

"The murder was so . . . public. Right in front of my shop. Who would dare?"

"Someone who was mad at Ed, is my bet."

I choked back a laugh. Lots of people in town were mad at Ed. He had wielded his power over each and every one, but none seemed guiltier than Grandmère at this very moment. I had to do something. *Think, think, think!*

Inspiration struck. If I had killed someone, I would have run. I thought again of Kristine. Surely she had to know something had happened in town. The crowd had grown to twice its original size. Where was she? Why wasn't she here mourning her husband?

I said, "Chief, would my grandmother have stayed around, huddling in the corner, if she was the murderer?"

"If she were in shock, she might."

Dang. I hadn't considered the shock angle.

"Charlotte, she is covered with blood."

"She pressed on the wound to stanch the flow of blood," I argued. Grandmère had explained that much to me in the sixty seconds before Urso arrived. During World

68

War II, though she had been a mere slip of a girl, she had saved a soldier's life the same way. He'd stumbled into their home.

Urso raised a hand. "Let's give her a chance to talk, okay? You can stand nearby, but don't cue her, got me?"

He lumbered toward Grandmère and Pépère. Grandmère clung to Pépère, her back to us.

"Mrs. Bessette, could I have a word?"

Pépère pried her from him and turned her to face us.

Grandmère's skin was ash gray and beaded with water. Mist-soaked hair clung to her face. "I did not do this," she whispered and clutched her hands so tightly that the blood drained from them.

Urso shrugged, as if everyone said "not guilty." "Ma'am, where were you for the past hour or so? Your granddaughter said you left the shop with Kristine Woodhouse."

"We . . . we . . ." She licked her lips. "I pushed her outside. She wanted to return. I told her no. She and her . . . friends . . . they were drunk. They strode across the street and disappeared into the diner."

"The Country Kitchen?"

"Yes. I . . ." She struggled for breath. "I took a walk."

"Which way?"

She pointed north, toward the Village Green. "I went to the clock tower."

"Really?"

I believed her. Why didn't Urso? The brick and white wood clock tower had been constructed as a monument in memory of Providence's war veterans who had given their lives to keep America safe. Grandmère went there often. Sometimes she spent entire mornings sitting beside the clock tower, reading a play or feeding birds. She said she found inspiration at the site where ashes of the fallen lay buried beneath the earth.

"Anybody see you?" Urso said.

"It was dark. The mist —"

"I need a name."

"But there was no one," Grandmère pleaded. She turned to Pépère. "Tell them you saw me."

"Oh, *chérie*." Tears pooled in his aging eyes. He reached for her hands. "I am so ashamed —"

"Ashamed of what?" Grandmère said.

I echoed her. Had my grandfather done something that might ruin his life? Or my grandmother's? I glanced at my grandmother. If I was feeling sucker punched, I could only imagine how she was feeling.

Urso put his hand on my arm. "Charlotte, please."

I shook him off. Beads of mist scattered into the air. "I need to know where my grandfather was. Pépère, please, what did you do?"

Pépère's shoulders heaved. "I had . . . a craving."

A craving? "For what?" I swallowed hard, not sure I wanted to know the answer.

Pépère blew out a long stream of air. "Ice cream. I went to the Igloo."

"But we had so many hors d'oeuvres at the gala," I blurted. "So much cheese."

Urso choked back a laugh. I shot him a hard look, realizing how ridiculous I had just sounded. Somebody had been murdered. Why did I care whether my grandfather ate ice cream instead of cheese? But his jaunt to the Igloo didn't make sense.

"I always eat cheese. I wanted . . . I had . . . a craving." Pépère brushed my grandmother's face with his fingertips. "I'm sorry, *chérie.*"

Grandmère's eyes pooled with tears. "It matters not, *mon ami.* I know how you like sweets."

Something flicked in Urso's cheek. Was he moved by their obvious love? His wife had left him three years ago for a tornado

71

buster. Tongues had wagged. He turned away from my grandparents and surveyed the crowd. "Anyone see Mrs. Bessette at the clock tower? Anyone?"

Everyone was as quiet as sleepy sheep.

Urso clasped Grandmère's elbow. "All right, Mrs. Bessette —"

"Chief Urso, wait!" I yelled.

Jordan slipped up beside me and rested a hand on my shoulder. "Charlotte."

"Not now," I snapped. I instantly regretted my tone, but I couldn't keep my frustration in check. "Chief, please, let her go."

"Sorry, Charlotte. I've got to do my job." The look in Urso's eyes said he truly was sorry. "Mrs. Bessette, ma'am, I'm afraid I'll have to place you under arrest unless we can find a witness who can give you an alibi."

Jordan whispered, "Charlotte." He spun me around and riveted me with his gaze. "If you need one, I've got a good criminal attorney."

I didn't have the wherewithal to ask why he would know a criminal attorney. I simply said, "Yes."

CHAPTER 5

The following day, as the rain disappeared
and the thermometer rose steadily outside,
so did the emotional temperature inside
Fromagerie Bessette. Customers, abuzz
with gossip, roamed the shop. The center
display table, where the olive-wood-handled
cheese knives had lain, was a popular spot
to convene. The crime scene tape that had
encircled the table was gone. By midnight,
Urso and his deputy had obtained all the
fingerprints they were going to catalogue.

"How is Grandmère?" Rebecca asked. She
stood at the cheese counter offering tastings
of Cabot Clothbound Cheddar and Crem-
inelli Salami Casalingo while I packaged
requests. Matthew had yet to appear.

"Not good," I answered. I had visited my
grandmother before opening the shop. The
attorney had arranged with Urso for Grandmère to be under house arrest and not
confined to a jail cell. While house arrest

73

wouldn't have been difficult for most, because Grandmère did so much outside her home — the theater production, the dance classes she taught once a week, and acting as mayor — she felt stifled and instantly had gone into a funk. Not that she could be mayor right now. She'd had to relinquish her duties while under house arrest. But sitting tight, as Urso had told her to do, was nearly impossible. Thankfully he hadn't insisted on her wearing an ankle bracelet. That would have put her over the edge. I had found her wandering through the house, wearing no makeup, her hair as messy as if she had brushed it with a scrub brush.

Rebecca said, "I'm sure this will all be resolved soon."

"I hope so."

Out of nowhere, customers started yelling questions rapid-fire.

"Charlotte, did she do it?"

"Did you see her do it?"

"Do you think she did it?"

No, no, and no.

"Did she have a motive?" asked Mr. Nakamura, the cherub of a man who had moved to Providence two years ago and opened a well-stocked hardware store called Nuts for Nails.

"Of course not," I snapped.

"I saw them coming out of the town hall together last week," a nun from St. Mary's said.

My dental hygienist waved her hand like a game show contestant who had the winning answer and yelled, "Me, too!"

I couldn't refute either of them. I didn't know my grandmother's every coming and going. She could have been at the town hall at the same time as Ed. She was the mayor. He did business with the city. All real estate transactions were handled in an office on the second floor.

"Were she and Ed having an affair?" asked the beekeeper, a transplanted Hawaiian who provided The Cheese Shop's stock of jarred honey. I was surprised by his query. He was a naturalist, not usually drawn in by town gossip.

Fearing the day could only get worse, I didn't grant him a response.

"Of course they weren't having an affair, sugar," Tyanne chimed in as she pushed to the front of the throng, her floral perfume cloying, her plump face looking smooth and unwrinkled but smug enough to pop with glee.

I was surprised to see her. Prior to hooking up with Kristine, Tyanne had often visited The Cheese Shop alone. I'd commiserated with her about losing her home to the hurricane and having to start life anew. We had chatted about good food and interesting books. At that time, I couldn't get enough of her honey-drenched drawl. But once she became a Kristine groupie, she stopped coming in by herself. In fact, I couldn't remember the last time I'd seen her without the others. Granted, I hadn't expected Kristine to come to Fromagerie Bessette the day after her husband was found murdered on the sidewalk, but it surprised me that Tyanne was there. Felicia and Prudence, usually at the forefront of town gossip, had yet to surface. Were they flocking together, trying to cement their alibis?

"I heard Ed and Bernadette were in love in high school," said the older woman standing next to Tyanne, an animal rescuer who had given me Rags.

"That's ridiculous." Like a clipper ship in rough waters, Vivian carved a path to the front of the pack and faced the crowd. "Bernadette was twenty years older than Ed."

And she didn't move to the United States until she was eighteen, I wanted to say, but kept my mouth shut. I was not fueling this gossip-fest any longer. I filled Vivian's order

76

first and thanked her for her defense of my grandmother. She patted my hand and said not to worry. She was certain Bernadette was innocent.

By midmorning, my stomach churned with excess acid and my jaw felt screwed together. I wished I could change out of the button-down shirt and long slacks I had worn into something cooler, but I had no time. A half dozen reporters from as far away as Cleveland had descended upon us, each with a camera crew. I had hoped Fromagerie Bessette would get attention from the press, but not for this reason.

In an attempt to dissuade the reporters, I set out a wooden platter arrayed with paper-thin slices of Double Cream Gouda from Pace Hill Farm, one of the smoothest tasting cheeses around. As the reporters and their crews munched, I talked up the new ownership of the store and its expansion. I enlightened them about how much my grandparents loved Providence and how much they had done to improve the town by adding color and vitality and a sense of joie de vivre, but in the end, the reporters clamored for a story about murder.

"Was Bernadette in love with Ed Woodhouse?" said a weasel of a reporter with bug-eyed glasses who I had seen at the gala.

"Did he reject her?" said another reporter, equally as creepy looking as the weasel.

"Was that why she killed him?" said the youngest reporter in the group, an overly made-up female whose suit was a perfect fit and whose hair was shellacked to a shine.

"No, for heaven's sake, no!" I shrieked. "My grandmother and grandfather are happily married. My grandmother didn't kill —"

Rebecca put a hand on my arm and whispered, "Charlotte, why don't you take a break? I'll handle this." With aplomb I didn't know a twenty-two-year-old could possess — I certainly hadn't at that age — she sidled around the counter and summoned the reporters to come closer. As she answered the first of their questions, she flipped her hair in a girlish way and smiled at the cameras as if she were a budding actress destined to star in one of Grandmère's productions.

At the same moment, the owner of Sew Inspired Quilt Shoppe, a freckle-faced forty-year-old who everyone called, no surprise, Freckles, trotted up. She was as cute as a button, loved the color orange, and was the kind of woman who relished life so much that she finished nearly every sentence with a chuckle. "Charlotte, a minute?"

I scooted from my spot behind the counter and followed her into the wine annex. Dozens of people browsed the wines that were for sale. Many carried our decorative six-pack holders. None seemed interested in us.

I said, "What's the matter?"

"You won't believe what Kristine Woodhouse is up to." A happy snort escaped through her nose.

I could always count on Freckles for the latest scoop. Every morning, she homeschooled her daughter. Afternoons and evenings, she worked at her shop and gleaned up-to-the-minute news from other homeschooling mothers and customers.

"What?" I said.

Freckles toyed with the zipper on her hot orange hoodie. "She's wearing a red, white, and blue dress with a banner strung across her chest like a beauty pageant contestant that reads *Vote for Woodhouse,* and she's handing out flyers."

The day after her husband's death? I groaned. Leave it to Kristine to take advantage of the situation while my grandmother languished under house arrest. I found myself wishing Kristine ill. Not death, mind you, but a bad hair day or even identity theft.

Choosing my words carefully, I said, "Basic black isn't always the way. Perhaps she's celebrating Ed's life in living color?"

"You are too kind."

If only she knew what was truly going on in my mind.

Freckles thumped the counter with her palm. "I want to help Bernadette. What do you want me to do? Knock on doors. Arrange a rally? I've got a quilting party this afternoon. And a sparkly T-shirt class at eight." At times Freckles left me breathless. Two afternoons a week, she taught quilting and quilting lore. Three nights a week, she taught women how to make T-shirts decorated with rhinestones. On Saturdays, she held children's crafting sessions and birthday parties. "But in between I could —"

"Do nothing."

"Nothing?" Laughter bubbled out of her. "Uh-uh. No, ma'am. It's guerrilla campaign time." She clapped me on the shoulder. "C'mon, we're all in this together. We cannot, I repeat, cannot let Kristine Woodhouse become our new mayor."

"Perhaps you haven't heard. My grandmother —"

"Oh, please." Freckles burst into giggles. "Like Bernadette could hurt anyone. Chief Urso will see that. Now . . ." She rubbed

80

her hands together. "Give me a job."

Matthew slogged into the annex with hangdog eyes and hunched shoulders, looking more like a basset hound than a Great Dane. His striped shirt wasn't tucked in. His stone-washed trousers looked slept in. He pushed a trolley filled with our latest shipment of wine.

I said to Freckles, "Let me think about it."

"I'll put my thinking cap on, too." She gave my arm an affectionate squeeze and scurried out of the shop.

Campaigning, worrying about my grandmother, and running a thriving business did not go hand in hand. My stomach felt as tangled as one of Rags's balls of yarn. But Matthew looked like he needed more reassurance than I did.

"You got home late last night," I said. After paying the sitter, I had shuffled upstairs, checked on the girls, who were sound asleep, and then stumbled into bed. But I barely slept; I tossed until three A.M. Matthew had wandered in around two.

"I was out . . . talking." He tied a chef's apron at the back of his waist. "Trying to make sense of . . ." He shook his head.

I cuffed him on the chin with my knuckles and said, "Perk up. The lawyer tells me everything is going to be okay." I wasn't so sure he was right, but other than working out a contract for the transfer of The Cheese Shop from Grandpère to Matthew and myself, I had never had cause to deal with a lawyer. Jordan swore by him.

"But what if it isn't okay?"

"It will be."

Matthew shuffled into the wine annex. I followed.

"Do the girls know?" I said.

"They heard something on the news this morning. I switched it off." He snapped his fingers. "Like that." He collected a few bottles of wine and set them out on the bar. Today's selections for tasting would include three white wines. A sauvignon blanc from Healdsburg, a chardonnay from Napa, and a pinot grigio from Italy. Michael had decided that we would offer limited daily samples, either white or red. He wanted the town of Providence to become educated on the variety of wines from all over the world. Any more than three in a short time span, he said, and the palate couldn't differentiate. We would offer more expansive tastings once a month and invite wine sellers from around the country to give lectures, staying within the limits of Ohio state laws, of course. "How's Grandmère holding up?"

"She's fine," I lied. I planned to visit her at noon with a picnic of Crackerjack Chicken and Caprese salad on a skewer and see if I could bolster her spirit.

"What's with all the reporters?" Matthew asked.

"Don't worry. Rebecca has things under —"

"No way!" Rebecca shouted above the din. "Charlotte's mother was not the love child of Ed Woodhouse and Bernadette Bessette! They were enemies. As a matter of fact, Ed Woodhouse threatened to evict the Bessettes from the shop."

My mouth dropped open. So much for Rebecca having things under control.

The reporters reacted to the news like piranhas in a pond full of raw meat. They shoved their microphones toward Rebecca's pretty face and shouted questions. She stumbled backward into a cheese display. Fifty-pound wheels of Morbier fell to the floor with a thud.

I smacked my forehead with my palm, then marched through the arch. "That's it. Anybody who's here for a story, get out of my shop." I shooed them like a flock of geese until each and everyone exited to the sidewalk. I shut the door and spun around. Customers were gaping at me. I forced a smile and said, "Who wants a taste of Humboldt Fog? On special today." Humboldt Fog was a gorgeous young goat cheese with a vein of vegetable ash, a white bloomy rind, and a clean lemony taste. "Half price," I added. I never offered Humboldt Fog at half price. Never. But I was willing to do just about anything to get my customers' minds off the fracas.

I replaced the Morbier wheels and headed for the cheese counter where Rebecca stood, red-faced, both hands covering her mouth like a spelling bee contestant afraid to speak. "It's okay," I whispered.

"I didn't mean to . . . I wished I had . . ." She clapped her hands over her mouth again.

I patted her shoulder. "Relax. The truth will come out. Grandmère is innocent."

But Rebecca simply shook her head and raced to the office.

Bozz came out seconds later, Rags dangling around his neck, and said, "What's with her?"

"Loose lips," I said as I handed out a tasting of Humboldt Fog to a regular customer. "What're you doing here, anyway? Don't you have school?"

"Teacher/parent conferences. All day, all night." Bozz snatched a slice of the Double

Cream Gouda from a wooden platter sitting on the tasting counter and popped it into his mouth. He swallowed it whole, as only a teenager could. "This is my favorite, I think."

I smiled. He said that about every cheese he tasted.

"How's the website coming?" I asked.

"Good. Some snags with the links you want on it, though."

"What kind of snags?"

"Some of the links are defunct. Probably means the companies have gone out of business or are about to."

I wanted links on the site to tout those companies who had helped us in the past. My customers could ideally become their patrons. It broke my heart to hear that some couldn't afford to stay open.

"All the artisanal farmers and wineries around here are good to go, though." Bozz playfully pulled on one of Rags's paws. Rags batted him on the ear. "My dad said to say thank you for thinking of that."

"No problem." Bozz's family was salt of the earth. His grandparents and mine had been friends for years. His grandmother was one of the first to visit Grandmère during her confinement. "Take Rags out for a walk, would you?" I hitched a thumb at the blue leash hanging on a hook by the rear exit. Rags, more often than not, thought he was a dog.

As Bozz exited with the cat, in strode Delilah Swain, the owner of the Country Kitchen. She was a curvy raven-haired beauty who had wanted to make a career as an actress and dancer in New York but had returned to Providence five years ago, heartbroken and penniless. Her father ceded his business to her, though he continued to work full shifts.

"Charlotte, your grandmother," Delilah said, out of breath.

She was not prone to panic. She had nerves of steel. She had weathered a blazing fire and a remodel at the Country Kitchen last year without gaining one new wrinkle in her pretty face. She had starred in a number of the town's plays without ever missing a line. Seeing her out of breath made my adrenaline kick up a notch.

"What about her?"

"I was passing the house on my way to work and, well, you should go see her."

"What's wrong?"

"Just go!"

CHAPTER 6

Worried that Grandmère might do something drastic if I wasn't there to stop her, I whipped off my apron, hurried to the back of the store, and ordered Rebecca to buck up. I grabbed the picnic basket filled with goodies from the walk-in refrigerator, slung the basket over my arm, and took off.

The late morning sun baked my cheeks as I raced down Hope Street toward Cherry Orchard Road. As I rounded the corner and drew near to my grandparents' old Victorian — an olive green beauty with white trim, a wraparound porch, and a red roof — my heart clenched. Townsfolk with protest signs were marching on the sidewalk. Their signs read *Oust Bessette.* I frowned at one protestor, a woman who ought not to throw stones seeing as she had been forced from her position as treasurer of the Providence Elementary PTA after she was seen pole dancing in a nearby town. She had the gall to hold her sign higher as I brushed her shoulder. Kristine Woodhouse wasn't among the crowd, but I was certain she had incited the dissent. I spotted a few of the reporters who had pestered me in the shop earlier. One, the weasel with bug-eyed glasses, sidled toward me, a tape recorder in his hand.

I brandished my palm and said, "No comment."

"But —"

"No. Leave me . . . and my family . . . alone." Teeth gritted, I pushed through the white picket gate, past the banks of flourishing red azaleas, and scuttled along the cobblestone path.

Pépère stood on the porch by the swing, wringing his hands over his belly, his face pinched with pain.

I gave him a hug and said, "Why don't you go to the shop, Pépère?"

"I don't want to leave your grandmother with . . . with this." He indicated the swelling crowd.

"I'll be here for a while. At least take a walk. Go to the Country Kitchen and get a cup of coffee."

"People will want to talk about . . ." He screwed up his mouth. "I do not wish to."

Gossip was never one of Pépère's favorite

things. He had often told me that Fromagerie Bessette was not designed as a gossip parlor, but there was nothing he could do about it. He wanted people to feel at home. I intended to encourage that feeling.

"Why not build something?" I suggested. He loved to tinker. Birdhouses of all shapes and sizes adorned the yard, for thrushes, warblers, wrens. Mr. Nakamura, who owned the Nuts for Nails hardware store, teased that my grandfather kept him in business with all the wood and birdseed he purchased. "Please?"

He nodded.

"Where is Grandmère?"

"Inside." His mouth twitched up on one side. "She is . . . not herself, *chérie*. Do not judge."

He tottered toward the garage where he kept his workshop, and I slipped into the house with caution. I stopped near the archway of the living room and peered between the blades of the potted palms.

Grandmère, clad in a pink marabou-trimmed robe and mule slippers, was pacing the Persian area rug like a caged animal. She held a tumbler in her hand, the foamy contents definitely not milk. A gin fizz, I assumed. She made a mean drink, a concoction that had left me so dazed one time that

I had sworn off fizzes for life.

"Hello, Grandmère," I said tentatively, unsure if I would upset the delicate balance that had to be at war in her mind. She could rebel to the house arrest that had been forced upon her or take her sentence in stride. "You look very pretty." I crossed to her, swung the picnic basket out of the way, and kissed her on each cheek.

"How quickly they forget all that I have done." She swiveled around, the robe wafting around her ankles. She swept a hand in front of the wall filled with photographs of Playhouse productions. *"Que'st-ce que je vais faire?"*

"What are you going to do?" I translated aloud, as I often did, to make sure I had understood her fast-paced French. "Fight, that's what."

"One cannot fight an evil that one cannot see."

I petted her shoulder, my insides clenched with frustration. What would happen if she was found guilty? How could Pépère survive if she was locked up in jail? How could I? Not to mention, what would Providence do? We would lose the one soul who cared about the town more than her own life.

No, I had to stop thinking like that. She was not guilty. She would be proven innocent. I would do everything in my power to ensure that.

"Grandmère, the people who truly know you haven't forgotten. The rest will remember when your name is cleared."

"What will I do?"

She spun back to face me, her eyes misty with tears, and my heart ached. My grandmother was the most stalwart woman I knew. Seeing her broken made me choke up.

"We'll figure out something. I promise."

"I did not kill him, *chérie*."

"I know."

She swept past the Queen Anne armchairs and the hem of her robe snagged on one of the legs of the maple coffee table. She yanked it free and slumped into the burgundy velvet couch. The down-feather cushions poofed up around her. The liquid in her glass swelled but didn't flow over the edges. "Ed Woodhouse was a vile excuse of a human being, but I would never . . ." She settled back and closed her eyes. Perhaps the liquor was affecting her more than she realized.

"Why don't you give me the drink." I held out my hand.

Her eyes blinked open. She stared at the glass, as if trying to conjure answers from the contents. "It calms my nerves."

"Your nerves are fine. They're made of iron," I said, keeping my hand extended.

After a moment, she struggled off the couch and relinquished the tumbler.

Relieved, I carried the glass into the kitchen, set it in the sink, and placed the picnic basket on the terrazzo tile counter. "I brought lunch. Your favorites. French fries."

"Freedom fries," she muttered.

I smiled. From the day my grandparents arrived in America, they had embraced everything American. Along the way, they had picked up a number of quirky expressions, and though some might be dated, they still used them.

"I also have Crackerjack Chicken, and Caprese salad on a skewer." Both were easy to make. For the chicken, I basted chicken breasts with olive oil, seasoned them with salt and pepper, sautéed them to a tender white finish, and layered slices atop a piece of Brie and a crispy sesame cracker. It was a melt-in-the-mouth treat with a crunch. The Caprese salad on a skewer was exactly what it sounded like: marinated vine-ripe tomatoes, buffalo mozzarella, and leaves of basil, alternately strung on a short wood skewer. "Which plates do you want me to use?" She had three sets. One with roosters, another with flowers, and —

"The plain white ones."

Usually she liked me to use the ones with the roosters on them. Her kitchen wasn't huge, but it was friendly, with high ceilings and a large nook fitted with a Shaker-style square table and benches. A few of the rooster plates hung in brackets on the walls as decoration.

Grandmère set the table with plain place-mats and paper napkins.

My lungs grew tight. I had to break her out of this mood. But how? Bursting into song might help, but I was a little rusty, and Grandmère could be a perfectionist when it came to tone. I would have to warm up my vocal cords first. Instead, I chose to do a little soft shoe as I fetched a pair of crystal water glasses from the see-through cabinets. Grandmère didn't crack a smile. I gave up trying to entertain and hoped food would do the trick. I filled the glasses with ice water and placed them on the upper right-hand corners of the mats. Every meal was meant to be an event, Grandmère had taught me.

"Where's your grandfather?" she asked

"I told him to make you another bird-house."

She blew a ruffled stream of air out her

mouth. "Him and his birds."

"Be glad he's not enamored of mice."

I noted a glimmer of humor in her eyes, but it quickly died. I combed my brain for a few quick jokes, but none came to mind, not that they would easily. I preferred wit to slapstick. "Sit," I said.

I arranged the contents of the picnic basket onto white platters, set the platters in the middle of the table, put a white plate on each of our table mats, and slid onto the bench. I eyed the food and instantly salivated. Grandmère barely gave the items a glance.

"You have to eat." I laid my hands out on the table, palms up. She placed her hands on mine, and the floodgate that had been damming her tears broke. The last time I had seen her cry was back in high school when I had played Wendy in *Peter Pan.* When she regained control of herself, we ate.

She lifted one of the Crackerjack Chicken sandwiches and nibbled at the ends.

As we moved to dessert — a plate of fresh fruit adorned with a scrumptious triple cream cheese from California — I said, "Can we talk about last night?"

She nodded.

"I heard you say to Ed that he would not

like secrets revealed. What secrets?"

"Bah," she said. "I was so angry."

"I need to know. What secrets did Ed have?"

"I saw him with that woman from the tour."

"The guide?" The brassy blonde who had set off Kristine big-time.

She nodded. "I delivered a basket of cheese to Lois's Lavender and Lace. That woman is staying there."

"The tour guide."

"Ed came to visit her."

Knowing what I did about Ed now, *visit* wouldn't have been the verb I'd have chosen. A womanizer didn't simply visit, did he?

"He didn't see me, but I saw him."

If he was actually having an affair and Kristine found out, would she have killed him? Right in front of my shop? Of course she would. People who committed crimes of passion didn't have control over where and when. Had Urso nailed down her alibi yet?

"Ed told me to mind my own business."

He had said the same to Vivian after she chastised him at the gala.

Grandmère rose from the table, shambled to the sink, and started a pot of coffee. As she waited for it to process, she fussed with the glass roosters I had given her last year for her birthday. They stood on the counter, catching sunlight, their cocks' combs glimmering bright red. A few minutes later, she returned to the table with two steaming mugs of not-so-great but drinkable coffee.

I pressed on. "After your spat with Ed, you pushed Kristine outside."

"She said horrible things. And that Felicia. She said worse."

Had Felicia incited the crowd on the sidewalk in front of my grandparents' house? Though she could be a nice woman when separated from Kristine, she could also take instruction well. One flick of Kristine's index finger and Felicia would follow. Why some smart and talented people didn't develop backbones was beyond me.

"What did Felicia say?"

"Just worse. I can't remember."

Grandmère couldn't remember? The woman, who, over her lifetime, had memorized as many scripts as Meryl Streep, couldn't remember a few simple sentences? I sighed. Stress was really eroding her spirit.

"Then what happened?" I asked.

"The three of them crossed the street and went into the Country Kitchen."

"Three? You mean four."

"No, *chérie,* three."

"Which three?"

"Kristine, Prudence, and Tyanne, of course."

"Not Felicia?"

"No, never."

"Why do you say never?"

"Because Felicia has not set foot in that restaurant since Delilah returned to town." She leaned closer. "At one time, Felicia was in love with Delilah's father."

"With Pops?"

"She'd wanted to marry him, but he never asked her. She's always resented that he gave Delilah the diner."

I leaned back in my chair. Felicia, a widow for thirteen years, had more than enough money to buy the Country Kitchen should it ever go up for sale. Why would she hold a grudge against Delilah? Sometimes the secrets our little town kept astounded me. "So Felicia went off on her own?"

Grandmère nodded.

"And you?"

"That is when I took my walk. In the opposite direction of Felicia. I headed to the clock tower. She strolled south down Honeysuckle Street."

Toward the museum. That would make sense. Felicia, an avid art lover and devotee of history, had established Providence's Historical Museum. It was located in the residential district, thanks to a special permit that allowed her to use a historic landmark house that had been built in the early 1700s. The museum boasted artifacts of the Indian tribes that once inhabited Ohio, as well as relics of the first settlers and original artworks of American painters. Ever since vandals attacked statuary at the museum last year, Felicia had been religious about double-checking to make sure the museum doors and gates were locked. Fearlessly, she did a walk-around with a huge flashlight at nine and midnight.

"You stayed at the clock tower for how long?"

"I have no idea. Long enough to be able to breathe again and realize I had left you in disarray, so I hurried back. That's when . . ." Her lower lip began to quiver. "That's when I found . . ." Her gnarled hand flew to her mouth. She bit back a sob.

I patted her shoulder.

"He didn't deserve to die, Charlotte. Ed was not a nice man, but he didn't deserve to die."

I'm not sure everyone in town agreed with her.

CHAPTER 7

Who could imagine that a tale of murder would make for gawkers and curious shoppers? For days, the uptick in business had me, Matthew, and Rebecca hopping. Townsfolk who had never shown an interest in purchasing cheese before became frequent customers. More tourists arrived, from Cleveland, Columbus, Millersburg, and Akron. Reporters from as far away as Pennsylvania continued to arrive, hungry for a lurid story. Whoever couldn't find a room at a local inn or bed-and-breakfast camped at the nearby Nature Reserve beside Kindred Creek. Luckily for them, the weather was cooperating. No rain was in the forecast for a few days.

For three mornings in a row, Matthew, Rebecca, and I had arrived early. Matthew would order vast quantities of wine. I would get the fresh-baked treats into the oven. Rebecca would pop together new gift baskets

of wine and cheese — all extravagant looking, tweaked with silk flowers and lots of
ribbon, a knack fast becoming her specialty.
Afterward, the three of us powwowed to
discuss what our collective response to
reporters and visitors would be. *No comment* hadn't worked. Not once. We all
agreed that putting the right spin on whatever came out of our mouths could affect
Grandmère's case.

Dear, sweet Grandmère. I had visited her
every day. No longer was she sipping gin
fizzes, but she still wasn't herself. I tried to
devise a plan to help her, but other than
proving her innocent, I couldn't come up
with one. My heart felt raw.

"Charlotte, how about this cheese?" Vivian had shown up on this particular morning, not to gossip like the others, but to
make food selections for the antique auction she was going to hold at Europa Antiques and Collectibles the next afternoon.
She wanted Fromagerie Bessette to cater
the event, which would be modest in size. I
suggested she ask Luigi Bozzuto, Bozz's
uncle, the owner of the four-star La Bella
Ristorante, to manage it, but Vivian
wouldn't hear of it. Apparently she had gone
to high school with Luigi and didn't care
for him. A boor, she called him. I didn't

agree. I had taken a number of cooking classes with him and found him to be a clever, witty, and talented chef, much more so than my ex-fiancée who, after two years of planning our wedding, had left me in the wee hours of the morning to pursue his dream of being a chef in Paris. His sudden departure had left me hesitant about opening my heart to anyone ever again. Last I heard, he was still working at a two-bit creperie and living in a hovel. Creep Chef, Meredith had dubbed him. Speaking of which, why hadn't she returned my phone calls? I had rung her numerous times since the murder. Instead of talking every other day like we usually did, we'd chatted only once. She had consoled me about my grandmother but ended the call quickly. I tried to cut her some slack. She was a tender soul. She had to be devastated after having seen Ed's dead body up close.

"Charlotte." Vivian navigated her way through the display tables. "You've told me I should always serve not one cheese, but a selection of cheeses." I followed in her wake, adjusting the gathered sleeves of my peasant blouse as I went. She pointed to a box of crackers and a round of Petit Basque cheese. "Good choice?"

"Absolutely." Petit Basque, a sheep's milk

101

cheese, was highly popular with my customers. The interior paste had a fabulous taffy-like feel and a mild caramel aroma.

"How is Bernadette holding up?"

Without going into the intimate details, I brought Vivian up to date. At the same time, I made notations on a pad of paper as she chose other items for her soirée. I would stock her order later in the day.

"And the case? How is it going? Do you like the attorney?"

"He said the wheels of bureaucracy turn slowly. Other than that, he's pretty tight-lipped."

Vivian clucked her tongue. "Your little assistant certainly isn't."

Standing amidst a handful of reporters by the cheese counter, Rebecca looked more poised than when she had arrived on our doorstep. For today's crowd, she had dressed professionally in a crisp white blouse and camel-colored A-line skirt, her hair pulled back in a clip, her daring red nail polish replaced with a refined soft pink to match her dusty pink lipstick. I feared she might be having visions of becoming an on-camera news reporter in the future.

The grape-leaf-shaped chimes jingled. Jordan sauntered into the shop, looking as handsome as ever, and casual, the top of his work shirt unbuttoned, one hand jammed into the front pocket of his jeans. I gave what I considered an understated wave of my fingertips. Far be it for me to let the man know I was still hoping he'd ask me on a date. I hadn't felt like this about anyone since Creep Chef left.

"Morning, Charlotte," Jordan said. "Morning, Vivian."

"Hello, Jordan." Vivian elbowed me as Jordan proceeded toward the cheese counter. "If you want my opinion —"

"We're just friends," I said quickly.

Vivian chuckled. "I wasn't talking about Mr. Gorgeous, but if I was, I'd tell you to ask him out yourself. Men can be so dense."

My cheeks grew warm. I had to stop assuming that everyone in town could tell I had a crush on Jordan. He certainly had no idea.

"What I was referring to," Vivian went on, "was if you wanted my opinion regarding what to do about your grandmother's case."

"The lawyer says he has it handled." He wouldn't discuss the fine points of the case with me, not yet, but he said he was reviewing witness statements. By my recollection, none of the witnesses had seen a darned thing. Shock, the lawyer said, caused people to forget things. He hoped that as shock

wore off, someone would remember something that would be beneficial.

"Has he hired an investigator?" Vivian
asked.

"What for?"

"To look into the why and wherefore —
the motives, if you will — of other suspects."

Rebecca sidled up, fetched the half-eaten
tray of Vermont Cabot Cheddar, and headed
back toward the counter.

I gripped her elbow. "What are you doing,
feeding the darned reporters?"

She nodded.

"No, stop now!" I didn't mean to shriek.

Rebecca set the tray down in a flash and
said, "She's right, you know."

"Who?"

"Miss Williams."

"Me?" Vivian cocked her head.

"About hiring an investigator. I heard . . ."
Rebecca's mouth quirked up on one side.
"Do you want to know what I heard?"

I sighed. If she couldn't be the belle of the
reporters, she would subject me to her
opinions. "Go on. What did you hear on *Law
& Order* now?"

"Quiet investigation is often more effec-
tive than what the police do, you know,
barge in and demand answers."

"You dig for dirt," Vivian said.

"Quietly," Rebecca added.

"We can't afford an investigator," I said, not when all the savings had gone into the renovation of The Cheese Shop.

"Then you do it." Rebecca poked my arm.

"Me, investigate?" What, did she think I had oodles of time on my hands? Both Matthew and I were run ragged looking after Grandmère and Pépère and the twins. On the other hand, who better than I to dig for dirt?

"You know everyone in town," Rebecca went on, echoing my exact thought.

"My money is on Kristine," Vivian said. "Ed left her everything. And I'd bet his insurance policy was paid up. Double indemnity."

"But she has her own trust fund," I argued.

Vivian raised a skeptical eyebrow. "Murder is not always about money."

"What about the election?" Rebecca said. "If Mrs. Woodhouse implicates your grandmother, she'll sail through to a landslide victory. I'll bet that's why she used one of the cheese knives from the shop."

Come to think of it, Kristine had hovered over the table where the knives had been displayed. Had she pilfered one? In her warped mind, stabbing her roving husband while putting the blame on my grandmother might have killed two birds with one cheese knife. It was a crazy theory, of course, but Kristine bordered on crazy, didn't she? I couldn't imagine a sane person committing murder. Sane people reasoned things out. Sane people worked through problems. What was she thinking, parading around in bright colors like a beauty contestant? And why hadn't she had a funeral yet? What was she waiting for?

"And don't forget her friend Felicia Hassleton," Rebecca said, her cheeks rosy with zeal. "She could be a suspect, too. I saw her flirting with Mr. Woodhouse. She was twirling her hair around her finger." Rebecca demonstrated. "What if he dumped her and she flew into a rage?"

I suppressed a smile. My young protégé was becoming entirely too enraptured with the investigative process.

"C'mon, Charlotte." Rebecca prodded me again. "You know you are more than capable of cracking this case. Just think."

"I wouldn't do that." Jordan slipped into the huddle, a gold Fromagerie Bessette bag tucked under his arm. He plopped a sample of Molinari Toscano Picante salami into his mouth and chewed.

"Do what? Think?" I pulled innocently on

the hair cupping the nape of my neck, caught myself doing it, and whipped my hand to my side. I was nothing like Felicia Hassleton. Girlish machinations were not my style.

"Investigate," Jordan said. "Chief Urso is a good man. He'll get to the bottom of things."

"I know that."

"Isn't Mr. Lincoln doing his job?" Jordan asked.

Mr. Lincoln, our attorney, was as gaunt and as tall as the historic president, and about as stoic.

"I heard he visited your grandmother today," Jordan said.

Mr. Lincoln had shown up at the house at the end of my picnic with Grandmère. He had brought Grandmère a selection of magazines to help her through the confinement.

Vivian said, "Doing one's job and being a kind neighbor isn't always good enough, Jordan, and you know it. Sometimes it takes extraordinary circumstances to make a person do extraordinary things."

Her words held an undercurrent of meaning that I couldn't decipher, and I realized that I didn't know beans about Jordan Pace. I cocked my head. What was his story? Did he have skeletons in a closet? Did Vivian know something I didn't? He wasn't home-grown. He had moved to Providence from California about three years ago with little luggage and no job. Within months, he had established his thriving Pace Hill Farm. Tongues had wagged, but that hadn't stopped a number of eligible ladies from dating him, all of whom were married now. Their husbands teased that Jordan was a little slow on making decisions in matters of the heart. I was willing to be patient, to a point.

Jordan faced me and riveted me with his gaze. "If your grandmother is innocent, there is nothing to worry about."

"If?" I asked, my tone sharp, his doubt ricocheting me out of Dreamland and back to the present. "If? Of course, she's in-nocent. She said she didn't do this. I believe her."

"I believe her, too," Rebecca said.

A muscle ticked in Jordan's jaw. My guess was he didn't like women ganging up on him. What man did? He said, "Talk is that she and Ed argued that night about him evicting you from the premises."

Rebecca turned pale. Her bravado with-ered.

Vivian's didn't. She squared her shoulders

and glowered at Jordan. "Talk is cheap, and Ed didn't evict them or anybody else."

"That's because he's dead," Jordan said.

We all went silent.

Jordan shifted his feet, probably realizing he had overstepped his bounds. "I'm sorry, Charlotte. Just —" He glanced at his watch. "I've got to go. Tread softly, okay?"

Tread softly? What the heck did that mean? Did he think I would go around town like Annie Oakley, wielding a rifle and demanding answers?

With an aching heart, I watched him leave the shop, wishing we could return to life before the murder — minutes before, when Jordan had looked ready to ask me out. His interest in me had obviously fizzled. Why? Because I was the granddaughter of a murder suspect? Or was it something else?

To put the quarrel from my mind, I finished up Vivian's order, bid her goodbye, then set about straightening the shop's various displays. More than half of our supply of homemade basil pesto had sold. I would have to make another batch.

Matthew strode up, his apron a mess of oily fingerprints. We laundered them daily to keep them looking fresh. "Charlotte, Rebecca is trying to get rid of the reporters. Will you take over at the counter? I'm going into the annex. I'll get it set up for this afternoon's tastings, then I'll visit Grand-mère." He checked his watch as if trying to figure out how to squeeze all his duties in. The girls, the shop, and a private life of some kind. Last night he had arrived home at two A.M. again. If he wasn't careful, he was going to burn out, but I didn't want to point that out to him. He was a grown man. He knew what he could and couldn't do. If life wasn't so tense right now, I would tease him into revealing who in town had caught his eye. Delilah Swain, maybe? Matthew had taken ballroom dancing lessons as a kid. He could cha-cha with the best of them. The past few mornings, he had entered The Cheese Shop with a coffee from the Country Kitchen. I'd also seen him talking to the bake shop owner, an apple-cheeked beauty.

"Hold up," I said.

He didn't.

I tracked him into the annex. "Business is slow. Let's chat a moment."

"About?"

"Who are you seeing?"

"None of your beeswax."

I perched on a stool by the bar and watched Matthew unpack boxes filled with bottles of wine, "Is that the pinot noir you've been hoping for?"

He nodded. "From Joseph Phelps in California. Hard to get. It's fabulous, with flavors of blackberries and balsamic reduction, and —"

"Are you kidding? Balsamic reduction?"

"And sandalwood."

I laughed.

He jabbed a finger at me. "C'mon, you talk about the flavor of grass in cheese."

I did. Which season a cow, goat, or sheep grazed during the year made a difference to the flavors inherent in the cheese. The younger the grass, the younger-tasting the cheese. If the animal ate clover, I could taste it in the product.

"It's the same with wine. The grapes draw their flavor from the earth." He sliced open another box and withdrew twelve bottles of Argentinean malbec, a spicier, edgier red wine than a merlot, so Matthew claimed. I had yet to taste it.

And I wouldn't today. I hadn't tagged along to get an education on wine. I wanted to grill my new housemate. We hadn't had a moment alone since Grandmère had been arrested.

"What's going on?" I said.

"With . . . ?"

"You."

"Nothing."

"You're not spending much time with the girls."

He bridled and exhaled through his nose. "Don't start —"

"I'm not criticizing. I'm not complaining. It's giving me time to get to know them." I had enjoyed the last few nights, reading to the girls and teaching them how to cook, although with Clair's allergies to wheat, gluten, and nuts, I was forced to be creative with recipes or make two of everything. Luckily, few cheeses caused allergic reactions, and Rags was the least allergenic breed of cat. Clair hadn't had an upset tummy or itchy nose and eyes since moving in. At times, I mused that she might have been allergic to her wayward mother, and with the shrew out of the picture, her symptoms had cleared up. "I'm just wondering what's up. Are you all right? Have you met someone already? Is it Delilah Swain?"

"I'm not seeing anyone." He didn't make eye contact as he set the bottles of wine on the bar.

"Or that gal who owns the bookshop?"

"Oh, yeah, I'm such a reader."

Matthew's reading consisted of books about wineries, grapes, and *terroir.*

"I'm intruding, I know, but you're acting differently. You're sort of shut down. I don't want you worrying about Grandmère."

"I'm not."

"Is it your ex? Did she call or something?"

"I'm fine, Charlotte." He twisted the wine bottles so all the labels pointed out. "Look, I'll come straight home from work tonight and make sure I spend time with the girls. Okay? Just give it a rest."

"Matthew —"

"Really. Don't mother hen me. I'm fine. Go tend to the customers in the shop."

"Rebecca's doing that."

"Then bake a quiche or something."

"Can't. I'm off to pick up the girls from school."

"Fine." He tromped across the hardwood floor and started inspecting bottles of wine in the slots we had built along the far wall. End of discussion.

A ball of frustration gathered in the pit of my stomach. I didn't like secrets. But Matthew had one, and I intended to find out what it was.

CHAPTER 8

I had been so focused on the shop and Grandmère's situation that I had neglected to restock the refrigerator at home. With the girls in tow, I headed to the farmer's market that took place once a week in the Village Green. It would close when the sun set.

A broad white-and-green-striped tent covered the market, which consisted of twelve rows of fruits, vegetables, artisanal breads, coffees, meats, sweets, and nuts. Half the townsfolk seemed to be browsing the goods.

Amy, who appeared to get her fashion sense from my grandmother — blue skirt and purple shirt, with a matching headband threaded through her dark hair, and light blue cape tied at the neck — skipped ahead of Clair and me. Down the aisle of fresh fruits. Up the aisle of vegetables. Twice she twirled and bumped into a customer. I didn't want to rein her in, her spirit being so much like Grandmère's, but I didn't want her to become the terror of Providence either. I gave a quick whistle. Amy flashed me one of her gamine grins.

I stopped, item by item, and filled paper bags with apples, salad fixings, and broccoli.

Clair, dressed in a subdued white blouse and mint capris, pulled idly on the long blonde tresses that framed her face as she studied baskets of strawberries. "These look good. Can I eat them without . . . ?" She wriggled her nose. "You know."

"Yes. You do fine with all fruits. Pick out the carton you like best. Look for plump and red, no tinges of lime green. Get a carton for Grandmère, too."

She picked up a basket, turned it in her hands, and put it back. She lifted another. Her hands began to shake. Then her shoulders.

"Clair, what's wrong?"

She looked over her shoulder at me. Tears dripped down her cheeks. "I'm . . . I'm so worried about Great-Grandmère. The kids at school . . ." She licked a teardrop off her lip.

I turned her around, brushed her hair back over her shoulders, and lifted her chin with my fingertip. "Sweetheart, your great-grandmother is going to be fine. Promise."

"Amy says . . . Amy says . . ." Clair hiccupped. "Amy says I should slug them."

I bit back a smile. "Using your fists isn't always the best solution."

"I know and I tell her that, but she doesn't listen to me." She shuddered beneath my touch. "I want to see Grandmère."

"We'll go for dinner soon, okay?"

She nodded.

Amy raced back to us and spun in a circle, eyeing the hem of her cape as it flared. "Did I tell you what happened at school today?"

"Not yet."

"Willamina Woodhouse got put in detention." Amy did a little jig.

I grimaced, hoping Amy hadn't been the one to spur on Willamina. "Er, what did she do?"

"She sassed the teacher."

"Miss Vance?"

"Uh-huh. She said . . ." Mocking Willamina, Amy fluffed her hair and in a nasal voice said, " 'My father is being buried in two days and you can't come.' "

So, Kristine had at last set the date. About time.

"What did Miss Vance say?"

"Ask her." Amy pointed. "Hey, Miss Vance!"

Meredith stood on the far side of the market by the organic coffee display. She glanced up, and then like a meerkat checking its surroundings, looked right and left and ducked down. She didn't have a hole to dive into, but she slipped from view. Where had she gone? Had she crawled away? I was positive she had seen me. Was she avoiding me? Something gnawed inside me, but I refused to take her actions personally. Not yet.

When the girls and I finished our shopping, I offered to take them to the Country Kitchen for a soda. I didn't allow them to drink soda during the week, but after the encounter with Meredith, even I wanted a little cooling-off period. A glass of soda would do the trick.

The fifties-style diner was packed and noisy, its red booths and red-checkered tables crammed with teenagers and adults. Rock and roll music played through overhead speakers. Customers made choices of music using the mini jukeboxes set on the tables. Each day, a song was chosen as the "song of the day." Whenever a customer selected that song, Delilah, the waitresses, and her father "Pops" would parade from the kitchen and sing along with the song,

Delilah louder and more on key than the others.

We settled onto three empty stools at the red laminate counter. I sat in the middle, with the girls on either side. Their forearms and elbows barely reached the counter. We each ordered a Mama Bozzuto root beer from the perky counter waitress. The Bozzuto Winery had smartly expanded its product line in recent years and had started making delicious natural sodas. With a thick head of foam and rich caramel flavors, the soda tasted like dessert.

As I sipped my drink, I noticed a few of the customers staring at us and talking under their breaths, but I shrugged off their attention. Gossip and googly-eyed staring was to be expected.

Delilah passed by, the red ruffled skirt of her uniform swishing around her knees, a tray balanced on her shoulder. She winked. "Got what you need?"

I nodded.

Amy tugged on my sleeve. "I didn't finish my story about Willamina." She made a huge slurping sound as she drank her soda.

I gave her the evil eye.

She shrugged an apology, then said, "Anyway, when Willie went to detention."

"Willamina," I corrected.

118

"Uh-uh, she prefers Willie."

That had to make Kristine cringe.

"Go on," I said.

"Anyway, she skipped past Miss Vance, and she stuck out her tongue."

"You're kidding!" I don't know why I expected good behavior from Kristine Woodhouse's daughter. The "apple falling far from the tree" metaphor would definitely apply. On the other hand, I didn't want the twins to be judged by their errant mother. That wouldn't be fair. "Then what happened?"

"Miss Vance started to cry and she ran out of the room."

Poor Meredith. No matter what, tomorrow I was going to track her down and —

"There she is again. Getting coffee. See her?"

I swung around on my stool. Indeed, Meredith was standing at the register, paying for a to-go cup of coffee. Had my presence forced her to retreat from the farmer's market? I didn't want to believe that. I couldn't. She had a tote bag from All Booked Up on her arm. Books poked from the top. Meredith was an avid reader. Maybe she had run from the farmer's market to buy her weekly stash.

"Girls, I'll be right back." I hurried to my

friend and tapped her on the shoulder.

Meredith spun around. Tawny hair flapped her face. Her mouth opened, but no sound came out.

"Are you okay?" I asked.

"Fine."

"Pretty necklace." I hitched my chin at the sapphire pendant hanging around her neck. "New?"

Her hand flew to it. Her cheeks turned crimson. "It's . . . an antique."

I could tell that. And it looked expensive. "From your grandmother's estate?" Meredith was the only girl in a family of boys. Upon her grandmother's death, she had received all the jewelry.

Before she could answer, Delilah, her spiky-haired father, and two waitresses paraded from the kitchen singing an Elvis oldie, "(Let Me Be Your) Teddy Bear." As usual, customers joined in.

Over the din, Meredith said, "I've got to go."

"Wait, Meredith, what's wrong?"

"Nothing."

"Why haven't you returned my calls?"

"I can't talk now."

"I heard what happened at school today. That Willamina —"

"Sorry, I've got to run. Parent/teacher

stuff." She scooped up her cup of coffee, and without another word, dashed out the door.

"Meredith, wait!"

But she didn't. I blew a stream of frustrated air out my nose. I distinctly remembered Bozz telling me that parent/teacher conferences were the other day, so why had Meredith lied to me? Was I now a pariah, unworthy of friendship because my grandmother was suspected of murder? Or was I being paranoid and trying to read the worst of every little encounter?

"Stop it!" I heard Amy scream.

Delilah and her staff ceased singing.

At the far end of the restaurant, Amy tussled with Willamina Woodhouse. The girl had her fingers woven into Amy's hair. Where in the heck was her mother? I raced to the girls and pressed them apart by the shoulders, then wedged myself between them. Amy continued to scuffle against me.

"She started it," Amy said.

"Did not."

Willamina looked like a street urchin, her cheeks smudged with dirt, her tumble of curls knotted and frazzled. When was the last time the poor girl had taken a bath? For a moment, I felt as worried as a social worker. Did the child need someone to intervene?

But then she bit me.

It took all my reserve not to pinch her back. "Where's your mother?" I demanded.

"Campaigning."

With Ed's funeral days away? The woman ought to be committed.

"What happened here?" I said.

"She called Grandmère names," Amy cried.

"Did not."

"Did so. You said 'the old goat is guilty.' "

Something inside me snapped. I tightened my hold on Willamina's arm and shook once. "Where did you hear such a thing?"

"I made it up."

"I don't believe you." She wasn't nearly clever enough. "Young lady, you tell your mother that she is not to say anything like that in the future, do you hear me?"

"My mother didn't say it. Mrs. Taylor did."

Tyanne? Why?

I leveled Willamina with my gaze. "I don't care who said it, you don't repeat it. Now, get out of here." I released her. "And don't touch Amy again."

Willamina began to blubber. She scurried out of the shop, knobby knees battering each other.

Delilah sashayed to my side, wiping her hands on her frilly apron. "I'm so sorry. That girl is definitely trouble."

Everyone in the restaurant was staring at us. My cheeks turned warm.

Delilah raised her hands over her head and clapped. "Okay, folks. Show's over. Lots of tension in this town. Let's not add to it. Everybody have a soda on me. Pops, re-cue 'Teddy Bear.'"

That night, dinner at the house was somber. Matthew sat hunched over, eyes dark, as if he was still angry that I had pressed him for answers at The Cheese Shop. Rags seemed to pick up on the tension. He did figure eights around my ankles, rubbing his head against my leg as he roamed.

While we ate our black bean soup laced with crème fraiche in silence, I fretted about Grandmère's situation. It didn't help that Willamina Woodhouse had attacked Amy, or that Ed Woodhouse's funeral would soon be upon us, or that Kristine was making a big to-do about it, playing the grieving widow, expecting everyone in town to come — even us. I'm sure she thought she could rustle up some votes if she cried crocodile tears.

"I saw Meredith today," I said, hoping

Matthew might jump in and give me a little perspective. "Funny, but I think she was trying to ditch me."

"That's ridiculous." Matthew dropped his spoon onto the serving plate with a clack. "Don't assume just because someone doesn't talk to you that they are hiding something."

"Best friends are supposed to confide in each other."

"Mommy used to be Daddy's best friend," Amy chimed in.

Matthew winced. I did, too. I reached for his hand to offer a silent apology, but he shook my hand away, shoved back his chair, and scrambled to his feet. Rags darted from beneath the table and out of the room.

"Where are you going?" I asked.

"I've got some research to do," he snapped.

"Can I help, Daddy?" Amy popped up from her chair and hurried to him.

"No."

"Please, Daddy?" She peered up into his eyes. "I'm sorry if I made you angry."

He softened. "You didn't make me angry, Peanut. I . . ." Sad creases bracketed his eyes and mouth. "I need a little alone time."

And what about me? What did I need? I hadn't signed on to be a single parent. Out of the graciousness of my heart, I had allowed my cousin and his girls to move in. What had I gotten myself into? If I rocked the boat, would I ruin our budding partnership?

Matthew bent to Amy's level and kissed her cheek. "Daddy has some business to attend to. That's all." He lumbered to the study at the front of the house and shut the door.

I frowned. So much for his spending time with the girls tonight.

"Why don't we read, Aunt Charlotte?" Clair said, her face pale, eyes wide. She was clenching her soup spoon so tightly that her knuckles had gone white.

Something inside me clenched, too. How dare I be so selfish? These girls needed me to be a sane adult. Just because their father was being a jerk didn't mean I had to be.

"Sure, let's read."

Her fingers loosened their death grip on the spoon, but her eyes and mouth remained tight. How I wished she could express herself more, but I knew I shouldn't expect miracles overnight. With loss came pain. With pain came all sorts of emotional complications. I had swathed myself in tension at the same age. Perhaps in time, Clair would relax and her beautiful soul would blossom.

"Leave the dishes and follow me." I set a tray with three mugs of hot cocoa and a plate of gluten-free cream-cheese button cookies, and the three of us headed for the attic. Amy sprinted ahead, sounding like an elephant as she charged up the squeaky stairs.

In the attic, I had created a nook with fake-fur pillows and quilted throw blankets that I'd purchased at Sew Inspired. A small rustic bookshelf held the books the girls liked the best. Brass lamps with pretty ruffled shades stood at various spots around the room. The familiar scent of dust and lilac hung in the air.

I laid the tray on a little side table beside the red oak rocking chair that had been my mother's. "Amy, open the window, please."

She cranked the handle on the circular dormer window. Cool night air wafted into the room.

"This one, please." Clair handed me the first in the Crafty Sleuth series by Didi Jackson. In the story, a teenage protagonist used the craft of beading to solve crimes.

I wondered if I could be crafty enough to solve Ed Woodhouse's murder. More important, would Urso have my hide if I got too crafty?

"Get your beading bags," I said.

Kit bags filled with colorful beads, needle and thread, and instructions for making a three-strand bracelet came along with the mystery. The girls settled onto their pillows, Amy preferring the blue set, and Clair opting for the aqua green. I nestled onto the cushioned rocker and set my feet on the needlepoint ottoman. A wealth of emotions raced through me. If only my mother was here to help me make sense of the mystery surrounding my grandmother. Or my father, to help me get Matthew to open up to me. Grandmère said my father had a knack for getting people to talk and discuss their problems. He had been the principal of Providence High School. A plaque hung there in his honor. Sadly, none of his wizardry had rubbed off on me.

Amy scattered beads onto the pillow between her legs. One beading strand was already strung and tied off. Clair wasn't as far along. She invariably got distracted by Rags, who chose her lap for his nest.

"Okay, start," Amy said.

I took a deep breath, then obeyed. " 'I couldn't find my aunt Bailey anywhere,' " I read from the text. " 'Now, I'm not the kind of girl who freaks out, but I have to admit, hearing a guy on the radio say the biggest blizzard of the century was coming to Lake Tahoe in less than four hours —' "

"Do we ever get blizzards here?" Clair said.

The weather had been quite mild since April. Rain was due later in the week. Maybe a thunderstorm.

"We get snowstorms," I said, "but don't worry. None in May. And the last really big blizzard occurred before I was born."

"We got some real bad storms in Cleveland," Amy said.

I wondered if she was referring to the weather or to the outbursts between her father and mother. Contemplating the latter made my heart ache. What drove a woman to hurt the ones she loved?

"Ouch," Clair said, drawing me back to the moment at hand. She'd pricked her thumb.

"Put on your thimble," I said.

"It's like a glove for your thumb," Amy added, reiterating what I had said nights before.

By the end of the first chapter, both girls were yawning. Stress could make even the stoutest sleepy.

Once I was nestled in my sleigh-style bed, I got to thinking about women hurting the ones they loved. How could I prove that

Kristine had killed Ed? According to Grandmère, Felicia had headed toward the museum, and Kristine, Prudence, and Tyanne had gone into the Country Kitchen. Had anyone seen Kristine after she'd left the diner?

I slipped out of bed and paced the floor. Adrenaline rushed through my veins, making my skin hot and prickly, as I counted off details on my fingers.

One: The gala opening of The Cheese Shop had continued after the fracas between Grandmère and Kristine.

Two: Guests had remained focused on wine and cheese and lively conversation. Hadn't anyone gone outside at just that moment when someone stabbed Ed, which had to be between nine fifteen and nine thirty?

Three: Grandmère told me that after her visit to the clock tower, she had returned. She found Ed on the ground at ten o'clock. She rushed to help, but he wasn't breathing. She said Ed must have been dead for at least a few minutes, maybe more. She looked around, but she didn't see anyone dashing into shadows.

Four: Meredith had appeared seconds later and screamed. Where had she come from? Had she seen something implicating my grandmother? Was she afraid to tell me?

129

Was that why she was avoiding me? Had somebody — Kristine — threatened her?

Five: If Kristine had killed Ed, she would have been splattered with blood like my grandmother and Meredith. Had she hurried to her boutique not far from the Country Kitchen to change clothes? Had she disposed of the dress and her gloves and then slipped out, wearing a new frock?

I stopped pacing and stared at myself in the mirror over the bureau as something Amy said to Clair came to me. About the thimble in the attic. *"It's like a glove for your thumb."*

Kristine and her girlfriends had donned gloves while at the gala. If she had been wearing gloves when snatching the olive-wood-handled knife, she wouldn't have left fingerprints on the gift box or the knife.

But that didn't matter now, did it? If she killed Ed, she would have had to dispose of the bloody gloves. Garbage collection wasn't due for three more days. They might still be in the Dumpster behind her store.

CHAPTER 9

The next morning, after I dropped the twins at school, I went to the Providence Precinct and strode into Urso's office. Sunlight cut through the vertical Levelor blinds and cast prisonlike bar shadows on the beige walls. I shuddered but didn't miss a step.

"Chief Urso." I gave a discreet tug to the seams of my split-neck shift — my prettiest, with a turquoise and brown swirl print — and I squared my shoulders. I had dressed for business, not confrontation.

Urso rose from his desk chair, dwarfing me, and offered me a seat in one of the hard-backed chairs.

I declined, and instead paced in front of his bulky desk, which was as neat as a pin, papers stacked just so. The walls were empty of anything that might be considered pretentious. A silver frame with a picture of his family, including his parents and brothers, stood on the metal file cabinet.

"A bloody dress and gloves," I blurted.

"What about 'em?" He remained standing, arms hanging comfortably by his sides.

I explained my theory.

"Now, Charlotte." Urso worked his tongue around the inside of his cheek. "I can't have you getting involved. You know that."

"I'm not involved. I'm theorizing."

"And I'm theorizing, as well," he said. "All day long. Not in between slicing cheese."

I bridled at the remark.

"I'm sorry," he said. "That came out wrong. I just meant . . ." He ran a hand down his thick neck, then held it out to me, palm up in a pleading gesture. "Aw, heck, it's my job. It's not yours. You shouldn't —"

"— bother my silly head about it?" I snapped. "You men!"

Urso bristled that time. He wasn't like other guys, and obviously didn't like me bundling him in with the others. He appreciated a woman with a bright mind. The one time he had asked me out in high school was after I had aced a history test. I had said no, not because he wasn't handsome — he was, in that teddy bear way, with kind eyes and a warm smile — but because Meredith had a crush on him, and I hadn't wanted to lose my friendship with her. Following his divorce, I had considered asking him out, but then Jordan Pace showed up, and, well, I was smitten.

"Charlotte, I assure you that I am taking every tip and witness statement under consideration. I am looking at suspects other than your grandmother."

"Where was Kristine at the time?"

"Picking up her daughter from Tyanne Taylor's house."

Tyanne, as Kristine's good friend, wouldn't deny that, but I didn't put it past Kristine to dump her daughter at home and return to the scene to kill Ed. "Did you test the knife that killed Ed for fingerprints?"

"Of course."

"And? Were my grandmother's finger-prints on the handle?"

Urso licked his lips. "We already discussed how long it takes for results to come through."

"Oh, sheesh, U-ey." I rapped my knuckles on his desk. "You know something!"

"The knife was wiped clean."

I groaned. That meant anybody could be guilty. Anybody.

I left, as frustrated as when I'd arrived, and went to open The Cheese Shop. Within minutes, I was overwhelmed by an onrush of customers. Rebecca and Matthew could barely keep up with slicing and wrapping

133

the orders in our pretty gold and white wax paper, while I printed off labels that included the country of origin, the milk source, the type of cheese, and the price per pound. By lunch, my brain, usually a steel-trap for figures and details, was fried.

At one point, Rebecca thumped my shoulder and said, "Girls' night out tonight? You look like you could use a little fun."

Rebecca, Meredith, Delilah, and I met once a week at Timothy O'Shea's Irish Pub, known for its international list of beers. However, the pub also offered a super-duper Cosmo, with a smidge more of Rose's lime juice, the glass rimmed with multicolored sugar. Rebecca had grown quite fond of Cosmos. She had also taken to watching whatever sport aired on the multiple televisions around the pub, favoring the Cleveland Indians over the Cincinnati Reds, and the Cleveland Browns over any other football team. She had a major crush on the hunky quarterback. I, being an alum of OSU, preferred watching the Buckeyes play. If there wasn't a football game on TV, I immersed myself in the live Irish music. My mother's family originated from Ireland. Listening to the soulful strains was one of the ways I could keep her memory alive.

"I'm in," I said. "But I'll need to change."

"Oh, no, you look wonderful. I love your dress. And your cute little sandals." She thumped my shoulder again. "They show off your legs."

I batted her away, then called Meredith and left a message on her cell phone telling her I missed her and needed to chat. I had never truly embraced using a cell phone, preferring conversations in person, but in dire emergencies a cell phone was useful. I hoped Meredith would realize I was desperate to talk and return my call between classes.

Late afternoon arrived quickly. When I had to leave to set up Vivian's auction party, the wine annex was unusually busy, so instead of Rebecca, I asked Bozz to help me carry platters of cheese, baskets of artisanal breads, and bottles of wine to Europa Antiques and Collectibles.

Vivian lived and breathed antiques and, if she could have, I believe she would have taken up residence in the store. She had created an international extravaganza inside the shop. Each section was decorated in furniture and gift items from a different country. Posters and photographs highlighting the country's most beautiful sites were hung on the walls. Italy was my favorite area, as it was decorated with photos of the Tuscany coast and posters of Michelangelo's most famous statues. Once, a few years ago, Pépère had taken me to Italy and France to further my cheese education. I yearned to go back. For now, until the shop's books were regularly in the black, my travels would be confined to tours via the Internet and practicing French with weekly brush-up classes using Rosetta Stone.

Vivian swooped up to me, her unbuttoned silk jacket billowing open. "Don't you look pretty? And aren't those platters beautiful! I love how you've arranged them."

I had set the three types of cheeses that she'd ordered — one each of goat's milk, sheep's milk, and cow's milk — on an oval platter. In between, I decorated with large helpings of strawberries, grapes, dried apricots, and cashews. The Barefoot Contessa would be proud.

Vivian said, "Set them over there, please." She had adorned antique end tables with vases of fresh flowers and placed doilies on a handsome Henry VIII Tudor-style dining table. "And Bozz, why don't you put the wine bottles on the sideboard." She pointed with one hand while strategically straightening price tags on a display of silver platters.

Bozz rested the six bottles of wine on the

lace runner that Vivian had set out. A dozen vintage-cut crystal wineglasses stood nearby, all beautifully etched with a leaf pattern.

"Bozz, be a dear and go into the storage room and fetch two more hard-backed chairs, the ones with the burgundy needle-point seats. They're just beyond the work-tables that are cluttered with rolls of bubble wrap." Vivian fluttered her fingers and Bozz trotted through a pair of black velvet curtains at the rear of the shop. "Charlotte, carving knives are in the sideboard's cupboard, beneath all the junk."

I opened the doors and had to remove a set of engraved linens, antique books, yearbooks, silver platters, and picture frames before I found a set of Bakelite-handled knives and forks stowed in a black silk box. I selected two of the knives and said, "These are pretty."

"Thank you. They're my mother's. That's my little mock hope chest. I won't sell anything that's in there."

I kept my parent's precious memories in my mother's maple hope chest. Once a year, I took them out to appreciate them. My mother loved white linen tablecloths. My father had a box filled with more than a hundred fishing lures, all polished and ready to go. Whenever I touched the items, I recalled my mother's smile and how my father's eyes crinkled with delight whenever he looked at me — bittersweet memories that brought fresh tears to my eyes. I brushed them away and gave my cheeks a quick pinch for color. No sense dwelling on the past. I couldn't fix it.

"Charlotte, help me with these." Vivian straightened cards that she had placed by the various items to be auctioned.

"Do you always serve food for these auctions?" I asked. I couldn't remember Pépère providing cheese platters for the antique shop before.

Vivian shook her head. "I wanted this one to be special. We have so much to celebrate. With all the tourism, business is picking up. Six wholesale buyers from Cleveland are due today. They buy huge lots."

"Why twelve glasses for wine?"

"Didn't Matthew say that I needed different glasses for tasting?"

"You can pour a red in after a white, just not the other way around."

Vivian clucked her tongue. "My, my, so much to learn." She started to collect the ones she didn't need.

"Leave them," I said. "They look lovely."

"Good, good." She rearranged them, put her hands on her hips, and stared at the

138

room. "Something's missing." She chewed her lower lip, then snapped her fingers. "Be right back." She disappeared into an office at the rear of the shop.

The door didn't close behind her, offering me my first-ever peek into the office. While the shop was tidy and organized, the office looked like a tornado had charged through. A trail of crumbs led from the door to a bureau. The bureau's drawers spilled over with vibrant blue and gold and crimson fabrics. The desk was swamped in paper, an old-style hand-crank calculator, and bric-a-brac. Oriental curios, Christmas ornaments, and teacups were crammed onto bookshelves. I smiled to myself. No wonder Vivian always kept the door closed. She didn't want the townsfolk of Providence to know she was a slob.

Vivian returned with white monogrammed linen napkins. She untied the ribbon holding the set together and placed the napkins by the cheese displays.

"Those are beautiful," I said. "The W's are hand-embroidered, aren't they? Did you do the work?"

Vivian blushed and stammered, "The W's are for my married name."

I wasn't sure why that embarrassed her. Maybe because she had made such a fuss over getting married only to have it fizzle in less than a month. Annulled. Last I heard, her ex-husband had moved to Chicago. Vivian never spoke of him. She had kept his name, but why wouldn't she? Her maiden name — with *K*s and *Z*s and far too few vowels — was impossible to spell.

Bozz returned with a pair of beautiful chairs with lions' paw feet. "Are these the ones?"

Vivian nodded and directed him to set them by the table. She squeezed my arm. "Thank you for helping out. This means a lot to me. I wish Bernadette could have come to —" She pressed her palm over her heart. "You know, she and I, we're the same . . . in here. We like the same music, the same theater." Vivian had always supported Grandmère's choices over Kristine's for the Providence Playhouse's season offerings. "We believe the town should grow and prosper, but that Kristine Woodhouse . . ."

Kristine had voted for isolationism. Naively, she believed she could have a thriving boutique with only the locals as clientele. At the prices she charged, maybe she could.

Vivian lifted the carving knife, cut off a slice of the cow's milk cheese, and sighed. "Mmmm. Morbier, my favorite." She peeled off the rind, tossed it into a basket expressly for discarded rinds, and slipped the morsel into her mouth. "Fabulous. Just the right texture. That nutty flavor. And do I detect a hint of hard-boiled eggs?"

I nodded. Morbier is a fabulous cheese, traditionally two cheeses, made at two times of the day, one section made from the morning milk and one from the evening milk, though nowadays it is made from a single milking. Vegetable ash is spread in the middle to maintain the visual appeal. I had imported Franche-Comté/Jura made *au lait cru,* from raw milk.

"It tastes even better if you eat it with a slice of the prosciutto I brought, and have a sip of the Estancia pinot noir."

"I shouldn't drink. Not if I want to keep my wits about —" She gaped through the opened window. "Oh, lordy. What in the blazes is Kristine doing now?" Vivian wiped her fingers on a linen napkin, tossed it into the basket with the rinds, and sailed past me.

Bozz and I followed her to the sidewalk, where dozens of people clustered around Kristine Woodhouse, dressed in a red silk dress, matching hat, and two-toned shoes. Her fists were jammed with flyers.

"Kristine," Vivian said. "Stop what you're doing this instant."

"This is public property," Kristine countered.

Oh, no, I thought. Here we go again. Was Kristine intent on fighting with everyone in town? Her flyers read *Elect Me, Not Bernadette*. I had to give her points for bluntness. No one would mistake her meaning. But people didn't seem to want her flyers. Many were suppressing a smile. Some were muttering nasty comments. Did Kristine realize that people were finding her zealousness ridiculous and her lack of etiquette appalling?

Vivian said, "I'm having a gathering today. I can't have —"

"You can have whatever I dish out, got me?" Kristine's jaw jutted forward. "I refuse to let the police bully me into hiding."

"Bully you?" I said.

"Raiding my home, peering through my closets, sorting through my garbage. The day before my husband's funeral, no less."

I wanted to cheer. Urso had actually taken my advice. I didn't care that he might have foresworn decorum for due process. I wondered if he would share his findings.

Vivian said, "I'm sorry to hear that, Kristine, but really, I need you to move along."

Kristine took a step closer and met Vivian eye-to-eye. "I'm on to you. You don't want your precious auction attendees to back out. If they do, you might not have enough money to pay rent, and that would leave you in, let's say, a tenuous position, wouldn't it, dear? We wouldn't want to make the new owner edgy."

I said, "What are you talking about?"

Bozz whispered, "A developer bought Miss Williams's building. The deal was all cash. It closed before Mr. Woodhouse . . . died."

I remembered Zinnia from *Délicieux* mentioning the sale, but I hadn't realized the sale involved Vivian's building.

Vivian's face turned chalk-white.

"Forget about Kristine." I gripped Vivian's hand. "Let's go inside. Bozz, go back to The Cheese Shop and see if you can help Rebecca."

As he trotted off, I led Vivian away from the burgeoning crowd and into the antique store. "It's going to be fine," I said, hoping it would be. Kristine and Ed had been bad enough as landlords, but a new owner could be iffy. He could hike rents or kick a tenant out for any number of reasons.

"If she has her way, I'll be ruined," Vivian said.

"If she has her way, everyone will be. She's a spiteful, nasty woman, and I wouldn't put it past her to have killed Ed."

"With the candlestick in the parlor, Miss Scarlet." Vivian dissolved into a fit of giggles.

I pressed her into a Victorian walnut gentleman's chair, its cushions a creamy silk with a diamond pattern. "Breathe. C'mon, like in yoga class. One long wave. Then repeat."

She knew what I was talking about. She was a stalwart yoga enthusiast, an avid runner, and she even worked out with a personal trainer.

When Vivian looked more relaxed, I uncorked a bottle of sauvignon blanc and poured her half a glass. She protested, but I ordered her to drink a sip. As she did, I caught sight of Meredith threading her way through the throng on the sidewalk, a silver gift bag tied with glittery ribbon in her hand. I called out, but she continued on, as if she was on a mission and couldn't spare a second.

Odd behavior, but I couldn't think about her now. I had to help Vivian get ready for what could possibly be a do-or-die auction.

CHAPTER 10

Two hours later, I gathered up the platters and baskets and recycled the wine bottles in the garbage behind Vivian's store. I returned to The Cheese Shop, elated that I could help Vivian sell every item she had hoped to auction off, most over the reserved bid. She swore the buyers were loose with their checkbooks because Fromagerie Bessette had provided such wonderful food and wine, and she promised to praise us at the next city council meeting. Word-of-mouth advertising was worth its price in gold.

I bustled to the back of the shop with the platters and baskets and deposited them in the kitchen. When I returned to the cheese counter, I saw the cute young woman who owned All Booked Up bookstore slipping out the back door. Matthew stood in the arch leading to the annex. He looked eons better than he had the night before, his shoulders back, his eyes and skin glowing with energy.

"Aha!" I grinned. "You are seeing her."

"Am not. She asked me to check out her books about wine at the store. She wants to make sure she has the right ones."

"Uh-huh." I winked.

He frowned. "Crowd's thin now." He removed his apron and smoothed the front of his pin-striped shirt. "But business was solid today."

Those words were music to my ears. Actually, just having Matthew talk to me put a song in my heart. Maybe we could clear the air. "Are you — ?"

"I'm leaving a little early. Rebecca said she was more than happy to take over in the wine annex. The girls are busy at an afternoon art program, and one of their friends' parents will drop them off at Grandmère's. You're going there for dinner, right?"

"So are you, I thought." I peered through the arch. The annex stood empty of customers. Rebecca was wiping down the bar with a fervor bordering on obsession.

"I'll be there late."

"Are you calling on the local wineries?" I asked, knowing that I had to visit all the local farmers soon. Maintaining public relations was one of my top priorities. "Or calling on a certain bookstore owner?"

Matthew didn't answer.

"Or are you going to see Zoe, who owns the bakery?"

"Charlotte, don't."

Why couldn't he admit he was dating somebody? Unless he wasn't and had something else to hide.

He slung his apron on the hook by the rear door, tidied the tail of his shirt that had come free of his slacks, and strolled wordlessly toward the front of the shop.

As the grape-leaf-shaped chimes jingled goodbye to Matthew, a wistful feeling toyed with my heart, and I hated myself for it. I was not my cousin's keeper. He had a right to privacy. Maybe he was doing something totally innocent, like attending some event at the Congregational Church down the street and he was late. I'd heard the bells ringing a welcome when I had left Vivian's shop. A little time spent praying might do Matthew a world of good. Maybe he could find a way to get past the hurt that his ex had caused him and reconnect with me.

I ambled into the annex and said to Rebecca, "Looks polished to a shine."

She beamed.

"Are we still on for tonight?" I asked.

"I am." She tossed her wet rag into the sink behind the bar.

"Any word from Meredith?"

"Not a peep."

The front door chimes tinkled again, signaling last-minute customers had arrived. I put off worrying about Meredith and hurried through the arch connecting the annex to The Cheese Shop to find Prudence and Felicia waltzing in, sunhats flopping, frothy floral dresses wafting up around their knees. The skirts settled down again as the door shut.

"Good afternoon," Felicia said, as if she hadn't a care in the world. Why would she? Her deceased husband had left her a mound of cash that covered a fairly extravagant lifestyle. A trip down the Nile. A hike up Machu Picchu. A ballooning escapade across the south of France. I dreamed of doing all three.

Someday . . .

Prudence, as usual, looked uptight and edgy. Maybe it was because she never had any fun. She was a well-known penny-pincher. In all these years, she hadn't purchased one ounce of cheese from Fromagerie Bessette. Gossip was that she had never married because she wasn't willing to share a dime with a husband.

Some people changed over time; some people didn't. I remembered being a gawky teen with acne and drab hair, ignored by the jocks, teased by the in-crowd girls. I had found my confidence and sense of style during college. Nowadays, I usually felt good in my skin, that is when I wasn't fumbling for nouns and verbs in front of Jordan Pace.

The two women paraded toward me. Prudence took up residence on one of the ladder-back chairs by the tasting counter and crossed her spindly legs. She tapped her manicured nails on the counter as if to remind Felicia that time was a-ticking.

"Charlotte, dear, lovely little dress you're wearing," Felicia said.

I fingered the neckline of my sheath self-consciously. Felicia wasn't prone to handing out compliments.

"How are you holding up?" Felicia didn't really care how I was. She simply didn't want me to boot her out of the shop. She perused items behind the glass, her gaze as focused as a rat surveying the contents of a mousetrap. "I'd like a half pound each of three of your favorite cheeses. Make sure that Tartuffo thingie I read about is included." The *Délicieux* reporter hadn't completed her interview with me yet, but she had written a blog on the Internet. In it, she had raved about the morsel of cheese I had fed her. Today the Tartuffo had almost sold out. I made a mental note to purchase more.

"How about a Vermont Grayson?" I suggested. I adored Grayson, which tasted like a Taleggio, a semisoft raw cow's milk cheese, excellent melted on panini with a slice of chicken and a dried cherry reduction sauce. Felicia liked cheeses with creamy centers.

"Sure. Whatever. I'm having a little garden soirée at the museum this weekend. A mini fund-raiser."

"Is the museum in financial trouble?" I asked.

"Nonsense!" Felicia hesitated then wiggled her fingers. "But reserve funds must always be in place. Ed was going to donate, but then, well, you know." Something flickered in her gaze. Sorrow? Anger? She flipped her hand as if to swat away the emotion. "Oh, if you have any of that scrumptious ham and pineapple quiche around, let's include that." She leaned in to Prudence. "Charlotte features a different quiche every week. You should try some."

At times, I wondered if Prudence ate anything other than lemons and grapefruit. She could do with a little sugar, a bite of cheese, and an extra dose of belly laughter in her diet.

"Let's see, what else?" Felicia wandered

away from the counter, dragging her tapered fingernails across the fronts of the basil pesto jars as she roamed.

The movement made me jerk to attention. I flashed again on the gala event when Kristine and her chums had marched in like a drill team. They had all come with gloves. Any could have put back on the gloves, grabbed the olive-wood-handled knife, killed Ed, and left the scene without leaving a fingerprint on the box or the knife. The killer could have disposed of the bloody gloves — at least one from the pair would have to be bloody — and purchased a replacement pair the next morning. Kristine's Boutique was the only shop in town that sold gloves. If she wasn't the killer, one of her friends might be. Would she reveal to Urso which of her pals had needed a new pair?

Itchy to be rid of my customers so I could call our chief of police with yet another theory, I quickly fetched a quiche from the refrigerator, set it into a cake box, and tied it with gold ribbon. "Is that all, Felicia?"

"Oh, no, I've got an extensive list."

Great.

"Pssst." Prudence, who hadn't moved from her spot, spanked the granite with her palm and beckoned me closer. "Felicia is

very upset, though she wouldn't let you know. Ed actually withdrew his offer to donate at the last minute. Can you believe it?"

"Why would he do that?"

"Why do you think?" Prudence rolled her eyes suggestively.

I gaped. Had Ed made the stipulation that, in order for him to give money to the museum, Felicia had to have an affair with him? Had she turned him down? They had looked pretty chummy at The Cheese Shop's reopening.

"Charlotte," Felicia called from the front of the store. "Let's throw in a couple of these jars of honey, too. I know how you suggest adorning cheese with yummy concoctions."

"Will do," I said in a light, airy tone, though my mind was churning with new theories.

"By the by, how's Bernadette?" Felicia went on. "I truly can't believe what everyone is saying that she's, you know . . ." She tapped her head with her finger.

My grandmother was nowhere near crazy. "She's holding up well."

"I saw her wandering the yard in her robe," Felicia said.

Prudence clucked her tongue. "Leave it to

152

Bernadette."

"She's taking advantage of a well-deserved vacation," I countered. That was the pat answer that Pépère and I had come up with, to counteract any rumors that townsfolk might start.

"And losing votes in the process," Prudence said. "The election is days away. She can't afford to look like a loony bird."

I bit my tongue. Prudence's pal Kristine wasn't looking all that sane lately either.

Felicia drew up to the counter, her arm loaded with jars. "Kristine's bound to win now."

I stiffened. Could Kristine have killed Ed and thrown suspicion on Grandmère simply to win an election, as Vivian and Rebecca had intimated?

"I wonder if she'll have time to do it all." Felicia set the jars by the cash register. "The dress boutique, being mayor, handling all the real estate deals. Ed hooked up with a new developer, did you hear? New blood is what the developer wants." She pulled a credit card from her vintage gold-filigree Lucite handbag but didn't hand it to me. She brandished it in the air as she made her point. "Ed was getting ready to evict your grandparents. The scuttlebutt is that Bernadette was so furious when she heard the news, she lost it."

My fingers formed tight fists. These women were never going to believe my grandmother was innocent until she was proven above suspicion. Eager to be rid of them before I punched each in the nose, I carved off wedges of cheese, bundled them, and placed them in one of our gold bags. Then I thrust them at Felicia.

"Oh, no, no, no, dear." She stopped me with her palm raised high. "I'd like you to deliver the order, on platters, just like you did for Vivian."

I resented her tone. I had taken Vivian's order to her as a favor to a friend. Felicia was business. I lifted my chin and said, "I'll have Rebecca deliver it."

"Fine. Whatever. You can add a tip to the charge, of course. Don't make a face."

I didn't know that I had. So much for thinking I was the model of discretion. But Felicia had a way of making a person feel like a servant. I wondered if people like her and Kristine simply couldn't help themselves. Even if they couldn't, that was no excuse for being rude.

"Pretty it up," she went on. "You know, add the fruits and things, like you did at your gala. Presentation is so important. I aim to impress."

"That'll cost extra."

She winced but recovered quickly, fluttered her fingers, and said, "Of course. You know, I really don't know what happened between your grandmother and Ed." She handed me a credit card. "Bernadette seemed fine when we parted ways that night. I mean, after the blowup with Kristine over that niece of yours."

"My grandmother did not kill Ed Woodhouse," I snapped as I punched in the appropriate numbers on the keypad to close out the transaction.

"But who else would have, dear?"

Kristine, or you, for that matter, I wanted to say, but I was smart enough to know a blatant indictment would make Felicia clam up. And how was I supposed to get answers unless I listened and scraped together information?

I said, "Prudence, I heard you and Kristine and Tyanne went to the Country Kitchen after the fracas."

"Mm-hmm," Prudence said, her face as unreadable as a marble statue's.

"And, Felicia, you went where?"

"To the museum, as I always do at the end of the day. Why do you ask?"

"I was hoping one or both of you might

have seen my grandmother at the clock tower."

"Sad to say, I didn't." Prudence slipped off her chair and clip-clopped toward a display table. She bent near a three-pound wheel of Brie, inhaled, then said, "Heavenly."

I knew for a fact that she couldn't smell a thing. I had recently refaced and rewrapped it.

"You and Tyanne stayed at the Country Kitchen for how long?" I asked.

"We listened to Kristine gripe for a minute or two, and then we headed home." Prudence snickered. "We didn't even buy a cup of coffee. Delilah Swain wasn't happy about that."

"And Kristine went to Tyanne's house to pick up her daughter?" I asked.

Prudence and Felicia nodded in unison.

They all lived in different directions, which meant only two had alibis for the time of the murder, if the alibis were to be believed.

"What about you, Felicia?" I said.

"Me?"

"See anybody on your way to the museum?"

She tilted her head, the feathers on her hat flopping to one side, and stared at me,

156

reminding me of a chicken who thought a rival hen was interested in stealing her seed. "Why, I stopped and chatted with my sister, Lois, at her place."

A tingling of hope shot through me. Lois was Felicia's alibi? Felicia couldn't have picked a worse person for corroboration. Lois was known to drink a little too much after five P.M.

CHAPTER 11

The instant the ladies were gone, I called the police department. A clerk said Chief Urso was out and couldn't be reached for the evening. I left a quick message about Felicia's flimsy alibi, closed the shop, and walked with Rebecca to our girls' night out.

As usual, Timothy O'Shea's Irish Pub smelled of rich, foamy Guinness and warm bodies. Locals and tourists stood two-thick at the antique bar, a beautifully hand-carved stretch of wood that Tim had purchased in Ireland. Most of the folks craned their necks so they could watch one of the televisions hanging beyond the bar, three of which displayed different sporting events. A fourth TV aired the latest episode of *Vintage Today,* a regional cable show starring a hunk of a guy who taught people how to update the interiors of their homes with new fixtures and appliances. All of the televisions had the sound turned off and the closed-captioning option turned on. If no sporting events were major battles, then Tim preferred to promote conversation, laughter, and rollicking Irish music. A trio — two on electric violins, one on an ancient drum — played in the far corner. I patted my thigh in rhythm and thought about taking up Irish clog dancing. The nearest class was in Columbus.

Rebecca nudged me. "Go that way."

Like a woman on a mission, she steered me across the hardwood floor, through the round claw-footed oak tables, to one of the rustic booths lining the far wall. The backs of the booths reached to the ceiling, ensuring a small degree of privacy.

"By the way . . ." Rebecca scooted onto the bench opposite me and pulled an appetizer menu from the holder on the table. "Delilah can't join us. She's got rehearsal."

I wondered if Meredith would show up. The Pollyanna in me said good friends should be able to talk about anything, but the cynic in me, that little voice that I so desperately tried to keep locked in a mental trunk, said perhaps there was something sinister brewing — what, I couldn't imagine. Did she want to break up our friendship? Had I done something to offend her?

Rebecca rapped the table with her knuckles. "Yoo-hoo. Are you okay?"

"I'm fine." I didn't like talking about my fears. Especially at night. After my parents died in the crash, I took to crawling under the covers of my bed with a flashlight and a book, and I would sink into utter silence. Grandmère never pressed me. Creep Chef once told me that, like a porcupine, I stuck my needles out to guard myself from hurt. I wanted to convince myself that Meredith was simply avoiding me because she had so much end-of-the-year stuff going on at school that she didn't have an ounce of time, but I wasn't that cavalier. And she'd lied about the parent/teacher conferences. To my face.

A waitress toting a tray filled with drinks paused at the end of our booth. "The usual?"

Rebecca nodded. A Cosmo for her, a glass of Guinness for me. Tim's boasted sixty beers on his menu, both domestic and foreign. I'd made it a quest to try every one at least once. I was up to twenty-two. Guiness was still my favorite. When the waitress left, I asked Rebecca if she would like to have dinner with me and my grandparents, but she declined, saying she actually had a date.

"With whom?"

Her face flushed bright pink. She had shown interest in a couple of local farmers, but I didn't think any had found the courage to ask her out yet, she being Amish and, in their minds, possibly too prim for them.

"C'mon, who?"

"A reporter."

"Oh, no." The first reporter that came to mind was the weasel with the bug-eyed glasses who had grilled me the day after my grandmother's arrest.

"Oh, yes, and Charlotte, he's very cute. He says he'll tell me everything he's learned about being an investigative reporter and how to get a good scoop and, well, everything. He said he'll show me his notes."

I'd bet he wanted to show her a lot more than his notes. I said, "Reporters don't divulge secrets."

"I know." She twirled a lock of hair around her finger. "I'm not naïve."

"Look, Rebecca —"

"Please, don't talk me out of it. Back home, I wouldn't get a choice of whom I got to date, you know? My marriage would be . . . arranged. I'd really like to —"

"I get it." A spurt of anxiety rushed through me. Rebecca reminded me of a young colt, growing up so fast, believing she was ready for wide-open pastures. I wanted her to slow down, be wary, but I feared anything I said would fall on deaf ears. Wary wasn't exciting. She wanted exciting.

"What about you?" Rebecca said. "Who are you interested in?"

She couldn't tell? Hooray for me. Perhaps I was subtler than I gave myself credit.

"Come on, there has to be someone," she prodded.

"Why does there have to be someone?" For the past few years, prior to meeting Jordan, I had been perfectly happy being single. Sure, I'd had an occasional date, but Creep Chef had done such a number on my confidence, constantly making me feel insignificant for wanting to become a cheesemonger, that when he split, I assured myself that if I ended up single for the rest of my life, I would be happy to fill the days with the things I loved. Work, cheese, good food, family, and travel. I yearned to travel — when the shop was a super success and the budget allowed.

"Charlotte, c'mon, spill."

"Oh, look, there's Freckles." I wiggled my fingers, eager to get the subject off me. "And Felicia."

Rebecca looked where I pointed. "Ewww. She's with that Prudence. The woman never smiles!" she added, her tone tart, judgmental. "Oh, and isn't that the *Délicieux* reporter?"

Zinnia, wearing yet another flower-decorated blouse, sat at a table with the stocky man who ran the farmer's market. Her tape recorder stood on the table. Was she interviewing him? Had she forgotten about me? Perhaps *Délicieux* had warned her off the Bessette family for now. Too much conflict. Except wasn't any publicity good publicity? My shoulders sagged. Perhaps not.

"Say, isn't that gal at the bar the one from the Cleveland wine tour?" Rebecca pointed.

Unable to see much of the bar from where I sat, I peered around the corner of the booth. The bleached blonde woman — her tight brown tour T-shirt replaced with an even tighter pink one, her jeans so snug they looked painted on — sat with her legs crossed and one arm slung over the back of the bar stool. A jaunty man in a loose-fitting suit joined her. A pencil wove through the shaggy hair above his ear. He looked to be at least ten years her junior.

"Oh, no, oh, no, oh, no." Rebecca covered her mouth with the back of her hand. "It's . . . it's . . ." Tears sprang into her eyes.

I could only surmise. "Your date?"

She nodded. "Quigley." She sniffled, then shrugged in a worldly way, well beyond her years. "Oh, what do I care?" She wiped tears away with her pinky. "He didn't like any of the cheeses I offered him. He has no taste."

A good measure of a man, I thought, flashing briefly on Jordan and how much he enjoyed cheese and a hearty glass of wine. And cooking. And Ohio. And, well, everything I liked.

Our waitress set our drinks on the table.

Rebecca took a big gulp of her Cosmo, then ran her tongue along her lips. "Say, do you think the tour lady might have killed Ed? I mean, the one night she's in town, and he dies. Some coincidence, huh?"

"Lots of people visit here," I said. "Just because someone dies doesn't make a happenstance visitor a suspect. Heck, if that were the case, then Zinnia could be a suspect."

"But the tour guide was flirting with Ed. Don't you remember how he fed her and she licked the oil off his fingers?"

How could I forget? At The Cheese Shop opening, Ed's blatant disdain for Kristine had bothered me. Grandmère said she had seen Ed visiting the tour guide at Lois's B&B. Were they having an affair? Had she killed him in a *crime passionnel*?

"Or better yet," Rebecca went on. "What if my date is actually the guide's husband or her boyfriend, and he got super jealous and he offed Ed?" She shuddered and shook her hands as if trying to get sticky leaves off of them. "Ew. That's just too creepy to contemplate. He's a killer and I could have gone on a date with him. Let's go find out." She started to rise.

I pinned her arm to the table and prevented her from leaving. "Are you nuts?"

"Please? We'll find out if she knew Ed, you know, for a long time. Like maybe they were lovers before Kristine married him. They were only married nine years. Ed could have been with a lot of women."

My mouth dropped open. Rebecca was learning way too much from TV and the Internet.

"Oh, look, there's Jordan," Rebecca said.

Instantly I released Rebecca and my hands went to my hair to primp. Rebecca took the opportunity to bolt off the bench.

"Ha! Fooled you," she said with glee.

Guess I wasn't as subtle as I thought. Rats.

Rebecca hurried toward the tour guide. I wasn't certain which was more important to her, getting the scoop on the tour guide or snubbing her erstwhile date, but before she could embarrass herself, I raced to her, slipped my arm around her waist, and steered her into a U-turn.

"But they have motive and opportunity," Rebecca protested.

"That's enough, my little flatfoot." She had watched entirely too many reruns of *Law & Order* and *NCIS* and who knew what else. "Trust me, you'll thank me," I said. Once we were seated back at our table, I said, "By the way, I need your help tomorrow putting together Felicia Hassleton's garden party order."

Rebecca looked chagrined. "Yeah, okay, I heard you talking before we left. You know, it's possible that when Ed Woodhouse pulled out of donating to the museum, Miss Hassleton got so angry that she killed him." She drank another sip of her Cosmo. "Maybe we should tell Chief Urso to go to her house and search for evidence. I mean, if she killed him, the flowery dress she wore that night would be all bloody. Garbage collection hasn't come this week."

Apparently I wasn't the only one clever enough to think of these things. No wonder Urso had bridled when I'd strutted into his office. I cringed at the thought of how he would react when he heard the message I left earlier. I was more of a novice than Rebecca, it appeared.

"Hey, maybe we should look in her gar-bage for ourselves," Rebecca said, her eyes bright with zeal. "Or better yet . . ."

I felt a panic rising in my stomach.

". . . we should scour through the muse-um's garbage. If I killed somebody, that's where I'd put it. In that big Dumpster out back." Rebecca hitched a thumb, which thwacked the back of the booth. "Ow." She rubbed and snickered. "Clumsy me." She wasn't snockered, but one Cosmo was her limit. "We could go now, on our way to din-ner with your grandparents. I'm re-inviting myself, if that's okay."

"It's fine." Grandmère and Pépère would welcome her with open arms. "But Rebecca, the museum is out of the way."

"C'mon. Don't be a ninny. Felicia won't do her walk-around until nine. It's only seven." She slapped cash on the table to pay for our drinks, eyed the front door, then leaned forward and whispered, "We won't go inside. We'll just take a peek. Deal?"

Maybe one beer was my limit, as well, because I wasn't seeing any harm in her plan. After all, garbage was public property.

CHAPTER 12

"Isn't there a ladder on the darned thing?" Rebecca left her lookout point at the end of the alley behind the historical museum and its neighboring homes and stole to my side.

Muttering to myself, I toured the perimeter of the Dumpster a second time. Why, for heaven's sake, did Felicia need a Dumpster for her small enterprise? Why didn't she have a simple little green Tupperware garbage can like all the other houses in the area? Perhaps she had done some renovating, except if she was running low on money, that wouldn't make any sense.

"I know," Rebecca said. "I'll give you a boost and you can look over the edge."

"Are you crazy?"

"I'm really strong."

"That's not the point." I blew a stream of frustrated air out my nose. A sheath and sandals were not exactly appropriate attire for scaling a metal behemoth.

"C'mon. Step into my hands." Rebecca bent down and laced her fingers together. "Don't worry. I've lifted my brothers this way. Promise. I won't let you fall. Just take a peek."

Feeling like a numbskull, I slipped my foot into the stirrup she formed with her hands, and grabbing hold of the corner of the Dumpster and one of the braces running top to bottom, heaved myself toward the upper edge.

"What is going on, Charlotte?" Urso said from behind me, his voice authoritative and curt.

I dropped from the Dumpster, heart pumping, goose bumps prickling my arms, and shielded my eyes from the blinding beam of Urso's flashlight. Why in the heck was he carrying a flashlight at dusk? To intimidate me, no doubt. The tactic worked. Rebecca huddled behind me, trembling. I shook off my initial alarm and poked her to do the same. Urso was harmless. At least I hoped so.

"Well?" Urso switched off the flashlight and slung it into a holster on his belt. "Did you lose something?" He eyed my dress.

I followed his gaze and my cheeks warmed. The darned sheath had bunched up around my thighs. What I would have given for a baggy overcoat and galoshes right about now. I tugged the sheath's hem down to my knees, then stood a little taller, but that didn't make any difference. I still felt like a pipsqueak around Urso.

"Don't tell me you're looking for more bloody evidence," he said. "Let me guess, Felicia Hassleton's dress?"

I caught the smug humor in his gaze and bristled. Why was I so sure it was a woman who had killed Ed? Because it was a crime of passion. The killer had stabbed Ed in the heart. Yet another reason I didn't believe that my grandmother was guilty. As organized and forthright as she was, she would have plotted to kill Ed and then shot him. She owned a little snub-nosed revolver, handed down to her from her father. I chose not to offer that little tidbit to Urso. He didn't need more reason to suspect Grandmère.

"Find anything?" Urso asked.

"Hard to tell with a mere nanosecond to peek over the edge." I didn't even try to keep the snarkiness from my tone.

"I already searched Kristine Woodhouse's boutique."

Did he expect me to gush with thanks?

"I didn't find anything incriminating," he went on. "I think she's innocent."

A series of rejoinders rattled through my brain. Innocent, my foot. Maniacal, maybe. Pretentious, definitely. I tapped my fingers on my mouth, as if to keep the words nailed inside. What other possibilities were there?

I said, "What if Kristine burned the dress and gloves? Or buried them?"

"Or stuffed them in the back of her toilet?" Rebecca popped from her hiding place, my confidence apparently spurring hers. "I saw that storyline once on *CSI*. It was drugs, not a dress, but it's the same thing. At least, I think it is. Seems the same."

Urso sighed. "It's late, Charlotte. Why don't you visit your grandparents and then go home? As for you, Miss Zook . . ."

"Yes?" Rebecca squeaked.

"You should know better than to orchestrate something like this."

"But I didn't —"

"Oh, but you did." Urso snorted. "I happened to be at the pub."

Rebecca and I gasped in unison.

"Yep, sitting in the booth beyond yours. I heard the entire plot."

Why, the rascal. Playing cat and mouse with us. Letting us go off half-cocked just so he could trap us. I'd have to keep his diabolical nature in mind when dealing with him in the future.

"Now go home." Without another word, Urso strode from the alley. His shoulders shook with laughter as he turned the corner.

When he was out of sight, I realized I had forgotten to tell him about the theory that any of Kristine's friends — not just Felicia — could have killed Ed, but I didn't call him back. He wouldn't be in the mood to listen. That conversation could wait until morning.

But dinner wouldn't. Rebecca and I returned to The Cheese Shop. I selected a bottle of Markham sauvignon blanc, and I boxed the apricot-cream-cheese coffee cake I'd made earlier in the day, gluten-free so Clair could have a taste, and then we strolled toward my grandparents, heading south. On our way, Rebecca was eager to hash around other theories, but I nixed that idea.

As we neared the corner of Grace Street and Cherry Orchard Road, orchestral music filled the air. In moments, I realized it was coming from my grandparents' yard. A crowd had gathered three-deep and ran the length of my grandparents' white picket fence. I groaned. Just what I needed, as if my evening's run-in with the law wasn't enough excitement for one day.

Mr. Nakamura, the Nuts for Nails owner,

waved and smiled. "I love a free concert," he said, his almond-shaped eyes glittering with humor. He always looked for the fun in life. He had seen too much as a young boy, he told me one day when I was buying nails by the pound. I didn't know what he'd seen, but I could commiserate. "Nice night for one," he added.

Yes, it was a lovely night. The temperature was a balmy seventy-five. Not too hot, not too cool. So why was I suddenly perspiring? I was too young for hot flashes.

I pushed through the crowd, and the pastor's wife, Gretel, a hearty woman with blonde braids who looked like she would be right at home yodeling in the Alps, grabbed hold of my arm.

"How divine of your grandmother to offer us a peek at a rehearsal for the new ballet."

Now I recognized the tune. "Good Morning, Baltimore" from *Hairspray,* a reedy string version, probably recorded by Providence's very own ten-piece orchestra, conducted by my very own bullheaded grandmother. What was she thinking, putting on such a spectacle when she was under house arrest?

"It's going to be quite a show." Gretel winked. "A little risqué, but that's all right with me." Like Delilah, she had spent considerable time in New York. She'd wanted to be a publisher, but after a few years, she returned to Providence looking for a simpler, more spiritually fulfilling life. She once confided that spending an evening walking the rolling hills beyond town and drinking in the beauty of the stars, like those twinkling overhead tonight, were all she needed to feel at one with God. I craved a night like that.

"Oh, my, look at her go." Gretel clapped her hands. Her braids bounced in rhythm.

Delilah, dancing the lead role of Tracy, was clad in a frumpy dress with slits up the legs. She pirouetted across the yard and threw herself into the arms of a local farmer who moonlighted as Providence's leading man. He bent her backward, and she raised her arms gracefully over her head. A gathering of other dancers, part of the Baltimore street scene, cheered.

"Isn't she splendid?" Gretel said.

I had to agree. Delilah was graceful yet athletic. Her face shone with enthusiasm.

"Your grandmother has such an eye for these things. I commend her."

Grandmère, dressed like Martha Graham in a chic black leotard and wraparound skirt, looked fit, trim, and back in control of her emotions. She pounded out the rhythm of the music on the porch.

"She's certainly resilient, isn't she?" Gretel went on. "Acting like she hasn't a worry in the world."

"She didn't do it," I blurted. "She didn't kill Ed Woodhouse."

"Of course not, sweetheart, but who did?"

That was the million-dollar question, wasn't it?

"I don't know . . . yet. But I will. Excuse me." I hoisted my tote filled with wine and dessert and gave a little nod. "We're expected for dinner."

"Please tell your grandmother our prayers are with her."

Rebecca traipsed behind me as I cut through the rehearsal to the front porch.

"Delilah," I said as I passed her. "Come join us for a bite when you're through."

She agreed and, in time to the music, did a little jig and clicked her heels.

Grandmère, her body warm with exertion, gave me a hug as I crested the top stair.

"You're looking better," I said.

She gave a perfunctory nod as if to say, why wouldn't she? "The twins are inside. They brought your cat."

Grandmère didn't care for Rags. I wasn't sure why. She'd never allowed me to have a pet while growing up. Through the screened door, I spied Clair rolling on the floor of the living room with him. Amy was sitting on the couch, an album laid across her lap.

"Your grandfather is in the kitchen baking," Grandmère added. "Zucchini and onion quiche. I had a craving." I had gotten all of my quiche recipes from my grandfather. He was a wizard with flaky pastry. "Rebecca, *chérie,* I hope you like quiche."

"I love it."

I inhaled the lush aroma of cheese and nutmeg. No doubt, Pépère was putting together one of his legendary salads, as well. I could hardly wait. My garbological adventure at the museum hadn't deterred my appetite in the least.

"Is Matthew here?" I asked.

"He called. He's running late."

"Hmph," I muttered, again wondering what Matthew was up to. He wasn't dating Delilah, because she was at rehearsal. The wineries had closed, so he wasn't making business calls. Had he gone to the movies? The gym? Had he found some kind of local card game? Did he have a problem that we should discuss? Maybe he had stolen off with my elusive pal Meredith, I thought, then I chuckled at the ludicrous notion. She said she was dating someone who recited poetry. Matthew's idea of poetry was what

he read on the labels of wine bottles. Not to mention, about an hour ago, I'd seen him chatting up Zoe, the bakery owner. She'd be getting off work just about now.

"What's so funny?" Grandmère said.

"Nothing." Tension melted from my shoulders. Laughter truly was the best medicine. "When is your rehearsal over? How soon do we eat?"

"Now." Grandmère pounded her stick again.

As she ended the session and bid everyone adieu, I pressed open the screened door. Rebecca followed me inside. Delilah joined us minutes later.

We ate dinner in the dining room, a charming space with burgundy flocked wallpaper, the most handsome country French Provincial dining table with a parquet top, and a matching hutch that housed a glistening set of Lenox white-gold-banded china. The table, fitted with burgundy placemats and napkins, set off the plates beautifully. The salad Pépère had made — field greens, slices of Roma tomatoes, thin slices of red onion, and a sprinkling of crumbled Humboldt Fog, with his special oil and vinegar dressing seasoned with crushed garlic, mustard, and a pinch of sugar — was mouthwateringly good.

We kept the conversation light. We didn't discuss Grandmère's situation. We didn't bring up Matthew or his ex-wife. Not in front of the girls. Delilah regaled us with stories about the mishaps that had occurred during the rehearsal. When she told us that the leading man had landed on her foot not once, not twice, but five times, we all laughed. Even Grandmère.

Delilah came into the kitchen while I was scooping homemade espresso mascarpone ice cream into bowls. She leaned her hip against one of the cabinets. "I'm sorry your cousin isn't here."

Aha! I had picked up that she was interested in Matthew. "He's certainly been in the diner a lot lately."

She nodded. "Likes his coffee black."

"Do you two . . . chat . . . while he's there?"

"A little. Mostly he comes in, grabs the coffee, and leaves."

Did I detect a note of regret? And if he wasn't hanging around Delilah, where was he spending the rest of his time? Before I could ask, Amy appeared. I recognized the picture album she had tucked under her arm, and the muscles around my heart tightened. There were photographs of Matthew's wedding in it. Which meant photos

178

of her mother.

"Are you okay?" I said.

She plunked herself onto one of the chairs at the table. "Mum never calls."

"She's probably very busy."

"Doing what?"

"I'll leave you two alone," Delilah whispered and sashayed out of the room.

"Well," I said, weighing my words carefully. "She's probably working."

"Working where?"

"Waitressing is my guess. That's what she did when she and your dad met."

"Was she a good waitress?"

"Sure, she was." Honestly, I didn't have a clue. The woman hadn't worked in the restaurant a week when she set her sights on Matthew, the sommelier. She quit waitressing and moved in with Matthew a week after that. Grandmère had called her a gold digger. On the other hand, she hadn't asked for a cent when she left him and the girls. Mumsie and Dad had plenty of cash to keep their little princess in pretty frocks and expensive shoes for decades to come.

"Now, why don't you help me serve this ice cream." I clipped the tip of her nose with my knuckle.

"What about Clair's allergies?"

I loved that she cared so much about her

sister, a result of the twin bond, I imagined, or perhaps the bond that grew stronger when a parent left. My bond to my grandparents had certainly cemented after my parents died.

"It's gluten-free," I said, "but that one's the biggest scoop, so it's yours."

She giggled, and leaving the album on the kitchen table, trotted out of the room carrying two dessert dishes.

By the time we finished our meal, it was close to nine.

"Bedtime," I said to the girls. "Gather your things."

Rebecca yawned, thanked my grandparents for a lovely dinner, and headed home. She lived a block away. So did Meredith. I considered stopping by her place, but dropping in unannounced was not my style.

Before Delilah could slip out, Grandmère clutched her arm and asked if she would teach the morning dance classes for the next week. The elderly students really needed the workout, she said, and, well, the women wouldn't want to exercise on the lawn.

As they negotiated hours and salary, Delilah insisting she needed none of the latter, I went in search of Rags and found him lying on the living room floor. He looked like the

Cheshire Cat, a grin on his silly face. Pie crust crumbs led from a little rooster plate on the floor to Rags's mouth. The scamp must have begged Pépère for a taste of quiche, and Pépère, knowing I would disapprove, brought it to him on the sly.

"Slob," I muttered and hoisted him into my arms.

Pépère appeared in the arch. He eyed the cat and his mouth tilted up on one side.

"She is better, no?" he said. "Your grandmère?"

"Yes."

"I keep replaying that night. How I wish —"

"It's not your fault."

"Chief Urso. He pressed me for the truth."

"As he should have."

"Ed and your grandmother argued, Charlotte, nothing more."

I patted his shoulder. "Pépère, do you remember seeing anybody running in your direction as you left the Igloo?" The ice cream store stood three doors north of Kristine's Boutique. If I had murdered Ed, I would have headed away from the crime scene. I would have weaved my way home on side streets. Someone had to have seen her.

"I saw no one." He tapped a finger to his

181

chin. "You know, I did see Ed with Vivian the night before he died. They were at his office. They were quarreling. I can't remember ever hearing Vivian raise her voice before. She is such a lady."

If disagreement was evidence that could hang a person, we would all be suspects in the murder of Ed Woodhouse. Everyone except Pépère. He never bickered. Oh, sure, he lambasted himself in French diatribes, but he never lashed out at others.

"She must have learned that Ed sold her building. I'd have raised my voice as well."

"*Oui,* of course. Oh, *chérie,* this is making me think like a crazy man." Pépère beat the side of his leg with his palm. "Vivian is as innocent as your grandmother, no? Everybody is innocent until proven guilty. That is the American way."

Usually, unless one was covered with the victim's blood.

I kissed him on both cheeks and said, "Get a good night's rest. I'm sure we'll find answers tomorrow."

"I'll drive you home."

"The girls and I can walk."

"I'll drive." He was adamant.

I gathered the twins, kissed my grandmother good night, and we headed for his Audi. As I opened the passenger door, I heard Jordan's voice coming from next door. I peered around the hedge of well-trimmed holly.

Jordan was standing on the porch talking to an attractive woman who had moved to Providence only last week. Grandmère had promised to get me the dirt on her but had yet to do so. I didn't know what the woman did for a living. She didn't own a shop in town. She didn't have a husband or a pet or any children, as far as my snoopy grandmother could tell. With a solid build, strong features, and athletic forearms, she looked like the kind of woman who could wrestle a Wall Street broker to the ground at the end of a day of heavy trading. Grandmère and I teasingly called her Mystery Woman.

So who was she, how did Jordan know her, and why was he hugging her?

CHAPTER 13

A night of tossing and thinking about Jordan Pace, his cowboy good looks, his husky voice, and his arms wrapped around Mystery Woman did nothing for my mood. Neither did dressing in a somber suit and tight heels for Ed Woodhouse's funeral. Determined to do something that felt constructive, I called Urso. He wasn't pleased that I was, yet again, his first call of the day. He reminded me that it was the day of the funeral, and he was on his way to it. I told him I was, too, but I wasn't going to wait to tell him that there had to be a witness who had seen Kristine leaving her coterie of friends on the night of the murder. I recapped my conversation with Pépère in three sentences, and Urso begrudgingly promised to check into the entire town's alibis. After the funeral.

The Congregational Church was packed to overflowing. Among the assemblage were many familiar faces: Delilah and her father, Meredith and other schoolteachers, Freckles and her group of crafters, Mr. Nakamura and his teensy wife. The last to enter was Urso, looking decidedly handsome in a dark blue suit.

Huge five-foot candles lined the curved apse behind the altar. Early morning sunlight gleamed through the six stained-glass depictions of scenes from the New Testament. The pastor and his wife Gretel sat in a pair of brown velvet, high-backed chairs in the chancel.

Kristine, for once appropriately clad in a black dress, strutted down the aisle of the nave, her chin held high, a black-veiled toque cupping her perfectly coifed hair. Willamina, also wearing a black frock, shuffled behind her mother. The poor thing looked as sallow as a corpse. Her nose was chapped and red, her eyes swollen. She twisted a handkerchief in her hands. Without a glance back at her daughter, Kristine proceeded to the first pew. As Willamina passed, I had the urge to swoop her into my arms and comfort her. I fought the impulse with all my might. The girl didn't need me to incite her mother.

Felicia, Prudence, and Tyanne followed Kristine and Willamina, each wearing a black chiffon sheath and black lace gloves. Each carried a black linen hankie. How much had Kristine charged them for those get-ups? I wondered, and pinched myself for such catty thoughts. They slid into the first pew, with Willamina squeezed between her mother and Felicia.

Urso had granted my grandmother dispensation to appear at the funeral, but Grandmère said she didn't think Kristine would want her there, so she had declined. Pépère sat beside me, Matthew and the twins beyond him, and Rebecca at the far end. Vivian came in late, wearing a dark blue suit buttoned to the neck, and wedged herself into the pew beside Rebecca. We shared a somber nod.

The pastor, with his sage voice and owlish looks, gave a lovely sermon about life in the hereafter and reminded the family that they should feel solace knowing that they were loved. I wasn't sure how much of that was true, but it sounded good. Attendees who had lost loved ones in the recent past were weeping. A tear slipped down my cheek in memory of my parents. I often wondered what my life would have been like had they lived, but Grandmère warned that dredging up the past could only lead to sorrow.

After the organist played a mournful tune

by Bach, the pastor offered Kristine the opportunity to address the congregation. If it was me, I would have passed, but Kristine practically leapt at the chance. She stood and cut a bitter look in my direction. I tensed. Would she attack my family? Were we wrong to have come?

Pépère grabbed my hand.

I squeezed his hard. "Be strong," I said. I had encouraged him to attend, to be the face of innocence for Grandmère. Our friends — our real friends — believed she would be exonerated.

Like a queen ready to be crowned, Kristine strode to the front of the church, lifted her mid-calf-length skirt an inch, and took the carpeted steps to the podium, one at a time, slowly, deliberately. She moved behind the pulpit and braced her hands on either side, gripping so hard that her knuckles turned white. She took a deep breath, glanced up at the ceiling, and then back at the crowd. I had seen an actress in one of Grandmère's plays do the same thing to prepare for her overly melodramatic monologue. She was panned for her performance, a critic saying she had run the gamut of emotions from A to B.

"My dear, dear friends," Kristine intoned. Her words echoed into the rafters. She scanned the crowd but avoided looking in my direction. "I can't begin to tell you how wonderful it is to see all of you here. Ed would be so . . ." She paused, licked her upper lip ever so slightly. "So . . ." She paused again, this time I was sure it was for effect. "So . . ." She began to wail. Huge, gushing wails.

The assembly uttered a collective gasp.

Kristine laid the back of her hand on her mouth, then held up her other hand as if to tell us she was all right, to give her a moment. Not a soul whispered. When she had composed herself, she wiped tears off her cheeks with her gloved pinky and began again. "Ed was the most wonderful man. I have never known another who was better than him."

I had. Dozens. Hundreds. I bit my tongue.

"He was a wonderful husband, a fabulous father." She didn't look at Willamina, who was hunched over in the front pew, shoulders shuddering. "He supported me in everything I tried to do. I know he would want me to —"

Here it comes, I thought. The pitch. The beleaguered widow wants my grandmother to go to jail, and she wants the town of Providence to elect her. I squeezed Pépère's hand harder.

"Ed would want me to continue in my quest to make this the finest city in Ohio."

I knew it. *Voilà!* People were so predictable sometimes.

"I promise you . . ." Kristine's hand flew to her mouth again, and she slurped back tears. A soap opera actress would be hard-pressed to emote like she did. "I promise you that I will keep his spirit alive by doing exactly that. I will make you and Ed proud. Thank you all for coming. Thank you, thank you, thank you." She actually blew kisses and I was reminded of scenes from *Evita,* when the insincere Eva Peron played the crowd like a fine-tuned fiddle.

As Kristine strode to her daughter and people roused to their feet, I sat frozen in my spot, too stunned to move. The cheek, the gall. Poor little Willamina looked mortified. No siblings to help her. No grandparents to comfort her. Kristine reached out to stroke her daughter's hair, but Willamina batted her mother's hand away and fled into the aisle.

When I finally found my composure, I stood with the rest of my family and made my way out of the church. As we passed Kristine and Willamina, who were standing in the chapel's foyer speaking to well-wishers, Amy and Clair whispered to Willamina that they were sorry. She mumbled the same to them, and my heart broke. The poor kid looked in dire need of a friend.

Outside the church, we kissed Pépère goodbye. I told him not to say a word to Grandmère about Kristine's brazen promise, and he agreed.

Out in the sunlight, I looked for Jordan, hoping to catch a word with him. I hadn't seen him in the church, but that didn't mean he hadn't come.

"Charlotte." Vivian tapped me on the shoulder. "I'm so sorry. What she did in there . . ."

"Forget it."

"It was unforgiveable. She has no class, that woman. She and Ed. They never should have gotten married."

But they did, and the rest, as pundits would say, was history.

"I still think we can prove she killed him," Vivian said. "Money is a powerful motivator. Do we know how much she inherited? Has Urso or your lawyer found that out?"

I didn't know if anyone had, but I was too upset to think about it right then. I told her I would confer with both of them later.

Matthew, the twins, and I trundled home. We changed clothes, grabbed Rags, ferried the girls to school in Matthew's Jeep, and went to the shop. Out of respect for the Woodhouse family, whether they deserved our respect or not, we had chosen not to open The Cheese Shop until ten A.M.

The rest of the day passed quickly. Rebecca and I tended to the customers while Matthew prepared for the wine tasting we were having tomorrow evening. We expected a large crowd. He didn't mention missing dinner last night. In fact, he didn't talk at all, and though I was dying to ask him who, what, where, and why, I kept quiet. I wasn't a harpy. Our business was running smoothly. The girls, other than the incident with Amy missing her mother, seemed happy. Why rock the proverbial boat?

Besides, I had bigger issues to contend with. How was I going to compete with Jordan's new flame, and how was I going to prove that Kristine Woodhouse was guilty and my grandmother was innocent of murder? I decided to deal with Jordan tomorrow when I made the weekly tour to local farms. Somehow I would get him to spill the beans about Mystery Woman and perhaps, if I was supremely lucky, I could snag a date.

I spent the afternoon filling orders and consulting with Bozz about new pictures to add to our website. He had done a spectacular job photographing an array of cheeses. Around three, I wrote the first of what I hoped would be a monthly newsletter to our customers. I had set a guest book by the register so friends of The Cheese Shop could sign up and give us their email addresses. It was nearly full. In the newsletter, I focused on three distinctly different cheeses — one goat's milk, one sheep's milk, and one cow's milk — and I shared a few tips on how to serve the cheeses. One of my favorites was Caerphilly, a soft, nutty cow's milk cheese from Wales, which tasted great with a drizzle of apricot jam and a sprinkling of chopped cashews. Matthew popped into the office and offered a suggestion for wine to go with the Caerphilly, a red Ada Nada Dolcetto d'Alba from Italy, a mouthful to say, but delicious.

At four, I returned to the cheese counter, and Rebecca asked if she could take a break.

"Before you go, grab another wheel of Morbier from the refrigerator, would you?" We had sold all of the wedges I had set out. Our customers loved specials.

Rebecca trotted off and I found myself humming for the first time in a long time. Until I heard a pounding sound. Then a kicking sound. Then a scream. Well, not a scream really. A fit of laughter. Rebecca had locked herself into the refrigerator. Again.

"Problem?" a customer with a peanut-sized child in tow asked.

"Nope." I chuckled. Rebecca would be angry if I rescued her. I'd give her sixty seconds to figure out her escape route. "What'll it be?"

Two more customers strolled into the store and headed straight for the wine annex.

"Don't you need to help her?" the customer with the toddler asked.

"She'll figure her way out. I promise." She had before.

The woman asked for a quarter pound each of Molinari Toscano Picante salami, prosciutto, and Manchego cheese. As I filled the order, the grape-leaf-shaped chimes jingled. Zinnia scuttled into the shop.

She strode toward me and said, "Got a tidbit for you," then she began playing peekaboo with the customer's toddler, seemingly content to bide her time until I was free.

As I moved toward the register, I heard a slam and then a muttering of French swear words. Rebecca had escaped her chilly dungeon. I would bet she hadn't a clue what she was saying and would blush when I told her. And I would. Later. Out of earshot of customers. I had no intention of letting my purer-than-pure helper go down a path she didn't understand.

She shuffled to my side, looking like she had grappled with a bear, strands of hair falling around her delicate face, her ponytail loose, and the apron that she wore over her shirred-neck dress twisted almost backward. She smiled her elfin smile. "I've returned, thanks to the stool." The inner handle of the refrigerator stuck every once in a while. It required a little extra oomph to open it. I had put a step-stool into the refrigerator just in case Clair or Amy got trapped. The extra height would give them enough leverage to open the door. Rebecca, as slight as she was, had to use it, too.

"Charlotte, got a sec?" Zinnia said, no longer willing to wait.

I sidled from behind the cheese counter and joined her by the display of balsamic vinegar and extra-virgin olive oil bottles. "What's up?"

"I'm going back home."

"But —" I sputtered. We hadn't finished the interview.

"Don't worry. It's my fault we haven't completed the interview. I'm writing the article, anyway, and I promise it'll be very positive."

194

That was a relief.

"Before I go, I wanted to impart a little more gossip that I gleaned at Lois's B&B." Zinnia snagged my shirtsleeve and pulled me close. "Get this. Kristine Woodhouse is trying to get control of her daughter's trust fund."

"What? Why?"

"Sounds to me like she might be a little hard up for cash. I don't think Ed left her much else."

I needed to talk to Urso. Money was always a motive for murder.

"I know you're trying to buy this place," Zinnia went on. "Maybe now you can get it for a song."

No matter how destitute Kristine Woodhouse was, I couldn't see her letting anybody get a bargain. But a meeting with my Realtor, Octavia Tibble, was in order. I'd call her on my way to pick up the twins from school.

Providence Elementary was a lovely one-story brick building sandwiched between the matching junior high school and high school. All three, thanks to Grandmère and the city counsel, had recently been spruced up with new gymnasiums, repainted classrooms, and lots of thriving perennials interspersed with glorious beds of deep purple petunias.

I drove into the turnabout driveway by the elementary school.

Within seconds Amy tagged the front door of my white Escort and yelled, "Shotgun!"

Clair clambered into the backseat and huddled over her iPod, her blonde hair falling forward like a curtain to hide her face. The day after their mother split, Matthew had given each girl an iPod and twenty-five downloaded songs. They knew each song by heart. Clair had the better voice. Amy sang the loudest.

"How's Grandmère today?" Amy said, kicking her blue backpack forward under the dash.

"Eager to see you. And she's prepared your favorite snack."

"Peanut butter apple pie?" Amy asked, and rubbed her hands together like a money-hungry miser. Peanut butter apple pie was a little sandwich Grandmère had concocted, made with bread, raisins, peanut butter, apple, and Cheddar cheese. Melt-in-your-mouth delicious. "Does she have milk?"

"Of course. And don't worry, Clair. You'll get the treat, too. Grandmère made your special bread." A gluten-free bread that was soft and didn't need toasting. I glanced over the car seat. Clair looked up at me, eyes moist. My heart tightened. "Are you okay?"

"Mm-hm," she lied, and resumed staring at her iPod.

I'd have to pry the truth out of her.

"Miss Vance asked about Grandmère," Amy said. "I told her she was sad."

I frowned. People didn't need to know that Grandmère was crying at the drop of a sunhat.

"How is Miss Vance?" I said, still worried about Meredith. She hadn't made eye contact at the funeral. *Why, why, why?* rang out in my head. What had I done wrong?

"She's happy," Amy said.

Children were so easily fooled. If a teacher smiled, she was happy.

"Kids are talking," Clair added.

"About?"

"About Grandmère."

I glanced in the rearview mirror. Clair stared back at me, her eyes now awash with tears. I pulled the Escort to the side of the road, switched off the engine, and swiveled in my seat. "She's going to be fine. I promise."

"But what if she's guilty?" Clair chewed her lip. "What if Mum hears? What if she comes and takes us away?"

Indignation rushed up my neck and warmed my cheeks. I understood Clair's concern, but I had no worries that the girls' mother would suddenly reappear. She had made her choice. She would not come to reclaim them.

Amy smacked her thigh with her palm. "I think we should investigate."

"Huh? Investigate what?"

"The murder, of course."

"You are not to do a thing," I said with the sternest voice I could muster. "We have lawyers —"

"But we might hear something at school."

I reached out to both girls and clutched their hands in mine. "Your grandmother is innocent. Do you hear me? Innocent! And no matter what happens, we are a family. Nothing will break us apart. Nothing. Do you believe me?"

Both girls nodded. Clair wiped tears off her cheeks with the back of her hand.

Amy said, "Just in case, we'll keep our ears to the ground, okay?"

"Where do you hear things like that?"

"Rebecca."

I bit back a smile. Of course. My budding sleuth, Rebecca.

I pulled back onto the road. We arrived at my grandparents' house a few minutes later.

Grandmère, dressed in cheerful red capri pants and a red-striped scarf top, had set up a puppet show stage — mine, as a little girl — in the living room. A wooden box filled with well-loved hand puppets sat beside it.

As the twins rummaged through the box to claim their favorites, I left for my appointment with my Realtor.

Octavia Tibble reminded me of a border collie, always in motion. She'd asked if, rather than meeting in her office, I would oblige her by coming to the local library where she doubled as the librarian. She had taken on the responsibility when the last librarian retired, saying it was easy to lock up the library and show houses. "These books aren't going any place without my say-so," she teased. She had earned a BA and PhD in English from Ohio State University and could have taught college-level students, but she preferred the looser hours of real estate to teaching.

I found Octavia standing, not sitting, in the pre-school section, a dozen moppets at her feet, all listening with rapt attention to her earthy alto voice as she read a Junie B story. When she finished, she set the book down and encouraged all the children to cheer for Junie. They obeyed with glee.

So much for decorum in the library.

As parents gathered up their children, Octavia beckoned me into a glass-enclosed cubicle merrily decorated with yellow, red, and blue paper balloons tacked to a wall-sized corkboard.

Octavia offered me a chair, but she remained on her feet and fiddled with the beautifully beaded cornrows of black hair that framed her chocolate-colored face. "So, my darling girl" — Octavia was a good thirty years older than me — "what we have is a mess."

"She's not selling? The court won't allow it because of the murder investigation? What? Is it a probate issue?" I was not a lawyer. At one time I had intended to learn more about the law than simply how to read and sign a contract, but, like creating a website, I hadn't been able to find the time.

"I'm afraid there's another offer on the table. And it's much higher."

CHAPTER 14

My answer to stress is a tasty meal, an hour of watching the Food Network, and a good night's sleep. I got the first two but not the third. I lay awake worrying about what I could do to save us from being ousted from our building. Could the anonymous buyer who had outbid me terminate the lease? Before renovating, we had extended it with Ed. Would a sale nullify the extension? Irrationally, I wondered whether the buyer was a he or she. Bozz's father had been hunting for a restaurant space for months so he could compete with his brother who owned La Bella Ristorante. And Mr. Nakamura was very vocal about wanting to expand his hardware store, whether the space was next door to his current place of business or not. After all we had done to improve The Cheese Shop, I didn't want to be booted out without a fight.

I rose and took a hot shower. The pelting

water did nothing to ease the tension in my head, neck, and shoulders. I dressed in one of my favorite summer dresses — aqua green with ecru piping around the neckline and bodice — donned gold earrings, and surveyed myself in the antique mirror. Sadly, the outfit didn't improve my mood, either.

Grumbling like Pépère, I shambled downstairs and into the kitchen. I stopped in the doorway and moaned. Sunlight slashed through the double-pane windows over the sink and highlighted the dishes from last night's meal of individual pizzas, still sitting on the granite counter. The girls had promised to wash the dishes and stow them in the dishwasher before heading up to bed. I decided not to rouse them and complain. There was no way I could enforce house rules today without sounding like a shrew.

Choosing the high road, I cleaned up, then I went outside, gathered the newspaper, and clipped a few sprigs of lilac. I returned to the kitchen, set the newspaper on the red oak mission table, slotted the sprigs of lilac into a vase with water, and put the vase on the windowsill. The scent was heavenly.

I made myself my favorite breakfast — a piece of sourdough toast lathered with Dalmatia fig spread, topped off with a thick slice of Perrin Haute-Savoie — and inhaled. The sweetness and lush aroma of late August grass and clover in the cow's milk cheese came through distinctly. I poured a cup of coffee, set it and my toast at the table, and nestled into a chair. I took a bite of my ambrosia, savored it for a moment, and opened the newspaper. A picture of Kristine Woodhouse addressing voters greeted me. The article to the right of the picture was an essay about whether my grandmother, guilty or not, could ever earn the voters' trust again.

I pitched the newspaper on the floor. "Rubbish. Pure rubbish." My appetite quashed, I covered the rest of my meal in plastic wrap, washed up, and told Matthew through a closed bedroom door to tend to the girls. He mumbled a response, which meant he wasn't entirely awake, but I couldn't agonize over that. The girls either made it to school on time or didn't. It wasn't my problem.

On the way to the shop, I deliberately walked the long route, circling past my grandparents' house. While yoga class and moving fifty-pound wheels of cheese from the refrigerator to the cheese counter were my main forms of exercise, I needed a more rigorous regiment. A good walk would help.

I found Grandmère and Pépère in the garden. Grandmère was pulling out weeds with a vengeance, while Pépère trimmed the woody branches off his roses in preparation for the summer's blooms. Grandmère actually appeared rested. Her face, shaded by a straw hat, looked gently tanned and healthy. Perhaps taking a little time off and not bustling through life was good for her. I thought she might even be happy not being mayor, if she wasn't under house arrest for murder. Pépère, on the other hand, looked thin, his cheeks drawn. He hadn't combed his hair, and his buttoned-down shirt, usually tucked in, hung outside his trousers.

Before pushing through the gate, I kicked their morning paper behind a shrub. No need for them to read about Kristine's latest adventures. Grandmère kissed me on both cheeks, then scuttled into the house to fetch some water for all of us.

"How are things at the shop, *chérie?*" Pépère asked. His face grew wistful, and I could tell he longed to be helping — not that he didn't enjoy his time with my grandmother — but he was not designed to languish around the house. With retirement, he had meant to cut his workload in half, not stop completely.

"We've been selling out of Morbier and

Brie," I said. "And we're low on that Dry Jack you ordered. It's a real hit." Dry Jack was a California cheese, made by aging Monterey Jack for about seven months, which resulted in a hard cheese with a sharp, nutty flavor. Great for sandwiches.

"Good, good." Pépère continued to clip branches. "And how is Matthew doing with the wine?"

"We have a tasting scheduled —"

"Morning, Etienne." Urso rounded the corner, in uniform, on foot. "Charlotte."

My stomach clenched. What was he doing dropping by so early? He wasn't known for taking daily constitutions. On the other hand, he wasn't driving a police vehicle with the siren whirling either, which meant he wasn't there to cart my grandmother off to jail. Not yet. I said a prayer of thanks for small favors.

"Morning, Chief." Pépère removed his gardening gloves to shake hands with Urso. He batted the gloves against his leg. Little dirt particles flew off the gloves and swirled in front of my face, and I thought of Felicia. Odd, I know, but flashing on the garden party that she was throwing to raise money for the museum got me to thinking about something else. Felicia's roses. She tended to over twenty varieties of red and

205

pink tea roses behind her house. She grew even more in the museum gardens.

I cleared my throat, adrenaline pumping like a geyser through my veins, then said, "Uh, Chief."

"Yes, Charlotte?" Urso tipped back his broad-brimmed hat and appraised me, head to toe. He grinned in a cat's-got-the-cream manner, and I realized he was thinking about our little encounter by the museum's Dumpster. Was he getting ready to blab to my grandfather, or was he imagining my skirt bunching up around my creamy thighs?

"Gloves," I squeaked, and wanted to kick myself for feeling like a ten-year-old caught playing with matches. I had every right to be hunting down clues that would free my grandmother. Every right. I drew my shoulders back. "Gloves," I repeated.

"You told me about Kristine Woodhouses's gloves already."

"Gloves?" Pépère looked perplexed.

"Party gloves," I said.

"Kristine Woodhouse wore gloves on the night of the murder," Urso explained.

"So did Felicia, Prudence, and Tyanne."

Urso folded his arms across his broad chest and raised an eyebrow, clearly at the end of his patience with me. "I figured that out already."

Of course, he did. He wasn't a dolt.

"I checked all of them. Spanking clean."

"Okay, but did you check their garden gloves?" I said with a hint of defiance. "It's a known fact that Felicia loves to garden."

"This is true!" Pépère said, jumping into the conversation with a fervor. "And one time, I saw Ed standing in Felicia's yard while she was gardening. They were discussing museum business."

"Maybe that isn't all they were discussing," I said. "Maybe they switched gears as Pépère approached because they were talking about their clandestine love affair."

"Clandestine —"

"Maybe she was upset that he was breaking it off, and —"

"Charlotte, stop! You're starting to sound like Rebecca." Urso squinted in an amused expression and slung his thumbs into the pockets of his trousers. "You've all been watching too much *Murder, She Wrote,* I'm afraid."

I stood my ground. "If Felicia, or Kristine for that matter, brought a pair of gardening gloves with her —"

"Whoa!" Urso held up a hand. "Cease and desist! I mean it. Do not go theorizing without some proof, you hear me?"

"But, U-ey —"

"No buts." He gripped my arm. "You sling around accusations like that, you could find yourself in a whole lot of trouble. Slander, for instance. And don't think Kristine Woodhouse wouldn't sue."

"Grandmère didn't do this."

"And I intend to see that she's set free the moment I have another viable suspect." Urso lowered his voice. "Listen to me, I adore your grandmother." Underlying his tone, I detected a deeper sentiment. Did he adore me? Could I change Grandmère's fate by going out on a date with him? He hadn't asked me. Maybe I was getting his signals wrong. I had been known to do that.

I wriggled free of his grasp. "Got it. You're in charge," I said, making sure I didn't bat my eyelashes. I didn't want to fan flames, especially when I had my eye set on Jordan Pace. "Oh, look at the time," I said without glancing at my watch. "I have to scoot."

Minutes later, I hurried into The Cheese Shop, out of breath and hating myself for being a coward with Urso. I had every right to stand up to him and press him harder. He had to find out the truth. ASAP.

I set about preparations for the day, refacing and rewrapping the cheese, tweaking the displays, clearing the register. Matthew strolled in an hour after me, a smile on his face, a spring in his step, and a cup of coffee from the Country Kitchen in his hand.

"Good morning," he said. "Girls got off on time. Can we talk later, say noon?"

He grinned, and a river of relief washed over me. We would hurdle whatever problems we had.

"How about this afternoon?" I said. "I'm on my way out to do rounds." Rounds meant visiting all the local farmers from whom we purchased cheeses and accoutrements. I wouldn't return until at least three.

"Not good for me. How about tonight, after the tasting?"

"Deal." Afraid to spoil his mood, I didn't tell him about the bid on our building or Urso's warning for me to keep my distance in the investigation. We would discuss all of it in private.

The first vendor I needed to see was the beekeeper, Ipo Ho, the naturalist Hawaiian who owned Quail Ridge Honeybee Farm and provided us with the most intense floral micro honey. We spent a good half hour reviewing product. Next, I visited Two Plug Nickels, tasted their latest mascarpone cheese, and then Sugar Maple Farms and Emerald Pastures, each of which let me taste their latest artisanal goat cheeses, one of which was laced with herbs. I saved my trip to Jordan's for last.

The drive to Pace Hill Farm took me along a series of brilliant green swales and knolls dotted with gigantic oak trees. I passed the Harvest Moon Ranch, where a midweek wedding was in progress in the gazebo on the rise beyond the ranch house. Before long, I found myself humming a silly song from *Snow White and the Seven Dwarfs:* "Some Day My Prince Will Come." What nonsense. I switched tunes, forcing myself to sing "America, the Beautiful" at full volume. Much better. I was not designed to be a sappy romantic. At least, I didn't think I was. And America, as seen through the eyes of a native Ohioan, was incredibly beautiful.

A breeze swept through the rolling hills, swatting the tips of grain and making them dance a hula. The leaves of the trees sparkled in the warm sunlight. The sweet smell of grass wafted in through the open windows of my car, and I shivered with revitalized energy. On a day like today, anything was possible.

I parked in the lot beside Pace Hill Farm's original red barn and bounded from the car. Red rock gravel crunched beneath my feet as I trotted past the thriving greenhouse toward the updated farmhouse that served as Jordan's home and office. The front door stood open. I slipped in and paused in the archway to the office on the left. Jordan sat bent over at his desk. He was marking up a document. The room was a wide-open space decorated with the simplest Amish natural wood furniture, a pair of leather chairs, and a beautiful redbrick fireplace. Awards for excellence and photographs of Ohio's rolling hills, abloom with wildflowers, hung on the walls. Afternoon sunshine gleamed through the broad windows. The hardwood floor squeaked as I stepped inside. Jordan looked up, and a thatch of hair fell lazily down his forehead. He brushed it away with a quick swipe of his hand, and something inside me twisted into a knot. A pleasant knot.

He set his pen down. "What a surprise." He rose from behind the oak desk and wiped his hands on his jeans, then offered his right one.

His skin was warm when we shook hands. I didn't want to let go. But I did. In a respectably short time, I might add.

"Are you busy?" I asked, every fiber inside me aching to know what his relationship was with Mystery Woman. I didn't have the guts to ask.

"Just completing loan papers to upgrade the facilities."

"Oho! So you're sticking around," I teased. When he first took over the farm, he confided that he had a five-year plan.

"Indefinitely." He grinned, and my stomach did a flip-flop. Did he know how much I wanted to hear about his past? About how he came to Providence? About what he had left behind? I urged myself to get a grip.

"So, what's up?" I said.

"I should be asking you the same thing." He jammed his right hand into his jeans and gestured with the left toward the comfortable-looking leather chairs on the far side of the room by the fireplace.

I declined, too antsy to sit. "You know me. I like to peek in on the operation every few months." I cozied up to the window and looked at the view. "It's so beautiful here."

Jordan came up behind me, standing close enough that I could feel heat peeling off of him. "Yes, it is."

I spun around, my heart pounding beneath my skin. I hoped he couldn't see the fabric of my sheath heaving. Big giveaway, if he could. I drew in a long, calming breath and said, "Why don't you offer me an up-to-date tour?"

One of the joys of my job was getting an

intimate insider's look into the world of cheese making. I had taken over this particular duty from Pépère a few years ago. Jordan's farm was the largest in the area and the first to offer an *affinage* center, a concrete structure buried into the hillside where Jordan and his staff took on the aging process for some of the smaller farms' premium cheeses. Not every farm had the facilities for the task. It said a lot about Jordan that other Ohio cheese makers entrusted the care of their cheeses to him.

"My pleasure."

We exited the office's side door, crossed a covered walkway, and ambled into a new brick and cement building. Inside was a vast aging room, with multiple man-made caves that pushed farther into the hills. I had stood in the aging room before, but this time I looked at it with a different eye. It was large enough for a party to celebrate all the orders we would get once the website was up and running. Maybe I'd throw a yuletide bash with carolers. Their voices would echo off the ceilings and walls. Grandmère could help organize it — if she wasn't in jail. My heart wrenched at the thought. What could I do to get my investigation cooking?

Jordan fetched two sets of paper booties

and two hairnets from a basket hanging on the wall and handed one set to me.

"For sanitary purposes," he said.

We put them on, then he pushed through a set of multiple doors, and we tramped into a cave. The floors were slick with water to help keep the area humid. I loved the dank smell of the various caves — the soft-ripened room, the washed rind room, the pressed cheese room. Each was brightly lit, with a new trolley system to help transport large quantities of cheese. Every cheese was labeled. There were aging charts in every room with schedules for maintenance.

"What are those?" I pointed at a trolley of steel shelving, new since my last visit.

"Turning mechanisms." He grinned. "Yep, that's the technical term. Anyway, each will help with the flipping of the wheels. Ten can be turned at a time."

"Wow!" In the past, all the wheels of cheese would have required turning by hand. The rinds looked perfectly dusty yet moist.

"Each batch of Gouda is made by hand daily," he explained as we continued our tour.

I adored the Gouda that came from Pace Hill Farms. It was earthy and creamy, with a fudgy texture that melted in your mouth.

"From fresh milk with no growth hormones," he went on.

I nodded. This was all information that I had heard before, but I listened attentively because many of my customers expected me to educate them about the histories of the cheeses they bought. Pace Hill Farm's cows were milked twice daily, the milk so fresh that it often came from the cows within the hour. The grass that the cows grazed on was from pastures free of pesticides, herbicides, and chemical fertilizers.

We sauntered into cave after cave, with Jordan enlightening me about each of the cheeses. One, from the neighboring sheep farmer, was new, a yogurty cheese called Kindred Brebis, with hints of caramel, pasture, and clover.

As we returned to the office, Jordan said, "How's your grandmother doing?"

"She's hanging in, but the lawyer hasn't been able to lift the house arrest."

"And your grandfather?"

"Not well. He's so stressed. I worry that he's not eating enough." I roamed the office, taking in the various awards Pace Hill had won for excellence and the photographs of Jordan shaking hands with a number of Ohio's celebrities. There were no photographs of him from prior to his move here.

For all I knew, he was in a witness protection program and had restarted his life. The thought sent a ripple of excitement as well as fear through me.

"Charlotte," he said. "I asked you a question."

I spun around, my cheeks flushed. I had to stop wondering about him. When he was ready to tell me, he would. Jordan perched a hip on his desk and folded his arms across his chest.

"Sorry. What did you — ?"

"How's business?"

"It's good. It's —" I sidled toward him. "Actually, it's not. I met with my Realtor yesterday. I was trying to buy the building that we lease. Anonymously. As a corporation." I flushed. "Anyway, Ed put the building up for sale before he . . . died, but it seems someone outbid me."

"Ownership isn't all it's cracked up to be."

"But a new landlord could kick us out."

"I doubt they'd want to do that."

I stopped a couple feet shy of Jordan, and for a moment we simply stared at each other. He, with his head tilted, a sly smile on his face. Me, my head tilted the other way, probably looking starstruck. Pinching myself to rouse from my daydream would have been a dead giveaway. I took a step back and hitched a thumb toward the door. "Well, I should get going. Thanks for the tour. Can't wait to tout your latest successes."

"Hold on a sec." He closed the gap and put his hand on my arm. His face grew serious. He drew in a long breath. Was he bracing to tell me bad news? I couldn't handle it if he did. "Would you like to, you know, go — ?"

"Jordan!"

Mystery Woman appeared in the doorway.

CHAPTER 15

I glanced from Mystery Woman to Jordan and back to Mystery Woman, who looked dynamite in a slinky tank top and wrap-around skirt, her left arm raised, hand propped on the doorjamb, dark hair tousled just so. Cue the wind machines and a model in *Vogue* magazine couldn't have looked more seductive. I would never measure up.

But that wasn't what really sent my get-the-heck-out-of-here signals on full alert. It was the glistening diamond ring on the fourth finger of her raised hand. Was she Jordan's wife? His ex-wife? Her gaze seemed so familiar, so intimate. With her well-toned physique, she looked like a perfect match for him.

"Sorry to barge in, but we need to talk about the loan." She broke her pose and rifled through her oversized designer purse. Her hand emerged with a document.

Jordan eyed the papers on his desk, then

looked at me. Had he bought the house next to my grandparents for Mystery Woman? Was he planning on moving in with her?

I blurted, "I've got to go. I'll . . . be in touch . . . okay?" I rushed past Mystery Woman and out of the office. As I drove from the farm, the skies opened up and rain teemed down, mirroring the tears streaming down my face. I wanted to kick myself for being jealous, but dang, I liked Jordan, secrets and all. By the time I returned to The Cheese Shop, the rain had stopped and my mood had elevated to something better than bleak. Only slightly better.

I slapped a smile on my face that probably didn't reach my eyes and told Rebecca to grab some fresh air while the sun broke through the clouds. We had one customer, Ipo Ho, the Hawaiian beekeeper whom I had visited earlier in the afternoon. He didn't seem to notice my arrival, too intent on reading the labels of every condiment jar in the shop.

"Where's Matthew?" I asked as I tossed on an apron.

"Out."

"Out, as in outside in the garden, or out as in gone?"

"Gone." Rebecca hung her apron on the hook and plucked the front of her light blue blouse to align the buttons. A new blouse, I noted, and wondered whether I should talk to her about managing her finances. Another day, I thought, too weary to have the conversation, not to mention it was none of my business.

"Do you know where he went?" I was a little concerned. Not that Rebecca couldn't handle a swarm of customers on her own, but Matthew and I had agreed that we would try to have two people in the shop at all times. With Pépère attending to Grandmère, we were a little shorthanded.

"Shopping," Rebecca said.

My mouth fell open. We weren't serving any appetizers with the wine tasting. We had plenty of napkins with our brown and gold logo on them. I strode to the arch and peered into the annex. Matthew had set up the bar, and he had put out tasting glasses. Cards identifying the different wines we were offering sat stacked on one of the mosaic tables. Matthew hadn't neglected his duties. I gave up worrying about him and returned to the cheese counter to inspect the appearance of our wares.

As I did, the grape-leaf-shaped chimes jingled, and Vivian glided into the shop, a dry umbrella in one hand, a number of festive bags looped over her left arm. "Charlotte, I'm so glad you're here." She slotted her umbrella into the brass stand by the door, then sailed to the cheese counter and set her purchases on the floor. "What's with Meredith Vance?"

"What do you mean?" I kept my face impartial, despite my current distress with Meredith.

"She snubbed me."

My ears perked up. Perhaps I wasn't the only one on Meredith's ex-friend list.

Rebecca scooted in beside me at the counter and said, "Why don't I stick around until Matthew returns?" Apparently gossip held a bigger appeal than a well-deserved break.

"I was helping out the economy a tad . . ." Vivian confessed.

Everybody except me seemed to be spending the fruits of their labors. Perhaps a day of shopping therapy should go on my agenda.

". . . and I stopped into the Silver Trader," Vivian went on. "Meredith was at the counter. The clerk was wrapping up some kind of locket, putting it in one of their pretty silver boxes. You know the one, with the luxurious bow?"

I nodded, wishing she would hurry to the end of her story.

"I said hello, and Meredith whipped around like I had caught her with her hand in the till. She didn't say a word, grabbed her bag, and red-faced, sprinted out of the store. It's as if she didn't want me to know what she had purchased."

"Or what she had been given." Rebecca lowered her voice. "I heard a rumor. From him." She gave her head a quick tilt, indicating Ipo, who was still studying labels. "He said that Ed Woodhouse was involved in some unsavory real estate dealings — leasing projects that were making a ton of money. And he had a partner who was his lover."

"Lover?" Vivian gasped. "Are you sure?"

"Meredith is not Ed's lover," I blurted.

"No? Get this." Rebecca tapped a fingernail on the counter to make her point. "Ed was buying his lover lots of little trinkets."

"You can't possibly think Meredith was his lover," Vivian said. "Why, she's young enough to be his daughter."

"No way Meredith was involved with Ed," I repeated, prepared to defend my friend to the end, except a chilly tingle shot up my spine. Could that be why she had been avoiding me? Was she embarrassed about her association with Ed? I flashed on Ed at the gala event, slithering up beside Meredith. He had placed his hand on her rear end, and she had rebuffed him. At the time, I hadn't even considered there was something between them.

No, no, no! I still wouldn't.

"Ipo," Rebecca called.

He had iPod buds plugged into his ears, the cord from the earplugs leading to his pocket.

"Oh, Ipo, yoo-hoo!" Rebecca flipped her hair over her shoulders and grinned. Ipo looked our way. Her dulcet voice must have cut through his iPod-o-sphere. "His name means *daring* in Hawaiian. Isn't that sweet?" she confided, then smiled brighter, like an actress auditioning for a toothpaste commercial. "Ipo, do you have a second?"

Ipo was a big, brawny guy who used to twirl fire batons at luaus, but when he looked at Rebecca right then, he reminded me of a puppy hungry for a lap to crawl into. Hers. How I wished Jordan Pace would look at me that way. Ipo unhooked the iPod buds and traipsed to us, his meaty thumbs slung into the pockets of his jeans.

"Hey, Rebecca," he said, his voice a husky sexy. "You look, really . . . you know, cool."

"Tell them what you told me about Ed Woodhouse. You know, when we were talking about that episode of *Murder, She*

223

Wrote." Rebecca tapped Ipo once on his shoulder, using her index finger like a magic wand.

He brushed a curl of black hair off his forehead and started in. "Oh, yeah, well, I was just saying that people think a beekeeper doesn't hear things, you know, with the hood on and all. Like it's made of metal or something. Anyway, like, I was at the farm and Lois, you know, from the B&B, comes over. She had to restock her honey. She's serving high tea nowadays." Once he got going, he couldn't seem to stop talking. His words ran together. "Anyway she was, like, in a rush, and —"

"Ipo." Rebecca cut him off. "The point."

"Oh, yeah, right, cool. See, Lois was with this other gal. Swoozie something from Cleveland."

The voluptuous tour guide who favored tight T-shirts and strands of silver necklaces.

"Lois was, like, giving her a tour of my farm, and they were talking about Ed and his partner and how they had some not-so-legit real estate deals in Cleveland."

"Not so legit?" I asked.

"They were landlords who gouged the renters," Ipo explained.

"He and his partner made tons of money." Rebecca rubbed her fingers together like a moneylender. "Not to mention, Ed was giving the partner" — she paused for effect — "aka *lover,* extra tokens of his appreciation."

Ipo nodded. "Swoozie told Lois to warn her sister because, like, see . . . Miss Hassleton had some business deal with Ed."

The museum donations, I'd bet.

"Swoozie didn't mention who the business partner was, but there you have it." Rebecca extended her hands like a magician encouraging Vivian and me to applaud her wizardry. "Meredith was Ed's partner."

I shook my head. "I don't believe it."

"Meredith has lots of new jewelry and new clothes," Rebecca countered.

"She doesn't make that kind of money, does she? For all we know, the partner could be Kristine," I said.

Vivian snorted. "I can't see Lois referring to Kristine as Ed's lover."

"What about the tour guide herself?" I said, desperate to divert suspicion from my friend. "Or Felicia? Maybe she already knew about Ed's lease-gouging practices and was in on it."

"But why kill him?" Vivian said.

"Because he was going to end the relationship and end the partnership," I explained. "He was selling off assets. This building. Yours."

Ipo shifted feet. "I saw on *Law & Order* where this woman killed her business partner because, like, he got the partnership invalidated."

"Invalidated?" Vivian said.

"That wasn't *Law & Order*." Rebecca huffed. "That was —"

"There are lawyers who handle those kinds of disputes," I cut in.

Rebecca raised a finger. "What if Meredith killed him because she's a teacher and she wanted to preserve her reputation?"

"Oh, please."

"Maybe she wanted to end their affair, and Ed threatened to tell the world that she was involved in dirty business," Rebecca said. "Can you imagine the headlines?"

"Ridiculous!"

"How else can you explain Meredith's odd behavior since Ed's murder?" Rebecca went on. "She hasn't returned your phone calls. She's raced away from Miss Williams. And she wore diamond studs to Fromagerie Bessette's gala event. Studs she couldn't have afforded on her teacher's salary."

I flashed on Meredith clapping her hand over the sapphire necklace when I'd asked about it at the Country Kitchen.

"And what about her new, expensive, off-the-rack clothes?" Rebecca said, cross-examining with the flamboyant flair of a TV attorney.

She had me there. To maintain her budget, Meredith sewed her own clothes. She was a master seamstress with a Singer. So, why had she purchased so many new clothes?

"It's not possible," I muttered.

"I agree." Vivian gripped my elbow. "Meredith is not a cold-blooded killer. You've got to look at Kristine as your suspect. If Ed had that many lovers, she might have killed him out of jealousy."

"Broken vows and distrust can drive a woman mad," Rebecca said, as if quoting from a *TV Guide.* "Why don't you go to Meredith's house and ask her, Charlotte? Isn't she home by this time?"

"Yes, but —"

The three of them stared at me like I held the key to some ancient treasure-filled tomb. If I wanted answers, I had to act.

I smacked my hands together. "Rebecca, you man the shop. Vivian —"

"I'll come with you," Vivian said. "I'm not letting you approach a murderer alone."

Didn't she just swear Meredith was not a murderer?

I whipped off my apron and grabbed my purse. "Rebecca, call Matthew. Better yet, see if he's hanging out at Providence Patisserie. If he is, let him know where I'm headed."

"What about Chief Urso?" Vivian fished in her purse and pulled out her cell phone. "Should I call him?"

The front door of the shop opened and Jordan hustled in. He looked flushed, as if he had run the ten miles from his farm to town. "Can we talk?"

"Sorry. I'm on my way out." I started past him, but he clutched my elbow.

"You sped off before I could —"

"I can't talk, Jordan. Later, please?" My love life wasn't important right now. Meredith was.

"What about calling Urso?" Vivian wiggled her cell phone.

"Why do you need to call Chief Urso?" Jordan released my arm and looked from me to Vivian and back again, his forehead creased with concern.

"No, Vivian, don't call him," I said. "Not yet. We don't have any proof."

I strode out the door. Vivian fetched her packages and umbrella and scuttled behind me.

Jordan followed us both to the sidewalk. "What's going on? Where are you headed?"

I hurried along the sidewalk, which was still damp with rainwater, and veered south on Cherry Orchard. Meredith didn't live far from my grandparents. Jordan kept pace.

"Charlotte, talk to me!"

Vivian filled Jordan in on what Ipo had said at the shop.

"Nonsense," Jordan countered. "Meredith is no more a killer than I am. You're jumping to conclusions. Did you ever consider that Ed's partner could have been a man?"

I gaped at Jordan. Maybe I hadn't considered all the people who had motive to kill Ed. Lois could have gotten her information wrong. Perhaps Ed's partner in his unsavory business deals was a man. Maybe the lover issue was a moot point. What did I know about Jordan? Everything about him was a mystery. His past. Everything.

Stop it, I told myself. Jordan was not a killer.

And neither is Meredith! a voice inside my mind shouted.

But something was up, and I intended to get to the bottom of it.

I reached the front walk leading to the baby blue Victorian that was left to Meredith by her grandparents. The leggy rosebushes required pruning. The chipped porch begged to be sanded. The roof sagged and looked in need of new shingles. The gate hung open, the hinge busted. This was

229

not the house of a wealthy woman.

Jordan braced me by the shoulders. "Don't go up there, Charlotte. You'll regret it."

"I need answers."

Meredith's car stood in the driveway. She was home.

"You're feeling the pressure of opening the shop and having your grandmother under house arrest," Jordan said. "Stand down for a moment. Give this a little thought."

I shook free of Jordan, skirted around the broken gate, and strode up the walk. The front door stood slightly ajar. I rang the doorbell.

No one answered. I didn't hear movement.

A flurry of panic cut through me. Had someone stolen into Meredith's house? I opened the door wider and peered around the edge. No one lay in wait behind the door. The study and hall to the kitchen were empty.

"Don't do it, Charlotte!" Jordan charged up the path.

"She could be in danger. The door's open."

"The lock might be damaged, that's all," Vivian said. "Listen to Jordan."

I stepped into the foyer and heard voices.

Coming from upstairs. It sounded like Meredith was trying to speak but someone was hushing her.

Fueled by adrenaline, feeling sure that Jordan and Vivian would run in after me, I sprinted up the stairs, taking them two at a time.

CHAPTER 16

I thrust open Meredith's bedroom door and came to a grinding halt. I stared at the brass bed in utter shock. A flush of mortification coursed through me.

Meredith shrieked and yanked the rim of the floral bedspread to her neck. My cousin Matthew sat beside her, bare-chested, his lips pressed together, his shoulders shuddering. Not with fear. With laughter.

"You're . . . you're . . ." I sputtered, heat rushing up my neck and into my cheeks. "Oh, my, I'm so sorry, I . . ."

Jordan and Vivian arrived and peered over my shoulders.

"What the — ?" Jordan breathed heavily in my ear.

"Don't say 'I told you so,' " I whispered.

He didn't. Instead, he slunk quietly back into the hallway. I heard his footsteps retreating down the stairs and felt a sinking feeling in my stomach. My rashness might have just cost me a relationship with Jordan. Vivian remained steadfastly to my right.

"Guess it's no longer a secret, huh?" Meredith pulled strands of her tawny hair around her face, then laid her arms on top of the covers, the sheet still snug around her curves. "We were trying so hard to . . ." She glanced at Matthew, love obvious in her gaze. "We've been together for a while."

"You read her poetry?" I blurted.

"A rose, by any other name . . ." Matthew chuckled.

Meredith elbowed him. "Stop laughing."

He tried, but failed.

"We worried about the girls," Meredith went on. "We didn't want them to think that I was acting friendly with them simply because I liked their father. I wanted to build my relationship with them slowly. Get them to trust me. They had such a bad row of it, because of their mother. And if this doesn't work out between us —"

"It will," Matthew said. "It has." He weaved his fingers through hers. His thumb caressed her forefinger with tenderness. "This is the real deal."

How could he be so sure? He had only known her a month. How could he possibly know that their love was going to last forever? He was way too quick with his affections, in my humble opinion, but that wasn't what bothered me most. Was I going to lose my friend? Had I? To my cousin?

Silence filled the room. I shifted feet.

Vivian whispered, "Perhaps I'll wait for you downstairs."

I gripped her arm and made her stay.

"Why are you here?" Meredith asked, curiosity replacing laughter.

I swallowed hard. I didn't want to tell my best friend that Rebecca and Vivian had suspected her of murder, but I didn't want her to think I was checking up on her and my cousin, either. Red-hot embarrassment crept up my neck and into my face.

Vivian said, "Ed Woodhouse had a lover who was his partner in some unsavory real estate investments. Supposedly Ed lavished gifts upon her, and when I saw you at the jewelry store, and you avoided me —"

"You kept ducking us," I blurted. I couldn't let Vivian take all the blame. I was the one who had led the march to Meredith's house.

"You thought I was Ed's lover?" Meredith's free hand flew to her mouth, knuckles against her lips. Her cheeks grew pink. After a moment, realization set in and she let her arm fall to her lap. Her gaze turned to hurt. "You thought I killed him?"

"Not Charlotte. Never Charlotte," Vivian said.

"Ed was old enough to be . . . I would never . . ." Meredith drew in deep, rolling yoga breaths. "Never . . . oh, my."

"I gave her the jewelry," Matthew admitted. "My ex —" He ground his teeth together. "She ran off with everything I had given her. My mother's jewelry. I wanted Meredith to know how much I cared."

Meredith fingered the chain that hung around her neck. She'd replaced the sapphire necklace with a pretty silver one that held a heart-shaped charm. "This was what I was picking up at the jewelers. Matthew had it engraved. Inside it says, 'I promise.' "

"A promise is the best I can do for now." Matthew swiveled in his spot and grabbed Meredith's other hand. "I promise to be loving, honest, and good in —"

Meredith elbowed him. He grinned, then they both broke into laughter, a joyous sound that eased the tension in the room. I could breathe again.

"Charlotte." Meredith sobered. "I'm sorry for dodging you. If I hadn't, none of this . . . I'm sorry."

"You don't need to apologize. I'm the one who should. It's my fault for letting them all jump to conclusions. Can you ever

235

forgive me?"

"Of course. We have too many years between us." Meredith smiled. "For the record, Vivian, at the time of the murder, I was behind The Cheese Shop kissing Matthew. I heard a scream. I told Matthew to return inside, and I ran to the front of the shop."

"I protested," Matthew said.

"But I'm trained in self-defense," Meredith countered. She had encouraged me to take classes with her and her fellow elementary schoolteachers.

I turned to leave, eager to get away so I could castigate myself without a crowd.

"Wait, Charlotte, what about the girls?" Meredith said. "You won't tell them, will you?"

I glanced over my shoulder. "You tell them in your own time. My lips are sealed."

Meredith and Matthew's giggles followed me as I descended the stairs, and I felt a pang of jealousy. What I wouldn't give for a little taste of love. I thought of Jordan and hoped he was waiting outside so we could talk, but he wasn't.

"I'm so sorry, Charlotte," Vivian said. "I never should have assumed —"

"It's not your fault. Rebecca fueled the fire, and I let her. Let's put it behind us."

As Vivian and I returned outside, thunder-clouds were gathering on the horizon as if preparing to wage another attack. I hoped the rain would hold off until after dark. I needed a little reassuring sunshine. We headed back toward the center of town, the twittering of thrushes and warblers replacing conversation, until I decided to broach another subject that had been eating at me since talking with Pépère.

"Vivian, my grandfather mentioned seeing you and Ed arguing in your store the night before he was killed. It's none of my business, but —"

"It's a long story, but it was about my lease." Her hand fluttered to her throat. "Ed could be such a toad about what was important to me . . . to my future."

"He told you about the sale?"

She gave a curt nod. "I've pleaded with Kristine to put in a good word for me with the new owner, but she refuses."

"Someone bid on our building. Was it you?"

"If only I had that kind of cash."

"Do you know who bought yours?"

She shook her head. "I could strangle Kristine, she's so tight-lipped."

"Perhaps it's Ed's partner, this lover the tour guide mentioned?" Who, thankfully, was not Meredith.

"For all we know, it could be Kristine pulling a fast one. Maybe she bought out Ed before he died, to get everything in her name in case creditors came calling on him."

"And then he was killed —"

"— which means she wouldn't have been after his money."

I nodded. "But as Rebecca said, jealousy could be a driving factor."

We reached the front of the shop, and Vivian pecked me on the cheek. "Please don't think ill of me. I hate gossip and, well, I should have kept my mouth shut."

"I'm relieved to know the truth."

"The truth shall set you free," she said in a tone a revivalist could appreciate, then trotted toward Europa Antiques and Collectibles, her purchases swinging on her arm.

Matthew returned to the shop around five P.M. with an easiness about him that had been missing since we took over the shop. He didn't mention a thing about my intrusion at Meredith's. I sure as heck didn't intend to raise the issue again.

Soon after, three regional wine representatives arrived, two men and one woman.

Matthew had invited them to give mini-seminars on the evening's twelve wine selections. Matthew guided them from wine station to wine station, sharing his thoughts on how to best present the wines. He set out cards he had prepared with wine reviews and pairing suggestions as he roved.

While they waxed poetic about wine, I returned to the cheese counter. "Rebecca, are you ready?"

She gave me a thumbs-up. "Your grandfather is in the kitchen."

I had told Pépère he didn't have to come in, but he said Grandmère had ordered him out of the house. Apparently, she and the twins were going to watch a chick flick and then dance the night away.

At six P.M., I strode to the front door and braced it open with a cheese-wedge-shaped doorstop. The cool evening breeze swept inside, as did a handful of townsfolk and tourists.

Delilah moseyed in with Freckles, and they strolled directly toward the tasting room.

The oldest wine rep, an overly-suntanned man from California, greeted them at the arch and directed them to his station.

Meredith sauntered into the shop and pinched my arm affectionately. "Bygones?"

"Bygones," I said. "I'm so sorry —"

She put her finger to my lips. "No more sorries. Say, I spied Jordan over your shoulder at the house. Are things going well in that department?"

"Not well at all." I told her about Mystery Woman.

"I'm sure there's an explanation. I saw the way he looked at you at the gala. He's interested with a capital *I*."

I as in iceberg, I thought. Especially after the day's fiasco.

"Charlotte," Pépère approached. "People are asking for you."

Meredith kissed my cheek, then left me to track down Matthew.

"What do they want?"

"To know how to tell a good Brie from a bad Brie."

I tweaked his cheek. "Pépère, you are perfectly capable of educating them. After all, you are my Yoda." By the age of seven, I knew ripeness was key to selecting a soft-rinded cheese. Pépère had provided a great example of an overripe Brie that was runny and reeked of ammonia. I hadn't thought my nose would ever revive. The underripe Brie, which had been thick and chalky-white in the middle, had been much easier to stomach.

"They asked for you," he said, his gaze wistful and heart-wrenching.

"Let's both do it." I tucked my hand in his and we ambled to the counter.

After ringing up the customers' purchases, Pépère was once again whistling to himself. Hopeful that all would soon be right with the world, I went to check how the wine tasting was going.

"Charlotte, over here." Delilah beckoned me to join her and Freckles, who was laughing so hard I thought wine might come out her nose.

"What's so funny?" I asked.

"Kristine," Freckles said.

"Ever since the funeral, people just can't seem to stop talking about her." Delilah swept her curly hair over her shoulders. "And not in a good way."

"Sip?" Freckles offered me her glass.

I tasted the white wine, a Groth sauvignon blanc, one of my favorites. It had just the right balance of citrus and melons.

"This would go perfectly with that salmon-mascarpone risotto recipe you gave me," Delilah said.

Indeed, it would.

Freckles hitched her chin toward the arch. "Who's the cute guy?"

"Which one?"

"With your protégé?" She chuckled.

Through the annex, I spotted the wine rep from New York talking to Rebecca, who was manning the register. Beyond them, I spotted Felicia sitting at the tasting bar. I was surprised to see her alone, without Prudence, Tyanne, or Kristine by her side. Kristine hadn't set foot in the shop since the murder. Either she feared giving herself away with a furtive glance at the olive-wood-handled knife display, or she couldn't bear to walk past the site of Ed's demise. I figured it was option number one.

"That girl draws men like moths to the flame, doesn't she?" Freckles said.

"Who? Felicia?"

"Rebecca. Haven't you been listening?" Freckles eyed her glass of wine and giggled. "I'm the one who's been drinking, not you."

"That's because Rebecca's not intimidating," Delilah chimed in.

"And you are?" Freckles batted Delilah on the shoulder.

"I hate to admit it, but yes, I am. I came home to Providence with hopes of finding my one true love. But in Providence, men can't handle a woman as seasoned as me." She tapped her glass to Freckles and took a sip. "Charlotte, you're the same, right?"

I didn't think of myself as seasoned. I

hadn't traveled the world other than my few trips to France and Italy with Pépère. But I was passionate about my job. I devoted more hours than I had in a day to it. Was that why Jordan kept his distance? I would have sworn that our mutual affection for cheese had created a bond between us. But how would I know? I couldn't stand outside myself and see what others saw. Perhaps Jordan thought I was intimidating. Perhaps he wanted someone more available. Like Mystery Woman.

"Earth to Charlotte!" Freckles elbowed me. "Where'd you drift off to now?"

"Huh?"

"We have returned to the discussion of Kristine."

"Kristine isn't up to anything," Delilah said in answer to a question I must have missed. She leaned closer and whispered, "She was crying at the diner earlier."

"Kristine, crying?" I couldn't imagine.

"I smelled a little liquor on her breath," Delilah confided.

"She doesn't handle liquor well," Freckles added. "Remember the night Ed died? Hooboy."

Did I ever! Kristine had waltzed past me, the smell of alcohol strong enough to knock over the stoutest bartender. Had she had so much to drink that she couldn't remember what she had done? Was that how she could convince Urso, without a hint of a lie, that she hadn't killed her husband? No, I couldn't believe anyone could erase such a horrid memory.

"There's definitely a crack in her veneer." Freckles popped a piece of bread into her mouth. Matthew had set baskets of torn bread around the room, to help cleanse the palate between tastings.

"From what I gather," Delilah went on, "Kristine is feeling the pressure of keeping up appearances."

"That's not what the gossip is. I heard" — Freckles snickered — "she had a fight with Felicia at the diner. Didn't you see Felicia storm out?"

"Wait a sec," I cut in. "Felicia was in the diner? Grandmère said she wouldn't set foot in it because —"

"— of Pops?" Delilah shrugged. "They're back on speaking terms."

"What was the argument about?" I asked.

"One owing the other money," Freckles said.

"Felicia owing Kristine, or the other way around?"

"Kristine owing Felicia, and Kristine telling her she wouldn't pay her a dime."

" 'Neither a borrower nor a lender be.' "
Vivian squeezed into the group, a glass of
red wine in her hand.

" 'For loan oft loses both itself and
friend,' " Delilah added. "Shakespeare,
Hamlet."

"I see Felicia's running solo tonight," Vivian said. "Kristine must be burning more
bridges."

Freckles giggled.

"By the way, Charlotte." Vivian raised her
glass. "This cabernet is fabulous. Beautiful,
dense, with the sweet aromas of black cherries and a subtle hint of roasted herbs."

"You sound like you've been memorizing
Matthew's cards," Freckles said.

"I have." Vivian blushed. "Only the one
glass, that's my limit. What cheese would
you pair with this, Charlotte?"

"Brie. It's the king of cheeses," I said out
of habit, though my mind was still stuck on
the phrase from *Hamlet* and Felicia and
Kristine's altercation. Had Felicia demanded Kristine give her the money that
Ed had promised to donate to the museum?
Why argue at the diner? That kind of conversation seemed much better suited to a
meeting at one's home. Unless, of course,
Felicia was worried that Kristine was a killer
and wouldn't risk a one-on-one meeting.

245

On the other hand, Felicia was also clever enough to raise a ruckus to divert suspicion from herself. Maybe she wanted the town to believe Kristine was unstable.

I eyed Felicia, who seemed content as a solo act. Was she the real killer, setting up her old friend to take the fall?

CHAPTER 17

"Breakfast in five," I yelled up the stairs and returned to the kitchen where I had one omelet pan heating for scrambled eggs and another for Parmigiano Zircles, a tasty crispy treat.

Morning had come with a bang. Literally. Thunderclaps at seven A.M., followed by Rags pouncing on my stomach, and a phone call from Meredith asking the girls on an outing. Meredith had decided last night during the wine tasting that private time with the twins would be a perfect opportunity for her to break the news about her blossoming relationship with their father. The storm would pass by nine, she said. When the girls heard about the excursion, they couldn't get dressed fast enough. The patter of feet overhead as the girls ran from their closet to the bathroom and back to their closet made me smile. I whipped eggs into a yellow froth and prayed that

Meredith and Matthew would last as a couple. I wasn't sure either girl, not even plucky little Amy, could handle another woman walking out on them.

Rags weaved between my ankles and mewed.

I said, "Yes, breakfast for you, too. I haven't forgotten." He loved a dollop of scrambled egg on his tuna.

Matthew traipsed in, tucking his shirt into his trousers, a huge grin on his face. "So far so good."

"You haven't told the girls the full story yet."

"And I won't have to." He poked my back. "Meredith said she'd do it all."

I clucked like a chicken.

"Got that right." He retrieved a loaf of bread from the refrigerator, sour cherry jam, and a wedge of Haute-Savoie cheese, and he set them on the counter. "You look good."

"Flattery won't get you a cup of coffee. You've got to pour it yourself."

He grinned. "New dress?"

"It's the same one I wore last week." A simple sheath with vertical green and white stripes. Very slimming. I added a pat of butter to the omelet pan and poured in the eggs. The mixture sizzled instantly. I stirred with a spatula, turned down the heat, and concentrated on the Zircles, spoonfuls of shredded Parmesan cheese dropped onto melted butter to crisp up like a pancake. A great substitute for bread any time of the day.

Matthew popped a couple of slices of bread into the toaster. "Hey, heard anything from that lawyer for Grandmère?"

I had, and I hated the news. "I didn't have a chance to tell you last night, since you went straight to bed. Mr. Lincoln left a message on the answering machine. He said Urso has agreed to let Grandmère continue staying in her house."

"That's great."

"But" — this was the part I hated — "he said he isn't hopeful about keeping her out of jail."

"Why not?"

"Urso hasn't come up with anything on Kristine Woodhouse that would suggest she killed Ed. No bloody gloves, no bloody dress, no evidence whatsoever."

Matthew groaned. "And he doesn't have any other suspects, other than Meredith, who is now in the clear —"

"Don't start." I wielded the spatula like a sword.

Matthew held up his hands and backed

away. "What about that trust fund thing? Didn't Kristine dip into Willamina's money?"

"How did you hear — ?"

"Talk is rampant right now, with the election just around the corner."

Less than a week away. Pépère had confided that Grandmère had cried herself to sleep with worry the past two nights. She was certain she would lose.

"You can kiss that gossip goodbye. Mr. Lincoln said Kristine has plenty of funds." I dished eggs onto plates and added slices of fresh oranges. "There was some snag with her own trust fund, but that's been resolved. She doesn't need Ed's or Willamina's money."

Matthew snapped up the toast as it burst from the toaster. "Hot, hot." He juggled the pieces onto a breakfast plate and made himself a sandwich with the jam and cheese as he continued his theorizing. "Double indemnity means a lot of cash. I don't care how much you've got in a trust fund. It's motive, with a capital *M*."

According to Rebecca, money, power, and revenge were the top three motives for murder.

"I heard Kristine had an argument with

Felicia," Matthew said. "What was that about?"

"Ed promised to invest in the museum."

"And Kristine doesn't want to make good on the promise?"

"Ed might have pulled out on his own."

"Well, that's motive, too."

Amy hurried into the kitchen ahead of Clair. "I know what a motive is."

Matthew eyed me.

I quickly changed the subject. "Don't you two look pretty?"

"Thank you." Amy, dressed in a blue checkered shirt and a polka-dotted red skirt, did a twirl and then a curtsey. Grandmère would have been proud of her eclectic taste.

Clair, who had opted for a more conservative shorts outfit in aqua, pulled her ponytail tight and plunked into her chair at the table. "Where are we going with Meredith?"

Matthew said, "To the river."

"Cool," Amy said. "About that motive thing —"

"To do what?" Clair cut in.

"Throw rocks, wade in the water, whatever you want." Matthew gave a playful tug on her ponytail. "Fun stuff."

"And we don't have to think," Amy added. "Today is a day for not thinking. Except for about motives."

"No," Matthew said. "No thinking. Period."

"But, at school, I heard Mr. Nakamura's son say that his father wanted to kill that Mr. Woodhouse because he sold a building, and —"

Matthew thrust a warning finger at her.

Amy pulled an imaginary zipper across her lips and looked sufficiently warned.

I wished I had a child's ability to block out thoughts about motives and double indemnity insurance and Grandmère crying and wondering about people's alibis and . . .

"Is something wrong, Aunt Charlotte?" Clair said.

I forced a smile. "Not a thing. Who's hungry?"

Both girls raised a hand.

"What are you doing today, Daddy?" Amy said, diving into her eggs as I set dishes on the table.

"I'm going to work."

More lighthearted chatter ensued. I joined them at the table, pushed my serious thoughts aside, ate heartily, and then washed the dishes and waited with the girls on the porch for Meredith to appear.

The moment they drove away, my mind started churning again. Motive. Who had motive other than Kristine? Or could the killer still be Kristine? She might not need money, but she did crave power. With my grandmother in confinement, Kristine had gained a free ride toward getting elected. Mr. Nakamura, Vivian, and a whole horde of other tenants would lose their leases because Ed sold the building. But according to Bozz, that deal had concluded before Ed died. There was no turning back the tide. On the other hand, without Ed's financial support, Felicia might have worried that she would lose the museum, so she resorted to murder.

Seeing a delivery truck pull into the neighboring driveway at Lois's Lavender and Lace set me to thinking again about what Ipo said Swoozie the tour guide had told Lois. Pure gossip, sure, but what if some of it was true? Ed had a business partner. A lover. What if Ed had decided to end his relationship with his partner? What if the mysterious partner killed Ed in a rage? What if Felicia, secretly in love with Ed, had found out about the lover and killed Ed in a jealous rage? The list could go on and on.

A screen door slammed. Lois shuffled onto her porch, her wispy hair wrapped in a purple bandanna, the hem of her lavender-colored bathrobe fluttering around her ankles, a feather duster in hand. She started batting the upper corners of her windows and arches, attacking imaginary cobwebs, no doubt. She hunted cobwebs daily with a wild-eyed ferocity. Even I didn't have spiders that were that industrious. As she dusted, I flashed again on Felicia's alibi of seeing her sister the night of the murder, an alibi that was shaky at best because Lois, on occasion, would have a little too much to drink. How clear would Lois's memories be in the light of day? In all our years of being neighbors, we hadn't shared more than a handful of conversations. Would she confide in me now?

In an effort to entice her, I snipped a couple of sprigs of lilac, plunked them into an old wine bottle stripped of its label, and filled it with water. I tied a piece of lavender ribbon around the neck and hurried to the bed-and-breakfast. I found Lois teetering on one of the many floral sofas she had set around the porch. She was stretched to the limit trying to dust the wooden beams beneath the wisteria that tumbled over the eaves. The lower portion of her robe had parted, revealing stark-white bony legs.

"Good morning, Lois," I said.

"Mornin', Charlotte," she said with crisp politeness.

"Gorgeous day, isn't it? Thought you might like some flowers for the dining table."

Lois glanced over her shoulder and tried to focus, which was difficult because she had a partially blind eye that blinked non-stop. "For me?" She smiled delightedly, like a little girl who never received presents from Santa. She clambered off the sofa, shoved her duster into the belt cinched at her waist, and reached for the flowers. "How lovely. Aren't you sweet? And the ribbon. It's my favorite color, don't you know."

I did. Everything inside the bed-and-breakfast was decorated in shades of purple: the wallpapers, the bedspreads, the drapes. Though forewarned of Lois's fondness for the color, B&B guests never ceased to be amazed.

"Come on in." She beckoned me with the crook of her little finger. "Have a moment for tea?"

"Do you have Quail Ridge honey?"

"I wouldn't have any other. That Ipo. He's a honey of a guy, don't you think?" She chortled at her little joke and shambled inside.

I fished in my pocket for my cell phone, texted Matthew what I was up to, and followed Lois inside. Matthew and Rebecca could manage to open the shop without me.

Lois hummed as she brewed tea. "You arrived at the perfect time. All my boarders are out and about. So much to do in and around Providence."

We settled into the wicker chairs on the sun porch, a fresh pot of English Breakfast tea and two dainty floral teacups on a tray before us. Lois was an avid teacup collector. Havilland, Limoges, Royal Doulton. She had at least one in every pattern. Most of our previous conversations had revolved around the history of teacups.

"I'd offer you a *nippa.*" She mimed drinking from a flask. "But I'm clean and sober going on thirty days and can't be tempted, you understand."

"Good for you," I said, though that wiped out my theory that she couldn't be relied upon for corroborating Felicia's alibi. "Speaking of Ipo," I went on as I sweetened my tea. "He was telling me about your guest. A tour guide, I think." I snapped my fingers as if struggling for the name. "Swoozie. . . ."

"Swoozie Swenten. What a name! Swoozie Swenten, Swoozie Swenten," she sang, then snickered. "Adorable girl."

I pictured the bosomy tour guide and her tight T-shirts bursting at the seams and

256

didn't think *adorable* and *girl* were the terms I'd use.

"Funny, too," Lois added. "She always gets me laughing."

"She's still in town?"

"Oh, sure. Her tour is here for a whole week. They're doing the Amish thing, don't you know. And the cheese farm tours. And the wineries. I think they're all at Quail Ridge today. Ipo must be reveling in that, what with his saucy bride running off with that artist and leaving him with the farm to take care of — a farm he only took on because of her." Lois fanned her face with her fingertips. "Poor, poor man. Can you imagine moving all the way from Hawaii and ending up in the middle of America alone? Although . . ." She leaned in close. "I think he has a thing for your little helper. Why, the other day, I saw him slip a note into her mailbox, the sneak."

"Rebecca?"

"That's the one. What a doll-baby."

"You know, that reminds me. Your sister —"

"Is no doll." Lois stiffened. Her eyes narrowed with something just short of hostility. "What about her?"

"Oh, we were talking at The Cheese Shop," I said, treading carefully so as not to

257

rile her further. I'd seen Lois chase off Rags with a wicker broom more than once. Nips of liquor drove her to it, I reasoned, but if she was clean and sober, perhaps I had nothing to worry about. I didn't see any brooms nearby. "You know how Felicia loves cheese."

"I like it myself, but I can't eat much. Too rich, don't you know."

"The soft-rind cheeses aren't. And a bite of cheese a day never hurt anyone."

"A bite? Who can settle for just a bite?" She chortled and eased back in her chair, wariness gone.

"Anyway, Felicia was in the shop, and we were talking about the night of Ed's murder."

"How is your grandmother?"

"She didn't do it," I said out of habit.

"I didn't think for a second she did." Lois clucked her tongue. "Nobody in town does."

Hearing that gave me goose bumps, the good kind. Maybe if Grandmère was tried by her peers, she would never be convicted.

"Felicia and I were pondering possibilities, talking about alibis, and she mentioned that Kristine —"

Lois slapped her thigh. "That woman makes me furious."

You and everybody else.

258

"Felicia said that Kristine went off on her own and she — Felicia — strolled to the museum, and then visited you."

"Me? That night? Oh, no, she must be mistaken."

"Really?" I said, doing my best not to overreact. I took a sip of my tea.

"I was out of town. Visiting our aunt. She's eighty-two. Poor thing's laid up with a broken hip."

"But the bed-and-breakfast was filled with guests."

"My husband takes care of things when I'm gone."

Her husband was a cube-shaped man with a ruddy complexion and thick red hair who puttered around the garden starting at dawn and hit the hay not long after dusk. When he wasn't at home, he was roaming the hardware store.

"I guess I misunderstood her." I paused. How could I broach the next question without accusing Felicia of out-and-out lying? "Do you know anything about Ed Woodhouse's promise to contribute to the museum?"

"You mean, money?"

"Yes, money. Did he — ?"

"Ed Woodhouse, that no-good, promised Felicia the moon. After her husband died,

God rest his soul, she was so lonely. I tried to console her, but sisters . . . well, you know. Anyway, Felicia turned to Ed in friendship, and the man preyed on her."

"Preyed?"

"Made her all sorts of promises. Lifelong promises." Lois winked her good eye and gave a little nod. "You know the kind of promises I mean."

"Like he'd leave his wife for her?"

Another nod. "But, no-o-o-o, nothing doing." Lois sat upright and folded her hands primly in her lap. "I happen to know he had other lovers."

"Like who?"

"Like Swoozie. She was his partner, as well."

"But —" I sputtered. Ipo sure hadn't picked up on that! I carefully set my teacup back on the tray and said as innocently as I could muster, "Partner in what?"

"Real estate deals. Felicia wanted to invest with Ed," Lois went on, "but she invested too much of her inheritance in some moneymaking scheme and ran through it. I'm always encouraging her to travel with me, get out of town, get a new perspective, but she turns me down flat. That's how I know she's strapped. She's so proud, she wouldn't tell me if she's in financial trouble, but sisters know things."

Lois fluttered her hand in the air. "In the end, she chose not to be Ed's business partner, and then he reneged on the promise to donate to the museum, and, well . . ." She covered her mouth with her hand and battled tears. "Felicia is an innocent sometimes, don't you know."

I was beginning to think that Felicia was anything but innocent.

CHAPTER 18

The air smelled deliciously sweet and there wasn't a threatening cloud in the sky, so I took the long route to the shop and swung by Grandmère's house. While walking, I decided that I would not share with Grandmère the news I had learned from Lois. I didn't want to give her false hope.

I found her barefoot, plucking weeds from the grass, dressed in her favorite pink-striped capris and a Billy Joel Revival Tour T-shirt. The polka-dotted bandanna around her neck was drenched with perspiration.

"How long have you been at it?" I asked as I gave her a hug.

"An hour, maybe more. Who knows?"

"Drinking enough water?"

She gave me a baleful look. She was usually the one making sure I was keeping hydrated.

"Where is Pépère?"

"At the coffee shop. He needs the conversation. I am not much joy."

"Don't say that."

"Time slips by, *cherie*." She shook her trowel at me. Flecks of dirt and grass scattered into the air. "The town needs me, but do they plead my innocence to Chief Urso? *Non!*"

"They will. I have." I petted her shoulder. "Any more plans for rehearsals on the lawn?"

The notion seemed to brighten her mood. "As a matter of fact, this afternoon we will have one. I'm going to broadcast the music as loud as I can." She giggled. "I hope our new neighbor won't mind." She hitched her chin at Mystery Woman, who was climbing into a shiny silver Mercedes in the driveway.

She waved at us. Grandmère waved back.

"Who is she?" I said, curbing the impulse to dash to the woman and grill her for information. I couldn't erase the sultry image of her leaning against Jordan's office door jamb.

"I assure you, I would know, if I was able to get farther than the gate," Grandmère said. "But I am shackled to . . . to this." She threw her arms wide.

Plenty of people would love to have twenty-four hours a day to tend to their gardens and homes, but not my grandmother. Not under duress.

"I have begged your grandfather to snoop, but he refuses."

"A name at least?"

"Jacky. I introduced myself the other day when the real estate sign came down. She said, 'Pleased to meet you. I'm Jacky.' "

"That's all? No last name. No, 'Gee, I'm moving here from Timbuktu'?"

Grandmère shrugged. "What more could I do? *Toute seule.*"

"You are alone, yes, I know." I watched as the Mercedes pulled out into the street and Jacky, the mystery woman from who-knew-where, drove away. "She's awfully pretty."

"She is handsome, yes, and strong. Perhaps too strong. She has broken one or two men's hearts, I would bet."

Was Jordan one of them?

Grandmère poked me with the trowel. "Why do you frown so?"

"It's nothing." I glanced at my watch. "I have to go. Deliveries are due." I had a business to run and my grandmother's innocence to prove. Details of my love life, or non-love life, could wait. "Would you like me to bring you lunch?"

"I have plenty. Go, run." She swatted me with the trowel.

Moments after I arrived at the shop and

slipped on my apron, the deliveries started to arrive. New shipments of soft-rind cheeses from France, jams and condiments from the Heaven's Bliss Farm, and artisanal cheeses from Two Plug Nickels Farm. Two new up-and-comer cheesemongers from Wisconsin also showed up, without an appointment, and pitched their blue-veined cheeses. They tasted divine and I ordered ten pounds. Matthew helped unload the wares, then returned to the annex to compile a list of wines to order based on last night's purchases.

As I added the condiments to the shelves near the front of the store, Kristine Woodhouse marched into the shop, a scowl on her face. What now? I wondered, surprised to see her. Instinctively, I peeked at the new set of olive-wood-handled knives sitting on the display table to her right. She didn't give them a passing glance.

"Charlotte, I heard you're providing platters of cheese for Felicia Hassleton's affair tomorrow."

Was she here to pit me against her friend? She couldn't possibly dream that I would choose to side with her on anything, not with all the anguish she had caused my grandmother.

"That's right," I said through gritted teeth.

"Well, just make sure that she pays you up front."

Without another word, Kristine spun on her spiked heels and stormed out of the shop. The grape-leaf-shaped chimes jingled merrily, but my insides went cold.

Rebecca ran to my side. "What was that about?"

"Got me." Perhaps Kristine had been taking a mental picture that she could share with whoever was bidding against me for the building. What was the status of that deal, by the way? I needed to call Octavia and get an update.

"Mind if I take a break?" Rebecca said. "I could use a little sunshine."

"Go ahead. I can manage the counter," I said, as my mind reeled with other possible scenarios for Kristine's sudden appearance. Had she hoped for a crowd? Had she wanted to make me and everyone else in town question the status of Felicia's finances?

As Rebecca headed toward the rear door, a couple of customers entered. Urso and our lawyer, Mr. Lincoln, followed them in. Mr. Lincoln had grown a beard since our last meeting, which made him look even more like our historic president. Neither he nor Urso looked happy.

Rebecca scurried back and whispered, "Go talk to them. I'll see to the customers."

I thanked her and strolled to Urso and Lincoln. "I take it you gentlemen are not here to buy cheese."

"Miss Bessette, I'm sorry," Mr. Lincoln said in a deep, reassuring baritone voice. "I've been trying to negotiate with Chief Urso —"

"Charlotte," Urso cut in. "There have been complaints."

"About?" I put my hands on my hips.

"The recitals in your grandparents' yard."

"Rehearsals," I corrected.

"Whatever. The noise. The frivolity." Urso ticked the points off on his fingertips. "The blatant display of . . . of . . ."

"Of what?" I snapped, bristling at the idea of Urso taking away my grandmother's one and only pleasure at the moment.

Mr. Lincoln stepped toward me, palms open. "Display of disrespect."

"My grandmother is not disrespecting a soul. She is trying to have a life, which you" — I pointed an accusatory finger at Urso — "have denied her. She is not guilty. You have absolutely no motive to connect her to the crime whatsoever. A jury will —"

"We have her holding the knife and kneeling over the body," Urso said.

"That's enough to put her in jail," Mr. Lincoln said softly, as if he was embarrassed to have to state the obvious.

"But —" I stammered. "Do something. That's why we hired you. Do something!"

"He can't, Charlotte." Urso took a step forward. "If Bernadette doesn't live a quieter life, I'm going to be forced to remove her from her home. I'm the good guy here, don't you see that?"

I did. He was. I had no right to blame him. "I will talk to my grandmother. In the meantime, I've come up with some other theories."

"No, Charlotte." Urso towered over me.

I withered beneath his scowl, feeling about as insignificant as a toadstool. Fine, I thought. I wouldn't share my theories. But I wouldn't stop investigating, either. And I would have a chat with our attorney, in private, and see if he could come up with some legal hocus-pocus.

They left and business resumed. Customers who had received the first of our newsletters came in asking about the cheese-of-the-month: Rolf Beeler Val Bagnes, a cow's milk from Switzerland. It was cured in white wine and tasted excellent at room temperature or, like a typical raclette, served warm and scraped onto a plate — *raclette* means

268

to scrape in French. I usually decked out the dish with potatoes, gherkins, pickled onions, and other tangy tidbits. Matthew had imported a lighthearted pinot gris from the Valais region to accompany the cheese.

Midafternoon, Rebecca elbowed me and said, "Oh-ho-ho, look who's here." She raised an eyebrow and jerked her chin to the right.

Swoozie Swenten, the blonde tour guide, and a group of tourists all dressed in jeans and red T-shirts with *I Love Ohio Wine* emblazoned across the fronts, stood in a semicircle by the gift table. All were laughing. Someone must have told a good joke.

I sauntered to them and smiled. "Care to share?"

One of the male tourists smacked Swoozie on the back. "You do it."

"Okay," Swoozie said, her voice husky from years of smoking. "How do you get a Scotsman on the roof?" She eyed her pals, then me. "Tell him drinks are on the house!"

The joke wasn't that funny. I had heard it told dozens of times with a different nationality affixed each time. But the crowd burst into another fit of giggles, making me wonder just how many of the local winery tasting rooms they had visited in the past twenty-four hours.

"Swoozie, do you have a sec?" I said.

"Yeah, sure." She bumped me with her hip and flourished an arm to steer me toward the far wall, as if she were the instigator in our little tête-à-tête. When we settled into the corner by the jars of honey, she licked her teeth and combed her pony-tail with her fingers. "What's up?"

"A friend said you and Ed Woodhouse were business partners."

She sobered instantly. Her gaze grew guarded. "Which friend?"

"And that you were lovers, as well," I blurted.

"Your friend got it wrong." Her tone was as clipped as a prison matron's. She turned to leave, but I gripped her elbow, feeling emboldened by the crowd roaming the shop. Swoozie wouldn't attack me with all these witnesses. At least, I hoped she wouldn't.

"How wrong?"

"I was his partner, yeah. I put every last bit of my savings into Ed's ventures, but I was not his lover."

I reminded her of The Cheese Shop open-ing, when practically everyone in town saw her licking olive oil off Ed's fingers.

She blanched. "It's not what you think."

"What should I think?"

She shifted feet.

"He's dead," I said.

"I didn't kill him. You don't —" Swoozie's eyes widened with dawning realization. "Oh, shoot, it's your grandmother who's suspected, right? I'm so sorry about that. My mind drew a blank. How's she doing?"

"Where were you that night?"

"Here. With my tour. I'd had a little . . ." She made a drinking gesture and cocked her head. "Goes with the job sometimes."

Seemed to me that a lot of people had too much to drink that night. I made a mental note to talk to Matthew about monitoring future tastings and refocused on Swoozie, my foot tapping the floor like a riveter.

"Where were you after?"

"After?"

"I don't remember seeing you after the argument that broke out between my grandmother and Kristine Woodhouse, and I sure as heck didn't see you afterward, at the scene of the crime."

A glimmer of fear flashed in her eyes. Swoozie glanced at her group of tourists and back at me. She fingered the strands of silver necklaces encircling her neck, then cleared her throat. "Look, Ed and I, we played around a bit, but it never meant anything . . . I mean, I never get serious with anyone, you know? It was just fun. We were partners."

"In shady deals."

"Shady?" Her hands balled into fists.

I wondered if I should duck.

"Lois told you, didn't she? Shoot. I should've known better than . . . Shoot. Okay, yeah, Ed and me, we charged excessive amounts of rent. I didn't like it much, but he said supply and demand allowed for it."

"I heard he was planning on invalidating the partnership," I lied. Anything to get her more riled up and spilling the story.

"Invalidating? He —"

"You stood to lose a lot of income."

Swoozie's shoulders sagged as if she was finally accepting her own truth. "But he didn't break up the partnership."

According to her. "The way I see it, you could have killed him for two reasons. Either to not lose the partnership, or to get your name disassociated with the deals in order to keep your reputation clean," I said, using the same reasoning my friends had applied to Meredith being guilty. "A gal like you, in a public business like leading tours, can't afford to sully her reputation."

"I didn't kill him," she blurted. "Ed's death left me with a mess. Ask Kristine."

"Ask her what?"

"Aren't you listening? Ed and I were partners. My name is on a lot of documents. I couldn't have kept that a secret. Kristine knew about me." Swoozie barked out a laugh. "I can see you're shocked."

Creep Chef said I had a lousy poker face. Guess he was right.

"Suffice it to say that Kristine" — Swoozie licked her teeth — "she's riding me hard to sell off these puppies, and she expects results yesterday."

Good old Kristine. How surprised she must have been, believing she had gotten rid of her philandering husband only to end up with his lover as her new partner. She soared to the top of my suspect list yet again.

"So where were you at the time of the murder?"

"I guess Ed won't care any longer, not like he cared then." A bitter sadness swept across Swoozie's face but quickly vanished. Maybe she really did love him. Why, I couldn't imagine. "I was with somebody else."

"Who?"

"A reporter from Cleveland."

"The man I saw you with at the pub? He

was wearing a jaunty hat and a shabby-chic suit."

"That's the one. Quigley. He was here visiting his mother. Sweet, huh? Twelve years younger than me but so much fun. Sex with a randy man makes a gal feel alive, you know?"

No, I didn't know, but wished I did.

"Like I said, Ed didn't care. Not that way."

I didn't get the sense that Swoozie was lying. Her eyes were clear. She didn't look away. Urso could probably corroborate the alibi.

"Am I free to go now, Officer Bessette?" she quipped.

"I'm sorry —"

"Nah, I don't blame you. You've got a lot at stake." She clapped me on the shoulder like we were old friends discussing the weather. "Don't worry. I won't boycott the shop. Best tasting cheese for hundreds of miles. Love what you've done with the place, by the way. The gold tones, the wood. I'd like my kitchen to look like this someday. If I ever have a kitchen." She sniffed. "If Kristine Woodhouse has her way, I'll be heading for the poorhouse sooner rather than later."

Swoozie started to head off, but I called out, "One more question. Are you a partner in this building?"

She glanced over her shoulder. "Nah. Nothing here in town. It's all in Cleveland or Columbus." She wiggled her fingers as a goodbye and strode across the shop to rejoin her group, full hips swinging, her gait confident.

I skulked back to the cheese counter, mumbling to myself, furious that, yet again, I had jumped to a wrong conclusion. But what was I to do? Urso was going to take my grandmother to jail if I didn't find out who killed Ed. Before I could flail myself with my typical string of rebukes, the door flew open.

Bozz darted in, his face tight with panic. "Hey, Miss B! There's a weird looking man outside asking for Rebecca."

CHAPTER 19

Like a mother bird, I flew outside to protect my chick. Bozz followed at my heels. I skidded to a stop when I saw a bearded older gentleman waiting beside his horse and cart at the curb. My racing heart settled down to a moderate thumpa-thump, and I glanced back at Bozz.

"Weird looking?" I said. "Bozz, he's Amish."

"Yeah, I know, but that hair and that straw hat. It's like, bizarre-o, don't you think?"

"You look weird to him," I hissed. "Did that ever occur to you?"

"Uh, no," he stammered. "But I'm normal."

"Young man." I poked him with my forefinger. "Do not let me hear you talk like that again. He is normal in his world. His world is simply not like ours. Got me?"

Bozz nodded.

"Now, go fetch Rebecca. Tell her that her

father is outside."

"That's her dad?"

I gave one of my most commanding gazes and, without another word, he turned tail and sprinted inside.

A crowd of lookie-loos had gathered, as always happened when an Amish person came to town. In their horse-drawn carts and common garb, the Amish folk were a novelty to the rest of civilization that seemed to be progressing at a furious pace.

"Mr. Zook." I strode to Rebecca's father. I had only met him once. He wasn't one of the regulars from the Swartzentruber Order who came to town to sell furniture and goods to the shops.

He did not proffer a hand. He did not smile. "Rebecca, she is here?" His liquid blue eyes looked stressed, his thin mouth as taut as piano wire.

Something was clearly wrong. My heart started to race again. Had something happened to her mother? I didn't expect him to fill me in. Rebecca told me how private he was, how he shunned typical society. Coming into town to locate her must have taken all of his reserve.

Rebecca appeared at the doorway, her apron off, her hands fiddling with the straps of the sweet peasant blouse that she wore over capri slacks. She secured her long hair in a clip, then approached her father and lifted her chin. He kissed her forehead but made no other physical contact.

"Why have you come?" she asked. "If it's to ask me to go back —"

"Your grandmother —"

"— wants me to come home?"

"No."

"Then what?" When he didn't answer, Rebecca's hand flew to her mouth. "Is she sick?"

Tight-lipped, her father surveyed the crowd.

"Papa, please explain." Rebecca gripped his hand. "Please. I'm sorry if I've hurt you and the family, but let that pass for now. You came to me. Please?"

He screwed up his mouth. "It was old age."

"Was . . . ?" Moisture pooled in Rebecca's eyes. "Do you mean she's . . . ?"

Her father held out a brown paper package tied with twine. He removed the twine and opened the package. Within lay an off-white lace shawl.

"Oh, my." The tears streamed down Rebecca's cheeks. "It's her wedding shawl."

"She wanted you to have this. She said to tell you that you are loved." He placed the package in her outstretched arms, kissed her once more on her forehead, and then he climbed into his buggy and drove away.

With slow deliberation, Rebecca draped the shawl over her heaving shoulders, the moment reminding me of one of my favorite all-time movies, *An Affair to Remember,* this scene so different yet strikingly poignant. I slipped my arm around Rebecca's waist, and we watched in silence as her father turned the corner near the Congregational Church.

As the crowd dispersed, I said, "Do you want to talk about her?"

"She was . . ." Rebecca hiccupped. "She encouraged me to leave the community. She said I had a hunger, and it wouldn't be satisfied if I didn't take the chance." Rebecca placed her hand on her chest. "She understood me."

"And now she's watching over you," I whispered.

Rebecca threw herself into my arms. I patted her back for a long while. When she came up for air, I said, "Why don't you take that break now?"

"I can't. The spinach quiches are in the oven."

"I'll handle them. Go read in the garden. Or walk to the clock tower. Grandmère always finds strength visiting the Village Green."

"Thank you." Rebecca gave me a hug, and clutching the ends of the lace shawl in her fists, wandered off.

I returned to the kitchen, and as I set the quiches to cool on racks, I revisited the moments after Ed's murder. Grandmère said she had gone to the clock tower. Where had everyone else disappeared to directly following the argument with Kristine? Urso must have canvassed the shop owners and the people who had attended the gala, but hearing their answers for myself was in order.

An hour later, Rebecca returned from her break, her eyes glassy but her makeup refreshed, and she ordered me to take my break. Although Saturdays are typically our busiest sales days, I said I could handle the cheese counter alone if she wanted more time. She refused. Work, she told me, was good for the soul.

Before sleuthing, I took an ever-so-needed moment to drink in the scent of the vine roses tied to the fences in the Village Green and the daisies and petunias planted in huge decorative pots that stood on every street corner, all of which seemed to have doubled in size overnight. As I did, I became aware of how much I needed to take a good hike with Mother Nature to revitalize my flagging spirit, and I set a tentative date in my mind.

For now, business first.

At the art gallery, the bakery, and a half dozen other shops, I talked to the owners and received the same responses. Those who attended the gala opening had seen nothing. Those who had worked at their shops had seen nothing. At Sew Inspired, Freckles reported that she had stayed in the wine annex with the group of knitting students she brought to the party. The bald-headed owner of the Igloo remembered seeing Kristine and Grandmère burst onto the sidewalk. After that, the ice cream store was inundated with customers, Pépère among them. Mr. Nakamura said he returned to the hardware store with his wife to take inventory. Not wise after a little too much wine, he advised me; however, as he unlocked the door to his shop, he recalled seeing Prudence and Felicia chatting outside the diner near the corner of Cherry Orchard and Hope. He hadn't seen either Tyanne or Kristine.

My last stop was La Bella Ristorante. I sauntered into the restaurant and let my eyes adjust to the dim light. With its arched brick ceilings and twinkling candelabras, La Bella was considered the most romantic place in town. I agreed, though I hadn't experienced the romance part firsthand. I hoped to one day.

"Come in, signorina. Welcome." Luigi Bozzuto clutched my elbow. "You look so beautiful today. The green, it matches your eyes."

Luigi was a sly dog. Though he was born in the United States and as American as they come, he insisted on calling ladies *signorina* and often spoke with a put-on Italian accent. With his handlebar mustache, dyed black hair, and devil-may-care eyes, he reminded me of the bad guy you loved to hate in old movies.

I told him about my quest for answers, but he refused to talk without feeding me. I followed him through the packed restaurant to the back room where the walls were faced in distressed brick. Historical photographs hung everywhere, the Bozzuto family pictures among them.

"Sit, Charlotte. I will return in moments with my latest dish." He pushed me into a cane-backed chair and clapped his hands once to draw the attention of a waiter. I was pretty sure that Luigi's dish would consist of a meal laced with cheese. He was always trying out new recipes on me, free of charge. I didn't squabble. My stomach was grumbling like a train hungry for coal.

He returned with a delectable appetizer of artichoke hearts drenched in melted Taleggio. I took one bite and thought I had died and gone to heaven.

"Wow. I detect nutmeg," I said.

"And white wine." He perched on the chair across from me, a smug smile on his lips. "But just a hint. Mama's recipe."

It tasted like fondue without the bread. "Next cooking class, you have to teach us this recipe." The thought of standing by Jordan's side, tasting something this scrumptious, made me shiver with desire. How I wished I could learn the truth of his relationship with the mysterious Jacky.

"So, what have you come to ask me?" Luigi twisted the flower vase on the table so the face of the bloom leaned toward me.

"It's about the night Ed Woodhouse —"

"Ha!" He spanked the table. "I wondered when someone would come asking. I know all of Ed's secrets. He and I went all the way back to high school, you know."

"No, I didn't know." Luigi looked eight to ten years younger than Ed. "And what do you mean, someone would come asking? Hasn't Chief Urso questioned you?"

"Why would he? I was here with a restaurant full of customers and had no reason to kill Ed."

I tilted my head.

"Okay," Luigi grinned. "So everybody had a reason to kill Ed. He wasn't a nice man. He was always two-timing someone. Interested in the short fix. That's why we couldn't trust him on the basketball team." Luigi crossed himself and glanced at the ceiling where dozens of strands of garlic and red peppers were hanging. "Sorry, Mama, I shouldn't speak ill of the dead." He gazed back at me. "Now, you are here to clear your grandmother, no?"

I nodded.

"What can I tell you?"

"You have a habit."

He cocked an eyebrow.

"After all the meals are served, you stand on the street and drink in the air."

"Don't be coy." He shook a finger at me. "I smoke a cigarette, and you know it. I am trying to quit."

"That night . . ." I said, leading my witness.

"I smoked one, maybe two."

"Did you see Kristine pass by?" I didn't add *covered in blood*.

Luigi tweaked the ends of his mustache.

"I saw your grandfather go into the ice cream shop. Mr. Nakamura and his wife hustled into their store, and Vivian went into hers." Luigi gazed into space for a moment, and I wondered if he was remembering the time when he had professed his love to Vivian. Why she hadn't thrown herself at him was beyond me. He was funny, sexy, successful. Perhaps her one-year marriage had made her sour on love forever. "Oh, yes, and I saw your grandmother walking south from the Village Green."

I seized on that information. "What time?"

"I did not look at my watch, but you could ask Vivian. She looked at hers. So did Mr. Nakamura. Perhaps they all wondered why they were working at such a late hour, unlike me, who works until two every night." He chuckled and tweaked my elbow. "It is the fate of a restaurateur, no?"

I nodded. "You don't remember seeing Kristine or Tyanne?"

"Let's see." He stroked his chin. "I noticed a very voluptuous woman walking hand-in-hand with a young man half her age. He wore a wrinkled suit and he had shaggy hair. They followed your grandmother. I'm not sure they would have seen her, however. They were lip-locked most of the way."

"A bleached-blonde wearing a tight T-shirt

and lots of jewelry?"

"That's the one."

Swoozie Swenten's alibi was now airtight.

Luigi sighed. "You were hoping for more?"

"Yes, but I don't want to sway your memory." If he hadn't seen Kristine, he hadn't. I wiped my mouth with a napkin and rose from the table. "Thank you for your time and for lunch. If you wouldn't mind calling Chief Urso and at least telling him that you saw my grandmother."

"It would be my pleasure. If there is anything else . . ."

"Yes, one thing." I pecked him on the cheek and headed to the front door. "Why are you still single?"

He laughed. "You know, I would date a lovely woman like you, even though you are twenty years younger than I, if you didn't have eyes for another."

"For another?" I cast a flirty glance over my shoulder.

"Speak of the devil." Luigi scooted past me and grabbed the front door of the restaurant as it opened.

I squinted into the sunlight that gleamed through the opening and caught sight of Jordan. On his arm was Jacky the Mystery Woman, looking radiant in a crimson sheath. Like a gentleman, his hand was cupped at the arch of her back. My heart started to gallop. My mouth went dry. What would I say? And how did Luigi know I had eyes for Jordan? So much for thinking I was good at keeping a secret.

Luigi embraced Jacky and kissed both of her cheeks, as he had done to me. "You look lovely."

"Charlotte, it's good to see you." Jordan released Mystery Woman and clutched my elbow. He leaned in close and spoke in a hushed tone. "After you ran from my office, I came by The Cheese Shop hoping to ask you on a date, but then there was the confrontation with Meredith and, well . . ." He worked his tongue inside his cheek. "Do you want to go out sometime?"

My mouth turned dryer, if that was possible. I couldn't speak.

"How about a picnic next Saturday?" he said.

I eyed his companion. She looked as good or better than she had at the farm. No wrinkles. A fabulous complexion. Striking features.

He followed my gaze. "Oh, sorry, Charlotte, let me introduce you to Jacky Peterson, my sister."

"Sister?" I blurted. I flashed on the awkward moment in his office. The real estate contract. He'd bought his sister her house. Jealousy skedaddled from my mind, but embarrassment for making a hasty assumption didn't. My chest, neck, and cheeks flushed with heat. I reached to shake Jacky's hand, but before we could, a shriek sliced the air.

Followed by, "You!"

I whirled around.

Kristine stormed toward me, a rally flag in her hand, a *Vote for Me* banner slung across her chest. "The hostess said you were here. I searched the kitchen, but no-o-o-o. You . . . you . . ." She shook a finger at me. "Outside. Now!" With her rally flag she prodded me into the sunlight.

Neither Luigi nor Jordan found the wherewithal to confront her.

I did. My dry mouth vanished as I batted the rally flag from her hands and dug in my heels. "Cut it out."

A herd of women, similarly dressed in rally clothes, gathered around us. Among them stood Prudence, as tight-lipped as a clam, and Tyanne, looking totally abashed. Reluctantly she picked up the fallen flag and handed it to Kristine, who tucked it under her arm like a riding crop and screamed, "You must stop her!"

"What did my grandmother do this time?"

"Not your grandmother. Felicia!" Kristine jutted her chin forward. "She's digging."

"Digging what?"

Into your past? Into your finances? Into your flimsy alibi?

"The ground," Kristine snapped.

"So?"

"Who knows what she could be burying!"

"Her garden party is tomorrow. She's probably planting. She takes pride in her garden."

"I don't believe it for a second." Kristine nearly vibrated with anger.

"Look, Kristine, I don't know what the beef is between you two —"

"Kristine, sugar, let's go." Tyanne tapped Kristine on the shoulder.

Kristine glowered at her and back at me. "Felicia could have bodies buried around that place she calls a museum."

"Bodies?" I snorted. "Oh, please."

"You tell Chief Urso to stop churning up my life and nose into hers, do you hear me?" With that, she beckoned her pals, and they marched south like a well-trained unit, all except Tyanne, who hung back for a moment, looking as if she wanted to say something. A moment passed, the two of us staring like old friends who wanted to make amends, but then she faltered and hurried off to join the others.

My breathing was staccato. My skin prickled with pent-up energy. What was Kristine's game? She had to be pretty desperate to cause a ruckus like she just did. I tried not to give her attack another thought, but I couldn't. She had upset me. I glanced at the front of La Bella Ristorante and decided now was not the time to return inside to ask Jordan about our upcoming picnic.

However, once I returned to the shop, I called Octavia Tibble. I left a message on her voice mail and asked her to find out more about Jacky Peterson. Call me crazy, but I was still curious about her. Where had she come from? Why was she settling in Providence? Next, I called Vivian, and like I had with Octavia, reached her voice mail. I left her a message to call me. If she had glanced at her watch, as Luigi claimed, perhaps she could corroborate my grandmother's clock tower alibi.

By midafternoon the crowd in the shop had thinned, and I realized I was exhausted. My voice was worn out from talking to customers about the origin of the cheeses and the ingredients for the special quiche of the day — white Cheddar with turkey and cranberry sauce.

I glanced at Rebecca, who was withdrawn

and subdued, and felt a tug on my heartstrings. Often, she eyed her grandmother's lace shawl, which she had hung on one of the hooks at the rear of the shop, but I kept mum. When she wanted to talk about her loss, she knew she had my ear. Matthew was chatting up one of the local vintners in the wine annex.

"Taking five," I said.

Before I could remove my apron, the front door shot open and the twins ran into the shop.

Amy charged to the counter. "Aunt Charlotte, we had the most wonderful day."

"We threw rocks," Clair said, her enthusiasm matching Amy's.

"Big huge rocks into the river."

"And we skipped them." Clair mimed the action.

"We did lots of skipping. And laughing. And we sang songs."

They broke into a round of "Frère Jacques," conducting each other with their index fingers.

Meredith trotted in a minute later, her skin and eyes glowing with energy.

Amy stopped singing and scooted around the counter. "And guess what else? We know a secret about Daddy and Miss Vance."

I peeked into the annex. Matthew was still

chatting with the vintner.

I said, "Um, what is it?"

Clair joined our little powwow. "Daddy and Miss Vance are going to go on a date."

I smiled at Meredith, who gave me a thumbs-up. She had handled the announcement perfectly. Matthew would be thrilled. One date would lead to another, and slowly the girls would adjust.

"That's wonderful," I said. "Now, who wants dessert?"

Each waved a hand in the air.

"Taking fifteen," I said to Rebecca, who was dabbing her eyes with a tissue. "Are you okay to — ?"

"Busy hands are a good thing. Go!"

Meredith, the twins, and I settled into the first booth inside the Country Kitchen, with Clair beside me and Amy beside Meredith. Delilah, Pops, and a pair of waitresses were roving between the booths and tables singing along with Van Morrison in a loud rendition of "Brown-Eyed Girl."

"Ew, look," Amy said under her breath. "Willamina is over there." She pointed and Clair twisted in her seat to take a gander.

"Amy, put your hand down," I said. "It's not nice to point."

"Why are they always giggling?" Clair asked.

Willamina, holding court like her mother, was surrounded by the wealthiest girls in town. Some, I knew for a fact, went to the beauty salon for highlights and to get their nails done. At eight-years-old. What mother in her right mind encouraged her daughter to be that vain? Willamina looked up, saw Amy, and made a sour face. Amy stuck her tongue out. So did Clair.

"Girls, stop it. I mean it. No more," I snapped. "Go wash your hands."

They obeyed, passing by Willamina's table and sharing another tongue-sticking-out moment before disappearing into the restroom. So much for following orders.

Delilah and the other waitstaff wrapped up the song, customers applauded. Seconds later, Delilah slid into the booth beside me. "Hey, ladies."

"Sounding good," I said.

"Man, there are days when I miss Broadway. Or at least trying to be on Broadway." She gazed at the ceiling with a wistful look.

"Maybe you should take Grandmère up on teaching more of her dance classes."

"We'll see." She thumped the table like a drum. "So, what's going on? I heard Kristine accosted you."

Meredith's eyes widened.

I quickly explained the encounter outside

La Bella. "Kristine's something else. She saw Felicia digging in her yard, and she intimated that Felicia could be burying bodies there."

"It wouldn't be that far-fetched," Delilah said. "There were rumors that she did away with her husband."

"What?" Meredith nearly shrieked.

"He returned from Europe in an urn. Pops said people talked for days."

I had been off at college when Felicia became a widow. I knew nothing about the incident. In all my brief conversations with Lois, she hadn't mentioned anything suspicious in Felicia's past. Until today. "Lois hinted that, at one time, Felicia had wanted to invest with Ed."

"When did you talk to Lois?"

"This morning."

Delilah poked me. "Look at you. Providence's very own Nancy Drew."

I moved the silverware on the table out of my way and leaned forward on my elbows. "Felicia wanted to invest, except she came into some difficult financial times."

"How would Lois know?" Delilah said.

"Felicia put off traveling with Lois, and when Ed didn't invest in the museum —"

"Shhhh." Meredith hitched her head at the girls, who were skipping toward us between tables.

Amy and Clair stopped for a moment at Willamina's table and exchanged a few words. No sticking out of tongues, which was a good sign, but when they returned to the table, Clair looked miffed.

Delilah scooted from her spot to let the twins slip back in. "Sorry, girls. Who wants a slice of caramel cheesecake?"

"I do," Amy said.

"How 'bout you, Clair?" Delilah asked.

Clair didn't answer. She was staring at Willamina, her forehead creased, her eyes hot with fury.

I laid my hand on hers. "What's the matter, Clair?"

"Willie said Grandmère's going to get killed."

CHAPTER 20

I glanced at the big-handed clock over the diner's counter and groaned inwardly. There simply weren't enough hours in the day to take care of a shop, guide my nieces, and chastise another woman's child. I patted Clair's hand. "That's just an expression, sweetheart. It's not nice, but Willamina means her mother will win the election in a landslide."

"A landslide?" Clair's face turned pale.

"Not a real landslide. Not dirt. She thinks her mother will win all the votes."

"Well, she won't. Grandmère will win."

"I agree."

While we finished our sodas, I glowered at Willamina and at the same time felt sorry for her during this challenging time in her life, robbed of her father and abandoned by her campaigning mother. At the very least, Kristine should hire a nanny for the girl. I didn't think she should be left alone to roam

Providence.

Feeling overly protective, I returned to The Cheese Shop and invited Rebecca for dinner. She didn't speak during the meal except to say how much she liked the risotto and to comment occasionally on Amy and Clair's account of their day at the river with Meredith. Rebecca, it turned out, was a master rock-skipper, which only encouraged the girls to expand upon their stories.

As Rebecca was leaving, I gave her a hug and said, "Take the day off tomorrow. Allow yourself to grieve." I felt her tears splash my shoulders before she scurried away.

The next morning, to my surprise, Rebecca arrived at Fromagerie Bessette at the same time I did, both of us in summery pink dresses, the frilly hem of mine touching my kneecaps, the tight stretchy hem of hers clinging to her slim thighs.

"We match," Rebecca said.

"Hardly," I said, stupidly wishing for the days when I was twenty-two, footloose and fancy-free, and had thighs of steel. I silently rebuked myself. Long ago, I had learned not to look back. The past was gone and could not be replayed. So why did I have regrets today? If only I could turn back the clocks to a week ago, before Ed was murdered, when Grandmère was undoubtedly innocent. I sighed and eyed my sweet associate. "Why are you here?"

"Busy hands."

"But I told you Pépère offered to help Matthew in the shop. The twins are spending the day with Grandmère making a scrapbook project of all the theater projects she's done."

"A scrapbook. That sounds fun."

"She said if she loses the election, she will become a squeaky wheel at city council meetings, if only to ensure that the theater program receives all the funding it needs."

Rebecca swept her hair over her shoulders and looked at me with earnest eyes. "Please, may I stay?"

Who was I to say no? Church bells pealed as I pushed open the door. In less than an hour, we created the platters for Felicia's garden party. Pépère arrived at ten A.M. with a worrisome look on his face and a cup of coffee from the Country Kitchen in hand.

"You look perplexed." I ran a finger along the scowl lines etching his forehead.

"Your grandmother was singing this morning, full voice. She has this plan —" He tapped his temple. "She's going to have a campaign rally in the front yard."

I gulped. Urso would not be pleased. But

once Grandmère got an idea in her head, it would be impossible to dissuade her.

"The election," Pépère went on. "It is in two days, you remember. You saw Kristine's posters as you came to work?"

How could I have missed them? Kristine and her legions had posted hundreds of posters overnight. Three feet by four feet with bold red lettering.

"Don't worry. The townsfolk will do the right thing. Promise." I patted his arm. "Now, Mr. Strong Man, fetch me a wheel of Morbier."

On his way, he sneaked a piece of Double Cream Gouda from one of the platters for Felicia's party and plopped it into his mouth. I smiled. At least he was upbeat enough to practice his old tricks and believe he was getting away with them.

Two hours later, even though I had made a point of telling Felicia that I, myself, would not be delivering the platters, I pulled the delivery van in front of the beautiful chocolate brown and white Victorian house that served as the Providence Historical Museum. For Rebecca, work was something she could handle in her fragile state, but attending a party was not. I'd hired Bozz to help me. Our arms loaded with trays of cheese and accoutrements, Bozz and I tramped up the cobblestone path leading to the entrance. The dozens of tea roses were starting to bloom. The smell of sweet mown grass and the perfume of lilac stirred something inside me as I climbed the steps to the front porch. Hope, maybe? Felicia's list of guests was extensive and included our attorney, Mr. Lincoln. Perhaps I could get a moment alone with him to discuss Grand-mère's case. I'd make a point of mentioning Luigi's sighting of her heading toward the clock tower.

Felicia must have been peering through the break in the gold brocade drapes, because she whipped open the door before I could press the doorbell. Dressed in an antique green crinoline dress and high-buttoned shoes, her curly hair swept up in a loose chignon, she looked like a lady right out of the eighteen hundreds. "Come in." She eyed the trays we were carrying. "Ooooh, aren't those pretty?"

"We have another six to bring in," I said. "And the wine, of course."

"Lovely. This way. Follow me." She trotted along the hall, her heels clicking the hardwood floor with precision. "Perfect day for a garden party, isn't it? Not a cloud in the sky. Seventy-two degrees." She glided past four marble statues of frontiersmen and disappeared into the kitchen at the back of the house.

As I followed, I peered into the rooms on either side of the hall with new appreciation. I had visited the museum a number of times, but I never failed to see something unique. Felicia did a nice job of moving the exhibits around with regularity. The wood-paneled study was filled with books and historical photographs. The living room was furnished with a mixed set of antique chairs and settees, its walls finished with dainty floral wallpaper. Glass cases held tomahawks and pottery and china. Much of the china had belonged to Kristine Woodhouse's great-grandparents. I wondered whether, in the wake of her argument with Felicia, she would demand they be returned.

Bozz and I staged the food and wine in the celadon-tiled kitchen, then set out a few platters in the rear garden. Felicia had strategically placed verdigris metal tables and chairs around the yard in shaded spots beneath magnificent oak trees. A string quartet tuned their instruments at the far end of the yard.

Within an hour, guests started to arrive. Couples at first: Mr. Nakamura and his wife, Freckles and her husband. Felicia greeted them warmly and discreetly tucked their donations into a glitzy handbag. A frizzy-haired female photographer for the *Providence Post,* who had arrived minutes before the guests, roamed the grounds snapping photographs.

I made my way to Mr. Nakamura and his wife. "Sir, a word, if you don't mind." I told him about Luigi seeing him entering his shop the night of Ed's murder. "Do you remember what time it was? Luigi thought you glanced at your watch."

"Nine fifty, remember, dear?" his wife said. "You said, 'Oh, my, it's ten to ten. I thought it was later than that.' " She eyed me. "Except his watch does run fast sometimes."

"Do you remember seeing my grandmother?"

"I'm sorry, I don't," his wife said.

"We were focused on one thing and one thing only: inventory," Mr. Nakamura said. "You understand."

Mrs. Nakamura glanced at her husband and gave him a curious look. "Perhaps Vivian saw her."

I caught sight of Vivian over Mrs. Nakamura's shoulder, offered my thanks, and headed toward my friend. She looked as brilliant as a spinnaker, in a white dress with bold blue stripes that showed off her shapely

frame. Luigi Bozzuto, strikingly good looking in a tan linen suit, appeared right behind
her. He batted Vivian gently on the arm.
She turned and, to my surprise, smiled at
him. Was she open to love after all? What
could she not have liked about him back in
high school? I chose not to intrude on the
moment.

Octavia swept in behind them, her linen
jacket flapping open, her beaded cornrows
bouncing on her shoulders. She scoured the
crowd and her gaze landed on me. She gave
a curt point of her finger for me not to
move, slapped a check into Felicia's outstretched palm, then bulldozed through the
crowd to me. Grabbing my elbow, she
steered me to an arbor of wisteria far from
the crowd.

"Jacky Peterson doesn't exist."

"She's got to. She's Jordan's sister."

"I'm telling you she's buried her identity."

"Buried?"

"Maybe she's running from an abusive
husband."

"Oh, my."

"Hush." Octavia wiggled her hand for me
to be quiet. She eyed someone over my
shoulder.

Jordan and Jacky were approaching our
huddle. Each carried a glass of wine. I had

303

to admit that Jacky didn't appear abused in the least. Not a scratch on her pretty face. She looked radiant in a warm yellow suit. Jordan was dashing in a rumpled linen shirt, jeans, and loafers, like something out of an Errol Flynn movie. He smelled good, too, like fresh mown hay. My heart did a little tap dance.

I think Jordan could tell, because his mouth quirked up in a half-grin. He said, "Seeing as we were interrupted at the restaurant yesterday, let's start this over. Jacky Peterson, please meet Charlotte Bessette, cheese shop owner extraordinaire."

I said to Jacky, "You must think I'm so rude."

She chuckled. "If I recall, you were being prodded by a woman with a flag. How do you do?"

As we shook hands, Octavia cleared her throat.

"Oh, sorry. Octavia Tibble," I said, "this is Jacky Peterson. I think you know Jordan Pace."

"Peterson. Is that your husband's name?" Octavia said, with all the subtlety of a bull charging a red cape.

"I'm divorced."

Octavia ogled me with a knowing glance.

Jacky smiled, unruffled. "Charlotte, please

tell me the history of this place," she said. "It's so lovely."

While I filled her in about Felicia's passion for documenting Providence's history, I thought about ex-husbands and divorces and found myself wondering about Felicia's personal history. I didn't for a second believe what Kristine had said about Felicia burying bodies in her yard, but rumors did circulate about Felicia's husband passing away while they were in Europe. Had she killed him? Would she have gone that far to finance her museum? After running through her funds, as Prudence and even Lois had suggested, Felicia could have seduced Ed Woodhouse to entice him to invest. Had she killed Ed when he opted not to keep her dream alive? I thought of the fight Felicia and Kristine had had at the diner. Perhaps Felicia had instigated it to cast suspicion on Kristine and to keep Urso from suspecting her of murder.

A blood-curdling scream cut through the air.

"Leave!" Felicia yelled.

Looking as livid as I'd ever seen her, Felicia charged toward Kristine, who swept onto the rear porch with the ferocity of a tornado. She was flanked by Prudence and Tyanne. Each wore elaborate outfits — tea-length, animal print sheaths, three-inch heels with matching clutch purses, and lacy black hats and gloves. If the frizzy-haired photographer snapped a picture and sold it to *Vogue,* she could label it *Sex in the City, the feral side.*

"What are you doing here?" Felicia demanded.

"I have an invitation." Kristine brandished an embossed card.

"I thought you, of all people, knew better than to come." Felicia's high-pitched tone revealed her dismay.

"You need money. I've got it," Kristine boasted. "Want to beg? I hear you're good on your knees."

I nearly choked. Had Kristine no shame?

Felicia, as pale as crème fraiche, raised her chin, collected the folds of her skirt, and dashed into the museum.

Nobody ran after her. Not Prudence. Not Tyanne.

Though Felicia was not my friend, I didn't think she should suffer such a humiliating experience alone. I excused myself from Jordan, Jacky, and Octavia, and chased after her.

"Felicia," I called as I hurried through the kitchen, but she didn't answer. "Felicia!" I glimpsed her fleeing down the hall. I caught up with her in the foyer and gripped her by the arm.

"Leave me alone." She wrenched free and raced out the front door, slamming the thing so hard that it rattled.

Meredith called, "Charlotte! Is that you?" She stood in the study by the far wall, one of the museum's books open in her hands. "What was that about?"

I paused in the archway and explained what had happened.

"What a horrid, horrid woman Kristine Woodhouse is."

"She's like a train wreck waiting to happen."

"If I didn't suspect she was the murderer, I'd worry she was next on someone's hit list."

"What are you doing?"

"Snooping." Meredith grinned. "Just kidding. You know me and books."

What she said gave me an idea. I glanced at the front door and then back at the mahogany staircase. Would something in Felicia's ledgers show me what Ed had or hadn't promised? Would that information confirm that Felicia had been so desperate for Ed's donation that, when he reneged, she — not Kristine — killed him? The office where she did her bookkeeping was upstairs. I remembered taking a tour of the museum once and seeing Felicia busy at work at a handsome Edwardian rolltop desk. I had remarked on the beauty of its ornately carved side supports. Circa the eighteen nineties, she had said. Would the desk contain documents that could pin her with a motive and absolve my grandmother?

"You won't believe all the stuff I'm learning about Providence," Meredith went on. "Felicia has done a great job with this place. Want to see what I've discovered?"

"In a sec." I stole to the front door and peeked out one of the stained glass panels that flanked it. Felicia was nowhere in sight. How long would she wander? If I had been as upset as she had been, I would have needed at least a half-hour walk.

"Charlotte," Meredith said.

None of the party people were touring the museum yet. I had to take the chance.

"I'll be right back." I tiptoed up the staircase, bypassed the Victorian costume display and the room housing an assortment of antique clocks, slipped into Felicia's office, and pulled the sheer drapes closed.

CHAPTER 21

Felicia's office was tidy and modest. The Edwardian rolltop desk and a secretary's swivel chair stood in the center, a small round table with an antiquated dial telephone and an iron lamp to the right. Oil paintings of Kindred Creek hung on the walls. There were no file drawers, antique or otherwise. No free-standing boxes or trunks.

I tried to open the tambour rolltop, but it wouldn't budge. I couldn't jostle open any of the three drawers beneath it. As much as I'd hate to ruin such a lovely piece of furniture, I needed something to jimmy the lock, or I needed a key. Preferring my second option, I ran my hand beneath the drawers. No key was attached with tape. I fingered the backside of the desk's frieze. Nothing had been stuck there either. I groped beneath the seat of the desk chair and came up empty.

I stood on the heart-shaped hooked rug

in the middle of the floor and slowly scanned every inch of the room. Had Felicia hidden the key somewhere, or did she have the key on her person to prevent nosy museum visitors like me from prying?

I wasn't ready to give up. I rarely did when on a quest. Perhaps she had stashed it in the lampshade. No.

Under the telephone? Again, no.

In the coat closet?

I scurried to the door and opened it. The hinges creaked. I froze. My heart thundered as I listened for movement outside the room. Nothing. But I didn't have much time before someone would note my absence and come looking for me. I peered into the small cedar-lined closet and saw a series of antique jackets, dresses, bonnets, and high-buttoned shoes similar to those Felicia had worn for the party. The shelf overhead didn't hold anything remotely resembling file records or a ledger. Frustration building, I rooted through the pockets of the jackets and dresses for the desk key and I was about to quit, when I suddenly remembered where I put my house key whenever I went to yoga class. Because my yoga clothes have no pockets, I stuffed the key in my shoe.

I turned each pair of shoes upside down,

and in the next to last pair, a sassy brown number with white-tipped toes, I found a scrolled key.

My pulse racing, I crept to the office door and listened again for sound of anyone approaching. Hearing nothing, I returned to the desk, slotted the key into the lock, and twisted. Success.

With a gentle shove, I pushed up the tambour rolltop. A pen and a set of reading glasses lay dead-center, at the ready. The stationery compartments to the right were filled with personalized museum stationery, envelopes, and panes of stamps. The twin drawers held paperclips. Certain I was looking for a ledger of some sort, I whipped open the tiny cupboard on the left, but it merely contained business cards and boxes of pens. A clock with a second hand ticked mercilessly on the shelf above the stationery slots.

"Hush," I muttered as I slid open the three front drawers. In the first and second, I found lined pads, void of notes or doodles. In the third, I discovered a green-spined book. I pulled it out, my fingers shaking with nervous energy, and flipped to the first page. Numbers and names of donors stared back at me, each entry dated. The same on the second and third pages.

Before I could read more, I heard foot-steps on the stairs. The clickety-clack grew louder. My adrenaline pumping, I searched for a hiding place. The room was too sparse, the closet too far away. I barely managed to pull the tambour rolltop down and stuff the ledger behind me as the door to the office squeaked open.

Feeling like a girl caught stealing money from her mother's purse, I forced a smile at Felicia.

"What the heck do you think you're do-ing?" she demanded, her eyes sparkling with suspicion.

"I . . . I . . ." Sputtering didn't become me.

"What's behind your back?"

"Nothing."

"Give it to me." Felicia charged me.

I wielded the ledger like a shield, reluctant to fork it over.

She snatched it from my hands. "I'm call-ing Chief Urso." She crossed to the tele-phone and lifted the receiver.

"Don't," I pleaded, my heart pounding so hard I could hear it in my eardrums, not because I was anxious about being alone with Felicia — people downstairs knew I'd gone to console her — but because I was worried about Urso finding out I'd been sticking my nose in where it didn't belong. Besides, she looked more intent on strangling the telephone than me.

She tapped her toe. "Well?"

I swallowed hard, then confessed, starting with my theories.

Felicia exhaled as if she were a balloon that I had punctured with a sharp needle.

I continued. "When your sister, Lois, said you couldn't afford to take trips with her —"

"Couldn't afford to? Heck, I didn't want to!"

"Didn't want to what?"

"Travel with her," she snapped, her righteous anger revived.

"But she said you didn't have the cash. That you have money issues. She said you ran through your inheritance from your dead husband." I didn't add that people were talking about the possibility that, to get his money, she had killed her dearly departed husband while sojourning in Europe. "And Prudence thought —"

"I don't give a darn what that penny-pincher Prudence thinks." She replaced the telephone receiver, then whipped open the ledger to the last page and stabbed her finger at an entry. "Five million dollars and counting. I'm flush. You can ask my banker, who happens to be downstairs."

"But Lois said —"

"I told my demented sister that I couldn't travel because she snores and talks in her sleep."

I thought of Felicia's alibi for the night of the murder. "Lois said you didn't meet up with her the night Ed was killed."

"Of course, I did."

"No-o-o." I drew the word out. "She was visiting your aunt who had broken her hip."

"Auntie broke her hip the week before. I visited her at the same time as Lois. Auntie will verify the date. She may be in her eight-ies, but she's not the one losing her marbles, if you know what I mean."

Hearing people shuffling about in the hallway emboldened me. I said, "Then why did you argue with Kristine about money at the diner?"

"We didn't argue."

"You demanded she pay you what Ed promised you."

"Who told you — ?"

"There were witnesses."

Felicia worked her tongue inside her mouth. "It was a matter of principle. Ed made a pledge."

"Some people say you were a woman scorned, and —"

"Oh, for heaven's sake, enough gossip! Whoever your *some people* might be, they're wrong. I am not a woman scorned. I despised that man."

I felt like I was stuck in a kaleidoscope, my theories a jangle of fractured colored pieces. "I don't know who started that rumor," Felicia went on. "Lois, I imagine. She hates me for being prettier and younger, like I could help either. No matter. It's totally false. Ed was a sack of bones who liked to flirt, and when he flirted with me, he always added money into the equation. I'm not stupid. This museum needs constant renovations. Why not accept money from the richest man in town? So many others in town wanted to match contributions. Who was I to say no? Luigi Bozzuto, Mr. Nakamura, those three buffoons on the town council who kowtow to your grandmother. If they want our town on the map, then they shouldn't mind giving a pretty penny to preserve our history, right? Ed was my link, nothing more."

"But if he bowed out, all the others —"

"They paid up. All the contributions are in the ledger." She shook the book. "I had no motive to kill Ed Woodhouse."

I stood there, heat suffusing my cheeks, unable to apologize quickly enough. "I'm sorry, Felicia. Truly sorry, I —"

"Hmmph."

"My grandmother . . ." I shrugged. "She's not guilty. I need something, anything, to prove her innocence. I thought you . . ." I shook my head. "I didn't think."

Felicia snorted. She had every right. I couldn't prove any of my claims. All I had was hearsay. But if Felicia hadn't killed Ed, then who had? There had to be something I was missing, right under my nose, but I couldn't see it.

"My money is on Kristine," Felicia said as she stowed the ledger in its rightful place and locked the rolltop desk. "She's hiding something."

"But what?"

"She cut me off after that night. Cut me off! We've been friends for years, but . . ." Felicia made a slicing gesture across her throat. "She's been picking at me ever since."

"To cast suspicion?"

"That's my bet." She strode to the door, stopped, and peered at me coyly over her shoulder. "You're a sneak, you know that? I never thought you had it in you."

I returned to the party, dazed and confused. Jordan and his sister Jacky had vanished. So had Kristine, but like the tornado that she was, she had left destruction and devastation in her wake. Prudence and Tyanne stood near the cheese displays, looking nothing less than shell-shocked.

For moral support, I searched for Meredith or Vivian among the guests, but they seemed to have departed, as well. When was I going to learn that I couldn't go off half-cocked? How many times over the course of my life had Pépère instructed me to believe the best of people first? Worrying about Grandmère was making me act irrationally and was eroding my natural joie de vivre, not to mention that my sleuthing had lost me the opportunity to discover more about Jordan's sister, Jacky.

Someone called out, "Tyanne, yoo-hoo!" The head of the PTA, a vibrant woman with a fondness for red, made a beeline for Tyanne and Prudence.

I stared at Kristine's pals again and couldn't help wondering why they had remained at the party. Had they broken ranks with her? Though Prudence had never shown an affinity for cheese while in Fromagerie Bessette, she was wolfing down slices of Emmental and chattering, her mouth full, to her friend. Her face looked grave. Her body language screamed nervous. Was she plagued by guilt for doing nothing to

317

help Felicia? Maybe now, while the PTA gal chatted up Tyanne, I could isolate Prudence and find out what really happened that night.

I strode down the stairs and was halfway to Prudence when Luigi clutched my elbow.

"I remembered something else," he said. "Ed Woodhouse came to the restaurant the day before he died. He met with someone. A lawyer."

"What kind of lawyer?"

"A divorce lawyer."

CHAPTER 22

Around five P.M., I returned to the shop and forced Rebecca to take off the rest of the afternoon, no arguments. Then I called Urso. The precinct clerk informed me that he was out, saying in a dismissive tone that he always visited his family on Sundays, as if everyone in town should know that.

I hung up, disheartened. What I had to tell him could wait, of course, but I couldn't stop tidbits of information from cycling through my head. Ed Woodhouse had consulted a divorce attorney the day before he died. If Kristine had known, she would have knocked off Ed to prevent him from following through with the divorce — not to get his money, but to save face. Status meant everything to Kristine. She might have looked the other way when he cheated, but she would not have allowed Ed to leave her for good.

At six, Bozz returned with the platters

from Felicia's soirée. I asked him to wash and dry the platters, then thanked him for his great work and said he would see a bonus in his paycheck. He was proving to be a terrific assistant. Thank heaven he liked his toys and was willing to work hard to pay for them.

As Bozz disappeared into the kitchen, Matthew poked his head into the shop, two bottles of wine in his hands. "I've closed up the annex. Did Grandmère reach you? Are you coming to their house for dinner? I'm bringing Meredith."

"And wine, I see."

"Carlisle zinfandel from the Russian River. It's big and jammy with the aroma of blueberries."

"Sounds yummy."

"Pépère's barbecuing."

"Double yummy." Every summer Pépère became a glutton for barbecue and watched Bobby Flay religiously on the Food Network. "Yes, I'm coming. Wouldn't miss it. You know how I love barbecue." I winked. "I think Grandmère knows something's up between you and Meredith. She had that sing-song lilt to her voice when she called me."

He grinned. "Yeah, she's always two steps ahead, isn't she?"

If only she had been two steps ahead on the night of Ed's murder, or at least a step ahead of me the other day so I wouldn't have barged in on my cousin and my friend and found them in an intimate embrace.

Matthew jerked a thumb. "Need help closing down the counter?"

"No, thanks."

"I'm done, Miss B." Bozz bounded from the kitchen. "See you after school tomorrow." He followed Matthew out the rear exit and let the door slam shut.

In the relative quiet, the hum of the appliances the only sound in the shop, I threw together an appetizer tray to take to Grand-mère's, then I stowed the cheese in the refrigerator, and turned off the lights. As I always did, I strolled to the front door and locked it from the inside. I peered through the plate-glass windows, my gaze drawn to the spot where Ed had been slain, which was no longer a shadowy corner. Late afternoon sun cast a warm, hazy glow on the sidewalk. And yet I shuddered. What were Ed's last words? Did he plead for mercy? He must have known his killer. Had the killer plunged an olive-wood-handled cheese knife into Ed's chest and held it there until he died?

"Aunt Charlotte, come see!" Amy, wearing a paint-and-glitter-splattered artist's smock, grabbed my hand and dragged me to the wooden picnic table that had been moved from the backyard of Grandmère's house to the grass in front. Cans of paint, paint brushes, glitter, glue, rags, nails, and thumbtacks had been strategically laid out on top. A stand of wooden poles, no doubt filched from Pépère's birdhouse collection, leaned against the far end. Strewn on the grass beyond the picnic table lay a handful of completed two-by-three-foot rally signs that read:

A vote for Bernadette is a vote of confidence.
Vote smart. Vote Bernadette.

I smiled. Apparently the scrapbooking project for the theater had morphed into a sign-making fest for the campaign. I could always count on Grandmère to keep little hands busy.

"Aren't they colorful?" Clair was also dressed in an artist's smock, her cheeks rosy with enthusiasm.

Grandmère must have sent someone to

collect the smocks from the Providence Playhouse art department, probably Freckles, who sat huddled between Meredith and Gretel, the pastor's wife, painting slogans on rally signs at the far end of the table. Amy and Clair were dousing the signs with glue and glitter.

I squeezed Clair's shoulder. "The signs look great."

"We talked her into it," Clair said. "We didn't want her to get killed."

Grandmère clucked her tongue. "Nonsense. No one is going to kill me."

"Grandmère will definitely win," Amy said.

Dressed in an artist's smock as paint-splattered as the others', Grandmère circled her campaign group like a doting art teacher while giving tips and encouragement. I loved how she had turned her house arrest into something productive. If Kristine Woodhouse got word, she would be steaming mad.

Pépère appeared in the driveway, a barbecue apron tied at his plump waist and long-handled tongs in his hand. "Dinner!"

Grandmère, her supporters, the twins, and I traipsed to the backyard. Pépère had decorated the garden with tiki torches and card tables covered with checkered tablecloths. Each of Grandmère's campaigners had supplied a dish. Gretel had brought her five-cheese macaroni and cheese, yummy with its broiled crust and the creamiest insides I'd ever tasted. She'd even remembered to bring a portion for Clair that was made with gluten-free pasta. Freckles had provided her favorite baked beans and a delicious fresh-from-the-garden salad. Pépère had made succulent ribs and chicken with a zesty sauce of his own creation.

I set the tray of appetizers on the patio table. Amy plopped a marinated olive into her mouth. Clair did the same.

"Hello, Charlotte!" Meredith strode from the kitchen, quickly followed by Matthew who let the screen door slam shut behind him. Meredith carried loaves of crunchy bread from the Providence Patisserie. She couldn't cook worth a lick. Matthew held two open bottles of wine.

"Girls, wash your hands!" he said.

The twins obeyed.

As everyone started to serve up dinner, Grandmère pulled me to the swing on the porch. She thumped the cushion, indicating I should sit, then gripped my chin with her gnarled fingers. "*Chérie,* you look tired."

"I've been busy."

"You work too hard. You need extra helpers."

"That's not —" I pressed my lips together. Grandmère did not need to know all that I had been doing in addition to running The Cheese Shop. I wanted to share what I had heard about Ed and the divorce lawyer, but I didn't want any more rumors starting, and I didn't want to fill her with false hope. I would go through the proper channels and reveal my findings to Urso tomorrow. I patted my grandmother's cheek. "I'm fine."

"*Très bien.* Now, you know who I saw today? Jordan and —"

"She's his sister."

Grandmère grinned. "I was about to tell you. We were introduced. I invited them to dinner."

"You what?"

She glanced at her watch. "He's due any minute."

I fiddled with the feathers of hair around my face and picked at the sleeves of my pink dress, wishing I had changed since Felicia's party. I was overdressed for a barbecue.

"Relax." Grandmère smiled. "You look adorable."

I wasn't sure a thirtysomething woman could ever look adorable, but I loved her for telling me.

"Besides, he can't stay. They have other plans." Grandmère rose from the swing with a little grunt. "Just so you know, his sister is troubled."

I stood and straightened the front of my dress. "What do you mean? Like tetched in the head?"

"No, *chérie*. She is worried."

About her ex-husband showing up? I wondered.

"I see it in her eyes," Grandmère went on. "There is something weighing on her mind, but she covers with that smile. So like Jordan, don't you think?"

I cocked my head. Was he troubled, too? My grandmother claimed she was prescient at times. Was this one of them? Perhaps when I solved Ed's murder, I could get back to handling my own life and delve into Jordan's.

"So tell me, Charlotte, do you love him?"

A laugh burbled out of me. "Oh, Grandmère, it's way too early for love." I didn't love him, did I? A woman needs to know a man to fall in love, right? I knew he made good cheese and took great delight in food. I had stood beside him at a couple of cooking classes at La Bella Ristorante, and we had flirted and shared tips on slicing and dicing, but I didn't know what books he liked. I didn't know what his favorite color was. I didn't know squat. "I like him, Grandmère, and I want to get to know him better, but life has gotten in the way."

"Do not let it." She gave me a stern look. "You must drive your life. Your life does not drive you. Remember this!"

"Yes, ma'am." I kissed her cheek. *"Je t'aime."*

"Je t'aime, aussi." Grandmère slung her hand around the crook of my elbow, and we strolled to join the others. "Matthew looks happy."

"Yes, he does." I eyed my cousin and Meredith, standing apart from the others, his mouth tilted to her ear, whispering. He did look happy. And so did she. I hoped it would last.

"Ah, there's Jordan, and he's brought cheese." Grandmère released my arm and swatted my rear end. "Go bat those pretty eyes of yours. It will do you good."

Jordan, who had donned a linen jacket since Felicia's party, strode up the driveway, a wheel of Gouda tucked under an arm, a ray of setting sun glazing his forehead. Handsome as ever. My heart did a little somersault.

I met him halfway and, laughing, took the wheel of cheese from him. "A wedge would have been perfectly acceptable."

"I figured your grandmother could use a little spoiling. It's her favorite." He inhaled. "Mmm, the food smells good."

"Pépère's special cracked pepper barbecue sauce."

"Spicy."

Silence fell between us. Was he upset that I'd abandoned him at Felicia's soirée yesterday? If we were going to get past this uncomfortable stage in our relationship, I had to find the courage to push through it.

"Um, you mentioned a date," I said, heart pounding. "A picnic. I'm game." I jutted a hip, a flimsy attempt at flirting. I needed more practice. "You said Saturday."

"Why don't I stop by the shop tomorrow, and we'll pin it down." He turned to leave.

Courage!

"Wait, don't go." I grabbed his sleeve. An impulse to run my hands down his chest swept over me. I released his jacket and anchored my hands at my sides. "Look, I'm sorry if I've been a little erratic lately, first with Meredith and then Felicia and —"

"Charlotte!" Vivian yelled to me from the sidewalk. "I've got to talk to you."

She raced toward us, bobbling a gold box from Fromagerie Bessette in her hands. I looked regretfully at Jordan. His features softened, his smile finally met his eyes, and I breathed easier.

He clipped my chin with his knuckles and whispered, "We'll figure this date thing out tomorrow, okay?" He strode to his sister's house, giving Vivian a passing nod.

Tomorrow. I would look forward to tomorrow.

Vivian skidded to my side, jamming a heel on the cement like an anchor grounding on the ocean floor. "What's this about Ed meeting with a divorce attorney?"

"Luigi told you."

"No, I overheard him telling Jordan as I was heading out of the museum." She thrust the gold box at me. "Bringing a bacon and shallot quiche from Fromagerie Bessette is cheating, I know, but I'd bought it for my dinner earlier, and I didn't want it to go to waste. Now, come on, tell me."

We moseyed toward the picnickers, and I filled her in with what little I knew. Her eyes went wide. I said, "Unless the divorce attorney has another specialty that Luigi doesn't know about, it appears that Ed wanted a divorce."

"Do you think that's why Kristine killed him?"

"It's certainly a strong motive. She would not have appreciated being the ex–Mrs. Ed

Woodhouse. I've called Urso."

"They never should have gotten married. They were like oil and water."

"Charlotte, Vivian," Grandmère said. "Come eat. *Mangez, mangez.*"

I unwrapped the quiche, put it on the table with the other potluck items, and placed one of the cake knives that Grandmère had set out beside it. Vivian handed me a plate decorated with a rooster and took one for herself. We filled them with good eats, both of us opting for ribs, coleslaw, and a slice of quiche. I poured each of us a glass of Matthew's remarkable wine.

"Thanks," Vivian said.

"Girls, over here." Gretel patted a chair beside her and motioned to another one next to it. "Join us. Freckles is giving me my quick fix of gossip. I'm so bad." She toyed with her long blonde braid, her cheeks glowing with good humor. "You know how my sweet hubby doesn't like me to chatter."

"I won't blab." Freckles nudged Gretel, then eyed me and Vivian as we set our plates down on the table and nestled into two empty chairs. "I was just telling Gretel what Kristine, Prudence, and Tyanne wore today to Felicia's party."

"Animal prints and black gloves. My, my." Gretel laughed.

"In other news . . ." Freckles offered a knowing chuckle. "Vivian, I saw you chatting up Luigi Bozzuto today."

"I did nothing of the sort." Vivian wrinkled her nose.

"He likes you," Freckles went on.

"One would wonder why, after all the times I've turned him down. I've never given him an ounce of encouragement." Vivian took a bite of quiche.

"Some men like a challenge," Freckles teased.

"Why is that?" Gretel asked. "Why can't a man like a woman who is throwing herself at him?"

"Exactly," Vivian said. "What do you think, Charlotte?"

"I don't have a clue." Was that what I was doing with Jordan? Making myself too available? Was that why Urso was so interested in me, because I wasn't giving him the time of day except to call him with possible murder suspects? Not happy being the focus of attention, I said, "Do I detect a note of regret, Gretel?"

"Oh, no. Never. No regrets. Everything has a purpose. Ecclesiastes 3." She blotted her mouth with a napkin. "I belong right where I am. Fate plays its hand, which, by the way, might be why I take walks."

I tilted my head. "I don't understand."

"Well . . ." Gretel said, drawing the word out like a talented storyteller. "On the night of Ed's murder, I was out walking the hills, as I always do. I saw lots of people. I didn't think anything of it. Didn't mention it to Chief Urso. He had no call to question me. Lots of people walk. But . . ." She held up a finger. "I woke in my sleep last night and realized that I had seen someone who looked just like Kristine that night on one of the bluffs."

"You're kidding," Freckles said. "Kristine?"

"A silhouette, mind you. The silver light from the moon skimmed her body. She was digging."

"Burying something?" I said, thinking of the bloody dress Kristine would have needed to ditch.

"I don't know."

"What time?" Freckles said.

"I always walk around ten. It calms me before I go to sleep." Gretel studied her fingernails. "Now, of course, I could be wrong."

"Why would you say that?" Vivian leaned in, a forkful of coleslaw suspended between plate and mouth.

"Because I heard, at the time, Kristine was

picking up her daughter from Tyanne Taylor's house, and yet I felt so sure. I believe God wants me to feel sure."

"Are you?" I asked.

"Yes, I am." Gretel nodded with confidence. "I'll swear on a stack of Bibles."

CHAPTER 23

That night and the next morning, I left one message after another for Urso. The man was impossible to reach. At eleven A.M., he stomped into the shop. The grape-leaf-shaped chimes jingled merrily, but he wasn't smiling. He stopped halfway across the floor, hands at his sides, right hand twitching by his holster as if he was ready for a gunfight. Not with me, I hoped.

I asked Rebecca to tend to the three customers, and I hitched a finger at the rear door. "How about some sunshine out back, Chief?"

Urso nodded and lumbered up to the counter, a scowl etched into his forehead. I removed my apron, smoothed the front of my pleated blouse, and grabbed a bottle of Pellegrino from the cooler. I pushed open the door at the rear of the shop and Urso followed.

The fresh scent of morning filled the air

and infused me with hope. We were going to get to the bottom of the mystery and free my grandmother.

"I'm so glad you got my message." I handed him the bottle of sparkling water.

He screwed off the top and slugged down a couple of gulps. "I didn't get any message."

That surprised me. "Then why are you here? Did Luigi call you?"

"No. Why would he?"

"Gretel?"

"Nope."

"Because . . ." I swallowed hard. "Why did you stop by?"

"You know why."

My stomach turned to jelly. Felicia must have said something to him about my raid on her museum office after all. Rats. I steered Urso to the meditation bench at the far end of the garden. "Sit."

"I'm happy standing." He folded his arms across his massive chest and glowered at me.

"I'm sorry," I blurted. "Felicia has every right to press charges. I never should have broken into her office and rifled through —"

"You did what?"

He didn't know? Felicia hadn't blabbed?

My cheeks felt hotter than hot. "Well, doesn't that beat all? Hoisted by my own petard."

"What the heck does that mean?"

"A *petard* is an old French bomb, set against a castle wall to —"

"I know what a petard is," he snapped. "What did you do?"

"Why are you here?" I countered.

"You first. Why did you break into Felicia's office?"

"I thought that Felicia . . ." I zipped my mouth shut. It didn't matter what I thought, I'd been wrong. "I made a mistake. She's forgiven me."

"Charlotte, if you don't stop prying into others' affairs, I'm going to lock you up. Better yet, I'll remove your grandmother from her cushy house arrest and put her in the slammer. That'd serve you right."

"As long as you throw me in with her."

"Don't be a smart aleck." Urso gazed at me with hard eyes as he swigged more of the water and wiped the back of his hand across his mouth. "What am I going to do with you?"

"Why are you here?" I demanded, angry that I'd given him Pellegrino water when I could have given him tap water for all the good he was doing to free Grandmère.

"Because your grandmother has a battalion of women parading around her yard with rally posters this morning, and they're chanting. I told you —"

"She has the right to have friends over."

"She's under house arrest. Don't you understand — ?"

I put my hand on his arm. "U-ey, that's not important."

"Don't call me U-ey."

"You've got to talk to Luigi Bozzuto."

He flipped my hand away. "I don't have to do anything of the kind."

"He knows something that's pertinent to the case."

"Charlotte —"

"Ed Woodhouse met with a divorce attorney."

"A divorce . . ." He blew a stream of air out his nose and growled, reminding me of a frustrated bear who couldn't reach a hive of honey. "Why didn't Luigi come forward?"

"Because he didn't remember until yesterday. He saw the guy at church and it came back to him in a flash."

"And he told you?"

"He came straight from church to Felicia's museum party. You were with your family." I paced in front of him and explained my theory about Kristine needing the status of

337

being Mrs. Ed Woodhouse and her dream of a political future. "That's motive, right? If Kristine knew Ed was getting a divorce, she'd have done everything in her power to stop him. And get this, Gretel Hildegard, the pastor's wife? She saw someone who looked like Kristine digging in the hills that night. After ten o'clock. Kristine claimed she was picking up Willamina. She lied. What if she was out there burying her bloody dress and gloves?"

"Man, oh, man, oh, man." Urso slumped onto the bench and set the Pellegrino bottle between his thighs. He squinted up at me.

Rebecca poked her head out the rear entrance. "Charlotte —"

"Not now." I remained focused on Urso. "Seeing Kristine out there casts doubt, right?"

"What casts doubt?" Rebecca hurried over and drilled me with her gaze.

I repeated what I had told Urso.

"Yeah, that's motive." Rebecca snapped her fingers. "I saw on *Law & Order* where this wife —"

"Now, Miss Zook —"

"Don't 'Miss Zook' me, Chief. You call me Rebecca like everybody else."

"Rebecca, let's not —"

"Let's not what, theorize? Find out the

338

truth? Prove Grandmère is innocent?" She plopped onto the bench next to Urso and rapped him on the arm with her knuckle. "It's your job, I repeat, *your job* to keep hunting until you have all the clues. Did you get evidence from the crime scene? Did you scour the financial records of your major suspects? Are you going out to that hill and look for a bloody dress and gloves? Well, are you? On an episode of *Law & Order,* this wife refused the divorce, and —"

"I saw the show. I know what happens." Urso leaned back and let out a deep, throaty laugh.

"Don't laugh at me." Rebecca popped up like a firecracker and faced Urso, hands on her narrow hips.

"Sorry. I didn't mean to laugh, it's just. . . ." He swallowed back a chortle. "I will check into Kristine Woodhouse's financial records and Ed's meeting with the attorney and Gretel's sighting, and I will do my best to pin down exactly what happened and when. Happy?"

"Ecstatic." Rebecca gave a curt nod. "Oh, Charlotte, I almost forgot. I came out to find you. Matthew's looking for you."

Panic swept through me. "Why?"

"There's been another altercation at school."

Matthew and I raced into the school's main office, a hectic place filled with children who had forgotten their lunches. A saintly receptionist advised us that Principal Yale was attending to the twins in the music room rather than her office. The principal doubled as the music teacher. Arts, thanks to special funds granted by the PTA, were an integral part of the Providence school system's curriculum.

The sound of our footsteps echoed off the floors as we hurried down hall after colorfully decorated hall, veering toward the music room at the far end of the school.

A teacher standing by the door to the library said, "Shhhhh."

Inside, a group of students sat bent over their desks, each with a test in front of them, and I wondered if Amy had been caught cheating on an exam. The end of school was near.

We raced past another room and I heard, "Charlotte, Matt!"

I clutched Matthew's arm and we backed up a pace. Meredith stood on a ladder, a cloud of dust billowing around her, a feather duster in her hand.

"What are you doing?" I asked.

"Penance for not telling you the truth about Matt and me."

I cocked an eyebrow.

"Just kidding. I'm taking every lunch hour to clean out our storage room of historical books. Seeing Felicia's wonderful museum set me to thinking that perhaps, with a little display of our own, we could get more folks to fund our special projects." She tucked a strand of hair under the red kerchief she'd tied around her head. "Why are you here?"

"Amy got into trouble," Matthew said.

"Oh, no. Why didn't Principal Yale tell me? I'm coming." She scrambled down the ladder, brushed dust off her clothes, and pecked Matthew on the cheek. "I'm sure it'll be fine."

Walking in rank, we pushed through a set of double doors and down the last hall. Sunlight slashed the big-paned windows on our left and made the area feel as warm and dry as a sauna. The sound of children playing scales, up and down, up and down, on more than one piano, and in varying octaves, came from inside the music room near the auditorium. I peeked through the windows in the door. The room was set up for a small orchestra, with metal chairs, music stands, and a conductor's podium.

341

Instruments were stowed neatly on shelves. A bass violin rested in a T-stand in the corner, with probably the same old apple box beside it that I'd had to stand on to play the "brown monster" when I was the twins' age. Bass violins were a rare commodity in schools. Not only were they expensive, but they were hard to play. Always up for a challenge, I'd latched onto the "brown monster" with the passion of a virtuoso. I wondered who was playing it nowadays.

By the upright piano on the near wall of the room stood Principal Yale, a fortysomething woman and mother of five grown girls, who reminded me of Ina Garten, the Barefoot Contessa, full-figured with a beaming goodness. She was advising the twins, who were perched on the bench playing scales on the piano keys. At another piano near a window with a view of the schoolyard sat Willamina and Tyanne Taylor's son. They, too, were playing scales.

I pushed open the door and strode inside with Matthew and Meredith at my heels.

Principal Yale spun around and offered a tight smile. "So good to see you."

The children stopped playing and peered at us over their shoulders. Clair offered a weak smile. Amy made a goofy face. Matthew looked at me, helplessness in his gaze.

"Meredith, good of you to join us," Principal Yale went on.

"I didn't know —" Meredith sputtered.

"A playground fracas. I didn't want to disturb you."

"I'm their teacher."

"You were so intent with your project, and I have been paying close attention to this matter, but now that you're here, perfect. Why don't we convene out in the hall?" Yale extended a hand to guide the way. "Children, keep up the good work, in sync with the metronome, please. Scales build strong fingers. Do the C scale three more times and then move on to 'Pomp and Circumstance.' Clair, you're the leader. We want to sound good at graduation, don't we?"

The children said, "Yes, Principal Yale," and began again, their little thumbs stretching beneath their palms to make the transition upward.

Yale pushed through the door and led us to the far end of the hall near the entrance to the auditorium, where she had set up a semicircle of metal chairs. "Take a seat, please. Meredith, grab an extra chair, please." Meredith obeyed. "We'll have privacy here, I assure you."

"What did Amy do this time?" Matthew said.

"Actually, it was Clair."

"Clair?" Matthew, Meredith, and I said in unison as we sank into our chairs.

Yale remained standing. "She got into a fight with Willamina Woodhouse."

"Oh, no," we intoned like a Greek chorus.

"What I gather from the other children is that Willamina started ranting about the vote scheduled for tomorrow." Yale folded her hands in front of her. "She marched around the playground and called to her friends to join in. When they didn't, she chanted louder, saying her mother was going to win. Your little Clair . . ."

"She's always so good," Matthew whispered.

"Even the good ones lash out. It seems that Clair rushed Willamina, her fingers primed like claws."

"Did you see her do it, ma'am?" Meredith asked.

"No. The other children . . . they're quite descriptive with their words, as you well know." Yale tried to stifle a smile but failed. "Anyway, my understanding is that Clair rushed Willamina, grabbed her hair, and tugged her to the ground."

The three of us gasped.

A choppy rendition of "Pomp and Circumstance" started up in the music room.

"They tussled. Amy tried to pull Clair off, but Clair insisted that her grandmother was going to win the election. Willamina, bless her disagreeable soul, continued to oppose." Yale checked her watch and looked down the empty hallway. "Politics can bring out the worst in people, don't you think?"

"Yes," we all agreed.

Yale lowered her voice. "Willamina is a handful, I'll admit."

"She's going through such a sorrowful time right now," Meredith said.

"I'm afraid she knows how to push your twins' buttons." Yale gazed at Matthew and me. "I'm hopeful that this will all blow over after tomorrow's results, aren't you?"

"I'm not so sure," Matthew said.

I wasn't so certain, either. Who knew what Willamina might do if Grandmère were to be elected?

"You know the Taylor child?" Yale went on.

I did. Tyanne often brought her son, Thomas — a shy, gangly boy — into the shop. She encouraged his curious nature. Like Amy, he loved to sniff and touch.

"He tried to break up the fight, as well. I was surprised. He's not, you know, very

345

spirited in that regard. He's a bit of a computer nerd, frankly."

Meredith said, "I think he has a little crush on Amy."

"Yes, probably so." Yale glanced at her watch again and huffed. "Anyway, I've asked Kristine and Tyanne to join us."

As if on cue, Kristine barged through the double doors at the end of the hall and stomped toward us, her high heels clickety-clacking as she drew nearer. A few feet from us, she planted her hands on her hips, bonier looking because of the skintight ecru sheath she wore, and screamed, "What in heaven's name — ?"

"Please, keep your voice low, Mrs. Wood-house," Principal Yale ordered. "The children are in the music room. I do not want them to hear us conversing."

"Why did you call me —"

"Willamina was in yet another altercation."

Kristine glowered at me and back at Yale. "She didn't start it."

"As a matter of fact, she did. I believe she takes her cues from you," Yale said. "Sit, please."

"Why, I never!"

"Sit!"

Kristine plunked into the chair beside

Meredith, and I bit back a smile, impressed by the turn of events. In a matter of seconds, our genteel principal had turned into a lioness defending her pride.

"Listen, carefully," Yale said, a muscle ticking in her jaw. "I will not have this school turned into a vetting ground for your political aspirations. Do you hear me?"

Kristine nodded.

"Your child is undergoing severe emotional issues. Even her good friends are shying away from her."

The double doors squeaked open again. Tyanne pushed through, her chin quivering, her hands clutching the strap of her oversized yellow purse. She slinked toward us like a dog who knew she was about to be punished. "What's happened, ma'am?"

"Please, sit, Mrs. Taylor," Yale said in a much kinder tone.

"Yes, ma'am." Tyanne perched on the remaining chair, the one beside Kristine. She straightened her honey-colored linen skirt primly beneath her bottom, fiddled with the flaps of the matching jacket, and set her purse on the floor with a clunk. Then she scooched her chair inches away from Kristine. The feet of the chair squealed in protest.

Kristine went rigid, probably realizing that

her friends, like her daughter's, were separating themselves from her, as well.

The principal began her account.

When she finished, Tyanne fetched a tissue from her purse and blotted the tears that had pooled in the corner of her eyes. "What do y'all need us to do?"

"I'm not doing a darned thing," Kristine said.

"Kristine, let me —"

"Not a word!" Kristine thrust a finger at Tyanne as she bounded from her chair. "It was not my child's fault. It was that . . . that . . . willful twin."

"Her name is Clair." Matthew leaped to his feet, too, his face red. I could see his hands, which were jammed into his pockets, balling up and releasing beneath the fabric.

"Hush, both of you!" Principal Yale said.

"She's incorrigible. They both are," Kristine yelled, heedless of the principal's warning. "They're wild children."

"That's it." Unable to rein in my own anger any longer, I jumped to my feet and glowered at Kristine. "Your daughter is the one running all over town unsupervised."

"She is doing no such thing!"

"Please, all of you, lower your voice," Principal Yale said. "You do not want the children hearing —"

"I've seen her on more than one occasion in the diner, by herself," I hissed. "When our girls aren't at school, they are with my grandmother and grandfather or with a sitter."

"Ha!" Kristine shrieked. "I rest my case." She jutted her index finger in the air. "Your grandmother cannot be trusted. She's a murderer."

"Take it back," I ordered.

"Now!" Matthew hissed.

A look of triumph crossed Kristine's face. She leaned toward Matthew, probably hedging her bet that he wouldn't hit her in front of so many women. "You tell your twins to cease and desist, or I'll . . ." She swung around and brandished her finger like a sword. "I'll . . . I'll —"

"— what? Kill me, too?" he snapped.

CHAPTER 24

Matthew and I, exasperated with the way we had behaved at school, returned to work bristling with manic energy. Luckily, customers were swarming The Cheese Shop and the wine annex and provided neither of us with the time to think about how we could have handled the meeting with Kristine better. I downed a Hershey's Kiss to take the edge off and offered one to Matthew. He declined. I pocketed another for later, just in case.

Throughout the morning, Rebecca grilled me like a masterful DA, but I didn't divulge anything about our encounter. Not one word. Grandmère would have been so proud of me.

Around two, when we ran out of Stilton, I said, "Did we advertise some kind of super-saver sale?"

Rebecca laughed. "I think it was the news-letter."

Thanks to Bozz, the first of our many newsletters had gone out by email yesterday. I had included a recipe for my Stilton-Mascarpone torte, and Matthew had written an entire page about Chilean wines. He had already put in an express order for more malbec to be shipped to the store.

"Perhaps we could suggest substituting Gorgonzola for the recipe?" Rebecca said.

"Good idea."

As if our newsletter-responsive crowd wasn't keeping us busy enough, we had to take care of minor emergencies, too. The Mystic Moon Candle Boutique owner needed cheese to impress her future in-laws, Gretel Hildegard absolutely had to have a bottle of the wine that she'd tasted at the barbecue so she could share the liquid ambrosia with the pastor, and La Bella Ristorante had run out of Taleggio. Could we bring over ten pounds, ASAP?

Needing a breath of fresh air, I opted to make the delivery. Luigi was waiting, arms opened wide, outside the restaurant. I handed him one of our gold-toned bags filled with cheese.

"Thank you," he said. "I was so certain we had enough, but the Taleggio and asparagus appetizer was such a big hit, we had to bring it back."

"I sure loved it."

"Who's that?" He hitched his chin.

I looked in the direction he indicated. Vivian stood outside Europa Antiques and Collectibles, laughing and gripping the muscular arm of what could only be described as an Adonis. Blond hair, tan, and twenty years her junior. He carried a hefty gym bag over one shoulder. "Her personal trainer."

Luigi's face pinched with concern.

"Don't worry. She's not dating him," I said. "He comes to the shop twice a week and takes her through a workout."

"In the store?"

"She spends all her waking hours there. She only breaks free for the occasional yoga class or Cheese Shop visit." I cocked my head. "Didn't you talk to her at Felicia's party?"

"For a second."

"And did you ask her out?"

"I don't know if she's playing hard to get or if she's not that into me." He forced a smile, but sadness rimmed his eyes.

I patted his arm. "Take her some flowers. Be bold. She's a very busy woman. I've always felt that Vivian appreciates directness."

He saluted with two fingers and returned inside his restaurant.

Feeling like I had done my Cupid duty for the day, I headed back to The Cheese Shop, a grin on my face. Around four thirty, my smile disappeared. Felicia, dressed in a mint green chiffon frock that made her red hair look like it was ablaze, strolled in with her sister. Lois, her arms laden with packages, looked like she had spent the entire day shopping Providence's wonderful boutiques. I braced myself for another diatribe from Felicia, knowing I deserved it.

I was surprised when all she said was, "Don't you look lovely, Charlotte."

"You, too," I stammered.

Something flickered in her eyes, but it wasn't hurt or anger. I detected amusement.

"Charlotte," Lois said. "I simply must have some of those soft-rind cheeses that you told me about. I've been telling Felicia that they're not all that fattening."

"Not *as* fattening," I said, stressing the word *as,* and fetched a wheel of Brie. "Try this." I carved off a thin slice.

Lois popped it into her mouth and hummed her satisfaction.

"Obviously, she loves it, Charlotte," Felicia said. "Wrap up a pound."

"A pound?" Lois chirped.

"You can afford it, Sis. Charlotte, why don't you sell Lois some of those condiments you included in your newsletter?" Felicia eyed me, and I started to understand her glee. She was making her sister spend a lot of money, punishing Lois through her pocketbook for not corroborating her alibi.

Lois was a grown woman. It wasn't my place to protect her. I suggested the chestnut honey for the Tartuffo, the basil pesto to match an artisanal goat cheese from a Wisconsin farmer, and a variety of jams to go with the Double Cream Gouda from Pace Hill Farms.

After Lois paid for her purchases, Felicia prodded her. "Do it."

"No."

"Yes."

"One last thing." Lois's cheeks turned crimson. "Felicia was right. I was wrong. I visited our aunt a week ago, not the night of the murder. Felicia was with me. And I did see Felicia the night Ed died. It was around nine thirty." She tittered. "Silly me. I can't blame it on liquor, can I? Just gettin' old, I guess."

"Satisfied?" Felicia said to me.

I didn't know how to respond. I wasn't the one she had to convince. Urso was. "Uh, sure, whatever."

They left, Lois bubbling over with excitement about tasting her new purchases, and

I couldn't help but wonder why Felicia had needed to corroborate where she was on the night Ed was murdered. As the door slid shut and the shop fell silent, Felicia's name edged back near the top of my suspect list.

Seconds later, Rebecca hurried to my side. "It's girls' night out. Do we have time before Grandmère's rally for a little . . . ?" She mimed a drink. "Matthew said he'll watch the shop."

I glanced at the telephone by the register. I'd been hoping Urso would call. I was eager to know what he had gleaned from his encounters with Gretel and with Ed's divorce attorney. On the other hand, I was edgy, business had slowed to a standstill, and Rebecca looked eager for an hour of gossip.

"Sure," I said.

"Oh, goodie. Freckles and Delilah are coming, too."

I gave Bozz, who had stopped in for two hours of tweaking our website, the job of taking Rags home.

As always, the pub was jam-packed. The electric violinists were having a dueling match. The crowd clapped in time to the music.

Rebecca, Freckles, Delilah, and I settled into a booth. I glanced at the appetizer menu. I had forgotten to eat lunch, and with the flurry of afternoon business, hadn't stopped to snarf a snack. A slice of Morbier didn't count. My stomach grumbled in protest.

"Look over there." Rebecca pointed.

"Where?" Freckles said.

"At the end of the bar." Rebecca wiggled her finger. "Isn't that Jordan's sister?"

All of us craned our necks for a look. Jacky Peterson looked incredible in tight jeans and a plaid shirt with a red bandanna slung around her neck. She hovered by the waitress station, her foot tapping in time to the music.

"She's a waitress here?" I said.

"Started yesterday." Delilah wagged her hand trying to get Jacky's attention. "Wish she'd come take our order."

"You in a hurry or something?" I grinned.

"Sometimes," Delilah snapped.

"Touchy, touchy," Freckles said.

"We're in tech rehearsal," Delilah explained.

"That's no reason to attack your pals." Freckles grabbed the appetizer menu from me. "What's your favorite dish here, Charlotte?"

"Tim's mushrooms stuffed with goat cheese and herbs." I needed a fix of those delicacies at least once a month. "And the potato skins, smothered in Cheddar cheese and chives." One would think that, working in a cheese shop, I would grow tired of food made with cheese, but I didn't. I craved it.

"Yum. I'm getting the potato skins." Freckles slid the menu back to the end of the table. "So the ballet opens next week?" she said to Delilah. "Is it any good?"

Delilah smirked. "Guess you'll have to come to find out."

"I've got a ticket." Rebecca flailed her hand like an overeager student.

"Me, too," Freckles said. "Charlotte, when are you going?"

"Opening night." I always went to Grand-mère's productions the first night, not because she demanded that I attend, but because there was an electricity in the air that I couldn't explain. I only hoped she would be able to attend this one.

I glanced at my watch. Eight minutes had passed since we sat down. Tim employed three waitresses, none of whom seemed to notice us. I joined Delilah with the hand-waving. Finally Jacky acknowledged us by holding up a finger, indicating she'd be there in a second.

Freckles drummed the table as if it were a set of bongo drums. "So, who's got the scoop?"

"On what?" I said.

"On Jacky Peterson. She's here a week and she already has a job at the most popular place in town." Freckles winked at Delilah. "Next to the Country Kitchen, of course."

"She's divorced, but that's all I know." I watched Jacky out of the corner of my eye. If she had changed her identity, like Octavia suspected, and was in hiding, getting a job at Tim's wasn't the best idea. Inside a week, everybody in town would know her or want to find out more about her. The guys, especially.

"Hush!" Rebecca flapped her hands to quiet us. "She's coming this way."

"What'll it be, ladies?" Jacky set four cardboard coasters with Tim's logo on them in front of us. "Oh, hi, Charlotte. How nice to see you again."

"Same here. You sure got a job fast."

"Jordan is friends with Tim. I was really lucky. What'll it be?"

We ordered our drinks and appetizers. As she glided away, her hair swinging sensually across her back, I reflected again how happy I was that she was Jordan's sister and not a significant other.

"Speaking of Jordan . . ." Delilah said.

"What about him?" Rebecca twirled her coaster.

"I wasn't talking to you." Delilah looked at me slyly and said with a leading tone, "Did I hear right? Did Jordan ask you on a date?"

"Oh, Charlotte, I forgot to tell you." Rebecca clapped a hand over her mouth, then spoke between split fingers. "He stopped by the shop while you were at the twins' school."

With the flurry of the day's activities, I'd forgotten about Jordan's and my resolution to fix "this date thing."

Rebecca lowered her hand. "Will you forgive me?"

"Is he pining for you?" Delilah drew out the word, pi-i-i-ining.

How did I know? He could have stopped by to cancel our date entirely. Eager to keep my concerns about Jordan to myself, I said, "Not like Luigi pines for Vivian." I told them about seeing Luigi earlier and urging him to take Vivian some flowers.

"You know," Rebecca said, "for a good looking man, Luigi lacks a little confidence, don't you think?"

"He's all bravado," Freckles teased. "Pretty hair, great smile, but not a lot to offer in here." She thumped her chest. "He could use a little retooling on his depth quotient, I think."

"Really?" Delilah said.

I looked at her sideways and was surprised to see that she seemed a little forlorn. Was she interested in Luigi? He was years older. There were plenty of other guys in Providence closer to her age who had shown interest. Luigi's younger brother, for one. I sighed. There was no accounting for who one fell in love with.

"Look, look," Rebecca said, jerking her head to the right.

Prudence and Tyanne, still wearing her linen suit and carrying the oversized yellow purse, tramped to a table and sat down. Neither looked happy.

"What's with the dour faces?" Rebecca said. "Do you think they just got wind of how people intend to vote tomorrow? I mean, customers at the shop today were adamant that your grandmother is the hands-down favorite."

I wasn't sure that Tyanne would care at this point, not after Kristine had lambasted her at the school.

"How do you think Kristine's handling the scuttlebutt?" Freckles said.

"In her usual way." Delilah framed her

eyes with her hands. "With blinders on."

"You know, I saw this rerun of *Matlock*." Rebecca pulled on her ear lobe. "Or maybe it was *CSI: New York* —"

"Big difference," Freckles cut in.

Rebecca giggled. "I'm addicted to all of them."

Jacky appeared with drinks and silverware setups. As she set a glass of wine in front of Delilah, then delivered Rebecca's Cosmopolitan, Rebecca continued.

"Anyway, there was a woman running for office, and she was so out there, you know, stumping all the time, and —" She threw her arms wide and landed a blow to Jacky's wrist. The glass of beer she was setting in front of Freckles went flying and frothy liquid spilled down the table and over the edge.

Onto me.

"I'm so sorry," Jacky cried. She tossed a silverware setup to me.

I quickly unfurled it, dumped the silverware on the table, and tried to stop the flow of beer, but the napkin was one of those fabrics that wouldn't sop up anything. Totally useless.

"Go, go!" Freckles scooted out of the booth. She yanked me after her and propelled me in the direction of the ladies' room.

I bent forward, trying to keep the beer from hitting my brushed denim skirt. I pushed the restroom door open, hurried to the sink, grabbed a handful of paper towels, and dabbed my blouse, but unless I did something drastic, I was going to smell like a brewery when I went to Grandmère's rally. Risking exposure, I unbuttoned my blouse, whisked it off, and ran water through the spill. I'd rather be wet than stinky.

At the same time, a stall door opened. Tyanne emerged and gasped. Hadn't she ever been in a women's locker room?

"Sorry," I blurted. "Beer spilled and —"

"Are y'all alone, sugar?"

"Yes, why?"

Her face was tear-stained. Her dark hair, which usually fell smoothly around her plump face, was a rat's nest like she had been massaging it trying to get blood to her beleaguered brain. She chewed on her lower lip, as if she wanted to say something but couldn't.

"Are you okay?"

"I'm so sorry about . . ." She shuffled to the sink and rinsed her hands, scrubbing as hard as she could. I thought of Shakespeare's *MacBeth* when his wife said, "Out, damned spot! Out!"

"It was not your fault the kids got into a scuffle, Tyanne." I wrung my blouse free of as much water as I could. Luckily, it was drip-dry and the pleats wouldn't pucker. "It wasn't Thomas's either."

"Thomas . . . oh, my sweet Thomas." She sucked back a sob. "He's such a darling child, isn't he?"

I nodded. He was.

"He deserves someone better than me. And his father . . . his father . . . deserves someone better, too. Someone who . . ." Fresh tears streamed down her cheeks. "Oh, my, where do I start?"

"Start what?"

She looked at me through wet eyelashes. "I have something to confess. It's . . . it's about . . ." She hiccupped. "It's about the night Ed died."

CHAPTER 25

I slumped against the sink and stared at Tyanne in disbelief. Had I gotten my theory all wrong? Had Tyanne, not Felicia, been the one in love with Ed? Had she killed him? It was unlikely she was the woman Gretel saw walking in the hills. She was as tall as Kristine but half again as wide. Was Gretel's sighting meaningless?

I drew in a deep, calming breath. "Go ahead," I said, not worried that Tyanne would attack me in a public restroom. She needed a confessional. I would be her priest. "Tell me about the night Ed died."

"I was so . . . flummoxed. In a flurry, you know? Ed was making eyes at everyone, and Kristine was getting as drunk as a skunk. She couldn't see straight and she was muttering under her breath to me, and . . . she . . . she . . ." Tyanne licked her lips. "She made me do it."

"Do what?" I felt light-headed. Had Kristine and her friends banded together for one evil purpose? I'd seen movies of such things . . . read accounts. "Are you telling me you killed Ed?"

"Lord, no! I didn't . . . Oh, no! I . . ." She whacked her chest with her palm as if to jump-start her sputtering engine. "I lied, sugar. Kristine made me lie. She . . ." Tyanne squared her shoulders and stabbed the air with her finger. "Kristine didn't pick up Willamina from my house the night Ed was killed. I drove her little girl home."

"Tyanne, that's wonderful news." I gripped her hand. "Not wonderful for Kristine, but for you and for Grandmère."

"But I lied." She drew the word out.

"To protect yourself from a killer."

"My family would be mortified."

"We have to call Urso. My purse is at the table. Have you got a cell phone?"

"I can't talk to him."

"I won't make you. Promise. I just want him to protect you."

She rummaged through her yellow tote and pulled one out. "You can try, but I warn you, the reception in this place is as slow as molasses."

After a long wait, Urso answered. I told him I had a big break in the case and to come to Tim's as quickly as he could, but because of crackling static, I was only able to hear him say, "I'm on my way." I snapped the cell phone shut and eyed Tyanne.

"Oh, Lord," Tyanne drawled, looking like a trapped animal, anxious to escape. She glanced at the door, at the narrow window beyond the sinks. There wasn't a chance in ten that she could slip through it. "If Kristine finds out —"

"She's not going to. I won't tell her. Urso will keep this confidential."

"She's so proud. And so strong. And . . . Oh, my. Chief Urso's going to want me to tell him everything. No, no, no. I can't do it." Tyanne shook her head like a child having a fit. "I just can't. I'm so sorry, y'all. So sorry." She barreled past me, using her shoulder like a defensive guard, knocking me sideways into the bathroom wall. Her jock of a husband would be proud.

By the time I was able to find my footing and put my clammy shirt back on, she was long gone. I hurried back to the table.

Rebecca said, "I'm so sorry, Charlotte. Hey, are you okay? You look like you're in shock."

"I'm fine." I slipped into the booth, my shirt sticking to the Naugahyde.

"We've got to get a move on," Rebecca went on. "Your grandmother's rally starts in

366

a half hour. Seven sharp, she said."

"We paid the bill," Delilah added.

"And took the liberty of eating your mushrooms." Freckles chuckled.

Plates, empty of appetizers, sat in the center of the table. What did I care? I wasn't hungry anymore.

"Are you okay, really?" Rebecca's forehead wrinkled with concern. "You're not mad at me or something."

I told them what happened in the restroom.

"I'll wait for Chief Urso," Rebecca announced. "You go ahead. No way are you going to miss your grandmother's moment in the sun."

Before I could object, the front door burst open. Urso marched in, looking steamed.

"Uh-oh. That's our cue," Delilah said. She and Felicia slipped from the booth and whispered that they would see us at Grandmère's.

Urso's warning for my grandmother to cease and desist public displays resounded in my head. Was that why he was here? With town gossip, he probably suspected what Grandmère was up to.

He trundled across the room while removing his hat with one hand and running his other hand over the top of his thick hair.

When he reached our table, I said, "Are you okay? What's got you miffed?"

He remained standing. "I've been walking the hills all day with Gretel Hildegard and a group of church ladies. They just about preached me to death." He slapped his hat against his thigh. "I must have memorized twelve Bible verses just to keep them searching." Urso was a staunch churchgoer. I'd bet he had memorized the Bible in its entirety by the age of twelve and was just mollifying them.

I offered a supportive smile. "Did you learn anything?"

"Besides my favorite, 'The truth shall set you free'? No." He grimaced. "Not a scrap of clothing. No freshly-dug holes. Nothing. It would take days and crews of people, not to mention a few search dogs with trained noses, to scour the entire area. Needless to say, Mrs. Hildegard was not as specific as she could have been. That woman is a saint and she means well, but she's a little in the clouds, know what I mean? Always sees the best in people. Always hopeful."

Two traits I used to treasure in myself prior to my grandmother's arrest. Could I become that way again?

"Before my adventure on the hill, I did meet with Ed's divorce attorney," Urso went on. "Although he can't divulge the specific details of his confidential meeting, he confirmed that Ed was planning to divorce Kristine."

Rebecca smacked the table with her palm. "So there you have it. Kristine had motive and opportunity. That's like a double whammy, according to Jessica Fletcher. You know, she's the character on —"

"*Murder, She Wrote.*" Urso sighed. "Yes, Miss Zook, it's motive, but not necessarily opportunity. Don't look so smug."

"It's Rebecca, remember? R-e-b-e-c-c-a. Rebecca."

Urso refocused on me. "What's got you looking like the cat that swallowed the canary?"

I told him what Tyanne Taylor had confessed. "Kristine's guilty, U-ey. She lied about her alibi. Please free my grandmother."

"Please," Rebecca echoed.

"Talk to Tyanne."

"Confirm her story."

Urso nodded. "I'll do that." He ran his fingers along the brim of his hat. "Look, Charlotte. When all this is over . . ."

I got the distinct feeling he was preparing to ask me for a date. Panicked, I stood up from the table and clapped him on the arm.

"Thank you for all your hard work."

He jerked his chin as a gesture of good-bye, donned his hat, and left the pub.

As Rebecca and I strolled into the waning sunlight, I felt a heavy weight lift off my heart. Soon, Kristine Woodhouse would be behind bars and my grandmother would be free.

When Rebecca and I arrived at my grand-parents' house, a modest number of Grand-mère's supporters waited in line on the sidewalk as if anticipating a standing-room-only Broadway show. More crowded the yard and had formed a semicircle inside a dozen rented lights that Pépère and Mat-thew were setting on the front yard grass. A picnic table stood in front of the throng — Grandmère's mock-stage, I assumed. Amy and Clair snaked through the crowd hand-ing out red, white, and blue pom-poms, rally signs, and party horns. The chatter was deafening, the cool evening air stimulating.

Rebecca and I ran to the front of the line, and with Mr. Nakamura's blessing, we pressed through the gate into the yard ahead of him.

My grandmother, looking like a human flag in her red ruffled skirt and blue T-shirt with white stars, climbed on top of the picnic table. Through a microphone, she said, "Ladies and gentlemen, may I have your attention? We'll start in five." She spotted me and Rebecca and scrambled off her mock-pedestal. She set the microphone on the table and embraced Rebecca. "Dear child, I am so sorry to hear about your grandmother. I want you to know that we welcome you as part of our growing family."

Tears sprang to Rebecca's eyes. She gripped Grandmère in a bear hug and wept for a long minute, her shoulders shuddering. When she came up for air, she looked sheepishly at me. "I'm not crying about . . . I'm not . . . It's just . . . your grandmother is going to be set free, and I'm so excited."

"I'm what?" Grandmère said.

Words spilled out of Rebecca.

"It's true, *chérie?*" Grandmère looked so excited she could pop.

I nodded.

"Magnifique!" She grabbed my hands and twirled me in a circle. "Oh, this is a red-letter day."

"I need a tissue," Rebecca said.

Grandmère petted Rebecca's back. "Go get one. I won't be speaking for a few minutes."

Rebecca tore up the porch steps and

inside the house.

"You have been blessed with that girl, Charlotte," Grandmère said.

"Don't I know it!"

She clapped her hands. "Urso believes I am innocent now. It is incredible, no?"

I nodded. "He's tracking down Tyanne. With her statement, Kristine will be forced to tell the truth."

Grandmère shook a gnarled finger at me. "You did not have faith. But I —" She jabbed her chest. "I never faltered. The American system works." She pecked me on the cheek, then grabbed the microphone and climbed to her post on top of the picnic table. "Ladies and gentlemen. Three minutes. At the stroke of seven, we will begin."

A huge roar from the crowd echoed through the night. I hoped if Urso was anywhere near, that the noise wouldn't make him divert from his mission to talk to Tyanne and nab Kristine.

At the fringe of the crowd I caught sight of Swoozie Swenten, wearing what seemed to be her uniform of jeans, tight T-shirt and strands of silver jewelry. She was chatting with Vivian. I approached her and said, "Did you hear?"

Swoozie looked bemused. "Hear what?"

"Ed was planning on getting divorced."

Swoozie blanched. "Not for me. I —"

"No one said it was for you," Vivian cut in.

"But you don't look surprised," I said.

Swoozie shrugged. "Ed wasn't happy with Kristine. I knew it. I'm sure she and her pals knew it, too. Ask her." She pointed.

I spun around, expecting to see Kristine, and spotted Tyanne marching toward me, her eyes haunted and red-lined. Her linen jacket was jammed into her bulky purse. The tails of her blouse hung free of her skirt's waistband. If I didn't know her, I would have sworn she was destitute.

I approached cautiously, Vivian at my heels. "Tyanne, are you okay?"

"I can't talk to Chief Urso. I can't." She shook her head erratically.

I reached for her.

"No. Don't touch me! You can't make me. I won't, I won't, I won't." She scurried off, bucking her head against anybody that got in her way. Why had she come to the rally? Why join the others in the yard if not to support Grandmère? She was clutching her purse like a life preserver. Did she have something tucked beneath the wadded up jacket? A gun? A bomb?

Fear peppering my bloodstream, I ran to her and grasped her purse.

"Let go!" she screeched.

"What do you have in there?"

"Nothing. Let go. Let —"

I yanked and stumbled backward with her purse in my hands. Though I despised myself for being such a bully, I rifled through the contents. I found nothing other than personal items. Perplexed, I handed back her purse and said, "Why did you come here? Why are you acting so strangely?"

"I can't tell . . . Tommy . . . I have to get home to my son." She started shivering and hiccupping, and she dropped to her knees.

"Tyanne!" I crouched beside her and clutched her in a bear hug. "Vivian, find Pastor Hildegard." I scanned the crowd for Gretel and her husband. "Over there. Hurry!"

In seconds Vivian returned with them.

"Out of the way, everyone. Give her some room to breathe." Pastor Hildegard knelt beside Tyanne, his chiseled face radiating warmth and concern. Prior to becoming a minister, he had worked in a mental hospital. He clutched Tyanne's hand, told her to focus on his eyes, and whispered words of encouragement. She calmed down, her body stilled.

"I think she might be having a breakdown," I said. Who knew what keeping a lie about murder had done to her, not to mention the scars a tragedy like Hurricane Katrina had left on her delicate soul? "Can you take her home and make sure her husband is there?"

"Of course, poor dear," Gretel said.

"Tyanne, let's stand up, darlin'." The pastor hoisted Tyanne to her feet and he and his wife wrapped their arms around her. Flanking her, they escorted her through the crowd and out the gate, where an even larger crowd had gathered and spilled off the sidewalk and onto the street.

Vivian brushed grass off the back of my blouse and whistled. "What in heck was that about?"

I told her about Tyanne's confession and she whistled again.

"Then it's done," she said. "Urso will arrest Kristine."

I nodded.

"That's wonderful news."

"Charlotte!" Octavia scuttled toward us, the briefcase slung over her shoulder banging her broad hip. "The deal went through."

"What?" I said, delight burbling inside me. I'd had enough bad news for one day. "We got the building?"

"No, just the opposite. You have a new owner."

"But what about our higher bid?" I stammered.

"I'm so sorry. Somehow, Kristine found out you were Q. Lorraine Inc. She turned us down flat."

"How did she find out?" I said. "Only Bozz, you, and I knew."

"And me," Vivian said. "But I didn't blab. What about Matthew?"

He wouldn't have said a word. I wracked my brain. Had I told someone else the name, or was Kristine just clever? Speaking of clever, had Kristine learned that Tyanne had spilled the beans to me? Had she threatened Tyanne? That could have been what had sent Tyanne into hysterics.

The rented lights snapped on, the glare blinding me for a moment. The crowd oohed. Then a spotlight illuminated the stage. Leave it to Grandmère, with her flair for the dramatic, to make a spectacle of the evening. The crowd of onlookers applauded. Their conversation swelled.

I leaned closer to Octavia and shouted to be heard over the din. "Who's the new owner?"

"Providence Creative Arts, or something like that. It, too, is a corporation. I believe it bought the building Vivian is in, as well, and has plans for renovating it."

Vivian moaned. "Well, there you have it. He'll close me down."

"He?" I asked. "You know who it is?"

"The generic *he*," Vivian conceded. "Whoever the new owner is will close me down."

Delilah joined us, her curly hair framing her face with wild abandon. "Who will close you down?"

I said, "Some corporation has bought my building as well as Vivian's."

Vivian said, "He'll boot me out. Rental space in Providence is hard to come by. The new owner probably has an antique store of his own or some scrapbooking shop. Providence Creative Arts. Sounds snooty, doesn't it?" She looked truly devastated. "Where will I move?"

"How about that space above Luigi's restaurant?" I said, "It's empty."

Vivian sneered at the idea. "I warned Ed that this would happen."

A niggling suspicion gnawed at the edges of my mind. Pépère had seen Vivian and Ed arguing. Was it about this very thing? Could Vivian have been so worried about losing her lease that she would have killed Ed to stop the sale? No, Bozz told me that the sale of her building happened before Ed died.

I pinched myself to keep from suspecting everyone. My friends were not guilty. Kristine was. With or without Tyanne's testimony, Urso would be able to put the pieces of the puzzle together now. He had to.

"Did Urso find out anything about the woman roaming the hills?" Delilah asked.

I told them about his adventure with the Bible-quoting volunteers.

Delilah roared. "Too funny. He was toying with them. He knows those verses backward and forward." Delilah knew more about Urso than I did. She and he had dated when she first returned to town. I always wondered why they hadn't gelled but didn't have the guts to ask her. "So that means they didn't find out who was roaming the hills the night Ed died, huh? What if it wasn't Kristine? What if it was Felicia? Remember Kristine saw her digging? She's about the same size as Kristine. What if Felicia had dirt from the hills on her shovel and, to hide the evidence, dug in her backyard to mix up the dirt?"

I raised an eyebrow. "You're starting to sound like Rebecca."

"It had to be Kristine," Vivian said. "Charlotte heard Tyanne's statement. Kristine

378

didn't pick up her child. Kristine killed Ed, then went to the hills to bury the evidence."

"What evidence?" Octavia said. "What statement?"

For the moment, I felt like we were playing the old game Telephone. I filled Octavia in.

"That should be enough for a jury," Vivian said.

"Should be." Octavia glanced at her watch. "Charlotte, I'm going to scoot. I just remembered there's a colleague of mine who might know how to find out who the principals of the corporation are." She hoisted her briefcase strap higher on her shoulder and dashed off.

As she disappeared into the crowd, Meredith joined the group, her face and clothes a dusty mess, her hair, tied in a ponytail, covered with cobwebs.

"Don't you look lovely," I teased.

"I didn't have time to change after cleaning the storage room. You don't think your grandmother will mind do you, Charlotte?"

"Not if you vote for her."

Amy and Clair, rid of all their rally doodads, ran up to Meredith and each grabbed a hand. "You're here!"

"Hey, you two," Meredith said. "If you don't promise to stay out of trouble at

379

school, I'm going to make you help me in the storage room." She plucked a cobweb from her hair and dangled it in front of them.

The twins screeched, "We promise," then ran in circles around her, their giggles filling me with hope for their happiness.

Meredith said to me, "I heard you talking about Kristine. Can we trap her?"

Amy and Clair yelled, "Let's trap her."

My good vibes vanished in an instant. The twins did not need to be part of this conversation. "Girls, go tell Pépère it's time to start. Put Grandmère on the podium. Chant for her like you practiced."

Once they were out of earshot, I drew Meredith, Delilah, and Vivian into a huddle and said, "Trap her how?"

Meredith whispered, "Get her to confess."

"She won't," Vivian cut in. "But a personal sighting by Gretel should be enough."

"True," Delilah said. "Add in Tyanne's lie and —"

"Tyanne didn't lie." A hunched-back woman in a black veil and dress pushed her way into the huddle between Meredith and me.

I peered through the veil. Kristine stared back at me with a malicious leer.

A firecracker exploded and crackled red

380

and blue in the sky. And then another popped. And another. Seven o'clock. Time for Grandmère's speech.

Frizzles of electricity ran up my arms. "What do you mean, she didn't lie? And why are you dressed incognito?"

"She's spying," Vivian said.

"Looking for political pointers," Delilah suggested.

"I hardly need pointers." Kristine's voice dripped with sarcasm.

"Then why?" I demanded. First Tyanne showed up with her bulging bag, and now Kristine, acting shifty. My nerves couldn't take much more. "If you're planning on sabotaging the rally —"

"Oh, please. I wouldn't have made it inside the gate if I had looked like me." Kristine stood to her full height and pushed back the veil. "I will win tomorrow's election on my own merit."

"You will not." Vivian charged at Kristine and stood nose-to-nose with her, her hands balled into fists. "Bernadette will win." I thought for a moment she was going to punch Kristine, but then her fingers relaxed, and she backed up a step. "You'll see. The town wants Bernadette."

"What do you mean, Tyanne didn't lie?" I said returning to my initial question.

"She told the truth," Kristine said.

"You didn't pick up Willamina that night?"

"That's correct."

My mouth dropped open. We had her. She confessed.

"I didn't pick up my daughter because I, too, was meeting with a divorce attorney."

"Who?" I asked. It wasn't like Providence was overflowing with attorneys.

Kristine pointed. "Him!"

CHAPTER 26

"Mr. Nakamura is your lawyer?" I blurted. I glanced at the man and his petite wife who were standing amongst the throng nearest Pépère by the picnic table. All of them were cheering and hooting for Grandmère to take the stage.

"But he's the hardware store owner," Delilah said.

"Not an attorney," Meredith chimed in.

"He can barely write up a contract of sale," Vivian said, sounding a tad snarky.

I was equally as stunned, but worse, I was disappointed. Kristine had a legitimate alibi. And Mr. Nakamura, who I adored, could corroborate it.

As if he knew we were talking about him, Mr. Nakamura glanced our way, offered a cherubic smile, and waved. Like a goofball, I waved back. What else could I do? Charge through the crowd and grill him right then and there?

Kristine said, "He was a lawyer in Cleveland. A few years ago, he decided law was not his calling and moved here. He likes to work with his hands, but he never gave up his practice."

In our many encounters, Mr. Nakamura and I had talked about a lot of things, like how to refinish wood and how to hang a chandelier without electrocuting myself and possibly frying my hair. Why hadn't he mentioned his previous career? How had self-centered Kristine found out? She was the kind of person who would always turn a conversation back to being about her.

"I have granted him permission to give the details to Chief Urso," Kristine went on.

I moaned. She'd granted him permission. Like she was the Queen of England. My blood churned like hot oil ready to burst from a geyser, but I didn't lash out because it was Grandmère's night and she was climbing onto the picnic table.

A cheer broke out from the crowd.

Grandmère tapped the microphone to get everyone's attention. "Ladies and gentlemen, welcome." The microphone hissed. She passed it to Pépère, who fiddled with the switch.

"That's my cue to exit stage left," Kristine said.

"Wait a second." I grabbed her sleeve. "Mr. Nakamura and his wife were seen hustling into their shop a short time after the murder. Is that where you and he met?" She couldn't have met them at the shop. Luigi would have seen her go inside with them. I'd trapped her.

"No, we met at his house at nine thirty, which I believe was about the same time that Ed was . . ." Her hand flew to her mouth to stifle a sob. Phony or not, I couldn't tell. She recovered quickly. "I wanted to keep the meeting hush-hush so Ed wouldn't find out. Mrs. Nakamura was there. She saw me. They left your soirée early."

How could I dispute her? I couldn't remember seeing the Nakamuras during the last hour of the gala opening. "How long were you with him?"

Kristine raised a skeptical eyebrow. "What are you, the district attorney?"

"How long?" Meredith said, edging to my side.

"Ten minutes. Maybe twenty."

That timing was in keeping with what Mrs. Nakamura said. At ten to ten, they had entered their shop to do inventory.

"Ed was selling off building after building," Kristine went on. "He wouldn't tell me why. I thought he had made bad business investments. I didn't know he was planning to divorce me. I had to protect my interests. Married, I would be responsible for any of his losses. I couldn't go through that, no matter how much I loved him." She glowered at me. "And I did love him."

"Why didn't the Nakamuras mention this to Urso?" Vivian asked.

"Or why didn't you?" Delilah pressed.

"Yeah," Meredith said.

I smiled at my little team of assistant district attorneys, proud to call them all friends.

Kristine cocked a hip. "Because Chief Urso never suspected me of killing my husband. He has Charlotte's grandmother as a prime suspect."

"Welcome, everyone!" Grandmère said, with no hissing from the microphone. "The time is now!"

"It sure is." Kristine cackled. "If you'll all excuse me, ladies, I'm off. See you tomorrow when you will bow to me in allegiance." She waltzed away, the black chiffon getup fluttering behind her. If she had flown off on a broom, I wouldn't have been surprised.

When I was able to calm my breathing, I

said, "So if Kristine didn't kill Ed, who did and why?"

"Swoozie Swenten had a lot to gain," Vivian said.

"Maybe that wasn't her that Luigi saw walking down the street with the reporter," Meredith offered. "He's got bad eyes, and he's too vain to wear glasses."

"And I wouldn't rule out Felicia, no matter what she says," Delilah added. "I saw the way she looked at Ed. Have you checked out her alibi with her aunt or reviewed her bookkeeping with her accountant?"

I hadn't. I had taken Felicia at her word. Was I nuts? "Vivian, didn't you see anybody running from The Cheese Shop when you went to your antique store that night?"

She shook her head. "I was too focused on getting a shipment ready for the next day."

"The killer had to be somebody who knew Ed, someone who had a history with him," I said.

"The time is now!" Grandmère repeated, her words echoing over the crowd.

Meredith gripped my arm. "Give it a rest and give your grandmother her due."

She was right. I put my theorizing on hold and turned toward the picnic table.

"I love the town of Providence," Grandmère went on. "We have prospered not only in business, but in education and the arts, as well. They are the three pillars of our society. Your vote for me tomorrow means you want to continue to thrive as a town. You want visitors to come and share in our excitement. Isn't that right?"

Rousing shouts of approval followed.

"Now, I have to admit . . ." Grandmère chuckled. I'd bet she had scripted every laugh and hand gesture for emphasis. "I'm a little nervous, for the first time in my life. I stand before you accused of murder."

"No!" the crowd intoned.

"I'm innocent. If you believe me, then vote for me."

"We believe," the crowd roared like revival attendees.

Out of the corner of my eye, I glimpsed Jordan ambling solo through the knot of people in the driveway. I left my friends and drew up beside him, pivoting so we were both facing my grandmother on stage. "Nice of you to make it."

"Wouldn't have missed it. She's won my vote."

It warmed my heart to hear that. "Where's your sister?"

"She has business to attend to." He looked up at the sky. "Nice night. A gentle breeze, perfect temperature."

"Lovely." The sky was smoky from the firecrackers Pépère had shot off, but stars shone through. However, a breeze was kicking up from the west and a storm was in the forecast.

Jordan slipped his hand around mine and good vibes spiraled up my arm. We stood like that, part of the night's tableau, for a full three minutes.

When Grandmère stopped speaking and the crowd started to disassemble, Jordan pecked me on the cheek.

"What was that for?" I said feeling like a schoolgirl who wouldn't wash her face for a week.

"Couldn't resist. Now, about that date. I missed you at the shop."

"Yes, about that —"

"Saturday, say, eleven?"

I couldn't believe it. We were actually setting not only the day but the time. "You're on!"

"Charlotte!" Pépère charged toward me, his face etched with panic. "Come quickly. Your *grandmère.*"

Jordan and I raced after Pépère. We found Grandmère slumped on the picnic table bench. She wasn't passed out, but she looked dazed. Jordan broke free and knelt

389

beside her. He clutched my grandmother's wrist and put his other hand to her temple. "She's feverish."

"Nerves," my grandfather said.

"Did she eat beforehand, Pépère? She might have low blood sugar."

"She was too excited." He wrung his hands together.

"We need some cold compresses," Jordan said. "And some juice."

As if by magic, Rebecca appeared with a glass of orange juice, wet washcloths, and a couple of Hershey's Kisses. Knowing about my weakness for the darned things, Grandmère always kept a bag of the tasty treats on hand. "Charlotte, take these."

I grabbed the items from her, knelt beside Jordan, and slipped the cool cloths around Grandmère's neck. When she could sit, I peeled off the Hershey's shiny silver wrappers and forced her to eat a couple of them and drink some of the liquid.

When her eyes cleared, she smiled. "Oh, *mon dieu*. I'm so sorry. I'm better now. Don't fuss over me." She waved a hand. "I was so nervous. I could feel my heart . . ." She pounded her chest. "I want to win. I never knew how much."

Pépère sat beside her and clutched her hand in his. "*Mon amie,* you are getting —"

"Don't say it," she snapped. "Do not say, 'You are getting old.' I am seventy."

"Seventy-two," he muttered.

"That is young enough to jump out of a plane and young enough to climb a mountain, so it is not too old to run a town."

Pépère winked at me. "She's better now."

Grandmère batted him on the arm and laughed. "You old goat."

"*Ma-a-a-a-a,*" he droned.

Rebecca giggled.

Jordan and I stood up, moment of crisis averted. He said, "Why don't we take a walk —?"

"Charlotte, *chérie,* I almost forgot." Grandmère scrambled to her feet and clutched my arm. "Delilah needs you."

"What for?"

"Tech rehearsal. Right now. We start full dress rehearsals in two days. Delilah isn't sure she's up to the task. She would never admit it, I know, but will you help her, please? You are so organized. You see the big picture." She released me and folded her hands in prayer. "It would mean so much to me. It is a very difficult production."

I glanced at Jordan, who offered a what-can-you-do smile. "Saturday, eleven," I said. "A walk and a picnic. I make a mean prosciutto and Tomme Crayeuse panini."

"Done." He pecked my cheek again, in front of Grandmère and everybody, and strode across the grass toward his sister's house.

When the moment of swoon passed, I said, "What about the twins, Grandmère?"

"They can stay here for the night. That will give Matthew and Meredith, you know, a little time."

"First, I need to go home and change." Even though my clothes didn't smell of beer any longer, a skirt and blouse weren't the right attire for hanging out in an air-conditioned theater. Providence Playhouse was only a few blocks from my house.

"Bless you. Bless you." Grandmère kissed me on each cheek and gave my chin a tweak.

"May I go with you?" Rebecca said. "I'd love to see what a tech rehearsal is like."

A howling wind kicked up as Rebecca and I rounded the corner to my neighborhood. My house, dark except for the sole kitchen light that I had left on for Rags, looked as ominous as a ghost house in a suspense novel. The willow tree in the front yard waved its arms like a banshee. A few loose shutters jackhammered the sides of the house. I made a mental note to fix them. I wasn't one to let things go to pot. It wasn't a good business practice.

I unlocked the kitchen door, and Rebecca followed me inside. Usually Rags flew out of nowhere and attacked my shoes. "Rags!" I didn't hear him scrabbling down the stairs. "Rags?"

"Could he have gone outside?" Rebecca asked.

"He's an indoor cat."

"But you have the cat door."

"He never uses it." I slapped the granite counter. "Ragsie!" When he didn't come running, I pressed down the lever of the can opener to fake a dinnertime sound. He still didn't tear into the room. A riddling of fear snaked up my back. "Rags!"

"Shhhh," Rebecca said. "Listen."

A faint mewing came from the direction of the laundry room. I hurried down the hall, flew into the laundry room, and whipped open a cupboard that stood slightly ajar. I found Rags huddling beneath a pile of towels and shivering with fright.

I scooped him up and scratched his neck. "Hey, bud, what's up? You didn't hear those firecrackers all the way on this side of town, did you?" Rags was a bit of a scaredy-cat. When he was a stray kitten, he was attacked by a bully of an alley cat. He was taken in by the local animal rescuer, who gave him to me. Not worried about tomcats in my neighborhood, I'd allowed Rags to still be an outdoor cat. That ended one night, after a horrific lightning storm hit, and I'd found Rags howling with terror because he'd been pinned beneath the fallen branch of a red oak. He hadn't had any broken bones, but I'd cried and apologized for weeks. "I'm so sorry, fella, for whatever spooked you." He purred and nuzzled my neck. I said, "Yes, I adore you, too." I handed him to Rebecca. "Crisis averted. I'll be ready in a second. Give him some kisses, will you?"

She retreated to the kitchen, cooing to him like a lover.

I switched on the foyer chandelier and trotted upstairs, the old steps squeaking beneath my weight.

Near the top, my foot skidded on something slippery. I lurched to the right and groped for the railing. Without warning, the banister gave way, opening like a gate and propelling me sideways.

"Yipes!" Heart hammering, I grabbed the rim of the second-floor landing. My feet dangled down. My palms felt slippery. I dug my fingernails into the wood, but I knew I couldn't hold on for long. "Rebecca!" If the post had broken outright, I would have fallen headfirst to the floor. As it was, I could drop and break an ankle, maybe a leg.

Needless to say, I didn't want to suffer either. My pulse thundered in my head as I repeated, "Rebecca."

She appeared, Rags in her arms, and squealed. "Oh, my, what — ?"

"Darned old house needs a major tune-up."

"Do you want a ladder?"

"No use. My feet wouldn't reach. Besides, I can't hold on that long. Grab some pillows from the living room. Pile them on the floor beneath me."

"Will do." She released Rags, who stood beneath me, mewling like crazy.

"It's okay, buddy. I'm okay. Move away. Go sit." He weaved a figure eight beneath me. How I wished he was a dog and obeyed commands. "Rags, split, darn it!" I kicked off my shoes. They hit the floor with a thud-thunk. Rags scampered under the foyer table and peered out at me, his eyes glistening with betrayal.

Rebecca returned with two seat cushions and as many throw pillows as she could manage to squeeze beneath her arms. She nudged my shoes out of the way with her toe, then she tossed the pillows on the floor. "Let go. I'll catch you." She jutted out her thin arms.

If I wasn't so panicked, I would have

laughed. Little ol' her catching slightly big-ger ol' me.

I landed on the pillows, heels first, then on my rear end. Rebecca braced my back. Rags leapt into my lap and dug his claws into my thighs. "Ouch!"

"Are you okay?"

"I'm fine." I booted Rags off of me and struggled to my knees, then my feet. The good news was that everything worked. I'd have some black and blue marks, but noth-ing was broken. The other good news was that I hadn't slammed my head on the hardwood and ended up with a concussion. I'd suffered one years ago in a rousing game of softball. The recovery had taken weeks. "Let's get some ribbon and mark off that section of the staircase. I don't want the girls or Matthew getting hurt."

I returned to the laundry room where I kept my sewing supplies and grabbed a spool of grosgrain ribbon and a washcloth. Giving one end of the ribbon to Rebecca, who remained at the base of the stairs, I gingerly climbed the staircase, hugging the wall. When I reached the top, I bravely ventured toward the banister, looped my end of the ribbon around the newel on the second floor balustrade and said, "Okay, Rebecca, tie it off on that newel down

there." Once that chore was done, I sank to
my knees to mop up whatever was slippery
on the stair thinking the girls, against house
rules, must have sneaked some kind of food
up to their room. But I was wrong. What I
saw made me shudder.

Sawdust.

CHAPTER 27

My stomach did a flip-flop. Either I had really professional termites or somebody had wanted to sabotage me. Because of the marks on the bottom edges of the banister posts, I voted for the latter. That's what must have scared Rags into hiding. Who had broken into my house? Was it with the intent to kill me? I couldn't believe an angry Cheese Shop customer would resort to a home invasion. We had comment cards by the register for passive-aggressive people and, to date, hadn't received one. Did Ed's killer think I was getting too close to the truth? I shuddered at the thought.

I grabbed Rags and said, "Rebecca, let's go. Out of the house. Now!"

"But shouldn't we call Chief Urso?"

"I'll call him on our way to the theater." I would not renege on my promise to Grand-mère.

"You're taking the cat?"

"Rags loves theater."

Trotting down Cherry Orchard, I punched Urso's telephone number into my cell phone. As usual, he did not answer, but I cut him some slack. It was after business hours. I left a message and told him where I was headed.

Halfway to the theater, thunder rumbled and Rags mewed in my arms. "Yes, buddy, a storm is brewing, but don't worry. I've got you, you big baby." I nuzzled his head between his ears and he purred loudly. I hoped the skies wouldn't open up before we arrived at the theater. The town's farmers would welcome a hearty downpour. Rags, Rebecca, and I, on the other hand, wouldn't. We had left the house without an umbrella. I could only hope the rain would pass by the time I returned home later tonight. If I returned home. The twins were staying with Grandmère. Perhaps that was what I would do as well. My insides felt a little queasy even thinking about sleeping in my house alone. Matthew was spending a little one-on-one time with Meredith at her place.

"You know," Rebecca said, huffing beside me, her espadrilles smacking the sidewalk, "I saw something on *Law & Order*. No, that's wrong, it was in a movie. That old one with

Glenn Close."

"*Fatal Attraction?*"

"No, not that one. Anyway, this woman . . . yes, it was Glenn Close and what's-his-name . . ." She snapped her fingers. "Bridges. Jeff Bridges."

"*The Jagged Edge.*" If I didn't have a good mystery to read and shows on the Food Network Channel didn't catch my eye, I would seek out a classic movie for entertainment. At last count, I had watched fifty of the American Film Institute's top one hundred movies.

"Anyway, she figured out what had happened to his wife because of a typewriter, but she couldn't prove it. She was certain that he knew she had figured it out. So she laid in wait for him. He came into her house that night wearing a mask, and he had this big knife and —"

"Rebecca, stop. I don't need you to scare me any more than I already am."

"I just wanted to say that, to prove he was guilty, she had to set him up. Sometimes if there's not enough evidence —"

"I don't know what evidence Urso has," I said. "He hasn't shared any of that with me." Why would he? For over a week, he had believed that my sweet grandmother was guilty. Well, she couldn't be any longer.

She wouldn't have severed my banister.

I cycled through my list of suspects one more time. Other than Kristine, I had three: Swoozie, who wanted Ed's love; Vivian, who had argued with Ed; and Felicia, who was certainly handy with garden tools. Could she wield a saw? And then I added one more suspect: Luigi. He had known Ed during high school. He admitted that he and Ed had been rivals for years. In high school, they'd played sports and probably vied for the same girls or student government positions or, knowing Luigi, prom king. Both had been building up real estate conglomerates in town. But Ed owned more property. Maybe Luigi resented Ed because of that. Maybe he killed Ed to eliminate the competition. Had Luigi put in an anonymous bid on Vivian's building like I had for mine? Ed might have found out and refused to do business with him. The night Ed died, Luigi could have gone outside for his cigarette, caught sight of Ed leaving Fromagerie Bessette, and seen his opportunity.

I nearly stopped in my tracks as I realized the ridiculousness of my theory. Luigi couldn't have gotten hold of one of the olive-wood-handled knives. He hadn't come to the gala opening. And I knew, for a fact, that the murder weapon had come from my shop.

"We're here," Rebecca said, stopping for a moment to catch her breath.

Providence Playhouse was located at the north side of town. It had been built in the late eighteen hundreds and should have been a run-down heap, but with funds raised by my grandmother and her cronies, the playhouse had shored up its aging stage, hung new drapes and stage lights, acquired a state-of-the-art tech board, and restructured its backstage environment, which included fabulous dressing rooms and a full-sized green room. The fundraising campaign for the auditorium, whereby townsfolk could donate a plush loge seat and have a gold plaque with his or her name posted on the seat, had reached its goal of replacing five hundred seats in less than a year. Grandmère had danced around the living room with Pépère to celebrate the campaign's success.

I pushed open the playhouse's gilded doors and stepped into the foyer. The inner doors leading to the theater stood open. The strains of "Good Morning, Baltimore" — in tune — sent chills down my spine. Good chills. *Practice, practice, practice,* was Grandmère's motto, not *practice makes perfect.*

Nothing could ever be perfect, she said, and to strive for perfection was setting oneself up for failure. Was that what I was doing? Practicing out my theories and setting myself up for failure? Had I voiced those opinions around someone who now wanted me dead?

"Wow!" Rebecca whistled as she stepped into the darkened auditorium. "The set is beautiful. And the dancers . . ." She let out another whistle.

On stage, six ballerinas pirouetted in front of a silhouette of the Baltimore skyline. Fake stars lit the gray blue sky overhead. Delilah, dressed in a red leotard and skirt, her hair loose and lush hanging down her back, paced the apron in front of the dancers and banged out the rhythm of the music with a pole. "That's it. *Jeté, chassé,* one-two-three-excellent," she intoned, as if she was channeling Grandmère. Why she needed my moral support was beyond me.

I strode down the left aisle, eager to let her know that I had arrived, but I was distracted by people talking at the back of the theater on the right. I recognized the voices and a prickle of apprehension shot through me. I set Rags on a seat in the front row and said, "Stay here, fella. Rebecca, you too."

She sat obediently and stroked Rags's fur. "Where are you going?"

"Back in a sec." I made a beeline toward the rear of the theater, stopped at the last row, and put my hands on my hips. "What are you doing here?"

Grandmère beamed up at me.

Pépère didn't look nearly so happy. He said, "I couldn't talk her out of coming."

"I thought you were going home to change," Grandmère said.

"Long story. Answer me."

"Isn't it wonderful?" Her eyes glistened with childlike joy.

"The ballet will be great," I conceded.

"No, *chérie*. Isn't it wonderful that I'm going to be set free? My house arrest is over."

"Grandmère, it isn't over until Chief Urso says it's over and he —"

"— doesn't say it's over." Urso cut across the back row of the theater.

I moaned. Why, oh why, had I told him to meet me here? The light from the projection room illuminated the upper half of his angry face and made the badge on his uniform gleam bright gold.

"What in the heck are you doing, Bernadette?" he barked.

She scrambled to her feet. Pépère rose and

propped her at the small of her back.

"If townsfolk see you, they're going to assume I shirked my duty," Urso continued.

"But Charlotte said —"

"She was wrong," he snapped, and glowered at me.

I gulped. Earlier, when Grandmère had swooned following her rally speech, I didn't dare tell her that Kristine had yet another alibi, and that the new one was solid.

"Let's go." Urso crooked a finger, urging my grandmother to move into the aisle. He pulled a set of handcuffs from his pocket.

"You're not going to cuff her!" My voice reached a decibel I didn't know I could hit.

"I'm taking her to jail. She's a flight risk."

"U-ey, be reasonable. She's not running from you. She's feeble."

"I'm nothing of the sort," my grandmother said.

"Please, U-ey —"

"Chief Urso."

"Chief Urso, sorry," I said. "Please give her twenty-four hours more at home. At least until the end of voting day."

"I can't, Charlotte. I have to —"

"No one is going to think you're shirking your duty. For heaven's sake, you never have and you never will. You are Mr. Reliable with a capital R." I restrained his arm.

"Please. Nobody in town believes she killed Ed. And I promise she'll stay put." I crossed my heart like a Girl Scout, hoping to appeal to the former Eagle Scout in him. The ploy worked.

He pocketed the handcuffs. "But she has to leave now."

"I've only seen the first act," Grandmère protested.

"Gee, life's tough, Bernadette," Urso said. "Go home, now, or I'll put you in my cruiser."

"I'm going, Officer." She muttered a few salty French words as she scuttled from between the seats.

Urso clinched Pépère's elbow before he could escape. "I know she's a handful. Do your best."

As Pépère escorted Grandmère from the building, Urso turned to me. He tried his best not to let a smile reach his eyes, which made me feel a whole ton better. He wasn't mad at Grandmère, just flummoxed as to what to do with someone as willful as she was. He said, "What was so important that I had to track you down?"

"Did you meet with Tyanne?"

He nodded. "She changed her claim. She's a wreck and on sedatives. And I verified Kristine's alibi with Mr. Nakamura. He said client privilege prohibited him from telling me anything further." He perched on the arm of the loge chair. "Your turn. What else have you done tonight to impede my investigation?"

"I'm not impeding anything. I'm getting close. I know that because someone sabotaged my house."

"Sabotaged?"

"Whoever it was cut the posts of my banister. It gave way. I almost —" I started to shiver.

"Let's go."

Minutes later, beating out the rain by seconds, I entered my house through the kitchen door, with Rags tucked under my arm. Urso raced in behind me and ordered me to sit at the kitchen table while he took a look-see. He returned, a frown creasing his forehead.

"House is clear."

"But you saw the flakes of sawdust on the floor."

He nodded.

I said, "Someone cut the wood deliberately."

"I'll repair it for you." He flipped a chair around and straddled it. "In the meantime, who would do such a thing?"

"Felicia comes to mind," I said, putting

voice to my thoughts. "She's handy with tools. Maybe she thinks I have a photographic memory and could figure out if something was doctored in the museum ledger that I rifled through. And . . ." I paused for effect. "I think she lied about her alibi."

"How so?"

"She told me she met with her sister Lois that night, but her sister said she was out of town visiting their aunt. Felicia wasn't happy when I told her what Lois said."

"You told her —"

"And then, earlier today, Felicia and Lois dropped by The Cheese Shop, and Felicia made certain that Lois revised her story, to the minute. I think Lois is lying."

"Okay." Urso took a pen and a pad of paper from his pocket and jotted notes. "Who else is on your suspect list?"

"That tour guide, Swoozie Swenten. She was Ed's business partner. I think she was in love with him. Maybe Ed was getting divorced so he could marry her and then reneged. And Vivian Williams was having lease trouble with Ed. I can't see that as a reason to kill him, especially since her lease deal was closed the day before he died. Killing him wouldn't have changed anything. And then there's Luigi Bozzuto, but I can't figure out how he would have gotten hold of the murder weapon."

Urso leaned forward, forearms on his thighs. "You've been busy working those little gray cells."

"Don't patronize me. What do you have?"

He jammed his lips together, flipped his notebook shut, and pocketed it.

"Not sharing, huh?"

He chuckled. "Look, I want you to stay with your grandmother tonight. I'll shore up your banister, and tomorrow we'll have a better idea of how to proceed, okay?"

I nodded. I was exhausted and ready for a good night's sleep. Rags and I left with an umbrella in hand.

Grandmère and Pépère fussed over me like I was three years old, and I let them.

I woke to a stream of sunlight peeking through the split in the yellow-striped drapes. Years ago, Grandmère had redecorated my old room, changing it from turquoise, my favorite color, to buttercup yellow, but it still smelled of lavender and made me feel safe. I rose and stretched, then braced myself for a long Tuesday. Voting Day. Anything could happen.

After a warm shower, I saw the twins off to school, bid Grandmère and Pépère goodbye, and with Rags slung over my shoulders, returned home. Urso had set the banister back in place and replaced my grosgrain ribbon with crime scene tape. He hadn't been by yet to do the repair.

I set out food for my edgy Ragdoll cat, but he shunned it and roamed the house like a curious detective. I ate an English muffin with a slice of tomato and melted Collier's Cheddar and drank a quick cup of coffee, then I changed into a pair of coral chinos and a matching ribbed V-neck. I added sparkly earrings, dabbed on some blush, and hurried to work.

By the time I arrived at Fromagerie Bessette, the shop was awhirl with activity. Rebecca stood behind the cheese counter, prettifying gift baskets. Matthew, the sweetheart, was tending to cheese orders. While waiting, customers talked about who they had voted for. I didn't hear anyone admit to having voted for Kristine. Most were certain that Grandmère would win.

Leaving Matthew and Rebecca in charge of the shop, I retreated to the kitchen and, for the next hour, baked fresh quiche. Afterward, I headed to the office and busied myself with writing a newsletter and calling our vendors and the local farmers to ensure this week's deliveries. I had a quick chat on the telephone with Jordan that made me warm all over. He told me he was looking forward to tasting my panini. I was looking forward to another taste of his delicious lips. I didn't mention the banister incident. I didn't need him to worry if, indeed, all I had were very hungry termites.

Midmorning, Rebecca rapped on the office door and hovered in the arch. Rags bounded from my lap and rubbed his head up against Rebecca's ankles. "Not you." She wagged her finger at him. "No more treats for you." He hadn't eaten breakfast at home, probably still sensing the stranger's intrusion, so I'd asked Rebecca to feed him at the office. Like a silly goose, she had hand-fed him. If I wasn't careful, I was going to have a spoiled cat on my hands. I had to get him back on a schedule fast.

"You know," Rebecca said. "I thought about you all night. There was this *CSI* on, and it was about someone poisoning somebody else."

"What does poison have to do with me?"

"The victim on *CSI* had put two and two together. The killer couldn't let him live." Rebecca stepped into the office and perched on the end of my cluttered desk, while using her hands to work through her theory. "See, I got to thinking, what if Tyanne,

411

knowing Kristine was otherwise occupied, actually killed Ed? I mean, her husband could have watched the children, right? He wasn't at the gala opening. And what if Tyanne thinks you've put it all together, so she sabotaged your house?"

I hadn't even considered Tyanne. Should I have?

"But then I thought, who did Gretel see on the hill?" Rebecca popped off the desk and left the room, her question creating a void I couldn't fill.

I closed the office door and returned to the desk chair. Rags leapt into my lap and kneaded my abdomen with his claws. I ignored him, laced my fingers behind my neck, and looked up at the whirling ceiling fan, trying to clear my head. Who did Gretel see on the hill? Certainly not Tyanne. She was shorter and wider than Kristine. Felicia was about the same size. So were a whole slew of people in town.

Someone knocked on the door.

I sat upright. "Come in, Rebecca."

Meredith rushed in, once again covered in cobwebs. She held up a book. "You've got to see this."

CHAPTER 28

Curiosity didn't propel me from my office chair. Meredith often brought me rare books. She wanted me to become an aficionado like her. She often talked about starting up a book club. "Is it something you . . . ahem . . . borrowed" — I cleared my throat deliberately — "from Felicia's museum?"

"No, it's from the room I've been cleaning out at school. It's a Providence High School yearbook."

"So?"

"I've found yearbooks dating back seventy years. I've been thinking I might scan pictures of the fun stuff about people still living in Providence. You know, prom queens and kings, Most Likely to Succeed, Most Persevering. I thought I'd make a video collage, and then show it at our next fundraiser."

"What an undertaking."

"You're telling me, but I think for historical value, it could be really cool. Maybe some of the old coots would donate just to get the picture out of circulation."

"Why would they — ?"

"A ton of them were really geeky back then."

"That's blackmail," I teased.

"Sue me." She winked. "So, speaking of geeky, which is why I'm here . . ." She opened the book and set it on my desk. "While I was hunting, look what I found. A picture of Ed and Vivian, voted Most Perfect Couple." Meredith snorted. "It had to be a joke of course. Look at Vivian."

I peered at the picture. Vivian, as thick as a sparkplug, was wearing a plaid skirt and sweater, knee socks, and big glasses. She had a bow in her hair and braces that glimmered in the sunlight — a nerd by all accounts. She stood stiffly beside Ed, who, though gaunt and spooky during his last days on earth, had been handsome in high school. He had that jock look, with strong cheekbones, smoky bedroom eyes, and a smile that would make girls weak at the knees. Slap a letter jacket on him, and he could have been cast as the cocky hero in any Hollywood movie. How life had changed him. Life with Kristine.

"I wonder how Vivian felt about being

mocked like this?" Meredith said.

I ran my finger around the borders of the picture and something clicked in my mind. I never would have suspected that Vivian and Ed were the same age. With her taut body and creamy skin, she looked way younger than fifty. Ed had been going to seed. Yet, there they were, a couple. I should have put it together earlier. Luigi said he and Ed had been teammates, and Vivian admitted that Luigi had tried to date her in high school.

"Do you think someone made them pose like this?" Meredith asked. "They're standing so . . ." She mimed the awkward pose. "Some jerk on the yearbook staff, I'd bet. Thank God whoever it was didn't make them kiss or something."

I remembered kissing my first boy about that age. He was always tugging my hair and telling me I was ugly, ugly, ugly. I stared again at the picture of Ed and Vivian. Had he teased her mercilessly and made her adore him? She looked like she might have welcomed a kiss. In the picture, she was gazing longingly at him. What if, after all these years, she had remained in love with him?

"Kids can be such toads," Meredith said.

I shifted in my chair as comments Vivian had made over the past few days started to make sense. She said that Ed and Kristine were nothing alike, that they didn't belong together, they were oil and water. Did she feel that she and Ed were better suited? Had she pined for him? When I'd asked her about her tiff with Ed, she said he could be such a toad when it came to her future. What if she had meant her future with him? She could have found out that he met with a divorce lawyer. What if he made her think she could win his heart, but at the last minute, he sold off her building, her livelihood? A final slap in the face.

"Meredith, what if — ?"

Meredith's cell phone rang. "Hold that thought." She fished her phone from her purse and answered. "Yes? Oh, no." Her face turned pale. She snapped the phone shut. "It's the school. There's a plumbing problem in the storage room. I have to go." She reached for the yearbook.

I grabbed hold. "Do you mind leaving it? I'd love to look through."

"Sure. No need to let another book get ruined by a stupid flood." She ran out muttering, "If it's not one thing, it's another."

As I heard the grape-leaf-shaped chimes tingle and the front door slam shut, another image flashed in my mind. I shouted, "Rebecca!"

That first day after the murder, Vivian had tootled into The Cheese Shop and had prodded me into investigating the crime. She was the one who had suggested Kristine wanted to win the election so badly that she would have killed Ed and set up my grandmother to take the fall. Eager to latch on to a theory, I had agreed, but now, something wasn't synching in my mind. Something about the afternoon when Bozz and I had taken platters of cheese to Europa Antiques and Collectibles for Vivian's auction event.

I replayed the sequence in my mind, paying attention to detail as if I were logging cheese data into my brain. We set out the platters. We searched for knives. We found them among Vivian's collectibles — her hope chest — located in the antique hutch. There were yearbooks and other curios there. I recalled the spines of the books, *Providence High School*. Why keep them so close at hand? Mine were at home. Why were hers at her shop? So she could view them often? And the napkins that she brought out. The moment would have flitted from my memory bank if she hadn't seemed embarrassed when I admired the hand-embroidered *W*s on them. She had made a point of telling me they stood for her married name, a marriage that had lasted less than a year. What was the real story? Had she actually made them because she fantasized that one day she would become Mrs. Ed Woodhouse? Was that why her own marriage had fizzled?

"Rebecca!" I called.

She poked her head in the doorway. "Sorry, customers were clamoring for Morbier. We've run out, and —"

"Where's Matthew?"

"Visiting local vintners." She glanced at her watch. "He should be back soon."

I gathered the yearbook under my arm, petted Rags once for luck, and dashed from the office.

"What's going on?" Rebecca scuttled after me. "Did you find a clue?"

I explained my theory as I rooted through my purse for my cell phone. "And then there's the fact that Vivian really shouldn't drink. She alluded to her limit a couple of times, once at her store and again at the wine tasting in the annex. I hadn't thought much of it. She could be one of those people who loses all inhibitions after a small amount of alcohol."

Rebecca snapped her fingers. "You're saying she drank too much the night of the gala opening because she was watching Ed

Woodhouse flirt with all those women, and it drove her crazy."

"Exactly."

At the end of the evening, after Grandmère and Kristine had stormed from the shop, Vivian had confronted Ed, and he had blown her off. She had retreated to the rear of The Cheese Shop for a bite of ham and pineapple quiche. Had she been unable to console herself with food? Had she, in a fit of passion, grabbed a knife from my display table and gone after him? On the day that I'd intruded on Meredith and Matthew, I recalled Vivian saying to Jordan that extraordinary circumstances made a person do extraordinary things. I thought the comment had held an undercurrent directed at Jordan and his past, but perhaps Vivian had been referring to herself. I headed for the front door.

"Where are you going?" Rebecca said.

"To Europa Antiques and Collectibles."

"Are you nuts?" Rebecca raced past me and blocked my exit. She bolted the door, flipped the open sign to *Closed,* and steered me back to the cheese counter. "Call Chief Urso."

"I need more proof. I can't risk him getting angry at me and locking up Grandmère. If I go over to the antique shop, maybe I can drum up some."

"You don't mean you'll frame her, do you?"

"No, of course not. I'm going to take pictures with this." I waggled my cell phone. "The day we set up the event at her shop, Vivian's office was a mess. I remember thinking that the town of Providence would find that hysterical, since she's such a neat-nik. Anyway, there were crumbs on the floor."

"Crumbs?"

"Pie crust crumbs. She ate ham and pineapple quiche right after her to-do with Ed. I'll bet pie crust crumbs clung to her dress."

Someone rapped on The Cheese Shop door — the elderly animal rescuer accompanied by a cluster of various sized dogs, all straining at their leashes. I pointed to the *Closed* sign. "Sorry, emergency," I yelled through the glass. "Come back later."

The rescuer, a patient sort, gave a mush signal to her pack and scuttled off.

"You're thinking the crumbs fell on the floor?" Rebecca said.

"Right."

"But that only establishes that Vivian was here and went there, and we already know Luigi saw her go to her shop."

She was right, blast it. "Okay, let's say she ran from the scene. Realizing there was blood on her dress, she raced to her shop. In a panic, she undressed — the crumbs fell to the floor. She stuffed the dress into the bureau. She wore blue that night, remember?"

"She always wears blue." Rebecca stabbed a finger at me. "She told me once it matched her eyes."

"Well, I saw something blue hanging out of the opened bureau drawer."

"Oh, my! But what did she put on?"

"Her raincoat." I ticked off my thoughts on my fingertips. "Remember she was wearing a raincoat at the crime scene?"

"She hadn't worn it to the gala event."

"Right."

Rebecca frowned and shook her head. "What about Gretel seeing someone on the hill that night? The timing's all off."

My confidence waned until another thought occurred to me. "If Vivian had stuffed the dress in the bureau, wouldn't there be trace evidence of blood in the drawer?"

Rebecca clapped me on the arm. "*CSI* techs would be so proud of you!"

Heck, I was proud of me!

"Call Chief Urso," Rebecca said.

"You call him. Tell him I'm on my way to the antique store." I pushed past her and unlocked The Cheese Shop door.

She barged in front of me again and grasped my wrist. For a wisp of a girl, she had a steel grip. I was strong, too, a result of hoisting dozens of seventy-five-pound wheels of cheese daily, but I couldn't wrench free.

"Let me go," I said. "You watch the shop."

"I'm coming with you. Vivian might try to murder you. She sawed through your banister."

"To injure me. To incapacitate me. To give herself time to get out of town. If she'd wanted me dead, she would have killed me by now." I really believed that. We had been friends too long. "I think Vivian realized that I would be able to put all the clues together, perhaps as she swept up the crumbs, or when I asked her to corroborate what time she had visited her shop, or when Gretel revealed that she had seen someone digging. That's why she persisted in making us suspect Kristine. Now, let me pass, Rebecca. I won't endanger you."

"Danger's my middle name." My sweet young assistant got a bullish look, something I'd bet she had learned from her taciturn father. Willowy or not, she was not going to let me leave the shop alone.

How could I refuse?

Minutes later, Rebecca and I peered through the window at Europa Antiques and Collectibles.

"I don't see signs of Vivian anywhere," I whispered. "She's not standing at the register."

"There aren't any customers, either. The place looks filled with boxes. Like she's leaving town. Maybe she's in the storage room."

A couple of tourists in tie-dyed clothes who were window-shopping at Mystic Moon craned their heads to gaze at us.

I smiled and tapped my watch. "Thought the shop was closed already. It's not." I cranked the door handle and slipped inside. Luckily, Vivian hadn't hung any cute little wind chimes over her door. Nothing announced our entrance except the squeak of hinges in need of oil.

As Rebecca closed the door, she bumped into my backside. "Sorry," she whispered. "What now?"

"We sneak into the office and poke around."

"What if she's inside? The door's ajar."

"I'll act like I'm in the market for . . ." I glanced around the shop. A lamp for the twins' bedroom? A table for the foyer?

"An old cash register," Rebecca chimed in. "That would look really good in The Cheese Shop, don't you think?"

I glowered at her. "We're not buying anything."

"I know."

I weaved through the clutter of antiques toward Vivian's office and, on a whim, made a detour to the antique hutch. I opened the cabinet door and rooted through Vivian's memorabilia. I snagged her copy of the Providence High School yearbook and flipped through the pages. Dozens of students had written good luck wishes for the future. I stopped on the picture of Vivian and Ed as Most Perfect Couple and my mouth fell open. Across the bottom left corner, in tight, barely legible handwriting, was scrawled: *I promise to be there for you forever. Ed.*

"What the heck does that mean?" Rebecca peered over my shoulder. "Be where, to do what exactly?"

"I don't have a clue." And I wasn't about to waste time trying to divine words from the past — I'd done that too many times in my own life, with items left to me by my parents. I stuffed the yearbook back in place, hurried to the office, and nudged the door open. The room stood empty. The floor was clean. The drawers to the bureau were closed. Teacups and teapots lined shelves behind the desk. "Stand guard, Rebecca, and if Vivian appears, say something."

"Like what?"

"Ask her to . . . I don't know, show you . . . a cash register. When she does, I'll slip out of the office and act like I was in the restroom."

Rebecca pointed at me. "You're devious."

I had never thought of myself that way, but perhaps I was. Once in high school, I had stolen out of my grandparents' house at two A.M. Another time, I had cheated on a history test. And I knew how to change the odometer reading on my car.

I slinked across the hardwood floor and opened the top drawer of the bureau. A royal blue tablecloth stared back at me. The tail ends must have been hanging out the other day. I searched beneath the cloth. No blue dress. But I did spot pie crust crumbs at the base of the drawer. A forensic lab would be able to corroborate that the sampling came from one of my pies. I seasoned every crust with white pepper to give it an extra zing.

I fished my cell phone out of my trouser pocket and flipped it open. Using the camera tool, I took quick pictures of the crumbs.

I opened an email to send the pictures to Urso, but before I pressed send, my gaze landed on Vivian's gym bag tucked into the corner of the room behind the desk. Jutting from a break in the zipper was a wooden handle attached to something shiny with serrated teeth. A saw. Would sawdust from my banister still cling to the metal?

As I tiptoed closer to inspect, the office door squeaked open.

"Rebecca," I whispered. "Take a look at —"

"I'm afraid she's indisposed," Vivian said, her words clipped and hard.

CHAPTER 29

I spun around and stumbled backward, my rear end hitting the edge of Vivian's desk as she brandished one of the Bakelite carving knives. Lucky for me, she wasn't as deft as a ninja. In fact, she looked nervous. Perspiration soaked the underarms of her summery dress, and her forehead glistened with moisture. But her eyes bristled with manic energy. Nervous or not, she meant to scare me. Maybe kill me.

Keep calm, I told myself, but despite my warning, my heart had crawled up the back of my head and was hammering an escape route through my ear. "What did you do to Rebecca? Did you stab her?" I didn't see any blood on the knife, but I wasn't brave enough to draw nearer and take a closer inspection.

"I thought I heard something while I was doing inventory in the storage room. I was surprised to see your little helper standing by my office door like a cigar store Indian. I captured her and put her in the storage shed. Don't worry. There's air. She won't die of suffocation. I grabbed this" — she waggled the knife — "when I noticed someone had been rummaging through my things. Was it you?"

Darn. I wished I'd had the wherewithal to grab one of the knives. I'm quite talented with knives. As a girl, I loved to whittle. "How did you get Rebecca away from the door without making a sound?"

Vivian wiggled a bare foot. "Stealth."

"She still would have screamed at the sight of you."

"She was text messaging, the silly goose."

Hopefully texting Urso. "Did you hurt her?"

"I might have squeezed the air out of her for a second. I'm very strong, thanks to my taskmaster trainer." Vivian flexed her biceps. "Poor Rebecca. I can only imagine how she'll feel when she wakes, tied up in that musty old storage room with a gag in her mouth. Even I get a little claustrophobic in there." She drew nearer.

I detected the fermented odor of wine coming from her, and I tensed. Had she been drinking?

I screwed up some courage and held out

my hand. "Why don't you give me that knife and let's talk?"

She shook her head. "By the way, I locked the front door. We don't want any shoppers to interrupt us, do we?"

I sure did.

"Give me the knife, Vivian. Please."

She glanced at it again as if admiring the gleam of the blade. "I don't want to go to jail."

"You don't want to go to jail," I echoed. After Creep Chef took off for Paris, rather than sink into the mire of believing I wasn't good enough for him, or anybody else for that matter, I went to a therapist who made me embrace change as a great opportunity. One of the techniques the therapist used was repeating what I said so I felt I had been heard. I tried to apply that technique now.

"It was Ed's fault," Vivian said.

"Ed's fault. Got it."

"He made promises. Back in high school."

"He promised to be there for you forever."

"How did you know that?" Vivian peeked over her shoulder at the main room of Europa Antiques and back at me, then cocked her head. I'd seen a raptor do the very same thing in *Jurassic Park* before attacking the humans. Her eyes grew hard. "Have you been reading my journals?"

"No. I . . ." I scrabbled for the right words. "You said something to me the other day. That Ed and Kristine were oil and water. I assumed you meant that you and he weren't. That you and he were made for each other."

Tears flooded the corners of her eyes. "We were lovers that summer right after high school graduation."

She had to be kidding. I had seen the picture in the yearbook. Ed was definitely *not that into her.*

"He promised when we graduated college that he would come back to me, but when he returned, he dismissed me."

"You'd planned out your life," I reasoned. "You saw a future with him. You embroidered those napkins."

She nodded. "He started dating everyone but me. I told myself I could wait. He wasn't marrying any of them. Men need to sow their oats. I bided my time."

I glanced around the office looking for something that I could use to restrain Vivian. There weren't any ropes, no packing string. I considered racing to the gym bag and grabbing the saw to defend myself, but what if the zipper stuck? I didn't want to make her lash out prematurely with that darned knife. "And then Kristine came along," I prompted, hoping Vivian would continue talking long enough for me to forge a plan.

"They weren't right for each other," she hissed. "Just because they were both born with money didn't mean they were compatible." She had said something similar that night at the gala opening. Why hadn't I picked up on it then? "Ed belonged with me, but she . . . she swayed him. She fluttered around like a stupid peacock, and for some reason, he liked that."

A pounding came from the back of the shop. Then a frantic scream. Rebecca must have awakened.

Vivian smiled. "Must have freed herself from her bonds. I never was good at tying knots. But no matter. She won't get out. I bolted the door. I also took her cell phone, erased all texts, and stowed it in my purse for safekeeping, if you were wondering about that."

I wasn't. Guess I should have been. I scanned the room for an object that I could use to disarm Vivian. Hurling something was out of the question. I stunk at softball, hence the concussion I'd suffered in high school. I would miss my mark. Besides, getting whacked by china teacups probably wouldn't make Vivian drop the knife.

"It didn't take long before Ed realized he

had made a mistake." Vivian tilted her head. "He confided that he was sorry he ever married Kristine. Even sorrier that he got her pregnant."

Poor Willamina, plagued by a self-indulgent mother and a father who hadn't given a whit.

"We were friends, you see," Vivian went on. "Ed told me everything."

Except that he loved you.

I didn't say what I was thinking out loud. As Tyanne would say, I hadn't just fallen off a turnip truck.

"But Ed liked how Kristine bullied the townfolk. He loved power. He thrived on it. It made him feel like a big man." Vivian licked her lips.

"Want a glass of water?" I said. A pitcher of water and an empty glass sat on her desk, out of reach. I didn't, for one minute, believe dousing her with water would make her melt like the Wicked Witch in *The Wizard of Oz,* but it might disorient her. If only —

"No!" she snapped and took a step closer.

Rebecca continued to pound and scream. I wondered why the owner in the Mystic Moon next door didn't come over to complain until I remembered it was voting day. She must have gone to post her ballot.

"It wasn't like that for Ed in college," Vivian droned on. "He was a small fish in a big pond. He came back to Providence, and with Kristine by his side, he was a big man on campus all over again. When he grew tired of her, he started wandering."

"But he didn't cheat with you. Why not?"

Vivian gave a look that could drill a hole in the hull of a ship.

I swallowed hard and kept my cool. Provoking her probably wasn't the best idea.

"He told me he cared for me too much to have an affair. He was a liar, of course. I would have accepted an affair and he knew it, but he rejected me. I couldn't sleep. Every moment of the day I was thinking about him being with somebody else. It hurt so much, I couldn't breathe. At the gala opening, I —"

Rebecca's pounding stopped. I wondered if she had run out of energy or had given up. I wouldn't blame her if she had. At twenty-two, I would have curled into a ball and admitted failure.

Vivian said, "I drank too much that night."

"You shouldn't drink."

"I've only had one glass today."

She shouldn't have any, not if it made her want to slash someone to ribbons with a knife. I said, "Why were you drinking in the middle of the day?"

"I have nothing to live for."

"That night you killed Ed —"

"He . . . he . . ." She chewed her lips as if trying to keep a flood of anger from erupting from her soul. "Seeing Ed, with all those women, acting so cavalier."

The word cavalier made a proverbial lightbulb go off in my head. If I could reach the floor lamp to my right and use it like a lance . . .

I inched toward it. "You grabbed the olive-wood-handled cheese knife."

"I tucked it up my sleeve."

"After you fought, you followed him outside."

"I yelled at him. I don't remember what came out of my mouth. He grabbed my shoulders and shook me. He said he sold my building just to see if I would finally leave town. He was . . . horrible."

"Horrible," I echoed.

"Take it back," she snapped.

"What?"

"He wasn't horrible."

"But you said —"

"Take it back!" She lunged at me with the knife. Her toe caught on the carpet. She teetered.

I dodged her and raced to the lamp. I batted off the lampshade, and using the stem like a medieval lance, I rushed her and whacked the knife out of her hand. Vivian tried to grab the lamp pole but missed. I flailed it again.

She threw her arms up in defense.

I withdrew but kept the lamp aimed. "You sawed through my banister. You endangered not only me but my family."

"I didn't mean . . . I couldn't hurt you. I . . . don't hit me!" She slumped to the ground. The skirt of her dress fell in a puddle around her knees, as if she had deflated without the wind of righteousness to billow her sails. "The night Ed died, I had a dream," she whispered. "I was hugging a small carcass wrapped in swaddling clothes. It was Ed. He apologized. For taking away my building. For stripping me of my pride. He said I was the best woman he had ever known. I believed him, but it was too late. Too late." She moaned. "I didn't mean to hurt you or implicate your grandmother, Charlotte."

I believed her.

Risking everything, unable to see an old friend in such bitter pain, I set the lamp aside, crouched beside her, and wrapped my arm around her shoulders.

"Kristine was supposed to be the suspect,"

she whispered. "I'm so sorry. So —"

Rebecca burst into the room, a candlestick raised over her head, and screamed like a banshee. She skidded to a stop and looked at me, at Vivian, and back at me. She lowered her weapon. "I guess you have it under control."

I wasn't sure what I had under control, but I didn't think Vivian was going to be a problem any longer. She buried her head against my arm. Her tears drenched my sleeve. "How'd you get out?"

Rebecca grinned. "You'll be so proud of me. I used the old refrigerator-at-the-cheese-shop technique. I boosted myself onto one of those antique tables and jumped on the door handle. It broke off and I pushed it out the other side with this." She brandished the candlestick. "I saw someone do that on —"

"— *CSI.*"

"*Magnum, P.I.*"

Television was educational after all. Who knew?

"Let's call Chief Urso."

CHAPTER 30

Urso charged into Europa Antiques and Collectibles with a scowl on his face and his gun drawn. His young, gangly deputy bounded in at his heels.

"Put your guns back in your holsters, gentlemen," I said, and beckoned Urso toward the office.

He told his deputy to hang back, and he crowded into the doorway beside me.

Rebecca was standing guard by Vivian, who remained on the floor, running her fingers back and forth along the hem of her dress while humming the Providence High School fight song.

In a hushed tone, I explained everything to Urso. Vivian's motive, her emotional admission, and what evidence corroborated my theory: the trail of quiche crumbs, the saw in the gym bag, the old yearbooks with promises from Ed to love Vivian forever, the embroidered napkins, Vivian in a raincoat at the scene of the crime. I told him why I thought her bloody dress had been shoved into the drawer but removed.

"Charlotte, what were you thinking?" Urso said. "I warned you not to take the law in your own hands. I . . ." He rubbed his hand down his neck. "You put Rebecca and yourself in harm's way."

He was right, and it bothered me that I had done so, but my grandmother's freedom — her reputation — had been at stake. "I've got to tell Grandmère."

"Not until I say so."

"But —"

"No." When Urso set his mind to it, he could be so stubborn. "Now, explain to me why Vivian let me suspect your grandmother."

"She didn't mean to incriminate Grandmère. She kept trying to implicate Kristine. She hated her so much and couldn't believe Ed would break his promise. She had such dreams."

Urso nodded, then ambled into the office and crouched beside Vivian. She didn't stop singing. Calmly, slowly, he explained her rights to her. "Do you understand, Miss Williams?"

Vivian glanced at me, her face smooth and unworried. "You didn't find the most important piece of evidence, Charlotte. Would you like to know where it is?"

"Your dress?"

She nodded. "I took the dress and I wrapped it in a tarp, and I buried it."

My heart clenched with sadness. "Would you show Chief Urso where?"

Vivian held out her hand. Like a gentleman, Urso helped her to her feet, and the two of them set off on their journey. His deputy trailed behind.

Rebecca and I returned to The Cheese Shop, forbidden from telling anyone what had happened until Urso came back with news. In the course of two hours, we cleaned every shelf in the shop, baked four quiches, and jotted out an inventory of the contents of the refrigerator. We had at least twice as many customers as usual because it was voting day and the townsfolk wanted to give us updates on the exit polls, most of which were favorable for Grandmère. I wouldn't rely on their say-so, of course. People could lie about anything.

When the grape-leaf-shaped chimes announced Urso's arrival, I perked up.

Urso looked exhausted, his face and clothing dusted with dirt. "We found the dress in a totally different spot than Gretel Hilde-

439

gard had thought." He shook his head. "That woman."

"She meant well." I crossed to the cheese counter, spread a thick swatch of apricot jam on a chunk of sourdough bread, and topped it off with an artisanal chèvre made by Urso's mother's farm, Two Plug Nickels. "Eat this. It'll give you a boost. Rebecca, grab a bottle of Orangina for the officer." I happened to know Orangina was Urso's favorite beverage, next to wine, but while on duty, he couldn't drink a glass of pinot grigio.

He downed half of his snack in one bite and made an appreciative hum. "This tastes great. I've got to tell my mom about adding the jam."

"She knows."

"Hmph." He polished off the rest of his meal, gulped down half of the Orangina, and set the bottle on the counter.

Rebecca disposed of the trash in the bin beyond the counter and handed him a napkin. "How's Vivian?"

"I've put her in jail."

"Do you think a county judge will be lenient?" We only had one judge in Providence, a seasoned female who had never presided over a murder trial. I couldn't imagine she'd start now. "I mean, will the judge allow a plea of insanity?"

"We'll have to see. I've asked a psychiatrist to take a look at Vivian and make an assessment."

"She wasn't faking, as far as I could tell," Rebecca said.

I grinned. Not only was she a master sleuth, now she was a certified physician. "Is it all right if I call our lawyer on her behalf?"

Urso nodded. "Something definitely snapped, but she is guilty, and she'll serve time somewhere." He flung the napkin into the garbage bin. "On the other hand, your grandmother isn't guilty."

"So, now, I can tell her." I dashed toward the front door.

Urso blocked my exit. "Not so fast. This is the part of my job I enjoy. You have to keep your mouth shut until I share the news, otherwise I tell her what you and Miss Zook —" He cleared his throat. "What you and Rebecca have been up to. Agreed?"

"Agreed."

"Agreed!" Rebecca whipped off her apron and wiggled her fingers for me to give her mine.

I did, then I flipped the *Closed* sign on the door and skipped out after Urso.

Townsfolk collected behind us, as if joining a citizens' army. A few who had seen Urso exiting Europa Antiques and Collectibles with Vivian in handcuffs started saying what they believed had happened.

Luigi caught up with me at the front of the line. "What's going on? Where's Vivian?"

I could tell by the look in his eyes that he knew something had happened to the woman he loved, and it pained my heart, but I wouldn't break my vow of secrecy until Urso spoke to Grandmère. "I can't say."

Luigi kept pace with the crowd, his face somber.

Block by block, the assembly grew into a swell of voices, each with a newer rendition of the story. By the time we arrived outside Grandmère's gate, the group had stopped theorizing and was only chanting, "Bernadette! Bernadette!"

As Urso pushed through the gate, with Rebecca and me scuttling behind him, the townsfolk went silent, no doubt hoping to hear a snippet of what the real story was.

Grandmère emerged through the front door. She paused on the porch, the skirt of her red silk dress dancing in the breeze, and she tilted her head, as if listening for the song of the morning lark but not hearing it.

I tried to make eye contact and give my

442

grandmother a heads-up, but she wasn't looking at me, only Urso.

After a moment, she yelled, "Etienne!" then, bracing herself, she jutted her arms out in front of her, wrists together, ready to be hauled off.

Pépère shot through the door, an apron tied around his waist, a spatula in one hand, a tray of his mascarpone chocolate chip cookies in the other, the aroma amazing and triggering all sorts of memories in me. The day my parents died. The first day of grade school. The first play I had ever been in. Pépère stared at Grandmère, her arms thrust forward, then at Urso, and his face wilted. I could only imagine the horrible expression Urso was putting on. I could have slugged him. Heedless of the heat emanating from the stone baking sheet, Pépère set the cookie tray and spatula on the porch table and wrapped an arm around Grandmère.

Urso marched to the steps and halted. "Bernadette Bessette, come here, please."

She crept down the steps and squinted up at him, the planes of her face glowing in the sun. She cut a quick look at me. "I'm sorry, *chérie.*"

I whispered, "Don't be —"

Urso glowered at me. I zipped my mouth shut.

"Bernadette Bessette, you are officially . . ." Urso drew in a long, deep breath, dragging out the moment for effect. I made a mental note to tell Grandmère to cast him in her next theater production. He was a born ham. "You are officially released from house arrest. You are innocent."

A moment passed before the news sunk in, then Grandmère shrieked with delight and grasped my grandfather in a bear hug. Rebecca and I raced up the steps and joined the hug-fest. The crowd cheered.

Over the din, I quickly explained how Vivian had confessed. I did not reveal that Rebecca and I had gone to the shop to find evidence. According to our agreement, neither did Urso.

"That poor, poor woman," Grandmère said.

"She apologized for putting you through this," I said.

"What will happen to her?"

"She'll be given a psychiatric evaluation."

"The heart, it makes us do crazy things, no?" Grandmère patted her chest.

Out of the corner of my eye, I saw Jacky Peterson sitting in a white rattan chair on her front porch. She caught my gaze and raised a hand in acknowledgment.

I said, "Grandmère, I'll be right back. I love you, and I'm so happy for you."

She wagged a finger at me. "When you return, you will tell me what role you played in all this."

Throughout my life, I hadn't been able to get away with a thing. Grandmère had a second sense about me. I smiled. "I promise."

I skipped across the yard, letting the well-wishers have their moment with Grandmère, most talking about the exit polls and certain that she was going to win the election. I trotted up the path to Jacky's front porch. She set a magazine on the matching rattan table.

"What're you reading?" I asked.

"*Victorian Houses.* I need to learn something about this place I purchased. It's a little ramshackle inside. I'm pretty handy at sprucing things up. Jordan said you'd made all sorts of improvements to your home. If you've got any tips, I'd love to hear them."

How would Jordan know that I tinkered? He'd never been to my home. Of course, Mr. Nakamura could have told him. I had relied heavily on Mr. Nakamura's expertise when it came to little fixes. A pang gripped my heart. I had also relied on Vivian for decorating tips.

I drew in a calming breath and said, "Is Jordan around?"

"He's busy at the farm. Why?"

"I wanted to share the good news about Grandmère." I told her briefly what happened.

"That explains the crowd and the roar. Shouldn't there be more good news soon?" She glanced at her watch. "The polls will be closing in two minutes."

"Yep."

Voting booths in Providence were traditionally opened from five A.M. until five P.M. for local elections because it was a farming community.

"The scuttlebutt is she'll win," Jacky said.

If only scuttlebutt could be relied upon.

"You'd better get back so you can cheer with the rest."

I nodded. "It's been nice talking to you." I started to leave.

"Charlotte, wait!"

I turned back.

She said, "I quit at Tim's."

"I'm sorry to hear that."

"I wasn't cut out to be a waitress." She toyed with her long black hair. "I'm a little too unstructured for that, know what I mean?"

I didn't, but I figured over the course of the next few months, if Jordan and I started dating, I would find out.

"I was thinking of opening up a pottery place," she went on. "You know, one where kids and their moms come for birthday parties and things like that."

"Great idea. There isn't one in town, and tourists love handmade items. I happen to know there are some rental locations coming available." I hoped mine would not be one of them.

"In the meantime," Jacky said, "maybe you could tell me what's fun to do around here."

I rattled off a list of my favorite activities, including boating, walking trails, tube rafting, farm tours, all of which I needed to take advantage of some time soon, once Fromagerie Bessette was running smoothly and the pressure of being the owner eased up.

"I meant for us girls."

"Oh, well, there's yoga, sewing classes, candle making classes, a reading group — if Meredith ever gets that going — and Fromagerie Bessette is going to offer some cheese and wine pairing classes."

"Is that all?"

I cocked my head. Was she begging for an

invitation to girls' night out? My friends and I hadn't had all that much fun at the pub last night, or at least I hadn't after the beer spilled on me. Perhaps Delilah, Freckles, and Rebecca had roared at my expense. Laughter could be a lure to a woman looking for new friends. "If you want, you could join me and my girlfriends on girls' night out at the pub."

"I'd love that."

"Side note, we have a tradition." I was lying, but she didn't need to know. "First time out with the girls, you're in the hot seat."

She smiled, a bit of the devil in her gaze, like Jordan, and she nodded. "Okay, I get it. Sure. I'm game."

Another cheer, twice as loud as the first, let out from the crowd at my grandparents' house.

Jacky said, "Guess that means she won, huh? Tell her congratulations."

I raced back and found Grandmère dancing in a circle with Pépère and other townsfolk.

"It's official," Pépère said. "You are looking at Providence's four-time-elected mayor."

I pecked Grandmère on the cheek.

Matthew pulled up in his Jeep and Meredith and the girls tumbled out. They raced up the front path, rally flags waving.

Matthew said, "We just heard on the radio."

"Let the voters prevail!" Meredith yelled.

Amy and Clair hugged Grandmère. Fresh tears of joy streamed down her cheeks.

"May your *Hairspray* ballet go as smoothly," I teased.

"Oh, tosh," Grandmère said. "It will be amazing."

CHAPTER 31

We celebrated with an incredible dinner. In hopes of a victory, Pépère had whipped up a fancy all-American dinner: a platter of cheeses, nuts, and fruit for the appetizer; fried chicken and creamy polenta enhanced with melted Taleggio, garnished with crispy basil for dinner; and a New York–style cheesecake, laced with melted caramel and sprinkled with crushed Hershey's dark chocolate, for dessert. Each course was paired with a wine chosen by Matthew.

When I returned home, I felt happy and calm and very, very full. Fear of the incident the night before on the staircase vanished. Urso had repaired the banister. Vivian was behind bars. No one wanted to harm me or my family.

Like a newshound eager for the story, Rags did a cha-cha around me as I let the kitchen door swing shut. "Yes, she won, you silly cat," I said. "I'm sure she would appreciate a good nuzzle of congratulations next time you see her."

The doorbell rang out.

"Amy or Clair, can you get that?" I yelled.

At my order, they had scuttled upstairs to get ready for bed. So much excitement had made them wired beyond belief.

The doorbell chimed again.

"Girls?" They didn't answer, and Matthew was driving Meredith home.

I gave Rags a good nuzzle behind the ears, then sauntered to the foyer. I turned on the porch light and peeked through the cut-glass window to the right of the door. Kristine Woodhouse stood with her daughter, both in matching patriotic dresses, their hands intertwined. Willamina stared overhead, like she was assessing the light fixtures. Kristine gazed stone-faced at the door.

I heaved a sigh. What now? I shook off the tension zipping through me and swung the door open. "It's late," I snapped.

"May I come in for a moment?" Typical Kristine, she didn't bother to wait for an invitation. She pushed past me, dragging Willamina with her.

The twins hurried to the landing above us and peered over the railing.

"What the heck are you doing here?" I

said through tight teeth.

Kristine glanced at her daughter.

I sighed, in for the long haul. "Amy, Clair. Please take Willamina into the study and show her your dad's photographs of trees."

Eager to stave off bedtime, the twins raced down the stairs and gripped Willamina's hands as if she were their new best friend. "C'mon!" As the threesome disappeared into the study and closed the doors, their energetic chatter rose to a crescendo.

"Quietly!" I shouted.

Their chatter turned into giggles.

Kristine almost smiled. Finally she said, "I'm here to say I'm sorry."

"For what?"

"For thinking your grandmother could ever be a . . . For taking potshots at . . . For . . ." She opened her hands. "For everything. I haven't been very nice. So much went on behind closed doors. I . . ." She dropped her arms to her sides. "Ed made our lives miserable."

"He made everybody's life miserable."

Her face pinched with pain. "Please give your grandmother my congratulations."

"You should tell her yourself."

"Yes, of course. I will. It's late and I . . ." Kristine squeezed her lips tightly.

"What?"

"You've done a nice job with Fromagerie Bessette. I'm sorry I didn't let you buy the building."

"Me, too." More than I would ever give her the satisfaction of knowing.

"Willamina!" Kristine said in a singsong tone. "Time to go."

"Do I have to?" Willamina shouted from behind the study's doors.

"Yes. Now."

Willamina slinked into the foyer. The twins followed.

Amy said, "See you at school tomorrow," and Willamina beamed.

I smiled. Kids. They could put their differences behind them so quickly. I glanced at Kristine and forced myself to be gracious. She had, after all, gone out of her way to come to me and apologize. "Stop by the shop soon. I'll introduce you to some new cheeses."

I closed the door after they left, switched off the porch light, and clapped my hands. "Okay, back upstairs, girls. I want you in bed by the time your father gets home or he'll give me what-for."

Sniggering, they sprinted up the stairs and disappeared into their room. I returned to the kitchen to turn off the lights, and the doorbell rang out again. What more could

Kristine possibly need to say? I tramped to the door, snapped on the porch light and peered through the cut glass window. Jordan Pace stared back at me and grinned, a downright twinkle in his eyes.

I ran to the mirror hanging in the foyer, checked to make sure my eyes, nose, and mouth were in the right place, as if I could do anything in a split second if they weren't. I finger-combed my hair, then returned to the door and whipped it open.

"You're a little early for our date, aren't you?" I teased.

Jordan kissed my cheek, then slung his thumbs through the loops of his jeans. A warm tingle of excitement suffused my chest and neck.

"I've been meaning to tell you something all week," he said.

That he loved me madly and passionately? I had to rein myself in. I did not live in a fairy tale.

I said, "Did you want to tell me that you like my cute button nose?"

"I bought your building."

"What?" My voice soared an octave. So much for being the epitome of charming and casual. "You're the Providence Creative Arts corporation that Octavia told me about?"

"Actually, the name is Providence Arts and Creative Enterprises."

I bit back a groan. Take the first letters and it was an acronym for his name — Pace. I felt liked I'd been blindsided by a delivery truck. I forced a smile, the wheels of my mind spinning as if generated by speed-happy hamsters, trying to figure out a way to make something positive out of the news. I couldn't.

Jordan stood straight and held his hands open, as if that would help him explain. "We bought it because we knew Kristine wasn't going to sell to you, and we didn't want to see you get booted out by some big developer with no sensibility about our community. You know the kind I mean, someone from Columbus and Cleveland."

"Then, how about you sell it back to me?"

"Uh, I can't."

"What do you mean? Of course, you can." I paused. He had used the word *we*. "Who else is in your partnership?"

"Jacky, and she really needs this, Charlotte."

"I need it, too." I hated that I sounded desperate, but Matthew and I had worked so hard to make the shop our own. Pépère and Grandmère had dedicated their lives to it. Owning the building would make the whole business that much sweeter.

"Jacky needs to hide her money."

"Hide?"

"We've buried all her assets in the corporation." He licked his lips. "Her husband isn't a nice guy."

Octavia had guessed right.

"Jacky ran out with all the cash she could find. She changed her name —"

"Peterson isn't her last name?"

"No."

"But won't he be able to track her down through you?" I only paused a nanosecond before I answered my own question. "Of course, he won't. Pace isn't your real last name either, is it?"

Jordan offered a half-grin and a shrug. "I've been setting up this identity for her for a while. A move here, a move there."

"I see." I didn't. Not at all. "Are you Mafia?"

"Nothing like that."

"A cop?"

He remained silent.

"Are you ever going to tell me? Why did you move here? Why are you into cheese? How did you get the expertise? I mean, that alone would be a clue for whoever Jacky's husband is, right? Have you really thought this through?"

Jordan laughed, that husky, wonderful laugh that I liked so well.

Of course he'd thought this through.

After a moment, he said, "Do you still want to go on our date?"

He ran a finger along my cheekbone, and I shivered. The good kind of shiver.

"Yes," I whispered, flashing on something Rebecca had said.

Perhaps *danger* was not only becoming her middle name but mine, as well.

RECIPES

SMOKED SALMON AND MASCARPONE RISOTTO

2 tablespoons unsalted butter
1 medium shallot, chopped
1/4 cup yellow onion, chopped
1 1/2 cups Arborio rice
1 cup dry white wine
2 3/4 cups chicken stock
1 1/2 cups spinach, julienned
1/4 cup fresh chives, minced
4 ounces smoked salmon, chopped into
   bites
1 cup mascarpone cheese
Salt and pepper

Heat 1 tablespoon of butter in 6 quart saucepan.

Add shallot and onion and cook until wilted, approximately 3 minutes.

Add rice and stir for 30 seconds.

Add wine; stir to sizzling.

459

Add 1 cup stock and bring to boil.

Turn heat down immediately and simmer.

When rice absorbs liquid, add 1 more cup stock.

Repeat until all stock absorbed, approximately 10 minutes. Add water if needed (up to 1/2 cup) to keep rice moist.

Add spinach, chives, and salmon.

Mix and cook 3–4 minutes.

Remove from heat. Add cheese and rest of butter.

Set on warm plates, garnish with chives.

Serve IMMEDIATELY.

HAM AND PINEAPPLE QUICHE

1 pie shell (home baked or frozen)
Dash of white pepper
4 slices thin ham (Charlotte uses Applegate Farms Black Forest Ham), diced
2 slices pineapple, fresh, diced
1 tablespoon brown sugar
2 ounces milk
2 ounces sour cream
2 ounces light cream or whipping cream
2 eggs
2 ounces shredded Edam and Cheddar and Monterey Jack cheese
Dash of cinnamon

Sprinkle white pepper on pie shell.

Arrange meat in pie shell. Arrange pine-apple on top. Sprinkle with sugar.

Mix milk, creams, and eggs.

Pour into pie crust.

Sprinkle with cheese. Dash with cinnamon.

Bake 35 minutes at 375 F until quiche is firm and lightly brown on top.

POLENTA WITH TALEGGIO AND BASIL
6-8 PORTIONS

4 cups water
1 teaspoon salt
1 cup polenta cornmeal
1 cup fresh basil leaves, separated
2 to 4 tablespoons extra-virgin olive oil
8 ounces Taleggio cheese, thinly sliced

Bring water and salt to a boil.

Add polenta cornmeal in a thin stream. Keep stirring until cornmeal pulls away from sides of pan (no lumps). Turn down heat to simmer for 25 minutes, stirring every 5 minutes or so.

While the cornmeal is cooking, stir-fry the basil in olive oil until crispy, then drain on paper towels.

Spoon hot polenta onto each plate. Lay a couple of slices of Taleggio cheese on each portion and finish with the fried basil.

PEANUT BUTTER APPLE PIE SANDWICH

2 slices of your favorite bread
2 tablespoons creamy peanut butter
10–20 raisins
2 slices sharp Cheddar or Edam cheese
   (Charlotte uses a delicious Edam made at
   Mississippi State)
2 slices of your favorite apple (Charlotte
   prefers a Pippin, skin on)

Spread peanut butter on one slice of bread.
   Dot with raisins.
   Layer on the apples and cheese.
   Add the other piece of bread, slice and
enjoy.

ABOUT THE AUTHOR

Avery Aames loves to cook and enjoys a good wine. She speaks a little French and has even played a French woman on stage. And she adores cheese. Visit her at www .averyaames.com.

We hope you have enjoyed this Large Print book. Other Thorndike, Wheeler, and Chivers Press Large Print books are available at your library or directly from the publishers.

For information about current and upcoming titles, please call or write, without obligation, to:

Publisher
Thorndike Press
295 Kennedy Memorial Drive
Waterville, ME 04901
Tel. (800) 223-1244

or visit our Web site at:

http://gale.cengage.com/thorndike

OR

Chivers Large Print
published by BBC Audiobooks Ltd
St James House, The Square
Lower Bristol Road
Bath BA2 3SB
England
Tel. +44(0) 800 136919
email: bbcaudiobooks@bbc.co.uk
www.bbcaudiobooks.co.uk

All our Large Print titles are designed for easy reading, and all our books are made to last.